THE LIBERATION OF LORD BYRON JONES

THE LIBERATION OF LORD BYRON JONES

JESSE HILL FORD

Foreword by George Garrett

Brown Thrasher Books
The University of Georgia Press
ATHENS AND LONDON

Published in 1993 as a Brown Thrasher Book
by the University of Georgia Press, Athens, Georgia 30602
© 1965, 1993 by Jesse Hill Ford
Foreword © 1993 by the University of Georgia Press

The paper in this book meets the guidelines for permanence and durability
of the Committee on Production Guidelines for Book Longevity of the
Council on Library Resources.

Printed in the United States of America

97 96 95 94 93   P   5   4   3   2   1

Library of Congress Cataloging in Publication Data

Ford, Jesse Hill.
    The liberation of Lord Byron Jones / Jesse Hill Ford ;
    foreword by George Garrett.
        p.   cm.
    "Brown thrasher books."
    ISBN 0–8203–1527–3
    I. Title.
PS3556.07L53   1993
813'.54—dc20   92–36797
                                                    CIP

British Library Cataloging in Publication Data available

The Liberation of Lord Byron Jones was originally published in 1965 by
Little, Brown and Company, Boston, in association with the Atlantic
Monthly Press.

To Marlene

Blessed are those who died in great battles,
Stretched out on the ground in the face of God,
Blessed are those who died in a just war,
Blessed is the wheat that is ripe and the wheat that is
  gathered in sheaves.

—Charles Péguy

Foreword

The Liberation of Lord Byron Jones is an important novel for a number of good reasons. When the book, Ford's fourth published book and his second novel, appeared in 1965, it received considerable critical attention, most of it highly favorable, some of it extraordinary. Ralph McGill called the novel "magnificent." Some reviewers allowed that they were troubled and confused by the multiple viewpoint, the shifting points of view divided and shared among a large cast rather than a single character. Some others, particularly in the South, were troubled by what they took to be the presented image of the contemporary South and by what they inferred to be the attitudes, the social and political positions of the author. But the novel was widely greeted with mostly favorable reviews in the United States; and it likewise received overwhelmingly positive and interested notice in Great Britain, Europe, and even Japan. Not a major bestseller in hardcover, it was nevertheless a highly successful book commercially, a rare joining together of the ways and means of "serious" fiction—what these days would be identified as a "literary novel"—with the accessibility and conventions (then and now) of the "popular" mode.

These days *The Liberation of Lord Byron Jones* would be called Jesse Hill Ford's "breakthrough" book. Certainly it made him, in the terms of those days, something of a literary celebrity. Later the story, the book, and its author received even more attention when the film based on the novel, written by Ford together with screenwriter Stirling Silliphant, appeared in theaters in 1969. Ford had already earned an enviable reputation as a serious literary artist. In his foreword to the published text of Ford's play, *The Conversion of Buster Drumwright* (1964), Ford's former Vanderbilt mentor, Donald Davidson, had cited the late Stark Young's definition of "a work of art that is pure," that is, the ideal of a work of art "free of considerations outside itself and untouched by the intrusions of another world of aims." Davidson went on to call *The Conversion of Buster Drumwright* "a remarkable example of the operation of this high principle, so generally neglected in our confused period of tendentiousness, dull absurdity and prurient sensationalism." Of the limited vision of many of Ford's better known peers, Davidson wrote: "Their connections are with libraries, publishers, agents, and cocktail-party-givers, rather than with the people of a living society, and certainly not celestial."

The story of *The Liberation of Lord Byron Jones* is a complex accounting of the network of consequences arising from the fact that a decent and finally heroic black undertaker, L. B. Jones, a man of honor whose young wife, Emma, has an affair with a white policeman, demands equal justice under the law—a legal divorce from Emma. This uncompromising demand is the trigger for violence, mayhem, murder, and great tribulation for those central characters left alive and outwardly untouched. Like most writers dealing with credible, "realistic" fiction, Ford made use of whatever was at hand. He had written about the imaginary west Tennessee town of Somerton (loosely modeled on Humboldt, Tennessee) in a number of short stories and in his first novel, *Mountains of Gilead* (1961). In fact, Lord Byron Jones and his Lord Byron Jones Funeral Parlour for Colored have a part in *Mountains of Gilead*. Somerton and its history and family networks have continued to play a crucial part in the later fiction of Jesse Hill Ford, notably in his most recent novel, *The Raider* (1975), a historical story concerning the Civil War. In an author's note for *The Raider*, Ford insists on the factual basis and rooted reality of his story: "*The Raider* is the story passed down to me through my father, my mother, and my grandparents; it is the story of my people and of the land as it was in the old Southwest, that territory which we know today as the South." Of course, whenever a fiction writer shapes and transforms "real" raw material, there is always a small audience of readers more or less familiar with the original models, an audience that may understandably be confused by differences and discrepancies from the factual reality as they perceive it. Writing in *The Georgia Review* ("What Are You Doing There? What Are You Doing Here?: A View of the Jesse Hill Ford Case," vol. 26, no. 2 [Summer 1972]: 121–44), novelist Jack Matthews pointed out: "When Jesse published *The Liberation of Lord Byron Jones* in 1965, a lot of people in Humboldt saw the book as an unmistakable version of an actual local murder case of ten years before, in which a Negro undertaker named Claybrook was shot and killed." This kind of reaction and perception might be entirely irrelevant except that for some time afterwards Ford continued to live and to write in Humboldt.

The popularity and success of Ford's novel allowed some readers who were uneasy both with the charged subject matter and its treatment to ignore the validity and the integrity of Ford's vision and, at worst, to misread his story. *The Liberation of Lord Byron Jones* was close to the times and the events that it deals with, so close indeed that it was easy for many readers at that time, myself among them, to misinterpret, to distort many elements of the story according to personal experience and the precise angle and point of view of the individual beholder. This kind of distortion often arises with a work of fiction that touches directly and deeply on things that matter; the artist takes the enormous risk that this version of events, the artist's vision of them, is not in itself a distortion and, finally, inauthentic, *untrue*. Though the story line in the novel ends with a full and satisfactory closure, the larger events of the time are even now far from finished. In the final chapter we learn of the death of President Kennedy in Dallas and the predictably mixed reaction to the news by the people of Somerton, Sligo County, Tennessee, and, too, of the personal inner feelings of Oman Hedgepath, the lawyer who is as near to being the central character and consciousness of this novel as its method of multiple viewpoints will allow. In a rare moment, naked of his characteristic defenses of irony, Oman tells us of "the dull pain I felt, the emptiness and sorrow and loss that filled me and sickened me," and relates those complex feelings to the story.

Not even a prophet could have fully imagined the sequence of brutal public events still to come in the years that followed close behind the publication of *The Liberation of Lord Byron Jones*. Nobody would have predicted (the phophesy would have been as outrageous as it was unbearable) that the racial conflict, and other attendant issues at the heart of the novel, would remain as serious and unsettled now as then.

Foreword

The Liberation of Lord Byron Jones is in no way prophetic, and yet the passage of time has proved it to be true, a true bill of particulars. Quite aside from its significant aesthetic virtues, it has a double historical value. It is an authentic picture of the early 1960s, of events, attitudes, the clashes between old and new, the beginning of much that followed directly and much that is far from finished even now. Because of its clear authenticity and its relevance to recent history the novel can also be taken, not unjustly, as a documentary background of how we have come to be where we are.

It is clear now that Ford was creating a tragedy in the classic model. One thinks, for example, of *Antigone*, where Creon's worldly wisdom and sense of justice clash head on with Antigone's abstract and uncompromising dedication to higher powers and principles. Neither is wholly right or wrong. Judged by the tragic results, both bear a burden of responsibility and guilt. Just so, judged against Steve Mundine's idealism or L. B. Jones's stubborn sense of honor and justice, Oman Hedgepath, defender not of the faith but of the status quo, seems compromised, unworthy. But he, too, is as wounded as he is wounding and, abstractions aside, has as good a case to make as anyone else in the story. All the principal characters make choices, some of them bad choices; but, much as in the working out of Greek tragedy, the end of things in pity and sorrow and loss seems to be inevitable, fated by the whole creaky mechanism of our society, a machine with history but without gods, things destined to be whatever they will be and become because of the conditions of character, the qualities of *soul*.

Ford's artistic method and choices emphasize all this. These characters, not puppets or stereotypes, are allowed to speak and to feel for themselves, to present themselves in third and in first person. Each viewpoint, no matter how firm in the mind of the character, is tentative, fragmentary. We are invited to join the chorus, to bear witness to the whole of it in a way no character can. Each of the characters is given a slightly different idiom and style. By the end, at the funeral ritual of L. B. Jones, we can easily recognize their voices.

Of all Ford's novels this one makes the most deliberate and intense use of sensory detail as filtered through the limited sensuous perception of the various characters. See how much odors and textures, the touch of things, matter here. The effect of the high level of sensory perception proportionately renders the characters vulnerable, alive, far from types or symbols of this and that. Sometimes, as in the case of the highly sensitive brute Mosby, it is a paradoxical characteristic, giving him a shadow, as it were. In all cases the sensuous intensity, created and dealt out as a gift by the author, adds to the pleasures and the pains as they are experienced by characters and, thus, by the reader.

Time has proved *The Liberation of Lord Byron Jones* to be a more mature, a sadder and wiser book than we knew at the time. Maybe even Ford couldn't have known it. He set out, as every novelist does with the first fatal step on the long march, to imagine a tale and to tell it in the best way he possibly could. Like every worthy artist he learned his way and earned his luck as he went along. Now it is, once again, in our hands and we are lucky to have it.

GEORGE GARRETT

ONE

1

Oman Hedgepath

No matter what, you always feel bad in the morning, anyway. To drink or not to drink, I say what's the difference? Go to bed at eight o'clock or stay up all night, the next day you'll still feel the way the billy goat smells.

Then, still lying there with the pillow under me like a knot of old jimsonweeds, it came to me what day it was and I got up and thought about it, that if she had married me she would be fifty-two by now, so why think about the wench at all? To hell with a habit anyway.

Outlive her, by God. Pick up the Memphis paper one day and read where she's finally gone to the last roundup. That's one way to stay alive yourself, waiting for some old slat buster to die so you can at least have the satisfaction of knowing the lousy dame is finally out of the way. Mine eyes dazzle.

For ten years you wait for her to come to her senses and divorce him. The next ten you wait for a car to run over him or lightning to strike him out on the golf course and set her free. After that it's too late. You've passed up every honest chance you'll have, by then. Even a toupee and a monkey gland operation wouldn't do you any good after that. Your satisfaction has to be that age has ruptured her too. That's how short life turns out to be. It's a sad commentary on the world, I say. I was fifty before I found out that all whores don't live in whorehouses, that there are whores of the spirit as well as whores of the flesh.

I wouldn't give you a dime for the difference. Appropriately enough, it was raining. I went downstairs. "You can get me a couple of aspirin," I said when he poured my coffee.

"Um," he said and put the percolator on the sideboard.

I unrolled the *Commercial Appeal* and it was nothing as usual but solid nigger news, from the Ole Miss campus to the march they were planning on Washington. He brought the aspirin on a little silver plate and served them on the left side, like hot rolls, but give him credit, I thought, he's trying. At least he has an eye for splendor even if the means to it were eternally pissed away a hundred years ago somewhere between Montgomery and Appomattox.

"Got your bus ticket for Washington?" I said.

"Sah? Faw where?"

"Washington, D.C. It says right here the colored folks are going to march on Washington next month, going to picket the White House just like they been picketing the Kroger Store in Somerton. I thought maybe you had your ticket bought by now."

"Naw sah. I reckon dey have to gawn widout me dis time. Dey wouldn't want no old mens nohow. Young crazy folks an' wild mens is all dey looking fer, ain't it? Does it say *how come* dey marching?"

"Jobs and freedom," I said. "You better go buy your bus ticket before they sell out, hadn't you?"

"Naw sah. Dey git me dey gonner have to come after me. Mens sometime take an' go off dat way and don't git back."

"You're missing your chance," I said. He went back after my eggs and toast and when he brought my plate I told him again, "You're missing a mighty fine chance."

"Um," he said.

"I've got a colored divorce case coming up," I said.

"Who fer?" he said, stopping and turning around like one of the figures on those European clocks, the ones that walk out when the hour is struck. Old Father Death.

"L. B. Jones, the undertaker, you know him?"

"Well, I seen Mr. Jones, but now I don't really know him. He sho' runs some mighty fine funerals. It take something rough to beat *him* when he put on a funeral, because when Mr. Lord Byron Jones *do* it now it's gonner be worth the price of man's eyes to witness it. Women troubles. That some sorry piece of news, ain't it?"

[4]

"He's got 'em," I said. "He's wading in 'em up to his butt, like a game warden in a briar patch."

"Um. Got him ever which away he turn. Some sorry comeup. I'm sorry fer him. You can git him out though, can't you?"

"I don't know, *she's* hired S. R. Buntin. Just the nearest thing to a Philadelphia lawyer this side of the Hatchee River, Mr. two-bit Sears Roebuck Buntin."

"She got the trash on her side."

"That great jurist," I said. "I might get you to prepare my briefs."

"Yes sah, well if I couldn't beat Mr. Buntin I'd be the onliest one in town can't beat him. He sho' full of tricks though. Mr. Buntin bear watching now when he fall down on them knees and commence to crying. The cote got to hear him den. Once he start to weep, watch out den!"

"L. B. Jones will be a free man Tuesday," I said.

"Any man can git out of women troubles I'm proud fer him. Can't nothing come in pot luck distance of a mean woman."

"Amen," I said. "Damn them every one."

I looked at the want ads and had my second cup of coffee. Section 144 is farms and plantations. There was two thousand acres in Arkansas "already set up for a chicken ranch," tractors and all, for three hundred dollars an acre. "Owner in bad health," which is only a little more expensive than saying "Heart attack, must sell." It came to me that I'd be better off to quit trying nigger divorce suits and buy up some thirty-dollar-an-acre land myself. Sure, throw up a fifteen-hundred-dollar barn, a government pond and a thirty-five-hundred-dollar prefab house. Blow three hundred dollars worth into a plank fence whitewashed just once over lightly with three-dollar-a-day nigger labor, and then hit some retired Yankee over the head for fifty thousand dollars. Anybody that would plant anything in the ground nowadays but capital gains, that would try to raise anything but Yankee buyers, ought to throw his brains to the hogs, I say. Any man that couldn't clear a million dollars that way every five years hasn't got sense enough to candle eggs.

But that's the nature of man for you, I thought, that he will think the most brilliant thoughts of a lifetime in five minutes, only to keep on walking the same old rut so many times over it finally looks like a trench where he's been all his life. Men worship their manhood, going after a challenge when a dollar would come easier. Finally they can't decide whether to spit or go blind.

And who would I leave it all to but Steve, and what would Steve do but leave one half to the Republican Party and the other to CORE or the NAACP, just according to which one walked in and asked him for it first? It's a shame he and Nella don't get a dime's worth of black shoe polish and pass over the color line, because if there's anything more pitiful than a grown-up man and woman bleeding all the time because they weren't born Africans, I'd like to know what it is. Steve saying:

"But you have to take his case." He busts in my office that morning.

"Why?" I ask him.

"Because he has a right to a divorce like any other man, doesn't he?"

"But," I ask him, "suppose I just don't want him for a client? Because the case stinks. Because it so happens I've been in the practice of law long enough to smell one when it's a little bit off, and this is one I can smell. What then?"

"Then you're prejudiced," he says. "I'm sorry for you, in that case. A Negro comes to you because he thinks you're the best lawyer in town. You quote him five hundred dollars when a third of that would be sufficient, and then when you can't price him out, when he still wants you because he can afford you and he still thinks you're the best, then you turn around and want to withdraw from the case."

"Which is my business if I do say so, or have I got any rights?"

"That's for you and your conscience," he says. "You have the experience, I don't. It's not one damn bit of my business or Nella's either, for that matter. I'd be the last one ever to offer you my advice, because if it turned out wrong you'd blame me for it the rest of your life."

"You're a full partner," I says. "What do you advise?"

He wouldn't fall for it, of course. Spent one whole morning looking and acting dignified, like he'd switched a magic dial in his belly button and added on ten years of age and forty years of experience with nigger divorce suits. He played Hamlet on me. When I'd walk in his office to say something he'd all but come to attention.

He looked like somebody had sneaked up on him and really passed

[6]

him the torch, as though to say, "Well, I put all my nuts in one sack and here I stand yoked to this fascist, Uncle Oman, for the rest of my life." Because I helped talk him into law school. I could see that he thought the sack was definitely wet and due to give away any minute. Nothing jerks a knot in my soul quicker than being blood kin to somebody anyway, and there he was with the blood gone out of his lips, his mother's picture beside Nella's on the wall under his law diploma and him shuffling papers like a chicken scratching shucks, acting so *exactly* like nothing at all had happened that I knew right away it had. Here was the only man I had ever wanted for my partner, and I was lowering the blade on him — and all for the sake of a nigger divorce suit I was going to turn down. My heart went down to my guts like a lit rag. When I reached for a cigarette my hand shook so much I stuck the package back in my pocket. I stood right there and swallowed pride guts, feathers and feet.

"Steve?" I says.

"Yeah, Oman?" Those gray eyes were like crystal steel and so steady; I'll never forget.

"Maybe I'm going through the menopause or something," I says. He didn't say anything. "Anyway, you're right about that nigger, Steve. He's entitled to a divorce just like anybody and it's my job to wait on him. So that's what I'm going to do. Maybe I'm not the best there is, maybe I can't do the best job for him, but then if he wants me that's his problem. I'll represent him. If L. B. Jones is satisfied that I'm the last word in legal mashed potatoes, then by God I'll get him a divorce nobody ever saw the match of before. I'll get him one that will make a twenty-five-cent valentine look like a pawn ticket." Still he said nothing. "And it's my own decision. I'll ream his wife for him so clean and fine that the two hundred bucks he pays me will be the last plug nickel he'll ever spend on her sorry, adulterous hide." It got as quiet as needles.

"You know, Oman," he says finally, still very much the man, but softening. "You know, I believe you will?" I saw relief popping out all over him like hives. And that was the first I knew about how deep he felt on the subject, that you could practically tell Steve you planned to dump some poor old white lady into the cistern and chunk her with brickbats and he'd just about so much as say, "Well, draw up the papers and let's go get her." But let him get the first whiff of some

[7]

damn nigger getting prodded and rodded a little bit and right away he'd have a brain hernia. He'd turn the world into green slime, but then when a Southern boy has to go all the way to San Francisco to find a wife and she turns out to be a half-Scandinavian to boot, I say what can you expect anyway; just be glad she wasn't a Catholic or some hotshot Filipino baby. If niggers are going to be a man's hobby instead of golf or whiskey, or something decent, like duck hunting, then I say learn to live with it. So I did.

So when I had a chance, after the worst of it blew over, I had them out home for a few drinks and kind of floated the point over to both of them that if they wanted to take a knife and cut the Hedgepath and Mundine firm's throat at the jugular vein, then by God the quickest way I knew to do it was to go around Somerton espousing the nigger cause.

I says, "Talk about it in the family all you please."

"Oh, I know. I know," Nella says, sitting there with her knees sticking out so you'd have to put on smoked glasses and a blindfold not to see her fanny, naked as usual, which is another thing Somerton doesn't take to.

"But it's so easy sometimes," I'm telling her, "if let us say you didn't have the misfortune to be born and raised here in the Tennessee backwoods, if you haven't been brainwashed the way I was, from the cradle up, in other words," I says. "It's so easy sometimes to forget and clean some old Confederate daughter's plow, let's say at a bridge luncheon, before you quite know what you've said. It's like building a bonfire with your own fifty-dollar bills." I explain it slowly, so there can be no misunderstanding.

"God," Nella says. "Don't I know — and really you didn't intend it that way. You're just making a sane, perfectly plain statement. 'All men are brothers.' 'Wouldn't it be nice if we could have peace in the world?' And they just gasp at the idea of such a thing! Oh, I've learned. A woman mustn't say anything. Above all, don't think. Mercy!"

She turns her head aside with that glamorous movement that's so virginal it reminds you of the medieval tower and the maiden in the peaked hat, so demurely does she close her eyes and bat her eyelashes. Maybe she practiced it in the bathroom mirror ten thousand times before she got it right, but anyway she's got it, and it is right. I'm laughing right along with her because when the sex is beautiful it's so fine there is nothing else like it, when it's so pure. I know why Steve married her, and if she told me to go rob a filling station and then turned her head aside and looked that way I'd probably do it. I'd shoot myself in the foot for a woman like Nella. But then all that got by me. All I have left is the memory of unreal beauty. That's what memory is, always too fine and pure ever to fit the real circumstances; and my coffee gone stone-cold in the cup and it raining this day of all days that an old nanny goat down in Memphis wouldn't half remember now. I thought: Who'd want a fifty-two-year-old ball and chain around his neck anyway — two chins and sixteen grandchildren?

I put aside the newspaper and went upstairs and brushed my teeth, fifty strokes upstairs and downstairs. You lose *them* next, I thought, and all because the gums draw back. He'd rummaged around behind his x-ray machine the last trip and gotten a skull to show me just how it happened. Every time he said "dentures," I felt like one of those Hollywood Indians on the late show, when the horse turns and you see the arrow in his buckskinned back. It was almost a real pain. Looking at the skull saved him from having to look at me while he talked about the gum tissue. When he said, "At your age . . ." it was like falling off the pony. Each time he said it I bit the dust. Of course I knew that it was just dentistry. Because he liked me and felt for me himself, as a friend, and because he wasn't just one of those clinical mechanics, he was letting me down as easily as he could. "Of course ultimately you'll probably have to have them out," he had said, as though it could be a thousand years off in the future.

Maybe one of these years I'll jerk up the telephone and call my old flame and say: "This is me, Oman Hedgepath, and I thought I'd just ring you up, Miss Mary, and say happy damn anniversary. If you had made it to the church we'd have been handcuffed thirty years today. That's right — it sure is July again, yes ma'am. Makes me want to grunt just thinking about it. Why don't you just sit down and tell me all about your hemorrhoids and your cancers and your grandchildren — every little detail — because I'm just a poor little old country lawyer sitting here trying to run up a long distance phone bill."

One day I'll do it. One day, I thought, looking at that cold coffee.

[9]

"Hey!" I yelled.

He came out of the kitchen. "Sah?"

"Dump this out and get me some hot coffee. You old witch doctor! Do you let your coffee get cold in the cup before you warm it up?"

"Naw sah, I *drinks* mine. I pays attention to what I'm doing, and when *mine* get right then I drinks it."

"Bless you," I said.

"Yes sah, all right sah," he said, taking my cup.

And some people will try to tell you they don't have any sense. They'll say with a straight face that they never saw a nigger in their life that had any sense, and if they told the truth they'd have to be the first ones to say they've never outwitted one yet.

Because it is the nature of a nigger that he will stay up all night while a white man's asleep, figuring out a way to get the best of him.

The train from Memphis was roaring in the distance, towards Somerton — the mail train.

2

Mosby

The black man, Mosby, had slept again. The white boy touched his shoulder. When Mosby saw the boy's bearded face it startled him the first instant. Something in him flickered a moment like the oily instant when a snake shows its tongue.

"I think they called Somerton. You get off here, right?"

"Somerton, that's it."

"Where's your suitcase?"

"I don't have one," Mosby said.

"Just your cigar box."

"That's right. This box is all I'm carrying, this and what I have on my back."

"A cigar box for your shaving kit?"

"Yeah," Mosby said, looking out the train window. "Here we come. That's the quarry ponds where they used to cut rock for buildings back in old-timey days. That's the colored cemetery where they buried my mother, on this side of the hill. Up higher, over the fence, that's the white cemetery. You can't see too much for the vines in the fence."

"Even in death . . ." said the white boy.

"Across yonder, south, you have the Mountains of Gilead, made by some real old-timey Indians."

"Mounds," the white boy said, trying to see through the window across the aisle, leaning forward.

"That's right," Mosby said.

"Now these are warehouses and we cross Main Street here. Up yonder's City Hall and Alf's gas station, he's the bootlegger, across the street. Eclipse Monument Works, where they cut gravestones. Cotton gin, fertilizer plant, feed mill — you can't see that other side where they are. But now if you just look I'll show you the house where I was raised at — see, yonder, with the garden, that's back of it, and the kudzu vine, where it climbs the balustrade to the second floor?"

"Yes."

"That's Lavorn's Cafe and Tourist, where I was raised at, and Lavorn's the lady I call Mama. Because see when my own mother died, Lavorn, she taken me. She didn't have no children see."

"Fabulous, terrific, really . . ."

"And here's the Crossing where I get off at, so . . ."

"Good luck," the white boy said, standing to let Mosby pass. "Unless I see you again, good-bye."

"So long." The black man fended his way up the aisle and pushed through into the vestibule between cars and got off the train. From sitting so long his feet felt like strangers to the ground. He was lightheaded a moment, standing by the tracks while the signal bells clanged. He crossed the street to a little grocery, all right as soon as he moved. He got out of the sifting rain into a smell of apples and raisins and plug tobacco as he entered the store.

"What for you?" said the white man.

"A bite of dinner, some meat."

"Bite of dinner," said the white man, coming from behind the front counter and going behind the meat counter and sweeping open the refrigerator. "Baloney? How much?"

"Two thick slices about like my finger."

"Two thick slices about like my finger," chanted the grocer, slicing the horsecock with his big butcher knife, slapping the slices up on the white enamel meat scales and noting the price on a scrap of paper. "And what else?"

Besides baloney Mosby bought souse and cheese and sardines and two cans of Viennas, two Pepsi's already opened, a devil's food cake, two quarts of milk, a small pack of crackers and seven slices of light bread.

"Why don't I just put this in a little box."

"Yes sir, that would be fine."

The grocer jerked a pasteboard box from behind the checking counter and toted everything on the adding machine as he put it in the box. "Candy? Apples?"

"Yes sir, I forgot."

"Okay." Without asking Mosby what he wanted the grocer threw six dime Baby Ruths and two apples in the box and made change out of the ten-dollar bill Mosby handed him.

With the box under his arm and the smell of food taking hold in his stomach like hands, the black man stepped outside again. The rain had nearly stopped but gray clouds stood low in the morning sky.

He crossed the railroad tracks and found a place to sit on one of the yellow public benches sheltered from the rain by the overhang of the porch in front of the furniture store. Old Negro men were already there, sitting and talking quietly. They watched him eat but politely tried not to be watching him if he looked up or looked around. If he glanced at them they quickly looked away. He finished the cake, drank a quart of milk and dusted the crumbs from his thick, fat hands. Then one after the other he ate the candy bars, alternating with big bites of souse and baloney and cheese, letting it all mix in his mouth as he wolfed it down, sipping at a Pepsi, sipping now because there was only one more Pepsi and a quart of milk left to drink, and he didn't want to run out of bellywash to take his food down. For now, he let it all go down easy, slower now and slower still as he opened the crackers and the Vienna sausages, sucking the gelatine from around the sausages first, while they were still stuck together and crowded in the can like nice little new pigs, taking care not to cut his lips. When the salty amber gelatine was gone he divided out the crackers and ate the little sausages two at a time, each mouthful like a little dream of good times that would go on and on forever, each baby sip of Pepsi almost like a plan every man ought to have in his mind for happiness, maybe a woman and some kids and a place to hang up his hat at night if he was smart and wise, somebody to help him save his money and prepare for the cold winter of old age. A schoolteacher would be the best, he decided, because then she could bring in money too and if the policy numbers got raided and failed why then two could live just as well and happy on a schoolteacher's wages as one. Maybe they might move deep in the South somewhere to some little sleepy old place where the frost never fell nor scorched the grass and where the police wasn't so hard on peoples and didn't always want to rob and beat everybody so much.

A couple of sparrows lit at his feet and dodged in at the cake crumbs and the cracker dust. Man's luck and prosperity and contentment sifted down and helped the little creatures too and they had just as hard and dangerous a time as man did trying to pick up their bread. They had to be bold too, like a man, and like a man they knew life was risky, but they kept coming. They had to have food or they couldn't make it either.

He ate the apples last of all. A man could plant the seeds in just one apple and have him an orchard if only he had him just a little plunk of land, if only he could find some somewhere that somebody wanted to sell right, a man not trying to get rich on other people and load them with the misery of indebtedness.

He drank the final quart of milk, and sated at last, feeling like a man on top of the world without a thing to worry his mind, he put the box between his ankles and leaned back on the bench with both hands snuggled for comfort against his belly — but then, just as his eyelids half closed, they opened; his eyes came wide and he felt of the bench down beside him on both sides. Then he looked in the pasteboard box, carefully at first, under the milk cartons, carefully everywhere once, and then hurriedly again. When he looked up and saw the old men looking at him, he shoved the box back under the bench and stood up, trembling.

Slowly then he walked into the wet street. He crossed the railroad tracks again, keeping his eyes on the grocery. No one entered or came out of the place. Flies troubled themselves against the door screen. He pulled the door open and went inside.

The grocer held up the cigar box. "*Forget something?*" he said, leaning one thin white elbow on the cash register. His lips curved in a nervous, glassy grin. Behind the clear, steel-rimmed spectacles his eyes were like dark, polished stones.

Mosby stood silent a moment. "Box with my shaving razor and things in it," he said then.

"*And* your loaded pistol?" The white man laid the cigar box on the counter.

Mosby nodded. When he stepped forward and reached for the cigar box the grocer pulled it away, out of reach. "Boy, don't you know a pistol's just gonna get you in trouble with the law? What if I must to phone the Chief of Police and tell him a nigger just walked into my place of business and laid down a loaded pistol in a King Edward cigar box on my counter. You want your ass in a sling?"

"Naw sah."

"Yet if I don't call the Chief and tell him, don't you know I'm failin in the dereliction of my duty? Because you've done broke the law and if Chief must to find it out, that I knew it and didn't tell him and didn't perform the dereliction of my duty by callin him on the phone and tellin him, then he can ride my britches around the block for an accomplish. If I don't tell him, I'm an accomplish, and that's just the plain law on it, see?"

Mosby nodded. Cartons of Tums and BC powders and a glass jar half full of bubble gum were crowded beside the cash register. The grocer's hand slid the cigar box farther back out of reach. The grocer was a wiry man with a long face and big veins showing in his arm, a quick sort of fellow who seemed sure of himself, but maybe was not quite quick as he thought and maybe was not quite strong as he used to be. He seemed to be the kind of man who will always remember himself stronger than he ever was and always think of himself still just that strong. Mosby sized him up carefully and measured the width of the counter with his eye. He felt the height of the counter with his right hand propped lightly against it.

"Man can get hisself another gun," the grocer was saying, "from where he got the first one at in the first place. Now and the man that found that gun will do him a favor to keep it. In the case of which it wouldn't be no use botherin Chief because it's no law against a man if he *finds* a pistol that says he can't keep it, see?"

The grocer grinned. Mosby lunged across the counter, grabbing both the man's arms above the elbows and going clean over the counter himself, going down hard on top of the white man. Under Mosby's falling weight the grocer gave a smothered grunt and a muffled cry. Something snapped like a green stick. The white man groaned. Mosby felt pain ripple through the man's body like knotted string. He cuffed the white man's face and backhanded him, slugging and backhanding by turns, quickly and thoroughly again and again, pounding until his hand stung. The grocer's broken steel-rimmed glasses lay ripped aside. Blood oozed from the grocer's nose. The stricken man groaned and made snoring sounds like the heavy, troubling sleep of a flopped-out drunk. Mosby grabbed the pistol from the floor and put it back in the cigar box. He got up quickly then and walked out of the store. Across the tracks on one of the benches the old black men had begun a checker game. Sparrows still dodged in at the scattered cake crumbs.

Like a stick drifting in a slow current Mosby took the direction home, up towards the railroad tracks again, and went left, off the paving into a puddle-pocked dirt street, bounded by new horseweeds deep in the savage green of July, bounded by coarse Johnson grass still dripping, shaking off the rain's burden and rising from under it. The railroad embankment slanted away from the dirt street on important business of its own and the street made a lazy curve, forever independent of the tracks now.

The scented, heavy promise of swine meat set over slow fires to barbecue, the air steaming wet and the ground by the road's edge soft underfoot — the ground was familiar now. From the automobile graveyard across the road the blind junkman's geese unfolded and sang out; the blind man's dog barked twice and was silent. The cries of the geese rose and swam an instant against the flat distance of the sky like a commotion of flaring birds, uncertain in flight; then the wild sounds settled back slowly like drifting feathers, and hushed; and the silence sent out ripples until he felt the dry taste of doubt slide under his tongue, until doubt and fear entered his belly together.

The two-story cafe and tourist was hedged on both sides by catalpa trees. It was sheltered by one big white oak in the yard. Drawn shades lidded down over the bedroom windows beyond the second-story balustrade. Down a way from the unpainted balustrade the porch roof jutted protectively over the front door like a pouting lip. The metal beer and headache and laxative signs nailed along the unpainted walls on either side of the door gave the building color and dignity, like postage stamps on a gray package.

Mosby looked back for one final glance at the empty street down which he had come before he opened the door between the bright tin signs. The sheltering darkness of the building blinded him momentarily. "Mama Lavorn?" He called softly. "Mama Lavorn?" He tried to push off the anger that stuck in his throat like a fist. "Mama Lavorn!" Footsteps stirred ahead of him.

"Mama Lavorn — it's me, Mosby!"

"Lord God!" says the deep voice of the woman, that any but Mosby would mistake for the voice of a man. He stands trembling. "Child, get on a light and let me look at you! Child, child!" Her lean arms catch him in a grip like death. The hard face comes against his own wet with sudden salt tears, warm as dripping rain from a barn roof, warm and sudden as anger, these tears. "Light," she says. "Let my eyes have light!"

Not since he was thirteen had he been in Tennessee. Thus at Memphis he had thought: "Well, I'm back." Mosby was twenty-six.

Mosby, the black man, had walked past the Negro hotel twice. He had walked up and down Beale Street looking in pawnshop windows like a lost soul. "Well, I'm back." It had been Friday afternoon when he reached Memphis and he had worn the same clothes he had lived in since he had left Kansas City Friday, a week before. Now and then on Beale Street he had stopped to consider himself in the reflection of a shop window. Except for his tan shoes and his brown suit he had decided to throw away everything and buy new clothes.

Then he would get a night's rest, get cleaned up, and continue his journey to Somerton by train in the morning.

Looking in a pawnshop window at a set of drums, Mosby had planned what he must do. At the same time he had thought how people got down on their luck. Horn blowers and drum players, he had thought, they got down on their luck and hocked their instruments. Other people hocked their radios and guns and watches and jewelry and the Jew put new pocketknives in the show window beside the unredeemed merchandise. People, thought Mosby, people got down on their luck because the most of them never learned not to want things. They got things and things turned about and got them. Looking in the window and again at his reflection and sometimes at the reflections of people passing behind him in Beale Street, the black man had thought and planned.

Hot July and the sun hazy behind clouds and the Memphis streets warm underfoot. The automobiles smelled hot and their tires squealed when they scratched off. Memphis had been just the same almost as Kansas City. Memphis reminded him of Kansas, where he had worked for the policy racket, walking hard, flat streets.

The cigar box.

He had bought the pistol back in K.C. from a fellow policy writer, also a Negro. He had told his policy numbers boss, an Italian, explained to the wop that he would be gone maybe a month, and Mosby had started south taking it easy the entire way. With the weather good he had walked quite a bit of the way because he had not been in a hurry. So down he had come through Missouri to St. Louis and from St. Louis down along the banks of the wide Mississippi River, dividing the earth like a ribbon of rolling sky. Now and then he rode a bus for a few miles.

Slept in a field, slept in a barn, slept in a nigger hotel. Bought his food mostly at little crossroads grocery stores along the highway. Always ate big because he was a big size. A sack of groceries made him a meal. Nothing contented him more than to eat that way until he was filled. He thought best when he ate. His mind ran on and was not worried.

Turning from the pawnshop window he bought a sack of bananas at the fruit stand and stepped on the penny scales to weigh. When he dropped in his penny the scales showed him at 266 and his fortune read: *Be sure of success. Think big.*

In the clothing store on the other side of the fruit stand he bought underwear and blue socks, a red tie and a white shirt, and then walked back up the street two doors to the hotel and paid three dollars for a room. The clerk handed him a key and pointed to the stairs.

The room was one flight up and had an electric fan on the wall, a bathroom, and a window that faced Beale Street. Mosby locked the door and undressed. He switched on the electric fan, ate five bananas and lay down on the bed and shut his eyes, but was too near his journey's end to sleep as easy as that, for his mind ran on ahead to his main hate and his main love.

He could not rest for thinking how the white man would be so surprised, the cop, Bumpas, who had beat him and beat him nearly to death. Bumpas, his hate, the man he had dreamed about for so long that the cop's face was no longer clear and distinct in his memory.

Since he had been gone from Somerton thirteen years no one would know who he was.

Mama Lavorn, his main love, who had adopted and raised him from

a baby, and would not know him until he spoke. Seeing her, a sweet
pleasure would rise and fill his lonely heart and fill a place of emptiness. Mama Lavorn would know that he had come to pay the white
son of a bitch the death that was owed him for the beating of William Sonny Boy Mosby.

So kill the one and kiss the other? Maybe, and maybe then he,
Mosby, could go back to Kansas or not, but go where he would, he
would carry inside him then a feeling of contentment and peace,
wouldn't he? *"It's me, William Mosby."*

With the box beside him so his left hand could rest on it he had
lain in the Beale Street hotel while the wall fan hummed and a quiet
seemed to fall on the entire city of Memphis.

He has to sit down. Mama Lavorn has to hear the whole tale of his
journey just as he can draw it out of his memory and tell her. "Tell
me how, Sonny Boy — how you come, *how!*" Thin she is, and not the
woman he remembers. He tells her how. Telling and telling her, telling how he came.

How before daylight he woke. He smelled rain and lay still and
hardly breathed until he knew where he was.

Memphis! Then he groped for and found his sack of bananas and
went to the window and stood eating while rain blew in on his legs.
He threw the peelings out the window and watched how the rain blew
in Beale Street around the signs and the lamps, warm and blowing
and thick. The big summertime drops jumped where they hit the
street. The banana peelings floated away in the street gutters. He told
how he smelled the bananas and the warm-wet streets and sidewalks
and the wind coming across the river from Arkansas. When he had
eaten the last of the fruit, how he stood for a long time, only half
awake, watching the rain, standing with his feet wet. When his hunger returned he went to the bathroom and turned on the light and
filled the tub and bathed himself. Then he got the safety razor and
shaved and afterwards washed the razor and dried it and put it back
in the cigar box with the .45 revolver and the piece of white soap.

When he had put on the new underwear and the new socks he
took the shirt and began removing the straight pins that held it
folded. When he unbuttoned the collar a pin there, that he had not
found, drew blood from his thumb and he wiped the blood on the

[19]

new undershirt, his blood almost black in the uncertain light of the bathroom. He drew out the hidden pin and dropped it in the commode.

When he had dressed he went quietly down the stairs and out through the lobby past the clerk, who lay stretched out snoring on a dark green sofa beside the hotel desk. Out on the wet sidewalk Mosby stayed close to the buildings as he walked down Beale Street to an all-night cafe.

He sat down at the counter and ate coconut cream pie and pancakes, then waffles and scrambled eggs, grits and sausage, bacon and biscuits and coffee until at last he was full. His breakfast came to nearly four dollars. When Mosby had paid the check the colored proprietor, a bald man with a grizzled gray mustache, gave him directions to the train station. He used a toothpick to point the way, taking it from his mouth while he told Mosby the way to the station twice, twice saying when he finished and put the toothpick back in his mouth: "Then you can't miss it. See what I mean?"

As the proprietor had promised, it was not a long walk. After the quiet deserted streets, the wet sidewalks, the dripping buildings, and the full gutters, the station by contrast smelled close and dusty, like hay in a barn loft. Mosby found the ticket window and bought a coach fare to Somerton, Tennessee. With the ticket held between his left thumb and the cigar box he sat down in the waiting room, where he had fifty minutes to be passed before the train would be called. He composed himself for a catnap. (How he slept.)

After a lull the rain showered heavily on the station roof, then quit suddenly again. With his eyes closed Mosby had listened, half dreaming, and heard the frail boom of weak thunder as it died trying to cross long, flat distances of sky, distances not even big thunder could cross, he knew, and live. He had heard the thunder trying and trying it over and over very far off, like iron pipes; falling and hitting, hitting and rolling on a hardwood floor.

(Back in Kansas in his furnished room on such a Saturday morning if he were not gin drunk such thunder might wake him with static on his radio by the bed, and long as he was awake anyway he would get up and cross the hall into the landlady's room if she hadn't already come to him, if she wasn't already there, when he opened his eyes, waiting on him.)

[20]

How, sitting in the Memphis train station, he dreamed.

How in his dream he saw Mama Lavorn. On rainy days sometimes Lavorn (did she remember?) had told him a Bible story about the Flood. Again he felt the warm comfort of the crowded parlor. Dreaming, he saw the little china dogs arranged in pairs and families on the knickknack shelves in the corner. Mama Lavorn let him touch the dried brown coconut and the baby stuffed alligator on the table beside her copper lamp. (Remember?) She let him take the cold brick-heavy elephant's tooth from her blue-tiled hearth and cuddle it in his lap, and when she lit the alcohol burner under her brass teapot he watched the broad blue flame tongue sway back and forth, licking the bright belly shining above it. The teapot shimmered. The sweet scent of the burner had hovered in her parlor like wings.

"*Two by two,*" said Mama Lavorn, who told him the tale maybe one thousand times, "*Father Noah marched the animals into the Ark. The dog and his wife, the cat and her husband, the boar hog and his old lady. Old billy goat had so many wives it grieved him to make the choice, but finally he took the youngest, a black little nanny with one white foot like a stocking and blue marble eyes. The stallion and the mare horse, a pair of fleas. Father Noah didn't forget nothing, and down come the raindrops big as washtubs. The river come out the banks and busted the levee. Pinecones and gum balls commenced to float. When they were all inside the Ark, Father Noah shut the trapdoor tight and barred it good with a red oak two-by-six. Fence rails commenced to float and the wicked, standing outside in the cotton field, commenced to holler. Noah had the songbirds to commence singing so he wouldn't have to hear all that swearing and blackguarding going on outside in the rain . . .*"

He woke. It was time then to get on the train. Thirteen years since I saw Somerton the last time, he thought. He walked out to the day coach cars, climbed on, and got a seat by the window. He was drumming his fingers on the cigar box in his lap when a white boy stopped in the aisle and put his suitcase in the overhead rack. "This seat taken?" the boy asked.

"No," Mosby said. The train lurched and began moving.

The white boy sat down. He wore a full beard, and this, with his deep-set eyes, put Mosby in mind of the face of Jesus Christ on calendars, the kind of picture which hangs framed on the wall in stuffy

[21]

apartments in Kansas City where the radio is always playing and the baby crying and it smells like burnt black-eyed peas when they open the door.

"I'm from Rhode Island," the boy said. Mosby pretended not to hear him. With eighty-odd miles to go now, he wanted rest, and preferred to look out the window. Besides, he was hungry again.

"I'm a student."

"Oh, yeah?" Mosby said, reluctantly. "That's real good."

"Thought I'd travel in the South this summer, you know? See what it's really like? The only way is to talk to people, of course. You're the first Negro I've had a chance to talk to down here."

He said it knee-grow so it sounded a little nasty. Yet when Mosby looked at the fragile face again, at the strange, clear eyes, he knew the white fellow hadn't intended it to sound that way. The boy kept on saying it, knee-grow this knee-grow that, not making too much sense.

"You must be a preacher, ain't you?" Mosby said.

The boy wet his lips and touched the beard at his chin with lean, white fingers. "I've considered it. Yet I wonder if the ministry is the place. There are many problems . . ." His voice trailed off. He seemed to draw back into his thoughts like somebody with a load on his mind. Maybe he's hungry too, Mosby thought. The kid was awful thin and dry-looking and he smelled like stale lightbread. He started talking again, maybe trying to keep his mind off his stomach, Mosby thought, and noticed that every time the white boy said knee-grow his voice went just a little off key, like that was one word he always spoke like talking through a hosepipe, like maybe that one word scared him and he couldn't get used to it. In the same way, Mosby thought, a religious man will sometimes stumble around a cussword before it finally pops out of him. The boy's pink, wet lips were so surrounded and hidden by beard that his mouth looked like a burrow. He had a habit of licking his lips, like he enjoyed tasting his words.

Mosby looked away from the stranger's mouth. The flat Tennessee country went drifting by beyond the rise and dip of telephone poles and flat-running wires. A sifting rain fell. Green water stood in the barrow pits beside the track. Water twisted like a yellow rope in the muddy drainage ditches between the levee banks; peaceful one place, angry the other. The train whistle blew.

Mosby

Remembering breakfast Mosby thought how easy it would have been to get an extra sausage sandwich or two in a sack along with some biscuits and candy bars and little pecan pies. He could be eating right now if he had used his head.

"I was guessing what sort of work you do," the white boy was saying.

"You was?" Mosby said. The rain fell on cotton fields, cabins, barns and cattle alike.

"I'm visiting some Negroes at Fisk University when I get to Nashville," said the boy. "I got their addresses at school. I was in Louisiana last week, looking around. Terrific oppression and poverty. Those patient, hungry, knee-grow faces. Do you know when I talk to white people they all try to tell me knee-grows are happy? I think they almost believe it — the fear, you'd never believe the deep feeling of fear these whites have. You have to witness it for yourself, otherwise you can't really believe it. Like a never-ending night. Nobody talks about it. They ask *me*, an American citizen, 'What the hell are *you* doing down here?' As though I need a passport to travel around in my own country. Do you know?"

"I hear you," Mosby said. "I know what you mean." He glanced at the white boy. They'd catch him out just once and he'd be in jail then before he knew what time of day it was.

He would be put in a cage then like a dog and hauled out on some country road and put down in the ditch, where every time he looked up he'd have to speak to the shotgun.

How, young as he was they'd dog him, this white boy, until he wouldn't never in this world be the same, Mosby had thought, until he couldn't speak without he'd stutter, without he'd taste vomit for remembering. And here he was, asking for what he didn't know he was asking for, like a man just eating out his heart for the chance to stretch out his hand and pick up a rattlesnake, like some crazy guy that heard the name of somebody called Mr. J. H. Death, and couldn't rest now until he'd shook the gentleman's hand.

"I have to stop and ask myself sometimes if this is the United States of America," said the white boy.

"I wouldn't travel this country alone if I was you," Mosby said. "It's a wonder you got out of Louisiana. You don't want to try to make it that way alone, not thinking the way you think and talking the way you talk."

"But that's the point — I have to find out for myself. I have to go alone. Otherwise it gets to be a guided tour. You stay with your traveling companion. You don't put yourself out to meet people and talk to them like I'm talking to you, eye to eye, man to man."

"But what about if the police get you?"

"I know my rights under the law. They can't just arrest a man, like that, for nothing. You see, I know that, and they know I know it."

Mosby nodded. He thought, Let him go then, because nobody can warn him; they tried to warn our Lord the same way but He wouldn't listen, He went right on because that was just how it had to be.

How Mosby couldn't bear to look at the boy's bearded face. Shifting down in the seat he had pulled the cigar box close up between his elbow and his side and pretended to doze.

"I think we must be coming to a town," the boy said. The train was slowing.

Mosby opened his eyes and sat up straight in the seat.

"Now what would that building there be, I wonder," the boy said, pointing.

"Cotton gin," Mosby said.

"And the long, low buildings by the side track."

"Fruit sheds — packing sheds," Mosby told him.

"They seem to be mostly all Negroes."

"Well, that's the colored part of town you're looking at there."

"What will the black man do to get his freedom if pickets and marches — if nonviolence fails, I wonder?"

"That's something I don't know," Mosby said. "God made the black and the white and he put 'em here on this earth, but he never wrote out no set plans how to make 'em get along. If God made the mess, how can man straighten it out and make it right? Man is helpless. I'm thinking man can't hardly help himself."

"No," the white boy said. "That's where you're wrong. It has nothing to do with God."

"Say it *don't?*"

"That's right. Man created justice and he created injustice. He made lies and he made the truth. He made hate and he made love."

"I thought God and the Devil divided all that up between their-selves. God made the good, old Satan made the bad. Didn't they?"

The boy smiled and shook his head. "Man," he said.

"Say he *did?* And who created man?"

"I don't know," the white boy said.

"Some say God spit in the dust and made him, shaped Father Adam out of clay. I believe that. I'm just a poor man, but that's how I believe it happened — he just spit, and rubbed his fingers in the dry soil, and then you know, he commenced to work it like biscuit dough? Then he shaped him out a man and blew air in his lungs. Adam woke up and he was alive, wasn't he?"

"I don't pretend to know," the white boy said. "One myth is as good as another. I believe like you do, in this terrific sort of non-violence and freedom. It's . . ." He hushed a moment to lick his lips. ". . . just that if nonviolence fails. I mean at what point do you stop taking it *lying down,* so to speak? There's tremendous integrity in nonviolence, this terrific sort of tremendous self-knowledge and self-discipline, you know? Like the leaders keep saying. Yet that one question — at what point? I don't know." The boy stroked his chin whiskers with a delicate hand, white as fresh corn. The beard was dark and curly and rust-red, like dry corn silks.

The boy's mind was worried, Mosby knew, and it was all something to do with the colored and white, but just exactly what it was eating the boy, Mosby didn't know. "Listen," said Mosby. "Just be careful what you say and who you say it to because this down here, this ain't the way it is up at your home, where you come from — see what I mean? A fellow has to be careful. He can't *be* too careful. So take it easy, and don't rush, because they can kill you and not mean to do it."

"The police?"

"Not just the police. Any of them. Why you want to take up for the colored man anyway?"

"Because he's oppressed. He's not free and I want to help him."

"I see what you're saying, but I don't quite understand all I know. In other words, why?" Mosby asked.

"Because if you're not free, then I'm not free. If you aren't pro-tected, I'm not."

"You can be a white man and say that? When the police and the law both looks out for the white fellow? But tell me, who looks out

[25]

for the colored man? One colored man can beat and rob another, or he can misuse another colored man's wife. White police don't pay it no nevermind — you know that, don't you?"

"That's what I'm saying — if it happens to you, then it's happening to me."

"You mean you feel for *me* — for colored peoples?"

"I feel for you — yes. It's a matter of personal integrity."

"Now I got you," Mosby said, more uncomfortable than before. He looked out. "I wish you'd look there how it's raining again. Coming down cats and dogs — hot a mighty!"

"Where are you going?" the boy asked. "What city?"

"Somerton," Mosby said. "Just a small little place. Maybe you never heard of it." (How the white boy was half crazy.)

How land sprocketed past. Great wedges of his home country — of cleared countryside alternated with long, lonely stretches of swamp where thick cypresses stood bell-bottomed in the dark, stained water. In the flat woods slender tulip poplars soared straight and tall, standing like clean gray columns beyond the close thickets of green willow and pale white sycamore saplings, white as the brittle bones of living men. The quick, hypnotic flirt of corn rows and the sudden shade and gloom of another swamp, where no living creature stirred anywhere to be seen — it put him in mind of the earth before God divided the water from the land, before the light was separated from darkness. He considered how it was back before the creation of man. The train was like a tune of music, playing in him the lonely song of how it was.

Thus, and the words coming as they would, thus Mosby tells Mama Lavorn the story of how he came back and the feeling of the lonely song of how everything was long ago and the troubling thoughts that have his mind worried and the uncertainty of himself even if he has the pistol. Even with the pistol ready and in the box.

Finally he tells how he leaned on the grocer and how he never aimed to do it, and that the police must be after him and on his trail even now. How he messed up — he tells that too.

3

Steve Mundine

In bed beside his wife, the young white man drowsed. He dreamed, and dreaming saw the cypress bottoms south of Somerton beyond the Mountains of Gilead, saw the rust carpet, the woods floor of cypress needles and the bell-shaped trunks, some standing in clear water, and thunder breaking the distance.

July thunder, like artillery fire, was driving the storm north. Then rain was beating the ground and cooling the summer night. The familiar pounding of the window air-conditioners suddenly muted. When the vibration ceased it was always like a ship shutting down her engines at sea.

The quiet woke him. A moment later the gutters filled. The spattering overflow of rainwater striking the brick walk brought him back to an awareness of necessities. He got up and in walking to the bathroom felt a stiffness in the ankles, in the Achilles tendons, and saw himself playing tennis under the lights at Price Park last evening, with Johnnie Price Burkhalter, the hardware dealer.

After three sets they had gone to the country club for beer and had ended up having several and staying late because Johnnie Price Burkhalter got wound up telling about the Negro demonstration at the white park:

". . . I says, 'Reverend, you can ride down to City Hall in the car with me,' extra polite. 'No need for you to ride in the police cars with the others,' I says. What he wanted was us to arrest him, make a martyr out of him. One arrest don't make a nigger hero. How is it

'One flower don't make a spring'? 'How can you arrest me if you ain't a police?' he says. 'Oh, but I ain't arresting you. I only said you could ride down to City Hall with me instead of going in the police car,' I says. 'So I am to be denied access to the city park because of the color of my skin,' he says. 'Nobody says you *can't* use the park,' I told him. 'Only we wouldn't want anybody hurt, see? If nigger people from your part of town use our white park somebody might get killed. We're just protecting you. It's no law says you can't use the park, though of course when my grandfather gave the city the land it wasn't his intention that niggers would take it over from the white folks my grandfather intended should use it. And also remember we collected private donations to build the tennis courts, private donations from private citizens, and they didn't intend for niggers to take the courts over from them. Maybe being a nigger yourself you might not quite understand what I'm saying, since I never heard of a single Somerton nigger contributing one thin dime to make the nigger park in your part of town a little better. Hell — pardon me, Reverend — but hell, you people won't even trim the weeds out of your own park when the city offers to let you use the mowing equipment free, if you'll just let me remind you of a thing or two, such as whether or not your race might have some responsibilities.' I let him chew on that awhile and then he wants to know where I'm taking him and I say well, just on a little drive around the city for a few minutes, to show him the kind of houses white folks live in, how white folks keep their park, how they keep up their school, how they paint their churches. I take him on a quick little detour, a little fast guided expedition, and I say: 'Now let's buzz over to your neck of the woods and see how you God-damned — pardon me — black demonstration-integrationists live. Then maybe you'll see why we don't want your little bastards playing in the park with our children.' 'I'm not under arrest, then?' he says after a minute. Now we're starting down into coonville. 'No, Mr. Reverend, sir, your Holiness, I'm just on the park board of directors. I'm no police force fuzz knocker. You got in my car voluntarily to take a ride to City Hall, just like your little nigger stooges got in the police cars voluntarily, for their own protection.' He grabbed the door handle. 'Then let me out of this car.' I hit the accelerator. 'Go on, hop out any time you want to,' I says. 'Jump, by God.' When he saw the facts — that I wasn't going to slow down, much less stop, he sat back. I had him up in the front seat with me so I could keep an eye on him, you know. I let him out at City Hall."

The listener who had egged Johnnie Price on had been S. R. Buntin, a lean, dull-eyed lawyer. S. R. had told a few nigger stories of his own:

About the nigger that used his wife dog fashion so much she got to chasing cars and that's why he kept her chained out in the back yard — to keep her from getting run over.

About the nigger that got to liking canned dog food so well he ate it every meal for a month. Then he turned up one morning dead, and when the doctor asked his wife what happened she said: "Well, Doctuh, he was jes settin yonder in the road, lickin his nuts, and a car run over him."

About the nigger whore who told the white man he could have some free, but just on one condition. "What's that?" And she said: "Raise my dress up high as taxes, pull down my britches low as wages, and give me the same screwing that Kennedy give Mississippi!"

About the Chief of Police when newspaper reporters questioned him after the street demonstration in which police dogs had been loosed on the nigger rioters, a reporter asking, "Chief, now why did you turn fire hoses on those niggers?" and the Chief replied: "We had to wash 'em off before the dogs would bite 'em!"

After each story S. R. Buntin's face flushed dark red. The lawyer's yelping laughter broke out of him like cries of pain, his round catfish mouth opening and closing, his dull, slick eyes looking away with a desert gaze, as though at some fearful but distantly approaching object; and always beneath the queer sounds of his mirth, mixed with the laughter of his faithful listeners, lay that strange fear, like hard, white bone, live and exposed and nothing hidden. For all their braying clamor, it was there.

When S. R. was out of stories and was through repeating the punch lines (he repeated the punch lines — "Had to wash 'em off before the dogs would bite 'em!" — as though they were sacred incantations, again and again, until the last hysterical yelp had been wrung from his listeners), he winked at Johnnie Price Burkhalter and said: "Oman Hedgepath is gettin pretty deep into nigger law practice."

"How's that?" said the hardware dealer. "Oman's practicing nigger law?"

"Ain't your Uncle Oman representing L. B. Jones, the nigger undertaker?" S. R. Buntin asked Steve.

"I believe so," Steve said.

"You believe so? I'd call that an evasive answer. I'm representing your nigger's wife. So when you see that high and mighty uncle of yours you tell him S. R. Buntin is opposing him and he's gonna have to prove each and every instance of all that damned adultery he's charging my little black client with. What I mean she's fighting that nigger son of a bitch and I'm representing her. Tell Oman, by God, S. R. Buntin's fixing to clean his plow if he ain't careful, by God! Hear?"

The round mouth had opened again and closed. "Hear me?" S. R. Buntin was laughing again, and the others with him. The idea of the nigger divorce suit! It had been too much for them. Didn't niggers just jump over a broom when they got married? "When did niggers start marrying and having to get divorces like white folks?" Johnnie Price yelled.

"Hear me?"

"I'll tell him," Steve had said.

"What surprised me was Oman ever taking that nigger's case," S. R. Buntin had said solemnly. "Oman don't practice a lot of nigger law, but I guess if a nigger's rich enough he can hire any lawyer he wants."

"Money talks," the hardware dealer had agreed. "What's his fee, Steve?"

"I don't know," Steve Mundine had said.

"Don't know your own partner's fee?" S. R. Buntin winked at Johnnie Price again.

"It's between Oman and his client," Steve had said. What cloaked his tongue, he wondered, the same fear that made the others laugh?

On the way home from the club with the hardware dealer beside him in the car, Steve Mundine had thought time and again that here was his chance to say something sensible, to defend the ideal of the law, and Johnnie Price Burkhalter might have listened to what Steve Mundine could have told him about the rights of man under American law, cold facts which Oman Hedgepath and S. R. Buntin ignored so conveniently as soon as the subject of Negro rights was raised. The facts that these other lawyers, officers of the court, ignored were the facts that he, in all perfect honesty, could have told forth on the way home to Johnnie Price Burkhalter. He never got up the nerve to speak though, Steve Mundine.

Instead of speaking up he had answered the hardware dealer's probing personal questions about the Negro divorce suit. Instead of striking a blow for freedom Steve Mundine had meekly betrayed a professional confidence by giving Johnnie Price Burkhalter certain facts and details.

"How much is that nigger really worth? Don't Oman, with his bank connections, have a pretty accurate idea?"

"About three quarters of a million dollars, close to it. He has a good deal of real estate."

"Who does Jones claim is screwing his wife?"

"I don't know," Steve had said, lying because he didn't dare tell Johnnie Price that this was none of an outsider's business, losing chance after chance to speak up, to defend the law.

"What's she look like?"

"Nice-looking, in her early twenties."

"And I didn't know that nigger was even married. Ain't L. B. kind of old to have such a young wench for a wife? Sure, he was asking for trouble, old as he is. Ain't he well into his fifties? Who's his wife shacking up with, Steve?"

When Steve had lied again the hardware dealer had supplied the answer for himself. "Some other nigger," Johnnie Price Burkhalter had said. "That's who. Some other nigger, because old L. B. couldn't satisfy her. I didn't know that old nigger was even married. Here he is getting divorced. Married to a young gal and she steps out on him. Fool old rich nigger."

"Yes," Steve Mundine had said and they had ridden the rest of the distance back into town in silence, into Main Street under the glaring mercury vapor lamps casting a strange light against the old green-shuttered houses, making the magnolia trees look blue instead of green. When Johnnie Price got out of the car in front of his house the lights had made the hardware dealer's face yellow, the pits of his eyes went black and his mouth looked as though it had been burned away. His flesh wrinkled like rubber. "Monday again?" Johnnie Price was asking as he swung the racket.

"I'll have to call you," Steve had said. "Meet at the club tomorrow?"

[31]

"Seven-thirty," the hardware dealer had said, the automatic response. The young crowd in Somerton always met at the club Saturday night at seven-thirty for a couple of drinks and then always drove to a road-house restaurant for steaks. Always.

"Seven-thirty," Steve Mundine had said, before driving away.

He sighed. His image in the medicine cabinet mirror revealed the quiet young man, calm and reflective, with shaggy eyebrows, tousled hair, and good-natured lines about the eyes. Dark irises, eyes neither blue nor brown, but green, dark, and flecked with hints of yellow.

Me. It was a troubling thought. After a last look at the mirror he touched the silent mercury switch on the wall and walked back again into the dark bedroom to the windows. The flickering, fitful flash of the rainstorm showed Nella's form on the bed. She lay on her side, still and asleep. Did she dream? He wondered.

His mind's eye lingered over the beautiful details of that slender feminine body. She was five-eight and weighed a hundred and twenty. She wore a nine shoe; sweater, 36; dress and coat, size 12; blouse, 34. Her favorite perfume was Shalimar; the fur she liked best, Persian lamb. She had fine, compelling brown eyes, and straight, blonde Scandinavian hair. And finest thought of all — she was his; she loved him.

He reached for his cigarettes from the bedside table and lit one. It was always a strange experience, smoking in the dark. His mouth felt a little dry. Looking out the window at the brief twilight flares of lightning, he saw the rain coming in gusts, lashing the house where the porch eaves projected below the windows. Each electrical flash glared on the white drop of the outside walls and outlined shutters dark as ink, edging the wavy panes of old glass in the windows. The oak trees waved thick, leafy branches, down and up again, in a gentle sway, ungainly metronome arms vainly attempting to order the chaos of the wind's symphony.

He was tempted to wake Nella, but something stopped him. He was conscious, suddenly, of the great slave-built house, around and beneath him, as solid as anything the early nineteenth century could build, weathering this storm as it had a thousand others. The thick walls and high ceilings, the white columns which reminded him of monuments in salt, by moonlight, the broad porches and log-burning fireplaces of

Glenraven. Rooms where generals and their ladies had slept; a hall where governors had danced.

Nella Mundine, the new mistress of Glenraven, lay asleep at his back. What must the South with its long, romantic history think of her, coming from San Francisco, Norwegian and second generation to America? She had rescued Glenraven though; she had restored it. Southerners had ignored the opportunity. It was the habit of Southern people to deplore ruin, to witness decay and watch splendor crumble without lifting a finger to stop it.

In the same way the Southerner deplored evil — passively. Both traits, Steve Mundine had decided, were a measure of the region's decadence, a definition of the South's defeated spirit. It invaded the souls of men like a secret, invidious disease.

It was, he had discovered, precisely the sort of disease that one prefers to hide and ignore, to shield and deny, as though these tactics were treatment enough. "Say nothing," said the faces of his friends, "and this trouble will go away."

Life in Somerton was dreamlike, in some respects. This ethereal quality of time itself, as time was passed here in Southern society, had appealed to Nella, once she knew of it, nearly as much as it had always appealed to Steve. He had grown up in it, after all.

He was a native Southerner to the core; she was Southern by choice, by marriage, and by adoption.

They both had worked faithfully at living the even, gracious life that Somerton offered. Nella had compared the year's calendar to the pattern of holy days prescribed by the church in the Middle Ages.

In September the dove shoot at Oman Hedgepath's farm, hunters surrounding the fields at midday, the sounds of shooting, pink and gray feathers of the mourning doves settling into the corn stubble; the bright colors of empty shot shell hulls littering the ground, and above this, the plaintive whimper of the feeding call, birds slicing and dodging through the clean dry air; Negroes gathering the stiff, feather-soft bodies and cleaning them, keeping only the burgundy-colored, heart-shaped breasts.

November opened bird season — bobwhite quail. Southeast then to plantation on the Alabama line. They rode to the coveys on horseback, making a gallery of the same ladies and gentlemen who opened the dove season at Oman's farm — the best lawyers, the big landowners, the state senators, the crack surgeons, the bank presidents and their hard, graceful women. For three long days they rode, dismounting only to shoot over the quivering backs of the Brittany spaniels, dogs trained and hardened through the summer in Canada. The dog handlers went quickly ahead on foot, like Indians; behind the riders came the Negro grooms, running up to hold horses when the hunters dismounted.

In the spring they fished. Summers they traveled and rested. Between times they had tennis and golf, bridge games and all-night dances with a band imported from Memphis, and always the same smooth faces of the ruling aristocracy, aging only slightly, and the same loud, arrogant voices once the patina of this culture was scratched. A few ounces of bourbon and the rough manners of cotton and lumber fortunes, of cattle and oil money, broke out of hiding.

Lived in a certain way, at a certain level, such a life could be quite charming, as Oman had pointed out when he offered Steve a full partnership in the law practice. Oman proposed what came to be Hedgepath and Mundine, names on the second-story windows above the Farmers and Merchants Bank.

Steve and Nella had made several visits to Somerton before deciding on the move. On the first visit they had seen Glenraven, abandoned then; gray; paint peeling off, boards torn away, windows smashed, doors broken and ajar, shutters hanging awry, the lawn a thicket of weeds, a shamble of rose vines, buckbushes, broom sage and unpruned orchard trees; dead leaves and fallen branches beneath the great oaks — a great house dying by the decade, with perhaps one decade to go before it would fall completely and molder, before the final murmur of penetrating rains broke in to bring everything to ruin.

Oman saying: "I'd be afraid to offer the heirs ten thousand cash. State of Tennessee should take it over for a museum . . . but of course." Meaning of course the state wouldn't and of course the offer of ten thousand would not be forthcoming either.

Thinking back, Steve had come to realize that in the end he, Steve, had maneuvered things about so that Nella had made the decision for both of them. Glenraven, forlorn and weather-riven, had been the lure he trailed before her imagination.

Not until they were packing, preparing to move out of their San

Francisco apartment to come to Somerton (where they had lived with Oman, at the old Hedgepath family place on the farm, until Glenraven could be restored for habitation), in the midst of preparations already underway, had he begun to have second thoughts.

By then the bargain with Oman had been struck. By then Nella had bought Glenraven for fifteen thousand dollars. By then, of course, it was Somerton — win, lose or draw; the South, the West Tennessee flat cotton country instead of the stone mountains of Chattanooga or the soft hills of San Francisco.

The slow question, forming in his mind of late, was how wisely he had chosen. Corrupt brutal police; grim versions of the third degree; two standards of justice predicated upon a sensible leniency for the white man and harsh sentencing of the black. The cotton country South, with dedicated help, so he had hoped and imagined, could put these shackles off — but could it?

He had faced the first test. He took a last deep breath of smoke from the nub of the king-size Chesterfield, and felt for the ashtray to tamp it out; groping for the package and his lighter, he lit another. He had convinced Oman Hedgepath that the Negro undertaker's divorce suit must be taken on and carried through.

His next task would be more difficult. He would have to change the mind and heart of a man, his own kinsman, Oman Hedgepath. Smoking and watching the storm, listening as the thunder rolled unevenly away like great stone wheels, he wondered if the Navy had been preparation enough for the task. As a legal officer he had often had to persuade a naval commander of the need for applying the Universal Code of Military Justice.

Even a decade after the law's passage there were still officers of high rank who believed discipline among deckhands was best maintained with fists; who had more faith in the brig, in bread and water and the captain's mast, than in any sort of fair trial procedure. Enlisted men had no rights, they said. Such ideas were not easily rooted out of an organization as old in tradition as the Navy, especially given the isolation and anonymity of the wide sea.

In a sense the cotton-growing South was the same. Small cities, little towns, bleak communities miles apart, ruled by supreme political commanders. In such circumstances, who heard the cry of the beaten, downtrodden victim?

Weekly newspapers dependent upon local advertisers? Rock 'n' roll radio stations? A grand jury of farmers dependent on a single ginner to buy their cotton, a single banker to loan them money? A sheriff who rounded out his income with rake-offs from bootleggers? Preachers dependent on the good will of their flocks for survival?

The police could be honest enough about it. When two or three clever applications of an electric cattle prod to a prisoner's testicles would let an officer sit in cool comfort and take down a confession, what was the point in tearing trousers and muddying shoes, in slogging and beating through snake-infested underbrush in hundred-degree weather looking for a ten-cent razor blade or a colored man's ten-dollar pistol? Sit in a soft chair, drink coffee, and get the same or even better evidence. In a pinch the evidence itself could be fabricated. It often was.

As one officer had told Steve Mundine (he was a young man just hired on the force and just in the process of being broken in to the system): "Police officers like to live modern just like the next guy — you know?"

They weren't all of them sadists and bribe hunters, these police. If they committed an occasional atrocity it was usually and mostly a matter of convenience.

The question was whether, once hardened to such Dark Ages justice, a man's conscience could be stung back to life. Could he, Steve Mundine, wake Oman's conscience?

The challenge was clear. Wake Oman's conscience and the conscience of the community would be awakened. Convince Oman; convince Somerton.

Otherwise . . . he didn't like to consider the alternatives. The trick, he thought, is not to be beguiled, not to become hardened to it yourself. He turned back to the bed and put out the cigarette. The trick, he thought, is not to lose your head.

He touched the bed covers. Nella stirred. "Steve?"

"Here," he said.

"Doing what?"

"Having a cigarette — watching the rain."

"What time is it? Love?"

"Early yet."

"Coming to bed?"

The waking awareness in her voice carried to his blood. For an answer he lay down and drew her slender, lovely body close in his arms. She came willingly, kissing him and snuggling tight against him as though for protection from the same uncertainties he had just been considering.

The bloom of desire swelled briefly and then urgently as she responded. He didn't like early morning lovemaking, however. He checked his impulse, though it was difficult, lying thus quietly and so close. She seemed to understand, for soon she drifted back into the tides of her regular breathing, still pressing his big hand gently against the smooth orb of her breast. She was not big-breasted. Her breasts were small but exquisite, and he liked this about her too. In every sense she pleased him. In every feature she was, to him, perfection.

The air-conditioners were still running muted. He lay and listened for the thermostatic click that would bring them on again full force. Here the machines were almost one of the necessities of life. Here the summers scorched and steamed.

In Chattanooga, to the east where he had grown up, air-conditioners were hardly needed, especially not on Lookout Mountain. Coming from San Francisco, Nella hadn't been prepared for Somerton's climate either, for such tropical, deadening heat.

For Nella though, the heat had been part of the adventure. She had that sort of spirit. Coming newly wed into strange territory hadn't daunted her. Sunday mornings, when she talked long distance to her mother and father in San Francisco, she spoke of this swamp country, fifty miles from the Mississippi River, as charming. The strawberry harvest in May delighted her. She cooked preserves. The fertilizer plant at the south edge of town, tossing out red smoke, was a novelty. Rain, blowing and thundering north from the storm coasts of the Caribbean, pleased her so that she sometimes walked out into it, fully clothed, and let it drench her through. These antics, and her flat, Northern California accent, dismayed the Negroes who worked for her. At first she had insisted on calling them "Mr." and "Miss" and "Mrs." as she felt befitted their rights. In the end though, she had given this up, and settled for Sam, Josie and Tiny. In this at least, the old customs had defeated her, to Oman's outspoken relief.

"Calling her house help Mr. and Mrs. just won't get it! That old dog won't hunt," Oman had confided.

"I know, but let her discover it herself," Steve had said. And finally, Nella had.

Only the white people really dismayed her. The strong, loud, hard-drinking men; the hard, spirited, beautiful women, a colonial ruling class accustomed to meek and worshipful Negroes. It dismayed Nella that the whites accepted the blacks for serfs without a second thought. She was astounded to find that system was as strong and unbending as brass, moreover; and so long established that it was never questioned in polite Somerton society. To question it brought either furious silence or furious response. Who was *she* to question three centuries and a half of history? At times, she said, she had begun to wonder if the South were really a part of the U.S.A.

If he saw it correctly, Steve also detected fear in these white Southern outbursts. Nella was learning to avoid such confrontations. But it was taking longer than he had thought it would for her to become accustomed to things as they were, things as they had been, always.

Because of her attitudes, Steve himself had begun to re-examine and reappraise a society which, until recently, he had always taken at face value. He was making discoveries himself. The process was painful.

Steve and Nella Mundine had not come to Somerton as evangels or reformers, not Steve and Nella. He thought, Surely not. With his mother born here and his uncle living here still and his mother's name as old as any in the whole country, Steve Mundine had been bringing his bride home, to the South. Coming to Somerton had been the fruit of orderly thinking and logical decision. There had been no wish to question the South. There had been no intention of doing so, for the South, as Steve and Nella were gently and frequently reminded, the South began in Virginia quite early in the seventeenth century and established itself in West Tennessee quite early in the nineteenth century. The South.

A state of mind, he thought, very like Democracy, or Christianity, Motherhood, or Patriotism and the Flag. He thought, The South, not a region, but a way and a means of life to be taken on faith and accepted; to be believed without questioning, for, like the existence of God, the existence of the South could not be proved.

Neither maps nor laws indicate its separation from the rest of the United States.

Call it myth, he decided, closing his eyes.

Give it Nella's name for it, Steve Mundine thought. Nella stirred again. The air-conditioners kicked back on full force and set him thinking again of Chattanooga, of boyhood, his sudden exile from youth, from law school to the Navy, from the Navy then to Somerton, to this law partnership.

So life in Somerton was begun, in fear, in silence. He thought, Speak up, and lose a client? Speak out, and lose a friend? Speak at all, and be stared at, whispered about, doubted, shunned? He thought, *But why didn't I speak?*

Be silent then. He thought, Consider your death. Lie still and ask yourself what difference it will make in a hundred years.

The lonely sound of a train came out of the distance as he lay very still; he lay considering his own death, his body lying someday still and insensate. Spend half your life waiting to grow up, he thought; spend the other half waiting to die.

Steve Mundine raised up and looked out. Day-dawn was come, risen like dust, as though chattered out of the shrubbery by birds. Pallid light, soft as smoke, gray as moth wings, pressed beyond the window curtains. The train whistled, breasting a far-off thunder which went rolling now, slowly and northward.

Thus came Saturday, raining.

4

Nella

Saturday.

He stands there and I hear the rain and I know he must be thinking of his home, of Chattanooga, on the Tennessee border just north of Georgia, and I can feel his indecision, like Chattanooga itself, having the flavor of East Tennessee about it. It is a flavor that is sometimes not so Southern because the city is also industrial and had certain New South elements move into it after the Civil War. Still, some of the oldest families of the South live there too. A great battle was fought there a hundred years ago on the slopes of the mountain.

He looks out at the rain, my Steve, and hangs in the balance between liberality of thought and conservatism of mood. The Confederate dead seem to brood over him on certain days just as they seem to brood over Chattanooga. The dead seem to hang suspended over him sometimes like the very mist on the mountains. Another day the air will be perfectly clear. Then there is a vision of progress. He stands very still and does not move. He is thinking. I love him.

Chattanooga. A Negro home may be bombed one day and a white restaurant voluntarily desegregated the next day. Steve's ancestry traces back into South Carolina and Virginia. You have only to look at him to see the blood of generals and statesmen and of three signers of the Declaration of Independence, even perhaps, as he will say laughing, of seventy-one horse thieves and nine hundred fugitives from the British debtor prisons, but I cannot see anything but the generals and the statesmen and the heroes. He is something too solid to be part horse thief.

Perhaps they taught him to stand that way at military school, or at Vanderbilt, or in the Navy, in all those places and times before I knew him even though I have loved him always before I even saw him; I have loved him. His doting mother, Eloise, perhaps she too taught him to brood, to watch rain coming down and to stand so perfectly still and so obviously undecided within himself, to stand that way not moving. I hear birds singing in the rain. Lazy, crazy, lousy bitch me, why won't he look at me, if birds sing in the rain? His Yankee, his little Abolitionist, his San Francisco baby with the Stanford accent, why won't he look at me, but if he does look at me I will close my eyes and pretend to be asleep. He must never know how much I love him because it would be ruinous and he could not stand the glacial ruin of being so smothered in so much love, so let him never know and let birds sing in the pouring rain; let it be summer in this God-damned swamp, this South of his and Oman Hedgepath's.

Oman, the poor, the unloved, the bitter, the man you'd go away with for a weekend to the mountains or to Carmel-by-the-Sea if you were not in love because he is just simply so God-damned miserable and so God-damned lost and so much like a little boy sometimes you practically want to cry just looking at him and yet you know that inside of him he's the biggest God-damned monster that ever put on a bed sheet and went night-riding, and yet he's handsome and princely sometimes, and attractively bigoted so that I can see Steve in him and I can see him in Steve. He has Steve's indecision about him too because Oman wants to be human, but his dead fathers and his dead grandfathers own him and he's guilty for something and disappointed about something and he's suffering. He needs a woman and the only one he ever loved stood him up at the church for no reason at all and here is Steve, my husband, the only son of Oman's only sister.

Eloise Mundine. Skin like Steve's own, very fair skin, but fair Southern, not fair Scandinavian. I'm fair Scandinavian, she's fair Southern, and she broods sometimes this same way and I know she dreams of having married a West Tennessean and settled here where she was born and reared with Oman, how she might have remained here, had she married a West Tennessean, and carried on a tradition. Instead she marries Andrew Mundine, a surgeon. They go to bed and have Steve. Thank God for that.

And I see her brooding sometimes and sometimes considering the outside chance that Steve might someday settle in Somerton and enter the law practice with Oman, her brother, thereby continuing what the Hedgepaths began in West Tennessee, through my womb and blood and marrow, and she can look at me as if to say: "Don't you *want* his babies? Two years and he hasn't knocked you up yet, my dear?"

My eyes always answering: "Let me have him a little to myself. More than that he is still undecided. The whole South is undecided and wouldn't you agree, Eloise, that no man needs children until he has stepped down from his vantage point of indecision and waded in and begun the fight?"

"Fight?" says her attitude. "Fight?"

And I look back at her and say: "Eloise" (but only with my eyes), "where have you lived all your God-damned life, Eloise? This is a hundred years after that war and you are no spring chicken and yet you act like somebody just spilled your chocolate malted if the Negro Revolution is even mentioned in your presence, as though the freedom and dignity of the black man were something too odious for polite conversation. Ignore it, Eloise, and make it go away?"

She sinks back into her own oblivion, my man's mother, satisfied to be the woman who once in her life postulated for her son that which came into the condition of fact; she hoped he would move to West Tennessee and go in with Oman. He did, but not before the Navy had him awhile first in Washington and after that in my city, San Francisco, the Pearl of the Orient, and I am the one to be brooding at the rain and wanting my city.

I can see him as he was. The sturdy young Southerner with those large hands and powerful arms (his arms folded now where he stands and watches the morning) and that broad honest face. I saw his serene eyes, neither blue nor brown but indecisively shaded like the original mold of a creature as yet untainted, as yet uncommitted, having in him the penultimate possibilities either for good or for evil, and ready, it seemed, to swing either way. He saw me, Nella Liseth. He saw me coming down the aisle at the Presbyterian Church with my father and mother, with my hair quite straight and simply worn, pulled straight back in a pageboy and me five feet eight and unadorned so that he knew at once I could not be anything he had known until then. Scandinavia, he knew it at once (he read it in my arms, my legs, he said afterwards), and of course he had my father to look at too, the original Liseth, my father herding and steering Herr Liseth's wife and Herr Liseth's only child into church with no earthly idea that his child's husband-to-be had just spotted her coming down the aisle and had already begun to letch and to itch and to yearn so fetchingly for her, this Southern outlander disguised as an American in the uniform of a lieutenant (junior grade), U. S. Navy.

The instant likely match, the engagement in less than a month, the prospect of a law partnership in San Francisco open for Steve. He takes his Nella, does Steve, home with him on a flying trip to Chattanooga and I charm Eloise and Andrew, not with my wit, my looks, not with anything I am or anything I think or anything I say. They approve of me at once because I'm so unusual — a blonde with brown eyes, and it leaves you thinking, it makes you wonder. If I'd been blue-eyed maybe they would have fallen in love with my big feet. Brown eyes, blonde hair, and for all else they cared I could have been a rabbit. They didn't otherwise seem to look or investigate me closely enough to be sure, even, of my sex. Hair and eyes satisfied them. *If this is the kind of tricycle our Stevie wants, by God it sure suits us. Have some turnip greens with your corn bread?*

Pardon me while I vomit and why won't he look, but if he does I'll be asleep and he might kiss me and if I can distract him maybe we'll do it, because that's another thing, that his indecision has got him choked up and he can't do it much any more without being all bound up.

My mother said when they stop performing — look out. She should know.

There is poetry in history. You think if he philanders you will throw him out but you won't because as every single girl knows, if she's had a chance at married men, she knows that married men never leave their wives and wives never let their husbands go.

You get to be a wife and you think, If he did, I'd die; if he did I'd throw him out; but you won't. Steve yawns. He is like a baby then.

Anything animal he does, that will make you realize we are all part animal, and he is like a baby. I see him yawn and I have to yawn. Still he does not look at me and the lousy birds sing in the rain.

Love me, that's what they sing; love me.

My grandfather in Norway, Grandfather Liseth. I visit him in Oslo and he serves me Martini vermouth and cookies and treats me like I'm about the most gorgeous dame he's ever laid eyes upon, his own flesh though I am, and it is ten years at least since he came to San Francisco and visited us and now suddenly I'm a lady and he is all lady manners and we sit there in his wonderful apartment with my grandmother on her deathbed in the next room and the Oriental rugs looking as rich and delicious as the Martini tastes, and the furniture the same rich, the same ornate and baroque sort of thing. I'm a good girl and I drink my Martini and tell dying grandmother who looks like a dried-up snake good-bye and I walk out of there on my way to Copenhagen and for the first time in my life I feel like a woman because an old man was gallant to me.

Eloise and Andrew saw nothing but my eyes. Yet coincidence is glue and coincidence wove and wrapped and taped itself on top of coincidence to hear Andrew tell it, until it seemed that the families Liseth and Mundine had been welded together by fate since the very dawn of time, let us say back when horses were the size of kitty cats and cockroaches grew a foot long and hunted rats. See the wedding invitations shooting out from San Francisco. Then parties and gifts from everywhere — Sweden and Norway, Denver and Minnesota and Tennessee and Alabama; Chicago and Maryland; Virginia and Hong Kong, until . . .

Until late of an evening then, at Carmel, when the moon stood like a pale flower blooming above the Pacific sea, love was let down between us, love came down between and upon and out of him and into me, this man of mine built so to carry burdens, to turn wheels, and fell forests and generally lay every God-damned thing in sight to waste; to burn stumps and whip slaves while he disputed his land's sovereignty in his ancestral memory even while it is between us and on us — God, God help the memory of that and hear my moans and love cries — even then in that race memory of his he is defeating them one by one — Indian, Frenchman, Spaniard and English Royalist, each in turn, defeating them all and then losing everything he had won, handing over everything at Appomattox, everything, including, as he will say, including two billion dollars invested in black slaves.

Southern man into Northern woman. "Am I hurting you?"

"Are you out of your mind?" I ask him. "Would you rather drink a malted?"

He tells me that I am turned to slenderness, with tapering wrists and silken skin (nobody ever told me before that I had silken skin), with narrow hips and small breasts built all for adoration (nobody ever made me happy with my small breasts until Steve Mundine), and the companionship of kings and sailors, said he, and talked about Viking men pulling each his oar with a will so sure were they of the women who waited, slender but strong withal for the bearing of children (he would have gotten me pregnant on my honeymoon), proud women (he raved and whispered) able to manage land and keep accounts, support the church and see to the increase of herds and flocks, women who could live secure even at war and despite poverty, the sort of woman to comfort and adore her man all his days, but independently of her own free will and desire until I thought my God does he really believe in Superwoman? Until I thought wouldn't he be happier sleeping with a history book! And isn't it a shame he can't instead of having to go to bed with me? But it was only the sort of passing ugliness that we all have to put down, and I knew it for that and I put it down.

The moon waned and we spoke secrets in the whispered breath of the night and we told endless stories, anecdotes, tales about ourselves that had no point and no beginning and no ending, things so trifling and so long forgotten (until just then) that only love and the night's depth could ever have brought them to mind. When I cut my foot, burned my arm, broke my nose. His temperature when he had the measles. The one time my father spanked me. I got clinical and timed these conversations and found that words failed almost every twenty minutes by the clock and I told him: "I'm ready for you every twenty minutes. Did you realize that?" I said, "Steve, darling, how can we go our whole lives this way, with me wanting you every twenty minutes?"

It came daylight and I couldn't eat and I got a champagne bellyache. The whole time at Carmel I hardly slept except sparingly during the day, lying on the beach, sunning in my red knit two-piece bathing suit, but he had the appetite of a Bengal tiger and he slept soundly for a few minutes without even thinking about it and then woke all fresh to see me watching him. I was in the range of his vision every time he woke and desire would turn back on him endlessly and over again and he would be helpless with it, saying: "I love you," those three words that mean nothing except from the man you love. I was never tired of hearing him say it.

When he was released from the Navy we came to Somerton. It was challenging; he wanted it.

Now Steve begins to have doubts about this caste system, these Negro serfs. He begins to have his doubts and he begins to brood and to wonder if such gawking, shuffling, stammering creatures can really be human, as he suspected, or are they, he wonders, are they really as Oman sees them?

He caught me watching him. He touched the bed. I spoke. He turned and came.

5

T. K. Morehouse

Never do you know these days when some somebitch will swing down on you. "Depedy Marshal T. K. Morehouse, Federal Process Server, Western District, Tennessee," I introduced myself.

He had done already admitted how as he was Johnnie Price Burkhalter, owner and proprietor of Burkhalter Hardware Company, Somerton, Tennessee. His face kind of stood up like dog's hair when the somebitch growls. He drawed out about the mouth white as a leghorn chicken at those words. Oh, I watched him close let me tell you when I reached inside my suit pocket under my raincoat, let me tell you I eyed him like he was a tree full of dad dern diamonds, because these days you take even if it is in a store so full of customers it looks like inside of your daddy's beehive, you ain't safe. Take in Heywood for instance not a month ago I'd done had the cold clabber knocked out of me and was down flat on my bottom before I could so much as say howdy and him just a cotton-farming sort of friendly-to-look-at peckerwood that never *had* give *nobody* no trouble before and then threatened he would start up his tractor didn't I git up and git going, that he'd run me down and plow me under like a snake. So don't you believe I wasn't careful, standing thataway in a hardware store with so many axes and guns and singletrees laying handy?

Like a wise old man will spy on his nineteen-year-old wife, just so I watched Mr. Johnnie Price Burkhalter. I never down even blinked. I says, "Want me to read it to you?"

"What is it?" he says. His lips went to jerking like he was wired for electric power. Oh sure, he already knowed who I was and what it was. Somethin warns them all in advance until it is worth a man's mortal frame just to serve a paper on one of them. You're about as safe I say to stick your head in a cage and kiss a bobcat under the tail.

"Just tell me by God," he says right short. I seen it had done already shaken him right to his nuts. "If by God you don't mind by God!"

I advanced back maybe two paces to the rear wherefore I'd have a clean patch down the aisle for a fair run at the front door and never once take my eyes off Mr. Johnnie Price Burkhalter. Then I says, "Niggers — it's just some more of this nigger business. I don't mind to tell you. The niggers thereon named say and testify you run 'em out of your white park whereas and they claim they have a right to use it and all, so that, whereas you are on the Park Board of the City of Somerton, you have to go down to Federal Court in Memphis and tell the man why. Why you don't let niggers in the white park and just about anything else. It names also any swimming pool and golf course which as I understood the Mayor to say you didn't have neither one of them for the public. Only this park where the Confedrit soldier stands at, where the monument is, I disremember the name, ah . . ."

"Price Park," he says. "My grandaddy give the land by God where it lies. Give the land to the city before ever he died — my own grandaddy by God, I oughta know where it's located at."

"Price Park, that's it," I says. "And like I say now it's only my job you see, and I have to serve a paper only as it is my job. Next year I retar and I can tell you I'm gonna be pretty damn glad to retar. I never bargained to have to do nothing on the order of this, don't you see?"

Yet all I seen was sweat pop out on his face. Then his eyes rolled. "Gah-God damn if I won't be a son of a bitch," he says. "I seen better heads than yours on a cabbage to walk in, invade a man's private place of business on Saturday, trespass his store. Gah-God damn if I wouldn't by God suck boils before I'd have your damn job so I would, to come in and spit on the grave of a man's grandaddy. Low-down Federal bastard you!"

And that's when he reached out to hook onto me but I was already too quick for him from that time in Heywood County. "I'm just a-leavin," I says and made a quick step and a skip out to the sidewalk where it was the first I knew of that it was not raining any more. I unbuttoned my raincoat and went by the barbershop and motioned at the nigger shoeshine boy inside to come to the door and he come and opened the door, a boy about forty, so he looked. I smelled how it was inside with the air-condition and powder and hair clippers goin. I says, "Boy, where's Lawyer Hedgepath's at?"

"Yonder over the bank, please sir. Cross Main Street and go straight upstairs over the bank, please sir." He pointed at the bank.

"That that Federal somebitch? Why don't somebody take and have him cut?" A voice in the shop spoke up. It was too crowded to know who. I couldn't see for sure, but I thought I recognized the Mayor. Some laughed and I seen the barber take his razor just then and start to strop it. Even if he was only foolin still my hole made a grab anyway. My hole grabbed the way yours will cut out on a rough back road and all of the sudden you ride your car over a rough place where it seems like it's going either to throw you out or turn the whole business over and your hole *will grab*, every time, like it's trying to grab hold a grip on the seat, just so it will tight up and grab every time, and that's just how mine done when I seen a glimpse of that razor. A little quicker than ordinary or usual for me I made a brisk walk to the corner and crossed Main. It was land office busy in the bank and I slipped right on through, slick as grease, and found the stairs goin up with no more trouble.

Goin upstairs I heard the siren.

TWO

1

Lord Byron Jones

The siren made the undertaker's heart jump.

The rearview mirror of the Cadillac showed him nothing but a blur of diffused, brain-colored light, without images. Then ahead, down Fort Hill, in the same direction he was driving, he saw it, the ambulance from the white funeral home. He saw the crowd then and the police car in front of the grocery and it came to him that perhaps it was a heart attack. The ambulance stopped and the white attendants jumped out and opened the rear door.

He parked the car behind the police cruiser and got out to the sidewalk in time to push into the crowd of older colored men, the usual bench warmers, in time to see the cart come out, to have a glimpse of a white man's bloody face before the ambulance doors closed and the siren growled again. The ambulance moved off quickly towards the hospital and the two policemen came out of the grocery next, jumped in the cruiser, and drove off after it.

"What happened?" he asked.

"Somebody mighty nigh killed Mr. Jimmy."

"Who?" the undertaker asked.

"Don't nobody know. Somebody walked in to buy somethin directly just a minute ago and heered Mr. Jimmy hollerin down under de counter. So they called the po-lice."

"Reckon could it been the fat man?" said another.

"Could be, cause he come out, you know, and eat his dinner. Then he went back, didn't he?"

"He went back in Mr. Jimmy's. I think he went back. Look yonder at Mr. Jimmy's blood on the sidewalk. Is you Mr. Lord Byron Jones? Ain't you?"

"Yes," the undertaker said.

"Yes sah. I sho' believed I recognized you. You doin all right, Mr. Jones?"

"Fine," the undertaker said automatically. The old men stood musing over the grocer's blood.

The undertaker took off his gold-rimmed pince-nez glasses and wiped the lenses clean with his handkerchief. Then he put the glasses back on and got back in his car and drove on towards Main Street, turning right, beside the Lion Filling Station. The sirens hushed.

Straight ahead of him at the end of the street stood City Hall. When court was held on the second floor next Tuesday morning he would be here, he thought, seeing the tall upstairs windows. The American flag should have been flying from the mast above the roof cornice. The pole, he saw, was bare, even though the rain had stopped.

From somewhere beyond the high steel girders supporting the silvery water tower behind City Hall and above it, sunlight burned a rift in the clouds and poured golden feathers of light into the still wet street in front of him.

He found a place for the convertible in the parking lot behind Main Street and in front of the First Methodist Church. Carrying his raincoat folded over his arm, he walked up to Main Street. The sun's brilliance was like a pressure. The warmth quickly pushed through his black clothing and he began to sweat between the shoulder blades. Saturday crowds pushed by him. The whites regarded him curiously, as usual. They resented him, he knew, for being a dressed-up nigger, yet they smiled too. They took his measure for a black preacher, that illiterate cockhound, that wench-swiver which the white man automatically beholds in his mind's eye, and with all too much justification, the undertaker thought.

The undertaker paused at the corner of Fourteenth and Main. Across Fourteenth the soda fountain was being carried out of Templeton's Drugstore and loaded on a red farm truck. Templeton himself came out carrying a fountain stool. The druggist wore a strange expression. The long fountain was like an amputated member. Twenty

Negroes staggered across the sidewalk with it, sweating and bulging with the work. They carried poles — ten poles in all spaced at intervals under the soda fountain in the same way that a big log is carried, each man straining so as not to get the short end of the stick and the white farmer going along beside, one hand propped against the fountain to steady it, saying: "Easy, boys!" The druggist stood at the edge of the little crowd that paused to watch.

"Ain't that hell?" said a voice behind the undertaker. "Yeah, but I don't blame Templeton. Did he not take it out the govmunt could make him serve niggers."

"Well," said the first voice uncertainly. "Still a shame though. Man can't buy a dope or a ice cream nowhere along Main Street no more. It's a hateful comeup."

"Otherwise he'd have the niggers a-settin in on him though. Damn demonstrators settin right down at the soda counter, wantin service. That's what they done ever place else."

"Yeah, I guess," said the first voice. "Oh, I don't blame Templeton."

The Negro workers slid the fountain off the poles as they loaded it inch by inch into the truck bed, heaving and shoving. The workers were laughing now the strain was off their backs. They went back in the drugstore and brought out the iron fountain stools with white porcelain seats. The stools had stood bolted to the floor in front of Templeton's soda fountain for thirty-odd years.

While the undertaker watched the loading, the poisonous scent of insecticides wafted from the farm supply store behind him. He had often gone driving with Emma in the country. She had always sneezed when they passed a crop field dusted with chlordane. Her throat swelled, her nose started itching. "Maybe I must be a bug or something," she had always said, thanking him for his handkerchief. He had said if she were a bug then she must be a love bug and she had bitten him. "Where?" Emma had said, laughing now. "Where did I bite you? Where, tell me?" making his ears burn.

She would still be laughing at his embarrassment, and she would still be sneezing when they got to the farm. They walked that day over the hayfield. She had been afraid of the harvest spiders, daddy longlegs she called them. The ground had been full of grasshoppers leaping and flying away from their (his and Emma's) shadows. Crickets by the thousands went threading through the cut-over stubble, hordes of them wondering where their safe world had suddenly vanished to, wondering why the sun suddenly scorched them. Emma had leaned heavily against his arm and said didn't he want to lie down right here with the sky for a ceiling, the cypress woods for walls, the sun their lamp? Push bales together for a bed, she had urged him. Did animals, cows and things, have to have all the breaks? Emma had asked, leaning, rubbing against his arm, wanting him to take her and the urge half in him to do it except that it wouldn't have been seemly, humping together in the outdoors like cotton pickers at the end of a row. He'd had to refuse her for having seen it before in the fields. He'd tried to explain his revulsion to her, telling her the way field hands coupled, the feeling he'd had walking up on them grappling in the dust, how it had dizzied him and made him sick to know these were his own people, his own race. Emma had thought he was joking. She had even begun pushing and tumbling one hay bale to place it beside another, so weak with laughing she had finally been almost unable to move the bale. She had sat on it and raised her dress, laughing and inviting him, showing nothing beneath but her nakedness, throwing her head back to show the curve in her throat and laughing at the sky and her hands going down to where her legs joined, with savage little movements. She made pelvic motions he had never seen a woman make before. Emma faced him with closed eyes and her tongue stuck out, her lips drawn back, showing her teeth, so that even when he had raised his hand he had known that she was defenseless, yet even knowing she would bite her tongue he had slapped her before he could stop himself. He had knocked her off into the stubble and stood over her then saying: "So that's what you are! That's what you are!" wanting to kick her if she moved while the sickness went down on him. "Whore," he had said, tasting the word until it came to him that she was crying, that she was hurt, that her head was moving back and forth and she was looking straight up, straight past him, and he was embarrassed for her asking him why, asking him if he didn't want her babies.

He had sat down on the bale then and tried to talk quietly, telling her here she was with her college degree, reminding her of the diploma on the wall in their bedroom, did she think where the thing was done made a difference? Was she a field slut that would eat melon seeds and sip sheepball tea next?

"If it would help," she had said. Her mouth was bleeding and her tongue was cut and swollen so she could hardly talk.

"But a field slut — like a field slut, Emma?" he had said, trying to reason with her, trying to help her then, but she wouldn't have it and she shoved his hands away and got up and jerked her dress down and said yes goddammit she was a field slut. She was so utterly like some frozen thing, so quiet in her rage, that he'd said if she were serious he'd do anything, even set the bales together against his better judgment and . . .

Saying a bad word he hated to hear from her she had said forget it, going on to other bad words, big God-damn bad worker he'd turned out to be! His own farm. His own wife. His own hayfield.

And him trying to tell her how his people for generations back had sweat blood and cracked bones to raise themselves out of the fields, he had said: "I hate those words in your mouth. You can see why I'm sensitive about certain things . . ."

She hadn't seen though. "Sensitive? You handle dead bodies. Maybe that's what you're so used to, and if I laid stiff and still, then you'd want me because that's all you know. Dead! Dead! Dead!"

"Only come home with me, in the bed like proper people!" he had pleaded with her.

"Just once I wanted to see the sky," she said then, quietly, pushing his hands away, saying: "I'm all right! I'm all right! I'm all right!" She had seemed to come to her senses so they could continue walking.

A little sadly, so it seemed, the druggist handed up the stool he'd been holding. One of the Negroes in the truck reached down for it. The remainder of the loading went briskly.

The white farmer climbed into the cab and started the engine. The Negroes climbed in behind to steady the load — tables, chairs, fountain stools, the fountain itself; the men in the back of the truck laughing, smiling, the little crowd of whites on the sidewalk watching, a little dismayed. Blue smoke roared out of the exhaust pipe. The truck moved and rounded the corner from Main into Fourteenth and passed out of sight. Wearing the same lost, stunned expression, Templeton went back into the drugstore. The pathetic little crowd of whites walked away, gone then as quickly as it had gathered. The traffic ebbed and the undertaker made his way across the street and through the crowded bank to the steps leading to Oman Hedgepath's office.

When he walked in the reception room the secretary frowned at him. "I believe Mr. Hedgepath phoned me about dropping by to see him this morning," he said. "I'm L. B. Jones."

She always frowned at the sight of him, as though except for him she hadn't a worry, as though merely the reminder of his being was enough to ruin her day and bring on a headache. She touched her forehead. "Oh yes. Just a moment," she said, leaving her desk and going into Oman Hedgepath's office. The door to Steve Mundine's office was open. The young lawyer was talking to a white woman who wore a high collar of steel and rubber about her neck.

The secretary came back to her desk and sat down without looking at him. "Go in," she said.

He entered the lawyer's office and saw Oman Hedgepath leaned back in the swivel chair behind his desk, his hands folded on his waist, his chin resting on his chest. The lawyer's face, a strange face with a jutting lower lip and brown eyes, turned towards him a second. An abrupt smile formed and drained away from the corners of his mouth. "Set down," the lawyer said in his bored, white Southerner's voice, his quail-brown eyes avoiding the black man's face. His tie, his hair and his suit were all blending shades of brown. "Have a seat," the lawyer said in the same voice, though the undertaker had sat down already and was already feeling out of place because the other man's eyes habitually avoided his own. Like the lawyer's clothing, the room itself was furnished in autumnal tones of brown — reminders of dead leaves, dying grass, bare earth, wet bark and dried wildflowers. The dead.

The lawyer clasped and unclasped his freckled hands, every movement compulsive and yet practiced. The grimacing set of his teeth, the tireless hands, the way he held a pencil or opened a book or put down the telephone — it all seemed so studied and deliberate. He did everything with finality, yet everything he did was grotesque, as though the world somehow were already doomed and he knew it, but was carrying on anyway. He gave the impression of someone given over to a delaying action, hopelessly efficient and hopelessly sad, and perhaps, finally, hopelessly evil, even without especially wanting to be so, but without especially caring one way or another.

Oman Hedgepath gave the impression of being so far removed from life that the capacity for love and hate were both burnt out of him. His feeling for others seemed a sort of imprecise indifference, and this had the effect of inspiring confidence in his legal ability, as though if he were human he would be the less reliable for being subject to the infection of folly. As he was, he seemed immune, saying:

"Your wife filed an answer. Came yesterday morning. What do you know about it? Anything?" The slow voice accused the undertaker, but kindly, as though every accusation were inevitable, as though it were granted he, L. B. Jones, was only a dumb nigger. Of course a *nigger* wouldn't know anything. Still, one went through certain tedious forms, one asked him about it . . .

"Nothing," L. B. Jones said.

"Didn't tell you she was getting a lawyer?"

"No sir."

"Didn't let on what she was doing?"

"What does it mean?"

"What does it mean?" The brown eyes seemed to look at him an instant and then to go dark and flat again. "Means she's going to fight it, I guess. That's what it says. She demands strict proof. Don't she have any sense either?"

"I beg your pardon?"

The lawyer sighed. "Strict proof would mean naming her boyfriend, wouldn't it? You heard the word strict? It's a kissing cousin to stern, explicit, detailed, exact. I don't want to consume Saturday with explanations, but now it won't help your case to have a white man named right out in open court as a colored man's wife's lover. On the other hand, would it help Emma in any way you can think of to drag a miscegenationous relationship out into open court and wreck Willie Joe Worth? Will it help any way you can think of to wreck him — married with little children to look after and help support?"

"I wouldn't care if it wrecked him."

"That's sensible. You wouldn't care. Maybe I wouldn't care. Emma obviously doesn't care, that is if she knows what she's doing, filing a piece of paper like this. I can tell you her lawyer doesn't care. I talked to him and he strictly doesn't care."

"Who is he?"

"Who is he?" the lawyer smiled. "S. R. Buntin, and he don't care." The lawyer's chin touched his chest again. He grimaced. "On the other hand I do care. Where there's any reason to stir up a stink such as this one, and this is one stink that would not be easily laid to rest — where there's any reason for it I'm generally willing to go ahead. But there's no reason for this, and if a lawyer thinks well of himself and his profession he won't hurt anyone unnecessarily. Sometimes you have to hurt people. It can't be avoided. In this case, however, it could be avoided, and therefore it should be."

"Because he's a white man, because he's on the police force?"

"White man, colored man, Indian chief. What his color is or what his job is don't matter. He's got a family. That does matter. If he didn't have a family it would be bad, but not this bad. But understand that I'd be against harming him in this way even if he didn't have a family, and now he's at fault, more so than your wife if you say here's a policeman charged with upholding the law, and he deliberately goes out and breaks it by sleeping with a colored woman, a penitentiary offense by itself. White and colored cohabitation is against the law in Tennessee, I guess you know that, didn't you? And her being married of course compounds the felony. Now what are we going to do?"

"What can be done?"

"Well, I've talked to S. R. Buntin. I can't talk to Emma because she's not my client. I can talk to you though, and I think it's my duty. The only problem is I'm trying to do the right thing."

"For me?"

The lawyer smiled. "Do you know what the right thing is, L. B.?"

"I know I haven't done anything wrong. I've had the injury," the undertaker said.

"I asked you a question — yes or no, do you know what the right thing is?"

"Maybe you better tell me."

"Since S. R. Buntin don't care I think we better withdraw your bill for divorce."

"After I've waited seven months?"

"You could have had another lawyer. You can still have one. I told you I was busy, didn't I? Did I make you wait seven months or did you just decide you wanted to have me take the case bad enough to wait that long? I think we need to get that much straight, don't we?"

"All right."

"Withdraw the bill?" The lawyer raised his eyebrows.

"No. I'll talk to Emma. I can, can't I?"

"She's your wife till you get the divorce. Can you talk to her? If you won't withdraw your bill somebody ought to talk to her. What I'd like to know is why she decided to fight it all of a sudden. What changed her mind?"

"I don't know. Maybe she's had time to think it over. Seven months . . ."

"But that would have to be your fault, wouldn't it. Didn't I warn you I had a backlog? You'd have to wait your turn?"

"Yes sir."

"All right, L. B." The lawyer sighed. "Anytime 'tween now and Tuesday morning, which don't leave much time. I'd rather you instructed me to withdraw the bill. Once you think about it you'll see that's what you have to do unless Emma backs down."

"No sir. I won't withdraw, Mr. Hedgepath. I'll talk to Emma."

"You can go now," the lawyer said. "Change your mind phone me anytime, at home or anyplace. Main thing is to do the right thing."

The undertaker stood up. The lawyer turned in the swivel chair facing the window overlooking Main Street. "Good-bye, Mr. Hedgepath."

"So long. Be in this office with your witnesses at eight-fifteen Tuesday morning — unless you see it my way and change your mind."

"At eight-fifteen Tuesday. Yes sir. I'll be here."

"The alternative, or one alternative I should say, would be to file for legal separation if she'd withdraw her petition. Trade her out of the notion in other words. That way you'd have separate residence, live apart. Have her out of your house."

"But I'd still be married to her, wouldn't I?"

"You would that," the lawyer said, still slumped in the chair, still gazing out the window. "You would that," he repeated. "As you go out and you don't mind, would you tell Miss Griggs to ask Mr. Mundine to step in here when he has a minute?"

"I will," the undertaker said. As he walked out of Oman Hedgepath's office the secretary frowned at him. "He said he wants to see Mr. Mundine," said the undertaker.

"All right," the woman said. "Mr. Mundine?" she called. She got up and started for the young lawyer's office. "Mr. Mundine?"

The undertaker went out through the hallway and downstairs into the bank still carrying the raincoat, holding it folded in front of him at the waist, as though for protection. His hand slipped against the clear plastic handle on the glass front door. His knuckles struck the glass.

"Pull, L. B. Pull the door," said a mocking white man's voice from the teller's cage, a voice with just the right edge of bored amusement burrowing under it, in effect saying, *Well, what can you expect from a nigger?* There was a good-natured bit of tittering white laughter from the crowded bank.

Pulling open the door at last the undertaker walked straight into Main Street. There was a shrill screech of tires. Horns blew. "Hey, watch it, boy!" a voice yelled. He made it across without looking either direction, looking only at the green painted cornice of an old building across the way, thinking that German artisans had carved the leafy cornices from wood, going from town to town as the railroads moved west apace.

He went on quickly behind the building to his car, got in it, slammed the door and slipped his sunglasses on over the pince-nez glasses he already wore. Then he started the engine, and only then, as he felt the sudden flood of cold surcease from the air-conditioner slide over his knees and seep through the thin tropical suit, drying the sweat on his body, only then did he feel secure again.

He drove slowly out of the parking lot and turned right, going past the post office, where he turned right again.

Negro pickets stood crowded together in the unshaded sunlight in front of the yellow brick Kroger Store. Watching from the shade near the store's entrance stood two young white policemen wearing cool, short-sleeved shirts. With crudely painted NAACP signs hung about their necks, the Negroes looked pathetic and thirsty. The policemen were drinking Coca-Colas and smiling.

The undertaker passed on without slowing down, thinking that pickets didn't really help anything. They were like a beggar showing off his sores, pulling his rags aside. Whites hardly paid the children any notice. Colored people passed them by, embarrassed for them. What good, he thought, what possible *good* did they do?

He turned left under the traffic light and parked the car in front of the old house that served for Dr. Ocie Pentecost's clinic. He entered the building through the colored entrance and sat down in the waiting room with the other black people to wait his turn. Negro children played quietly on the floor with the waiting room toys. When the baby in the lap of the girl beside him whimpered she unbuttoned her blouse. The little mouth closed about the dark brown nipple. The calm little eyelids fluttered and closed.

The undertaker took off his sunglasses. Across the room a black peasant in faded bib overalls sat dozing. His big feet had burst his shoes at the sides. The old man's huge black hands curled palm up in his lap as though poised, even in rest, to lift something. He slept like a pack animal that takes rest where rest is found, in the deep slumber of a lifetime's exhaustion. The head slumped forward nodding, the brow was as smooth, as untroubled as polished granite.

2

Lavorn

I told my brother, Benny, I said and me sick and I prayed to God. The prayer was answered. Sonny Boy Mosby come home. After this I will not see him again. Not again, after this.

Benny said, "Hush, Lavorn, you only doing poorly and lost some weight. You ain't eating the right food."

But I said I know. It is a feeling when it is in you, a feeling. And you don't want to admit it but finally you have to be the one to admit it yourself. The time is near. Death is in you like weevils.

Like corn or wheat or any kind of grain, I said. You get ripe. It is time. And you are bound to go. Death is in me.

Benny said, "Hush, ain't we got to use our heads? Sonny Boy done beat up and put Mr. Bivens in the hospital."

I said Sonny Boy he couldn't help it because he was scared. I said, Benny, you know yourself what Sonny Boy done been through. Before he left out of here you know what they done to him. So he went wild. He had to beat that ole man up.

"His brain is concussioned. Mr. Jimmy might die," Benny said. "We must use our heads and hide Sonny Boy. The fuzz going to be picking up everything and everybody they can find. They going to shake it until something rattle. When death and murder happen they got to have a boy down in that jail. They going to have a body in that jail."

I said maybe he won't die. I asked Sonny Boy. "You didn't lean on him very hard, did you, Sonny Boy? Tell me just how hard you leaned on him."

"Pretty hard," Sonny Boy Mosby said. "I don't know why I done it. He had the dog."

I said, "Dog?"

"He mean pistol," Benny said, brother said. "Dog, that mean pistol."

"He had it. I know I couldn't go back to jail here another time. I couldn't do it. I jumped him before I knew it. Something told me I better shut him up. I leaned on him pretty hard, Mama Lavorn."

I said, "It's all right." Sonny Boy looked around the parlor. I seen he was trying not to look at me how my flesh hangs on me so loose. It was once so full. Once I was such a fat, stout woman. That is how he remember me. He goes away. He comes home to find me this way, thin. I'm drying out fast. Going down in a hurry. Every day can't I feel it? Every day, every night?

Sonny Boy sat on the sofa with Benny. They talked. Sonny Boy telling Benny about Kansas, telling what he done on the road and things. How he made it after he left out from Somerton. It was so many years ago. I thought about it. So many years ago.

I lit the alcohol burner under the teapot to make tea. That's like we used to do. Me and Sonny Boy when he was only a small child. I said, "I'll fix us some tea. That will bring back old times, how they used to be."

"Bring them back. Lord, bring back them old times," said my brother Benny.

Benny told Sonny Boy about the undertaker, L. B. Jones. Sonny Boy didn't even know L. B. married. Here L. B. getting a divorce. Me and Benny already consented to be his witnesses to tell and testify on how Emma laid around with Willie Joe Worth. Sonny Boy didn't know it was any cop by that name. Sonny Boy never heard of Emma. It was very strange for Sonny Boy. He nodded his head and pretended to understand. It was all new to him and Somerton was not how he left it. Somerton was changed. I was changed. Benny was older. Sonny Boy was growed up a huge, big man. "Lord," I said. "Lord."

The tea was ready. I served in my good china cups with the peacock painted in the bottom. Benny saying: "One thousand times I asked myself what Bumpas had on his mind. Why he done a little boy that way? Why a police would take and whip a boy like he wanted to kill him. Beat him until the absolute shit and the absolute water run out of him! Time passed. All that time nobody knowed where was Sonny Boy run off to. Sister calling me, saying where's Sonny Boy at? We gone crazy out of our minds. The patrol car come. They got Sonny Boy in the trunk. He's so beat up, beat up so bad until his shirt stuck on him. You couldn't hardly get it off his back."

I said to Benny, "Hush!" He wouldn't hush, saying:

"Sure, Bumpas that white bastard got him a farm now. White sons of bitches, they all taking money and bribes. Bumpas got him a farm. Got him a used car lot operation. You tell me how a cop able to buy that kind of stuff. Then I have to tell you it is because he take money off everybody. Rob the poor! If the color of the poor peoples' skin turn out to be black Bumpas gonna use 'em any way it please him to do. And ain't nothing gonna be said about it!"

I said, "Brother, don't pressure up your blood. You bound to get your blood high if you go on that way!"

"Anybody want to run a little beer bidness, little barbecue place — they got to pay Stanley Bumpas! What kinda jive is that?" Benny said.

Sonny Boy just drank his tea. He said: "I'm gonna let Bumpas have some kind of payoff treatment. He ain't looking to get what I have for him."

"I'm with you!" Benny said. "Peoples laying down payoff money in his damn paw every week. I'm with you on it, Sonny Boy. Beating a child half to death. Knocked the brains plumb out of Mrs. Osborn."

That is one man you got to pay every Saturday, Stanley Bumpas. Every Saturday. Peoples all fears him. To make examples he take first one and another. He beat them that way. He let them go tell the others how it feel when you don't pay. The rest gonna pay.

Sonny Boy saying: "Who? Mrs. who?"

Benny, my brother, saying: "Mrs. Osborn."

"Do I remember a Mrs. Osborn?" Sonny Boy said.

"Sometime back they beat her up. She had a cafe like sister?"

"I remember now," Sonny Boy said. "They beat her up?"

"She hooked up to an arrangement with the Sheriff. Mrs. Osborn paid the Sheriff in the place of Bumpas. They taken and made an example of her. Now she look like something burnt in the fire. They knocked and beat her out of shape."

"Yes," I said. "They fixed her, Sonny Boy. They wrecked her."

"Beat her senses out of her. She went crazy. She never been right since," Benny said.

"But that happened after you left, after you went away from here, Sonny Boy," I said. Sonny Boy looked down. He shaken his head like he couldn't understand it.

"Doing Mrs. Osborn that way," he said. "I don't know."

Benny nodded. "I taken the call. One evening the po-lice said a colored woman done had a bad accident out to the quarry ponds. I took out there in the ambulance. I pick the woman up and take her to the hospital. Don't even know *who* she was she tore up so bad. Didn't know till later she *was* Mrs. Osborn. Where is she, sister?"

"Yonder asleep on the daybed," I told him.

"Let Sonny Boy look at her, sister."

"Come on," I said. We set our cups and saucers down. We all tip-toes into the hall across to the cupboard room under the staircase where Mrs. Osborn laid asleeping. The electric light bulb shining in her face. Sonny Boy looked and saw it was like I said where her futures had run together like candlewax with scars that come out of her hairline like roads on a map. She slept with her hands folded together like she was praying. Her futures was ruined.

"Don't know nothing," Benny whispered, pointing to his own head. He put a finger to his own temple.

"I remember her now," Sonny Boy whispered. We backed out of there. Back we come to the parlor. "Sang in the choir at the Taber-nickel," he said. "Wasn't she here when they brought me home that evening?"

"Yeah," I said. "She came. She set up all night with us nursing you. When we didn't know if you would make it and pull through or not, Sonny Boy," I said, "she come and sat up all night. She watched at your bedside."

"Thirteen years. That's a long time to be gone from a place," Sonny Boy said.

Me thinking, how I thought when they did bring my little Sonny Boy Mosby home that evening, my Sonny Boy, dear, I said to my-self he will die tonight from this beating. Or he will live to kill that white man one day. I said if this child lives through the night; and it come sunup. I walked outdoors. I saw the sun coming like a ball of chicken blood. Up it come above Cucumber's Automobile Graveyard, the blind man's place across the road, rising. I said, I hollered through the door: "How is Sonny Boy Mosby, brother?"

Mrs. Osborn come to the window and raised it and she said: "Lavorn, Benny say tell you Sonny Boy still breathing." I said: "He'll make it then."

I knew he would kill that white man because Sonny Boy, his daddy was a killer. His daddy was slain by a railroad foreman. His daddy was a big man that never took nothing off nobody. Never said much. Maybe he killed several niggers. Peoples feared him, Sonny Boy Mosby's daddy.

I said when he went off: "This is his daddy's child. He will come back." He come back. I could not look away from him at anything else. That is how I loved him. I could not look away.

Sonny Boy looked into his teacup. The room smelled like wildflowers and hay and cinnamon. The kettle made its simmering sound like little sharp straight pins dropping and striking glass, so tiny. I could see Sonny Boy's weariness come down. It settled on him. I said: "Sonny Boy, don't worry. For we are going to hide you. We going to keep you safe. You don't have to worry about nothing."

"I'll hide him at the funeral home," Benny said.

"We will think," I said. "We will all think and think of something. The police must not have him again."

"They won't," Sonny Boy Mosby said. "Don't worry about that. They won't never have me again." He sighed.

I told myself, my prayer is answered. My baby boy come home. I said thank you God, amen.

3

Oman Hedgepath

Every train that comes through Somerton sounds like a damned iron goose. It don't whistle. It honks. I pulled out my watch. The train was three minutes late. I looked around at Steve and then back out the window.

Looking out the window is about the only entertainment left that the Federal Government hasn't figured out a way to tax. I thought, they'll tax that next. Then they'll tax jumping too — looking out and jumping out, except in Somerton you'd have to walk up Main Street to the Bayliss-Murray Furniture Store and ask them to let you in the attic. If you finally did manage to get up on the roof it is still only four floors above the street. I thought maybe a man could stand on an egg crate to make it four and a fraction. Or maybe he could get a stepladder and make it four floors and a half.

"Nobody with a grain of pride should settle for anything less than ten stories," I says.

"Ten what?" Steve says.

"If he were going to jump," I says. "Can you see some bastard bailing out of a second-story window into Main Street?"

"I'm serious," he says. "So she's got S. R. Buntin. What can she accomplish? You have the witnesses."

"Sure, " I says. "A whorehouse madam and a professional mourner — the madam's brother. Lavorn and Benny. Couldn't ask any more than that in the way of witnesses. I'd like to see anybody try to im-

[69]

peach witnesses like that. If I just had a nigger pimp and a Chinese bootlegger on reserve I wouldn't have a worry in the world."

"Whorehouse?" he says.

"Pardon me, Steve. You'd call it a knee-grow house of prostitution. She's Mama Lavorn of the Look and See Cafe and Tourist. Benny, her brother, is L. B. Jones's general handy man. Benny is the professional mourner, ambulance driver, and chief corpse dresser. Benny Smith ain't prezactly what you'd call a mental giant."

"He knows what he saw, doesn't he?" Steve says.

"That's right. Until yesterday all Benny saw was a white man wearing a pistol belt jazzing Emma Jones wearing her birthday suit. They got out of the back of the ambulance while it was parked in the garage one evening. Benny needed the ambulance to answer a call. A city police car was parked in the garage next to the ambulance. The white man pulled his gun and wanted to know what the hell Benny was doing in the garage. Emma was saying: 'Baby, it's only Benny, baby. Don't get mad, baby. Baby, Benny needs the ambulance to go get some old corpse or some old wrecked up nigger out on the highway.' Until yesterday that was all Benny needed to say. All Mama Lavorn had to say was Emma Jones and an unidentified white man played house in one of her rooms at the cafe and tourist. Just the one time was all she had to tell — yesterday." I lit a cigarette and blew smoke at the window.

People went shoving up and down Main Street like cattle in a slaughter pen. I thought, It will all be over in a hundred miserable years. Who will know the difference — just a pile of bones, that's all. Give it a bleeding century.

"What's so different now?" Steve was saying.

"S. R. Buntin will *insist* that the white man be identified," I says. My cigarette tasted like rubber. "The judge will back S. R. up. The nigger witnesses will have to say right out in open court — 'Mr. Willie Joe Worth, please your honor!'"

Steve still didn't see it. "You've already got the pistol belt and the patrol car," he says. "Folks will know it's a Somerton policeman anyway. Where does naming him make any difference? Doesn't it exonerate the rest of the men on the force, naming him?"

"Those details in the bill I drew up were a sort of warning. When I drew up the bill I said a man '. . . *who will be named at the hear-*

ing if necessary.' It's clear to the court then that we're not hiding a damn thing. It's also clear that it's a city policeman who's involved. It's clear that there is no use naming him. Long as she wasn't protesting the divorce."

"Then he's *got* to be named," Steve says. "That's all there is to it."

"That," I says, "or she's got to back out or L. B.'s got to back out."

"What did L. B. say this morning?"

"He won't back out," I says. "He's wild as an ape."

"Good for him, by God!" Steve says.

"Yes, good for him. You and I may have seen our last white client, too. If this happens we can go down to the Crossing and rent a corner in Mr. Jimmy's grocery and wait on his clientele. Hedgepath and Mundine will have seen their last white face when the first nigger witness of ours shoots his thick mouth off in court and names the white policeman who's been sleeping with Emma, the nigger undertaker's wife. You can kiss that white gal's broken neck good-bye. The next whiplash you see, that is, if you ever see another one again, will be black as my socks."

"You're exaggerating," he says. "I can tell."

"You'll see if I am," I says. "You *and* Nella."

"I know miscegenation's touchy," he says. "I'm a Southerner."

"Steve," I says. "You're a white man, Southern born. But for the sake of my mother — your grandmother — I'd feel a whole lot better if you didn't call yourself a Southerner. When you apply the term to yourself, it nauseates me. If you'd respect my feelings that much — can you?"

"If that's how you feel," he says. "Well, I got you into it this time, didn't I?"

"No. I walked into it on my own," I says. "I knew better."

"I made an issue out of it," he says. "I couldn't stand seeing you put him off that way. Time and time again. It had the appearance of a sort of unholy contest. The richest Negro and the best lawyer in town, both determined not to yield. The issue didn't really seem to be justice so much as the color of a man's skin. I couldn't sit still under the circumstances, Oman, because . . ."

"I know," I says. "It's done now. Now the point is to fix it somehow. Maybe you'll learn something out of this. I don't know. If I retire at sixty-five we've got thirteen more years of practice together.

That's a long stretch. I've only been in this office minding my p's q's for eighteen years. Are you ready to sit down and reason with me, Steve?"

"All right." He sat down where the nigger had been. You hate to see your own flesh sit where a nigger's sat, where the chair's hardly had time to cool off from the heat of a nigger's body. It hurts when your own flesh sits down there. Not that I'm prejudiced because I'm not. It goes deeper than that. Taboo is the word. If I touch a nigger or anything that belongs to a nigger, then I've got to wash my hands to get the nigger off them. I can't wash quick enough — and nobody could call anything like that mere prejudice. I've lived with it all my life. It's nearer to being a sort of magic than it is any kind of prejudice.

"Listen," I says. "Let me tell you something about me. I mean first off. Let's take all the time we need to talk this thing out — once and for all, *now.*"

"All right," he says.

"The first time I was ever in Philadelphia I rode in a taxi driven by a nigger. A white man shined my shoes. I could take the taxi driver all right; I didn't like it, but I could take it. But when I walked in the men's room under the hotel and there was a white man shining shoes, it got me. Steve, I went on through with it. I let him shine them. Then I went up to my room and puked."

"Maybe it was something you ate," he says. "You can't jump to conclusions."

"No," I says. "It wasn't anything I ate. That's the terrible point, because another time in Chicago —" (I almost got sick again thinking about it.)

"In Chicago about a year after that I was riding down State Street in a cab, in pretty heavy traffic. I happened to look out and on the sidewalk in broad daylight was a big buck nigger walking with his arm around a white girl. I puked all over the backseat of the cab. Shot my lunch right then and there, just like you'd press a button to set off a charge of dynamite. I couldn't stop it any more than you could stop the beat of your heart. Now I'm a Southerner. Do you begin to get some inkling of that definition, Steve? Because I'm going to tell you what I never told another living soul in my life. If it wasn't essential to tell you this in order that you might understand me, and

perhaps, along with it understand the South, and this particular law-
suit, I'd never in this world say a word about it. I need your promise,
your word of honor, that this will be kept in strict confidence."

"You have it," he says. He looked away. He was embarrassed for
me, I guess.

"When I was going to law school in Nashville I lived off campus,"
I says. "Moved out of the fraternity house and got a room with a
Mrs. Clyde, out in the country, in Belle Meade. She didn't have to
rent a room but she was a widow. It gave her a man in the house.
She had a cocker spaniel and a parrot. She went home to New England in the summer and I was expected to keep the house open, pay
the maid and the yard man, and see that the dog and the bird got fed.
It was one of those Spanish architecture places. Six acres of blue
grass lawn, oak trees that must have been saplings when De Soto
passed this way. I had a big upstairs room over the porte cochere
off from the rest of the house with shelves for my law books, a pipe
rack, my gun case against the wall — the gentleman scholar's abode. I
won't bore you with details."

"Go on," Steve says. "I'm listening."

"When Mrs. Clyde left that summer for Connecticut there was a
nigger gal that cooked and swept and waxed and dusted — young, she
was nineteen. If Mrs. Clyde hadn't left perhaps I never would have
noticed her. Her name was Cassie."

"I see," he says. He blushed right down to his ears.

"Not quite," I says. "Being young and always reading and studying
is no excuse. I was always around the house that whole summer. It's
no excuse. I don't excuse myself. All I'm saying is I spoke to her one
day. One morning I stayed in my room while she made my bed. She
saw the books everywhere. What she thought I was, I don't know.
Anyway we talked. Her husband had beat her up and run off, she
said. She had all the usual nigger problems. The first thing I knew one
day right after breakfast I was following her upstairs to my room so I
could answer a question she had. Maybe she thought I was a doctor.
She wanted to know if she were pregnant, 'Gaining weight,' was
how she put it. Maybe she was innocent, maybe she had it in mind
all along. Anyhow you know what happened. I laid her upstairs and
downstairs all summer long, morning, noon and night. The cocker
spaniel followed us around. He was the only witness. After that first

time I couldn't stop. Steve, where I made my mistake, was *when I stopped seeing Cassie as a nigger and saw her as a woman — a person.*"

"You mean you fell in love with her."

"God forgive me. Maybe I did. Anyway it went on after Mrs. Clyde came back and it ended the day Mrs. Clyde happened to notice the dog scratching the door and trying to get into the attic room. Mrs. Clyde opened the door. Poor lady — she couldn't miss it. I packed up that same day and moved out like a brass locomotive. I never saw either one of them, or the dog either, again. I'm saying this can happen to a Southerner. It hasn't happened to me since."

Steve was quiet. He sat picking at the skin around his fingernails. "Since then you never made the mistake of looking at a Negro as a human being," he says. "All you've seen since have been niggers."

"I didn't say a human being, Steve. I said a person as opposed to a nigger. I know it sounds pretty damned crude," I says.

"Why tell me all that unless you're somehow proud of it?" he says. "Do you know, Oman, *I'm* proud of it for you. At least you've seen one Negro as a human being. That's progress. My grandparents and their grandparents for generations back probably never saw a single black individual as a human being."

"I don't want you to take it this way, Steve," I says.

"Then just how am I supposed to take it?" he says, looking at his fingernails. "Tell me. Then we'll both know."

"I don't want you to judge Willie Joe Worth so harshly," I says. "Under the right circumstances nearly anybody can get tangled up with some nigger bitch. When he does it's no sign you have to ruin him — take his job, shame his family. Is it? Now do you see? Don't Willie Joe Worth deserve a break, Steve?"

"How do you mean? A break?"

"I mean a little consideration," I says.

"But you said yourself he's broken the law, Oman."

"Well so have I, God damn it! Who hasn't broken the law at one time or another, I'd like to know! You don't want to see an innocent white man get his cods razored over a God-blessed nigger divorce, do you? You got something against a man because he's a white policeman?"

Steve didn't say anything. I turned back to the window.

Down in Main Street a battered old green tractor, pulling a trailer load of hay bales, had stalled.

The son was driving, a hulking boy with fat red wrists reaching out of the sleeves of an old brown army shirt about two sizes small for him. The old man, who would be his daddy, thin and sharp-nosed and hump-necked, wearing a black felt hat even in the middle of July, and on top of that limping because one leg was shorter than the other, limped around in front of the tractor as though somehow to coax it forward from that vantage point. The machine started bucking and stalling each time the boy got it started. A knotty bunch of people gathered suddenly around like flies, from nowhere.

"Must you really protect him?" Steve said.

The tractor moved. It jerked up the slope in front of Alf's filling station with the old man beside it now, pushing against the engine cowling with both hands, as though helping the tractor along, limping and jerking and straining more like a bug in his frantic movements, more like an ant than a man.

I caught myself saying: "Not just him, not merely the man for his own sake, Steve, but for Somerton — our town, our community. This whole region of the civilized world."

"The South," he says. "Go on — say it! Admit it. It's the business between Negro and white that mustn't come out, isn't it? But can't you see? That's an outdated notion, Oman — who cares any more?"

"I do," I says. "I know the man. I know the people Willie Joe Worth came from — you don't. What you don't realize is that we have two things at stake. Our law practice and Willie Worth's well-being. Now it might take a little finesse to put it over to him, but I believe I can show Willie Worth that what's in our best interest is in his best interest. What's better for L. B. Jones is also better for Willie. If Willie Joe can't talk Emma out of fighting this divorce then tell me who can? If he's getting in her pants, the least he should be able to do is talk her out of this damned fool notion — or don't that make sense to you either?" I spun around to look him in the eye. Steve was looking in another direction. "Well?" I says.

"How well do you know Willie Worth?"

It was his first sensible question. "Steve, look here," I says.

"I'm listening," he says.

"All right. He's no plaster saint. You're not going to hire Yale graduates on the kind of money the City of Somerton can pay a police-man." He was looking at me now. I turned slowly and looked back out the window. "Willie Joe's from what I'd call pretty decent peo-ple though. He's your old overseer class. Maybe he's got a ninth-grade education. He started out driving a school bus. Drank on the job; wrecked the bus. Got on as a helper on a beer truck, which was like turning mice loose in a corn crib when you get right down to it. So he lost *that* job. See?"

"I'm beginning to," Steve says.

"Here you have a man. He's got a wife and children to support. Somebody got the bright idea he belonged on the police force. So we hired him."

"From whipping niggers in the field he graduates in the next gen-eration to whipping them in the streets. That's logical."

"It's a distortion," I says. Could I convince him? I wondered if I could. Across the way in the second-story room over the farm store the indistinct shadows of the Elks Club members went tottering and fum-bling around under the light over the pool table. Most of Somerton's Elks are in their early seventies or their late eighties now. They are men who've outlived their wives, like my father did. They wear the BPOE belt buckles. They carry that tooth on their vest chains the way he did. And they drop dead in midsentence one day, like Ernest Hedgepath did, around the pool table and in the midst of his brother Elks. Between chitterling dinners and coon suppers they talk about the pleasures of World War I. They don't have time to worry about changes in the world. To hell with it, they won't be here that long. They do what they please. They say what they think.

"Didn't you in fact use your influence with the Mayor to get Willie Worth on the police force, Oman?" Steve says. "And before that wasn't he a falling-down-drunk bum, a Crossing derelict? Not to change the subject."

"You might call it a concerted effort on the part of this community to save Willie Worth, my friend. I had a part in it, yes. We did save him, didn't we? He's on the force. He's doing a good job. Can't we show him some kindness?"

"He's broken up a marriage —"

"His mother came to see me about Willie. If you could have read the sorrow and the hardship in that old lady's features, it might change your attitude. 'If only somebody'd give Willie Boy a chance.' That's what she said to me, sitting right where you're sitting. See those old men over yonder?" I says, pointing out the window.

"The Elks?" Steve says. "The Elks again, Oman?"

"If you lived that long would you want the shame of Willie Worth's innocent children on your conscience? Would you want to live as long as those old men have lived and take along the realization that you could have prevented a tragedy — and you didn't prevent it? Sure," I says. "So it takes a little extra effort to do the right thing. I could say to hell with it — let the chips fall like they will. What's the reputation of a daddy of little girls mean to me anyhow? No, Steve, I'm going to look Willie Joe up. I must try to talk sense to him. Maybe you wouldn't do it."

"I wouldn't, you're right — and *you* shouldn't," he says. "Your duty goes no farther than getting a divorce for Lord Byron Jones. Excuse me, but I think what you're about to do comes under the term of meddling, Oman. It's also a sort of dishonesty, isn't it? Attempting to get someone to intimidate an opponent's client? Trying to make her withdraw a petition she has every right to file?"

"Intimidate — Can't he be asked to reason with her?"

"A white cop reason with a Negro woman — here, in Somerton? If it weren't such a pathetic, tragic notion, Oman, I'd have to laugh. Oman, can you really be serious?"

"Sometimes you remind me of a pain in the tail," I says. "If Willie Worth was black I'll bet my legs you couldn't jump down there fast enough to warn him. You've sort of got a prejudice against white men, Steve. Do you know that?"

"Maybe I have," he says. "I hope not. But maybe I have." In another second he would start preaching. I felt it coming.

"Can you believe I'm trying to do the right thing in a difficult situation?" I says.

"Yes. But I have to say I think your wisdom is a little blinkered." He was underway then. All he needed was a pulpit. "It's hard to express the frustration I feel, Oman. This business of protecting one man because he's white and putting off another because he's black; of going out of one's way to do a favor here only to withhold a favor there. I don't understand that kind of conscience, Oman. Do we really owe it to the idea of the Old Confederacy to persecute one people, to deny former slaves and favor former overseers — as you call them? How many generations of intellectual cripples is the South going to produce? Where's the break-off point?"

I knew if I didn't interrupt him he'd start believing it himself. He paused and I opened up on him with both barrels.

"That's what I like to see," I says. "A grown man who will curse his own grandfather's memory and spit in his law partner's soup. Milk your neighbor's cow — so long as your neighbor ain't a nigger — through a crack in the fence, and steal the pennies off a dead man's eyes, provided the corpse is white. By God, just express your opinions outside this office once. Then neither of us will need a bus ticket to get out of town; believe me or don't believe me!"

"Oh, I believe you," he says. "I just don't share some of your medieval opinions, that's all. In the end perhaps I'm an idealist. I'm sure I'm a coward."

"Yes, and the idealists will end up blowing this world to shreds," I says. "Between Fidel Castro and Earl Warren and foreign aid the United States is about to be washed right down the God-damned drain. I don't know why we don't just deed the son of a bitch over to Russia now. Why not have it done with, instead of handing them the world a mere five billion or so dollars at a time. Do you?"

"First we've got to turn the country over to the niggers, Oman," he says. "And that may take a little time." He had me there.

"All right," I says. "But you have to admit it's a gloomy prospect. Did you see that bastard that was in here —"

"The process server? Miss Margaret told me. Who all was served?" he says.

"Me, as City Attorney, the Mayor, and Price Burkhalter. Governing board of the city parks in other words. Steve, I'll be honest with you. I just don't know where it will end. Nigger divorce suit this morning, nigger trial this afternoon. Now in walks that old fool from Federal Court in Memphis and serves a paper on me, by God . . ."

Miss Griggs buzzed my phone. "Tell whoever it is I'm busy, will you, Steve? Tell them you and Nella just had me committed to Bolivar for fascism."

Steve answered it. "Mr. Hedgepath's busy right now," he says. "All right — yes, Bob. I'll give him the message." He hung up the receiver.

"Well?" I says.

"It's the Mayor. Mr. Jimmy Bivens just died up at the hospital, he said tell you. He said to remind you about the trial."

"Poor Mr. Jimmy." I got up and walked out to Miss Margaret's desk. "Mr. Jimmy died," I told her. "Send flowers and put mine and Steve and Nella's name on them." Steve came out of my office. He got his hat. I looked at my watch. It was noon right on the button. Steve wasn't so upset he was forgetting lunch. I thought well let him go home and give Nella an earful. Not every man can claim a nephew who thinks you're Adolf Hitler. I says: "Miss Margaret, you know what today is?"

"Saturday?" she says. "Don't forget the trial."

I got my own hat. "That's right," I says. "Saturday," and walked out. A cocker spaniel would show more interest than that. At least the dog would wag his tail.

I went down the iron stairs on the outside of the building instead of going down through the bank. It was like an oven outdoors. I was across the street and into Templeton's before I remembered that the soda fountain was gone. I was ready to sit down at the counter for a bacon, lettuce and tomato sandwich and a Coca-Cola. All I saw instead was a long, new cosmetics case with a candy display on it. Rather than walk right back out, like a fool, I bought a little box of aspirin and some cigarettes. Looking at the place the soda fountain used to be was like being suddenly dropped out of the sky into a foreign country. The whole world might be that way for me someday soon — the whole lousy world.

I pushed back out into the heat and walked down to the City Cafe where anything you order is bound to come either raw, cremated, or not quite ripe.

I had already sat down on the stool next to Johnnie Price Burkhalter before I knew what was happening. "By God," he says, unfolding his subpoena and laying it out in front of me. "Just the man I want to see, by God, if you don't mind to explain a little bit about the meaning of this, by God." He acted like it was my idea to have it served on him in the first place.

"Why your meat is just in a sling, Johnnie Price, that's all," I says. "You've had it, my friend. The Feds have caught you."

[79]

"By God," he says, "you're looking at one somebitch that's about ready to move to Australia! This kinda nigger stuff makes me tired, know what I mean? When my own granddaddy . . ."

"Burn me a couple of hamburgers," I told the waitress. "And give me a Coke in a bottle — repeat, bottle. None of your fizzy imitation junk."

"We don't have the bottles. We can send next door to the filling station though."

"Then send next door," I says. "God only gave me one stomach." She sniffed and switched off, poking at her hairnet. "Now what's your problem, Johnnie Price?" I says, like I had forgot all about him.

"I mean seriously," he says.

"Seriously," I says, "we've all had it."

4

Lord Byron Jones

"The hearing is Tuesday," the undertaker said.

"Tuesday?" said Dr. Ocie Pentecost. "Good, then it will be all over Tuesday. Over and done with."

"Maybe after Tuesday I can sleep," L. B. Jones said, "without having to take pills."

"Two at bedtime," the doctor was saying. He counted out the little red capsules and put them in a paper envelope which he licked, sealed and handed to the undertaker. "Emma won't reconsider?"

"No. The other man's got her. He took her away from me. The rest of my life I'll wonder if it was in any way my fault . . ."

"Excuse me," said the doctor. He picked up the phone. "That's the hospital. Mr. Jimmy Bivens just died."

"Then you have to go?" said the undertaker.

"I can't help him now," said the doctor. "What were you going to say?"

"I wonder if it was my fault."

The doctor propped one foot on the treatment table and looked at his knee. "Perhaps the two of you weren't suited, L. B. This might have happened in spite of anything. If it hadn't been Willie Joe she might have taken up with some other man. Maybe not a white man, but then maybe so. Emma's not stable. She's always been immature, romantic and fanciful. Emma never really grew up."

"You saw all this, then?"

"Yes."

"*Before* I married her?"

"Yes," the doctor said.

"Why didn't you say something back then?"

"Unasked-for advice is something I don't offer. She . . ." The doctor shook his head. "It probably couldn't have been helped," he said. And then: "Love is blind, they say."

"You started to tell me something, didn't you?"

"It wasn't important."

"Something about Emma?"

"She hasn't told *you* anything recently, I suppose?"

"We talk but we don't communicate. She hasn't told me anything, no."

The doctor shook his head. "It couldn't have turned out any other way," he said. "Still you could try one last time, couldn't you, to bring about some sort of reconciliation?"

"I intend to try. You'd try again if you were me?"

"If I wanted her, yes. I would, if I still wanted her," the doctor said slowly.

"I still want her."

"I know. It couldn't hurt to try again," said the doctor. "Could it?"

"Is there some reason why she might come back to me?"

"Maybe there is."

"You can't tell me what?"

"Put it this way, I wouldn't tell you. If I were *sure* there were something I'd have no right. She's my patient."

"I understand perfectly," the undertaker said. He felt the envelope in his coat pocket. "Two at bedtime?"

"Yes. I wrote instructions on the envelope."

"Excuse me . . ."

The doctor smiled. "By the way, I've been meaning to call you. You're worried and overburdened just now, but you could do me a favor?"

"Of course I will if I can," the undertaker said.

"Not that there's any particular hurry. Lavorn Smith — do you know Mama Lavorn?"

"Lavorn and Benny, my assistant at the funeral home, they are witnesses for my divorce."

"Well," said the doctor, "Lavorn's got a malignancy. She knows she's dying."

"I knew she was sick."

"She's dying," the doctor said. "This morning she phoned. She wants her funeral planned and paid for. She asked me to tell you and ask if you would see her. Today, preferably. Because Benny's such close kin, she doesn't want to discuss it with him."

"I see," said the undertaker. "I'll call on her. The end is near, then?"

"Getting near," said the doctor. "Benny and Lavorn are your witnesses. They must think a lot of you. I mean, considering the black and white involvement. You might well have been hard put to find anyone to testify."

"They're very loyal," said the undertaker. "I'm lucky there at least, I have loyal friends. I'll see Mama Lavorn today," the undertaker promised.

"Thanks," the doctor said. They shook hands. "That should be a great comfort to her."

As the undertaker was getting in his car Ocie Pentecost's car came from behind the clinic. The old doctor waved and sounded the horn, driving quickly away up Main Street, headed east to the hospital where he would sign Mr. Jimmy's death certificate. The doctor, always wanted everywhere at once, seemed always just to be leaving or just returning, a man never still, never in any one place for long.

The undertaker got in the black convertible and drove back to Fort Hill, back past the Negro pickets still standing under the broiling sun in front of the Kroger Store.

Like the cowards they were, they didn't picket in front of the locally owned groceries, only the chain stores. If they picketed any other kind the owner might come out with a gun. Somebody would be killed.

A Negro picket had stood on the sidewalk in front of the Burkhalter Hardware Company until Mr. Johnnie Price Burkhalter had discovered that the man was there. The hardware dealer had walked out then to where the picket stood, so the story went. The white man had said he was going back in the store after a gun and if, when he came back to the sidewalk, the Negro were still there, he, Johnnie Price, would have to kill him. Much as Johnnie Price *hated* the idea, he would *have* to do it, so he said.

[83]

Turning then, so it was told, he went into his store. Just as he had promised, the white man had come back out to the sidewalk with a loaded twelve-gauge shotgun. The picket was gone.

It had been either leave or die. It was either retreat at once or be shot down. The white storekeepers in Somerton were on their honor to shoot to kill. The Kroger and A & P managers, on the other hand, had an excuse. If they shot down a picket they would lose their jobs.

So the Negroes and the Somerton police had come to what amounted to a practical understanding. Only the chain stores would be bothered by pickets.

And somebody, thought the undertaker, a Negro, perhaps, had beaten Mr. Jimmy to death. Thus no matter how carefully and tactfully things were arranged, still somebody would get hurt now and then; now and then somebody would get killed.

Retreat, or die.

Demand nothing more than equal treatment and you had, then and there, demanded too much. For that the white man was on his honor to shoot the black man down. The black man, then, could take his choice.

Retreat, settle for less. Or die.

Picket the Kroger and A & P so as to take the moral out of the issue, he thought, and remove the issue from the moral; token resistance in the place of resistance all out; playing it safe instead of playing it for keeps. The pickets decided on half-measures instead of making the storekeepers face a decision.

Such, then, that if one Negro had stood his ground and waited for one white man in front of one store, then, at least, the issue would have been joined. Such, then, that the *white man* would have had to decide, one way or another, and accept the consequences of his decision. *Shoot, or back down.*

Johnnie Price Burkhalter had done his part. The nigger ran.

Run, nigger, run.

And the nigger ran.

Just as well. For all he proved, he might have stayed at home. Better he had never agreed to picket in the first place. Or was he solicited? Did he agree? Or was it, rather, his own idea?

Did he, rather, whoever he was (nobody named him, because niggerlike he ran and nobody wanted to remember his name), decide on his own and letter the placard himself: JOBS AND FREEDOM. DON'T TRADE WHERE YOU CAN'T WORK! Did he take his placard without anybody urging him to it, and walk to town that morning and stand in front of the Burkhalter Hardware Company, square on the sidewalk in front of the store where there could be no doubt about it, where every customer and passerby had to see him and read his sign? Had he decided then himself, on his own?

Because it is one thing to let down some alphabet organization. To act for it on account of its urging, to be sold and coerced into something, and then at the moment of truth to run; yes that was one thing. To decide though on your own, without moral pushing and shoving from others. To decide on your own and then to run, was something else again, he thought.

Men could take the long view, if they so chose, saying: "Let's wait a hundred years and see what happens, see if things get any better." No one could blame men for that.

Or the short view: "Freedom now." Nobody would blame them.

But regardless, a man must not run away. Did he run, then he wasn't a man. Then everyone could blame him justifiably. Fear, he became; fear running off with reason.

The Negroes themselves said it, they told the story too, at the end saying: *The nigger ran.*

In effect saying: "I might not have gone there in the first place, but if I had gone, then I would have had to stay there and wait for Mr. Johnnie Price Burkhalter to come out of that store. If I went that far, then I'd have to see it on the rest of the way through."

He parked his car beside Emma's under the carport and entered the house through the back door. She was in her bedroom, half dressed, on the bed reading. She hardly looked at him. "Get out of here," she said, her legs sprawled wide and careless, without shame. That nether face confronting him because she didn't care. She knew besides that her nakedness taunted him. He averted his eyes.

"Emma, if I could just say something."

"Scat," she said, her voice hard, bored. "Scram."

"If you would promise me you won't see him again."

"Christ, oh Jesus Christ," she said. "Man, are you out of your mind?"

"If you could promise me, I'm willing to call it off. I'll take you back and we'll never mention it again. It isn't too late, where I'm concerned."

"Listen," her voice came flat and level from behind the book, "if you're going to do something, do it. But don't come to me crawling, don't come begging. You screwed me, so now I'm screwing you. That's life, Daddy. Spell it l-i-f-e. It's my turn, if you understand what I'm trying to tell you."

"How have I wronged you? At least you could . . ."

"Dear oh, dear shit," Emma said. "The man wants to know how! I couldn't quit Willie if I wanted to. You know that. Don't you know that? Haven't I told you that forty thousand God-damn times already? Get out of here, *please, Mr. Jones?*"

"I want to hear you say no. If you say no, I won't ask you again. Will you give him up and come back to me, Emma?"

"Never, Dad. Never happen."

"Say *no*, then. Tell me *no*."

"I'll tell you, *No! Hell, no!*"

"Then why must you fight me? Can't you let me have a divorce gracefully?"

"Mind your business," she said. "Maybe I like things the way they are."

"You must have a reason."

"If I do," Emma said, "that's for me to know and for you to find out."

"All right, I won't bother you again."

"Thanks," she said. "You never bothered me before. You got nothing to bother with and probably couldn't even bother yourself. Could you? Hey, Daddy!"

He walked out.

"Hey, old man!" She was laughing.

Outside, when he closed the door, he couldn't hear her. He got back in the car quickly and started the engine and switched on the cool flood of the air-conditioning and slipped on the dark glasses again. Then, as the sweat chilled and was dried on his legs, he backed the car out into the street and drove slowly down Fort Hill to the Crossing, waiting inside the car's protection and behind the protection of the sunglasses, waiting for his nerves to settle. *Run, nigger, run.*

Niggertown Saturday when The People came to town, when one

could see what was left of the Chickasaw blood. One saw the image of The People by whom and through whom the black and the white became kin and cousins. The eagle brow, the straight long nose, the copper penny skin either washed out yellow or itself washing out blue-black to brown. Thus The People remained in their children. Slowly he drove and circled through the district where the young men walked in pairs, narrow hipped as antelopes in high-waisted black trousers, broad shoulders bulging their red polo shirts, ropy, muscled arms swinging. They walked like proud warriors and wore black, narrow-brimmed straw hats with white bands. Sure that the women were watching them, they looked neither to the right nor the left, but always straight ahead.

Behind the Crossing the older men sat dozing in cane bottom chairs on the little sloping porches while their women worked — chopping stove kindling, hanging out the wash, weeding the little kitchen gardens while the man napped on the front porch and the children played on the hard, swept, compound-like earth in front of the house.

Women working, children playing, and the man without work, above and somehow outside of it in a way The People could understand. Did They rise up suddenly out of death's exile and return, this They could comprehend, he thought.

Not the cannery, however, where a line of sweating black men loaded a freight car, passing the heavy cartons hand to hand with a flowing, apparently endless rhythm, the cartons passing like chips into the half loaded car on the rail siding and the cannery crashing and steaming behind them. The black men were working because the work was there, because it would always be there and could never be conquered. This, he thought, this much The People never understood.

The black man worked, but he built nothing. Afterwards he could not see anything. Everything was the same as before. The work remained endlessly before him and all his children.

Had the black man worked this hard to build a mound, then could The People, his cousins, understand. Had he worked thus to honor the God Sun and protect His People's dead, building a high earth mound to exist forever, to protect bones and to speak to his children's children a thousand generations hence, something which would forever say: *We were*, then any amount of bone weariness were made sensible.

[87]

The black man, however, like the white man above and over him, made sweat fall trackless into trackless dust. Despite rivers of the sweat of men thus shed, thus fallen, these men left nothing behind.

Like the nigger carnival, burning and wheeling four nights during strawberry harvest and cotton planting, four nights fluttering like a death of mayflies, and gone then and the field empty, as though nothing had ever stood there.

As suddenly almost it would be midsummer and the carnival trash, the faded confetti and mashed Sweetheart Cups like hulls lay littered alongside the roads until the fringing grass, like time itself, hid and consumed this too, the eternal, the immortal grass.

Past the carnival grounds, past the Negro high school, the heavy car lurched crossing the railroad embankment which led the trains west, for Memphis. Slowing down, he drove the car into the dirt lane. He parked across the way from Mama Lavorn's Look and See Cafe and Tourist, in the shade of the sycamore saplings which hedged Cucumber's Automobile Graveyard. He cut the engine, and lowered the window glass beside him.

The stench of lower niggertown entered the car. The smoky stink of burned garbage drenched by the rain. He lit a cigarette and waited, giving the odor time to fade. He watched the collection of life in Cucumber's henyard, beyond the makeshift fence of tin signs and rusty wire.

The piebald, tethered goat; the white cock rooster and his mixed harem — one red, and two black hens. In this midst the dog, chained to his kennel, appeared back end first from his tiny house, spine bowed, legs shifted for balance like a mechanical thing moved upon levers. The dog strained and crapped. The feces fell shiny and still as dead black beetles. The dog's spine relaxed. He turned around and sat back aloof, smelling the wind while the geese and a gosling tirelessly paced the edge of the fence, reaching through it to pluck grass.

In the shade of a junked refrigerator cabinet the white cock briefly trod one of the black hens. Across the lane sparrows sang under the eaves of the cafe and tourist. Tin signs on the building advertised "Drink Double Cola" and "Goody's Headache Powders."

He got out of the car. Down beyond the building, towards the railroad tracks, past Mama Lavorn's plum trees and her rose arbor, her garden flourished in a tangle of bean vines and weathered tomato sticks. Corn waxed green beyond, a jungle to itself. He smelled the heat.

Reluctantly, because he hated his mission and had never before set foot in the place, this gin-den whorehouse, he crossed the road. Allow the nigger his fun, his drunk-whoring Saturday night cut-scrapes, his self-debauching crime world. Allow him that. Urge it on him because this is black man's fringe benefit. This lusting immorality helps keep him quiet, helps keep him down, helps keep him broke and satisfied with the eternal exchange — six days of his labor for one night here.

Justify thus his reputation for a black, wick-dipping, drunken son of a whore.

Justify thus his white boss. For taking pity on him and taking the pains to rob him.

Justify the police force, the jail, the courts, the Mayor.

Justify his two-thousand-dollar funeral because until he died or was killed he was never once the center of attention before. Not once in his whole life.

The undertaker pulled open the screen door and stepped cautiously into the seeming darkness of the cafe.

"There you are, Mr. Jones." Mama Lavorn took his arm and guided him through the slow emerging twilight to the bar. The initial impression of pitch darkness faded until he could see beer signs and then Mama Lavorn's ravaged, smiling face, and finally, against the far wall, a slender prostitute, barefooted, wearing a yellow dress, white hat and white gloves. She was playing a pinball machine.

"Either we can sit here or back in the parlor," Mama Lavorn was saying in her pleased voice.

"Here is all right," he said. "I'm comfortable here."

"It *is* cooler, because out here we have the ceiling fans," Mama Lavorn said. "I guess doctor told you? About my going away?"

"Yes, it's sad news."

"Later or sooner we all come to the harvest. Like wheat," said Mama Lavorn. "We stand up to be cut down. Won't you drink a beer with me, Mr. Jones?"

"No thank you, I . . ."

"Wait," she cried, going behind the bar. "Wait! Don't I know what

[89]

would please a geneleman better than beer. Rum!" she said, coming up with the bottle and making sure that he saw how she broke the untouched seal herself.

"I . . ."

"Do you take Coke or Seven-Up? Mr. Jones?"

"Coca-Cola," he said, after a pause.

"On the side?"

"Ah . . . yes," said the undertaker.

She was getting the glasses. "You don't mind celebrating with me a little while we talk and make plans?"

"Definitely not. You are very kind," he said. "Not too much," he was saying, but she had poured him half a glass of rum already. Mama Lavorn was opening the Cokes, moving with a forced swiftness, smiling a forced haggard smile, and not quite succeeding with any of it. He saw how pain was underlying it. Soon she would be bedridden. Her death-sickness was an odor, like green, rotted leaves. Though he might sense it a thousand times over again, yet always it carried with it the same helpless feeling of fright. He wanted to reach out his hand to her and pull her back away from doom, back towards life. Feeling thus he had no heart to refuse her hospitality.

Still smiling, she reached for the bottle. Her hand was withered, like a claw. In health Mama Lavorn had been a great spice mound of a woman. Now in her taut face, however, he read the outlines of her skull. Her feverish eyes were bright and gone deep in their sockets. "Tell me about it," she was saying. Her deep-set eyes moved. She turned her head. "My funeral."

"Of the four policies the Elipsed in Christ," he began, "is the most economical. In your case, any service you choose will be entirely free of charge."

"Wait," she said, "just a minute. I want the best. I have the cash money to pay. I *want* to buy and pay for it. Understand? Mr. Jones?"

"For Benny's sake, since you're a relative of his," he said, "there will be no charge."

"Hush, Mr. Jones. I *have* to buy this."

"As you wish, then," he said, trying the rum. It had a dark, sweet, fiery taste. "Benny being your kin, I'm wondering if you would want him as the mourner."

"I want Benny to mourn for me."

He nodded. He took a brochure from the inside pocket of his coat. The light was too dim to read by, but he held it for Lavorn to look at anyway, saying: "The policies are four in number. Home to Jesus is simple and sweet. Hallelujah Farewell is the most popular. That's the blue flag burial. When paid up in advance we fly blue flags from the front fenders of both the hearse and the leading mourners' sedan."

"That's nice," said Mama Lavorn."

"Finally there's the Angel Chorus, one we've never sold, a luxury item like the one big diamond ring in every jewelry store. The Angel Chorus is too expensive, that is, I would say, high out of all reason, still we stock it just to show a client what the *ultimate* possibilities are."

"How much?"

"Five thousand dollars, cash money. For the Angel Chorus the grave at the cemetery is dug twelve feet deep instead of the usual six."

"Deep," said Mama Lavorn. "Let me go deep when I go!"

"A band of singers, the Gospel Beale Ramblers, is hired from Memphis. The object is to omit nothing that would glorify and beautify this service, no expense would be spared, of course . . ."

"I'll take it," said Mama Lavorn.

"Very well." He took out his pen and his note pad. "Shall the deceased be smiling?"

"Only a faint, sweet smile of rejoicing, please sir."

"What color dress?"

"Shining gold. But I have the dress."

"We'll need it now."

"Wait a minute, Mr. Jones. I'll get it." She went through the curtain door beside the bar and up the stairs. She was no sooner gone it seemed than something touched his elbow. Startled, he turned. Beside him the little prostitute stood plucking at her white gloves.

"Play some music. You got a quarter? Lemme taste." She took his glass and drank from it. "What you drinking?"

"Rum," he said.

"Give me a quarter for the gash box," she said, handing him back his glass. She had a delicate, impassive face. She wore her hair in a feathery fringe about her fragile features.

Her hat was an imitation of small white flowers. She took the rum bottle in her gloved hands. She tried to read the label. "*Ron?*" she said.

"It means *rum*," he said.

"*Ron*," she said. "Gin is better, you know? Because gin will stay with you. Mama Lavorn likes *ron* though, huh?" Taking his glass she took another swallow, handing the glass back, saying: "I don't know about *ron*, Papa. Maybe it needs something with it so it will stay with you."

Boston rum given in barter for African slaves, he thought, loading off slaves in the West Indies and loading on sugar cane molasses to be swapped in Boston for another load of rum. Rum for colored slaves for molasses. She was saying: "You coming upstairs now? You want to go upstairs with me? Say, Reverend, are you a preacher?"

"Funeral director," he said.

"Come upstairs."

"No thank you."

She was moving her hips. "No?"

He shook his head. She poured rum in his glass. "Not too much," he said.

"I don't know what I'm doing here when I got friends in Memphis," she said. "I got girl friends in Memphis that visit the used car lot once a week, you know? For that they get a car to drive all the time just like it was their own, you know? So what am I doing here?"

"How old are you?"

"Old enough," she said, "but not too old. Young enough, but not too young. What makes you so unhappy? It's Saturday, Papa Daddy. Don't you like me?"

"I'm married," he said.

"So twist your arm! Ain't you Benny's boss?"

"Yes."

"That married Emma. I know you," she said. "You got yourself a mess. Didn't you *know* Emma was going to put your leg in a sling? Didn't nobody try to tell you nothing about her?"

Lavorn came back carrying the gold dress. "Jelly, dance for Mr. Jones. Play some music and show him how you can dance. Jelly can dance real good," Lavorn said.

The undertaker handed Jelly a quarter. She dropped it in the juke box and stood a moment in the middle of the dance floor, poised, waiting. The music came and she began twisting. She danced over to the pinball machine and put her hat and gloves on it.

"Jelly and you been passing the time of day," Mama Lavorn was saying. "That's good because Jelly's all right. She's got a good heart. Twist, Jelly!" Mama Lavorn said, close to his ear: "Is your mind worried?"

He felt the rum like an edge, a thin warmth.

"I can tell. Your mind's worried," she said. "The cop, Willie Joe, have you seen him? Has he bothered you, Mr. Jones?"

"Do you know something?"

"I know Benny said Emma's got her own lawyer. Benny said we might have to tell Mr. Willie Joe's name when we testifies."

"If you're scared, you can back out."

"I told Benny, I said: 'We'll testify anyway.' Benny and me agreed on that."

"Willie Joe might blame me," said the undertaker. The rum's edge was becoming more defined. He felt a lightness in his arms. Cotton padding seemed to collect just behind his face, making a thick insulation. "But do I need a white man's permission to divorce my own wife?"

Mama Lavorn bent closer to his ear now, almost touching him. "You know better! When me and Benny tell that! Don't you know Willie Worth would kill you, Mr. Jones?"

The undertaker shook his head and smiled. "Run, nigger, run. Eh?" He felt the rum running, beating in his blood. He thought: *Kill devil rum bullion the old anaesthetic. Getting fool drunk, eh? Drowning it?*

"Run, nigger, run — is that what you say?"

Mama Lavorn cupped her glass in both hands, looking down. "Why stick your head in the fire?" Her thin hand clutched at his arm. He felt the black clutch of bone and rot and withering. She seemed to be pulling him, pulling and pulling him towards something. Her black deep-lined face came close to his. He saw the Face he had not seen before, the Face no man wanted ever to see, a Face which he instantly recognized. "Why, Mr. Jones?" she said. "Don't common sense sometimes tell a man to run while he still has a chance?"

Bumping like a pulse beat the music ran on, muted now. Mama Lavorn released him but he felt her hand's imprint almost as though it still gripped him. He took a long drink. "There's a reason," he heard himself saying. His heart began beating faster. "A very good reason."

For the first time the undertaker saw that other people had entered the cafe. Other people were dancing. A little apart from the others, Jelly danced alone.

"Benny and me," Mama Lavorn was saying, "we believe you ought to have protection."

Snakelike, Jelly danced and wiggled, but slowly. She was Sybaritic now, like an eel slowly moving down in deep water. She was like a fragile, untroubled sea plant, purely sensuous, moving in the blue darkness, swaying in the dark sea-stillness.

Run, nigger, run.

THREE

1

The Trial

The Mayor crosses the street to Alf's service station at two o'clock and while he is having a few drinks of Early Times from the half-pint Alf opens for him free because he is the Mayor and Alf is the Bootlegger, a courtesy extended, in other words, between city officials, as it were (the Mayor joking and carrying on about the nigger trial he's about to hear in a few minutes), he, his Honor the Mayor, happens to notice that the American flag has not been raised on the flagpole on the City Hall roof and he has Alf phone across to the police station and ask somebody to please raise the God-damn flag.

Alf and the Mayor are watching when Willie Joe Worth, ordinarily on the night shift but working days too now, double-timing some nowadays to keep an eye on the nigger demonstrations, shoulders his way through the little crowd of blacks already gathered in front of the police station in hopes the trial will be held in open court so they can hear it. Willie Joe goes up the City Hall steps and inside the building. In a minute the Mayor and Alf see him appear on the roof. The first try Willie Joe gets the flag on upside down and he has already raised it and Alf is already phoning the clerk's office in City Hall to have Miss Rosa catch Willie Joe on his way down and tell him he's got the flag upside down when somebody hollers from the sidewalk and gets Willie Joe's attention.

The flag comes back down. Willie Joe switches it right side up and hoists it again, this time not quite *all* the way to the top of the pole. The lines are fouled up some way. He fiddles with them a minute, can't get the flag raised any higher, gives it up and leaves it like it is.

Already the crowd of niggers in front of the police station is larger when Willie Joe Worth comes down the front steps of City Hall and goes back next door into the police station — a new building with glass across the front like a department store or a restaurant, so you can see the desk and the police and the others waiting around inside for the trial to start.

Alf opens another Coke. The Mayor has run out of chaser. "I don't know if I should phone the highway patrol or not," the Mayor says. He has a round red sunburnt face and fat cheeks, like a tomato. "Just in case they get smart alecky. Would you say it's a hundred of them over there now?"

"Fifty maybe," Alf says. "Or even less than that. You take niggers always seem more than what they are." Alf works halfheartedly on the black half-moons under his fingernails, using the little blade of his pocket knife. "Anything black looks bigger than what it is."

The Mayor nods, not halfway listening, feeling better now, feeling warmer inside himself and like he is maybe two people — himself, the Mayor, and another man calmly taking it all in and not himself involved, this other man. Everything gets clearer. The Mayor begins to see everything in depth instead of flat like he was seeing it before. He hands Alf the empty half-pint and Alf motions to his nigger, Washington, who takes the half-pint from Alf and slips it in his pants pocket and goes slowly out the front door of the station and on around behind the building where he will break the empty in the vacant lot — mainly just several acres of broken half-pints, weeds, and a few empty oil cans.

Washington is back in a minute. He leans against the counter again in his usual place beside where the kerosene heater stands in the winter, next to the flashlight batteries and the cans of household oil and lighter fluid. He's always there like a piece of furniture and he never says anything. He is one nigger who never smiles, never frowns, just goes about his work which is the way Alf likes him to be — there, but not something you have to notice. Washington is like the face on a dollar bill or a sign you don't have to read, you've seen it so much.

"Well, I guess I better get over there," the Mayor says.

"Give them bastards hell," Alf says.

"Don't worry," says the Mayor. He turns on his automatic smile, gives a broad wave, and crosses back over to the police station.

The little crowd of niggers doesn't quite make room for him to pass. The Mayor stops before them, nods and smiles. He doesn't see a single black face he recognizes.

"They having the trial in open court upstairs please sir?" says one.

"That's up to the City Attorney, Oman Hedgepath," the Mayor says.

"We axed him and he said it was up to you."

The Mayor takes a deep breath and smiles. "Now what we got here is just a hearing, not a regular trial. See what I mean? So it's gonna be in the little conference room. That's how it's gonna be. It isn't room for spectators. I mean that's how it is, on that." The Mayor smiles. "Fair to both sides, that's the way it's gonna be, if you'll just excuse me." The mayor clears his throat.

Sullenly they step aside and the Mayor enters the police station. Once inside he looks back. The crowd is still there. "Wanna move 'em from out in front?" a policeman asks.

"Let 'em be," the Mayor says. "Just interested in the outcome of the hearing, that's all. We ready?"

He walks back to the little conference room where the police sometimes question prisoners, a nice windowless room with mahogany-veneer paneled walls, fluorescent lights, and a neat green-carpeted floor. Cardboard boxes of recovered stolen merchandise line the floor along one wall so the Mayor must step carefully to get by to his place at the head of the conference table. Oman Hedgepath and the nigger lawyer are already seated. The Mayor sits down. Everybody has a green armchair, same color as the carpet, very comfortable and modern. Willie Joe Worth comes in smiling and shuts the door and takes a chair next to the wall on the Mayor's right. Down straight in front of him, beyond the end of the conference table, are the four defendants side by side in conference chairs against the wall — two girls and a boy, and the ringleader, the Reverend Goodman.

The Chief of Police opens the door and comes in followed by three more officers.

Oman Hedgepath clears his throat and stands. "I believe we are ready, Mr. Mayor, your Honor. The defendants are Lonnie Shepherd, nineteen; the Reverend Goodman, forty-one; and Misses Caroline Tucker and Beatrice McCaslin, both eighteen. I believe these warrants so identify them. I will swear in now as witnesses the arresting officers — all at once." Oman Hedgepath looks down at the Beale Street lawyer. "Is that all right with Counsel for the Defense?" Beale Street says, "Yes." The Mayor thinks "Yes, sir" would sound a lot nicer. Willie Joe Worth goes around the table to stand with the Chief and the other officers to be sworn in. They are all neat in their short-sleeve blue shirts and darker blue worsted trousers, each wearing a .38 special pistol holstered at his side, a blackjack in each right hip pocket, a hat held in each right hand, all heads crewcut and all swearing to tell the whole truth and nothing but the truth. They sit down and Oman Hedgepath asks the Chief of Police if he has been Chief of Police since October 1, 1957, if he is thirty-seven years old and a Somerton resident, and if his name is George Jenkins Fly. The Chief says yes, he is all of that.

"Would you then tell the court what happened Saturday a week ago," says Oman Hedgepath.

"Yes *sir*," says Chief of Police George Jenkins Fly, very muscular and blond, speaking in his high husky voice like a football player being interviewed on the radio, being in fact a former Somerton High School fullback, saying:

"Twenty-six niggers paraded up and down Main Street carrying signs and hadn't no permit to parade. I seen 'em the second time they come past City Hall and we went out and told them they was arrested for parading without a permit. Among 'em was those four yonder, Mr. Reverend Goodman, Miss Tucker, Miss McCaslin and Lonnie Shepherd."

"Thank you, Chief," says Oman Hedgepath. "How many in all?"

"Twenty-six niggers," Chief Fly says.

The Beale Street lawyer sticks up his hand without raising his eyes from some papers he has spread on the table in front of him beside his briefcase. "I prefer knee-grows if the court please. Do you mean knee-grows, Chief?"

"That's what he said, didn't he? Niggers?" the Mayor asks.

Beale Street is making a note with a sharp yellow pencil. "I will not quibble over the pronunciation of the word," he says, "but . . ."

"Chief is employing the old pronunciation," says Oman Hedgepath, "historically valid and correct. I believe learned Counsel for the Defense will find that 'nigger' is British English. I could refer him to several examples from history and literature should he wish it."

Beale Street raises his pencil. "It reminds us however of, and connotes unhappy conditions under, slavery, that particular pronunciation. However I've said we will not quibble."

"Well knee-grow reminds me of certain Scandinavian sociologists and others who have assumed an authority and published inaccuracies concerning racial matters which I find not only distasteful but provocative as well. However I will not quibble. Your witness." Oman Hedgepath sits down and takes off his glasses.

Beale Street stands up and slips his glasses on and looks now and then at his notes made with the sharp yellow pencil. "Now, Chief, they were parading. Anything boisterous?" The ordinance is so new it is still a fold-out piece of paper cellophane taped into the city ordinance book. Beale Street holds the fold-out with his left hand and looks down at it. "Any loud noise or anything?"

"Naw, sir," says Chief Fly, when Beale Street looks at him.

"That's all," says Beale Street. "I would like now . . ."

Oman Hedgepath stands up and slips on his glasses. "I'll just make an opening statement if I may, your Honor, and say that clearly the ordinance was violated. They were parading and they did not have a permit."

"I'll plead now," says Beale Street.

"Okay," says the Mayor. "You plead guilty or not guilty?"

"Not guilty."

"The law, the ordinance is there in the book. Defense Counsel has read it," Oman Hedgepath says.

"I have a statement," says Beale Street.

"Go ahead," the Mayor says. "Somebody gimme a cigarette."

Beale Street puts his hand over his heart: "Since slavery times we have had certain problems come down to us. There is great unrest all over America today on account of minorities wanting their freedom. In the paper I see where the Russians and the United States are going to sign an A-bomb treaty. That's what we need. Talk over the table. Not war. Here in this case these people were expressing themselves — what's in their hearts — by marching, demonstrations. That's all. Not bothering anybody. Just marching. This is the first time they have been arrested . . ."

"But they've marched several times before without a permit," Oman Hedgepath butts in, "haven't they, Chief?"

"At least six times or maybe seven," says Chief Fly.

"Yes — " Beale Street continues, his hand still over his heart. "But you try the bootlegger for the half-pint you catch on him, not for all he's sold. So this time it is justice to try just this instance. Leniency is in order today in the name of restraint and justice. Our trouble has been that the two races have not talked to each other in the South. Now it is getting better. Now we are at least talking. Nobody is going to get all he wants, but at the same time somebody's going to have to give up a little something. Talk has been about blood running in the gutters. I don't think that kind of thing is going to happen in Somerton, Tennessee. I been talking to different ones and I don't think any blood is going to run over this thing. Yet this is a sign of the times, a sign of the unrest that is more violent in New York City than here, and I hope I am not one of those causing unrest. I hope I am one who speaks with the voice of peace and moderation. What these accused persons have done is . . ."

"How're they pleading? What was it again?" the Mayor says. Willie Worth puts an ashtray down at his elbow. The Mayor uses it.

"Not guilty, your Honor," says Beale Street.

"All right, get on with it," the Mayor says.

"Thank you. All they have done is get out and walk to express their feelings. They want freedom. Everybody wants freedom. They express it in this way and they have a right under the Fourteenth Amendment to gather and express themselves. I'm not saying the City of Somerton doesn't have the right to an ordinance against marching without a permit, but at the same time I'm saying that if moderation is exercised and mercy is shown maybe this whole thing will die down and go away — but if the law is applied in a harsh way it may serve to aggravate a situation that is already a *bad* situation. I plead for a dismissal."

"You got anything else?" says the Mayor.

Oman Hedgepath stands up. "As City Attorney I could not find a dismissal acceptable. A light fine, yes; dismissal, positively no. We have this ordinance on the books and it is a clean, honest, wholesome ordinance. All it says is that in order to parade in Somerton you have to apply for and get a permit from the Mayor's office, that's all. Now these defendants knew about the ordinance and they violated it coldly and deliberately six or seven times before they were finally arrested. They are charged just this one time, it is true, but let me say that there is a reason for this ordinance. The City of Somerton must operate with a limited police force — fifteen men to keep law and order, both night and day. We don't have the money to hire a beefed-up police force. So far we have kept law and order and we are going to continue to keep law and order. Our police are first-class officers doing a first-class job. But for the protection of both races, for darkies and white folk alike, we're going to have to have advance notification as to when a march will be made, the day — and the hour, and the line of march. Then we can protect these people. Otherwise law and order cannot be kept. Somebody would get hurt. What we have here is a just charge against premeditated violators. Your Honor must make up his own mind, but I would not condone dismissal."

"Okay, anything else?" The Mayor looks around at everyone. Willie Joe winks again. Nobody speaks. "All right," says the Mayor. "The law says I can fine you and give you thirty days. I'm going to take off the jail sentence and leave on the fine — I fine you each one fifty dollars and costs, and by God don't let me hear of any of you marching again."

Beale Street has looked down again, that way he has of looking down and holding his hand to the breast of his blue suit, maybe not holding it over his heart so much as drying off his sweating palms. The Mayor decides against making a long speech.

"If everybody understands what I've said then court's adjourned."

The defendants, the police, the attorneys, all stand up and begin to move out of the room.

"We'll appeal," the Memphis lawyer says, so the Mayor can hear him.

"Why don't you do it right now then? Next door in City Hall. I'll show you where," Oman Hedgepath says. "You'll have to file a separate appeal bond in the General Sessions Court office."

"May well as to do it now then," says the nigger lawyer.

The Mayor walks out of the room and right away sees how the

crowd outside has swelled, all of them looking in the windows instead of home and minding their own business or working at jobs like honest folks. He opens the door and looks at their black foreheads, nothing else. He steps out and the crowd moves a little on the sidewalk.

"It all over," says a nigger voice.

"Light fines, that's all. Just light fines, if you see what I mean," the Mayor says. "Now if you'll excuse me." They make way and he crosses Main Street to Alf's and ducks inside the station and sits down on Alf's sofa made out of an automobile front seat with iron pipes welded to it. Alf opens another Early Times and another Coke and Alf and the Mayor both sit quietly and watch the nigger lawyer come out of the police station and wave to the crowd. The crowd falls back and they wave at him like a mob waving at a baseball player. Then Oman Hedgepath is beside the nigger lawyer and going with him up the steps into City Hall.

"Don't it make you want to vomit? Look yonder," says Alf. "Oman's talking to him."

"Sure," says the Mayor, "but he'd find the General Sessions Court office anyway and file his appeal. Oman ain't doing nothing only walking along to see what he's up to — to watch him in case he makes a mistake. Hell, it ain't no way to keep the black bastard from finding the office, Alf."

"Yeah, but it makes me want to vomit. Looks like you could arrest him for trespassing where he ain't wanted at or shoot him or something."

"That's just the trouble," the Mayor says. "Nothing's legal any more. Nothing you wanna name's legal. It's all for the nigger and getting worse ever day that goes by. If they don't hurry up and impeach Earl Warren I don't know what this God-damn country's coming to, Alf."

The Mayor feels the heat beginning to ease off from what it was when he first stepped out of the air-conditioned police station and crossed over to Alf's the second time. The whiskey and Coke stops him from sweating so much. After a minute he phones his office and tells them they know where they can find him if they need him, which of course he knows they won't need him but anyway it's a courtesy on his part, letting folks know where they can find him — just in case.

Then the regular bunch of cronies starts drifting into Alf's and pretty soon it keeps Washington busy just quietly taking the empty bottles out back and busting them. The Mayor tells about the trial over and over again. Each telling gets funnier and better.

"By God I told the somebitch," says the Mayor. "I says by God I don't care if you've got a hundred God-damn law degrees you ain't walking into this court and telling me how to run it. By God you're just a nigger to me and by God don't forget it!"

"Cleaned his plow, did you?"

"By God, lemme tell you, I lowered the blade," says the Mayor. "Another smart word out of that black lawyer somebitch and I'd of had him altered — and by God he knew it!"

And even if it's a lie and more than half of them know it is, anyway it's what they all enjoy hearing more than anything else. Each time he tells it they all feel a little better and a little braver.

There is a quiet pause and a farmer from out near the Knifebill Community speaks up softly. "That was a bad thang about Mr. Jimmy."

They all agree with him, that yes, it sure was. "I heard it was a nigger done it," Alf says. "Ain't that right, Mayor?"

"Awful thing, awful thing," the Mayor says, shaking his head. "I got to go down to the funeral home this evening."

"They'll have him ready by this evening?"

"That's right. The funeral's tomorrow. You wonder what it's gonna come to when a nigger can walk into a man's place of business in the broad daylight and knock his brains out."

"It was a nigger?" the same farmer asks.

"Well, now we got a lead that it was a nigger, I'll put it that way. Before he passed on Mr. Jimmy mentioned something about nigger. Course, like Lawyer Hedgepath said, it's a motive in every crime. So we're asking around to see if we can locate a nigger which had it in for Mr. Jimmy Bivens. It narrows down a little because the nigger we want is fat. Put those two together and you got the bastard that did it, see?"

The Mayor looks around. "Hell, somebody'll arrest his carcass before midnight. We got a bulletin out to the other towns and all. Then they'll pick him up."

Alf takes out his keys from his pants pocket. They are on a brass chain fastened to his belt. He unlocks the Coke machine and swings back the door. He takes some cold half-pints of Early Times out of the bottom of the machine.

"I'll take another half-pint while you get the door open, Alf," says the Mayor.

"All right," Alf says. "Coming right up."

A car pulls into the filling station from Main Street. Four white men get out of it and come in. Alf has to unlock the Coke machine again even though he has just locked it back. Business is good. "Tell about the nigger trial, Mayor," Alf says, unlocking the machine.

The Mayor smiles. The rest laugh. "Well," says the Mayor beginning, "I asked Alf if he thought we'd need the God-damn highway patrol and Alf says hell no, just tell them black somebitches by God to go home. So I walked across to where they were standing with their eyes all rolling and showing white you know. The NAACP had told them they had to stand out there and God, oh, they was scared stiff. You never saw such a scared bunch of niggers."

The faces around him are relaxed again. "Tell it, Mayor!" somebody says. "Amen!"

2

T. K. Morehouse

"Beat his brains out and he died at the hospital. Died of a brain concussion so they claim. Woke up onct they said and was talking pretty good. Then just as quick as a blink, the fellow says, that concussion hit his brain and down the hill Mr. Jimmy went."

"Mr. Jimmy who," I says.

"Mr. Jimmy Bivens. Where are you from?" It was a combination gas station and grocery on the outside edge of town. I was having two Powerhouse candy bars and a big Dr. Pepper, just a snack to hold me for I never believe a white man should eat much in the heat of the summer's day.

"Memphis," I says. "Mr. Jimmy who?"

"Bivens, runs a grocery like me, or did till somebody whanged his brains out. They give him ox gin and artificial restoration maybe two hours or more but it never provided a bit of hep for he was done beyond it onct that concussion hit him."

He sounded just a like a doctor talking. "What's *your* line of business?" he says.

I put the last bite of Powerhouse in my mouth and made out like it was too much to chew. Then I says: "You're Mr. Dan Dashazo, ain't you, owner of this grocery?"

"I shore am," he says. "How come you to know that?"

"Well," says I, "you know. The nigger business." I felt inside my coat for his paper.

"Yes," he says. "I told them, I says now boys if you want to vote that's fine with me, but now just one thing, don't come back to Dan Dashazo asking for no credit, no tars nor gas nor fertilize nor cotton seed, I says for after you sign up in that vote book it's cash on the line, if you know what I mean, and ever note I've got on a colored man who decides he's got to vote, why then that's due and payable now. So if you want me to call in all my paper, just go on and register up. Told ever last one just that, so I did," he catches his breath. "Yes sir." He smiles. "And what kinda business might you be engaged in doing?" he says. "You said Memphis?"

"Depedy Marshal T. K. Morehouse," I says, and handed him the papers. "You'll kindly appear in Federal Court in Memphis on the date cited."

"What fer?" he says. "Court?"

"Well, it's all wrote down there. Don't mean nothing only that they're gonna let niggers vote," I says. He takes a minute to study it.

"This here's onconstitutional," says Mr. Dashazo. "It ain't worth the paper it's wrote on, you know that?"

"Well," I says. "That's up to you on that part. Understand when they hand me one I have to deliver it."

"It's all right. It's all right, but my only point is something like this don't mean nothing. You can't tell a man who he can extend the credit to and who he can't, no more than you can tell a man who he must wait on in his own store, who he must work for, because this country's free. Onconstitutionallery will never win the day. It's bound to blow over and be forgot about. You take the latrine court, what power do they have over a man?"

"Well," I says, "some say—"

"Now, listen. Mister, I went all the way through World War I and never heard one word about no latrine court till it was brung up just a few year ago. Next thing they'll be wantin a nigger to go to the bathroom in the same place as a white man. My God, sir, don't you know what an impossible thing that is?"

"You won't git no argament on it outta me," I says. "But they're saying —"

"And Earl Warner, who in thunder is Earl Warner?"

"You mean Earl — "

"Listen, mister," he says. "I don't care who Earl Warner is, but if

I hear one nigger I hear a thousand talkin about Earl Warner like he's the next thing to John the Baptist."

"I better go," I says.

"Well you come back," he says. "Come back and visit anytime."

3

Oman Hedgepath

Look up and it's sundown. The day's over and you haven't been anywhere. You haven't done anything, it seems.

I heard Miss Griggs tell Steve good-bye. He came in my office. I
heard her steps on the stairs, on the way home to her mother.

"You ready to leave?" he asked.

"Don't have time to go home," I said. "We got a Citizens' meeting
in City Hall. I'm to sit at the speaker's table with the speaker."

"Who is he?"

"Dr. Burroughs from Mississippi. Why don't you come hear him?"

"No thank you."

"He might change your mind. Maybe if you'd listen to him once all
coons would start looking alike to you. Maybe you'd regain your sense
of mental balance. Dr. Burroughs has the facts at his fingertips."

"So I hear," Steve said. "Do you have to endorse those cross burn-
ers, Oman?"

"Citizens don't burn crosses," I reminded him. "If you'd just come
to a meeting."

"Nothing doing," he said. "God, no."

"Afraid you might get convinced?"

"Fat chance," he said. "I don't want to hear him because I might
talk back to him and make a fool of myself. I might get carried away
and heckle him."

"You probably would," I said. "Just like a Communist."

"Do you agree with what he says?"

"Partway," I said. "I agree with what he aims to do. Maybe some of the things he says are extreme, but he's a showman. Where organizing resistance to race mixing is concerned showmanship helps. Those points count just the same as any other. I haven't noticed any liberals or Communists worrying about the means they use. Should I?"

Steve shook his head. "You amaze me! You know exactly what you're doing. Those others, that mob, they don't know. But you know, and still you go along with it. You lead the others — or I should say you mislead them. Don't you have any misgivings?"

"Never a single qualm. I don't worry and neither did the Morgans, the Fords, the Mellons and Rockefellers worry when they stole the South. They chiseled it right out from under its rightful owners. Every power company, every railroad, every stick of wood, drop of oil, lump of iron, chunk of coal. We lost our war in Dixie and those colonialists bought everything we'd ever owned at two cents on the hundred dollars. Maybe you enjoy being disinherited, but me, Steve, I'm one peckerwood that has never liked it. They can screw me all right, but they can't make me like it. So I'm going to fight them — how about you?"

"Always toting that same anvil," Steve said. "Today it's colonialism and absentee ownership. What's it going to be tomorrow?"

"Don't worry," I said. "I'll think of something. It ain't hard. Did you ever stop to wonder why the South is the poorest section of the United States right now, today, when it comprises a third of the area of the United States and contains eighty per cent of this nation's natural resources? Don't that kind of give you boils where you sit down? It worries exploited people everywhere else in the world — why not us?"

"That's all over," he said. "And the issue besides . . ."

"Over hell," I said.

"The issue is freedom and equality for the Negro. That's something we can do something about. On the other hand, we can't correct these other things you talk about. When the Confederacy lost, all this was decided."

"At Appomattox," I said, "and the way the Supreme Court has ruled ever since. Can the State of Tennessee take back her coal and her iron and her forests, her phosphate lands?"

"I've said that couldn't be undone. It's a fact we've got to live with

[111]

— no state can secede. No state can confiscate from absentee owners. Isn't this law, and aren't we bound and pledged to uphold law and encourage respect for it? What else are we here for?"

"Are you serious?" I said.

"I'm serious," he said. "Oman, can't you see that what's held the South down this long is racial bigotry? Don't you know by the same token that when the black man is raised up, the white man will be raised up with him?"

He really believed it, the doctrine of the great, infallible Rastus Mc-Gill. Maybe he thought I wasn't wise enough to recognize where all this came from, thought I couldn't hear it trickling out of those Republican hills above Chattanooga where the first carpetbaggers took hold. I let him run on with it. I sat back and closed my ears and smiled at him and then said: "You haven't cited me a single fact. No statistics. You're all theory."

"There's nothing theoretical about a lynching," he said. "I don't call that theoretical."

"Well then," I said, "account for this. Account for the fact that in 1929 when the average per capita income tax of the population of Delaware was forty-four dollars and ninety-three cents, the average in Mississippi was thirty-nine cents! If the reason is anything other than the fact that everything of value in Mississippi was owned by some Yankee capitalist sons of bitches outside of Mississippi, then I'll throw my brains to the hogs right now. Mississippi is, was, and always will be as segregated as you can get. Does Jim Crow make that much difference?"

"I think," Steve began. "I think . . ."

"Wait a minute," I said. I raised my hand to him the way a policeman stops traffic. "Before the Civil War, if I mistake not, Mississippi had the second highest per capita income in the United States of America, second only, I believe, to Louisiana? Now does that say anything to you? Give me an honest answer."

"I think Hitler probably used many similar arguments to unite Germans behind the Third Reich. I'll grant you the South was raped after the Civil War. I'll grant you that radical Reconstruction was the greatest error and, even, perhaps, the greatest national crime ever committed. God knows we're still suffering from it, but none of this excuses what's been done to the Negro, Oman. None of it!"

"Well where, in the first place, did you get the idea I'm out to hurt the nigger or hold him back? I'm proud of every nigger that gets ahead in this world and I've got plenty of nigger friends. When the richest nigger in town wanted a divorce, who did he have to have — or bust?"

"Who talked you into taking his case?"

"You did. But I took it, and no matter how I took it, that point counts in my favor too."

"I'm not saying you're all bad," he said. "I'm just saying you're wrong. I'm saying the Citizens are wrong. Why take out your frustrations on the Negro? Must you punish him for what you imagine the North did to you? It's the worst sort of intellectual bigotry! It's insane, Oman, wrong!"

"But anyhow you'll grant me that the South's had a raw deal. That we were robbed?"

"I don't deny it, but tell me what your aim is, what is this driving madness of yours all about if it isn't simply an all-out effort to keep the Negro down and punish him for being black? What else, if not this, Oman?"

"Race purity," I said, "is part of it. But the larger thing is the return of Southern independence."

"You can't be serious, Oman!"

"But I am," I said. "One day the North is going to give us back our oil fields and our forests and sulphur mines and everything else because now we're going to organize and agitate! Hell, yeah! The other white conservatives, millions strong, and one day this country will have given us back what's ours by rights anyway. And when the North does finally cough up, when we do get ownership of the railroads and everything else in the way of a strategic resource located in the states of the Old Confederacy, the North is going to think it's a cheap price to pay. Watch and see! I haven't any illusions about it coming to pass in my lifetime, but it might very well come in yours."

"What makes you think the North would give all that up?"

"For the sake of peace," I said. "Racial peace. Because until we get it back I can guarantee you one thing. I can guarantee you the North won't have anything but solid nigger troubles. The Citizens and the other organized whites are going to agitate the niggers in America, and especially in the North, until the sheer blood and chaos will bring every Northern city to its knees."

[113]

Steve thought it was ridiculous, of course. Still, though, he listened. I could see him wondering.

"Sure," I said. "They'll want laws and appropriations and troops and a lot more to solve their problem, but one third of the states and a majority of the white people in this country will be working against them. When the riots and the terror have whipped them to their knees up there north of the Mason and Dixon we'll have the second Appomattox."

"Are you out of your mind?"

"We'll swap them the troops and the laws and the appropriations — we'll swap the bastards peace — for the return of the South's natural and strategic resources into the hands of Southern legislatures. From there it will be only a short step to getting it all back into the hands of white Southerners."

"And then what?" he said.

"Then we'll run this God-damned country the way we did before the Civil War. Why not? Strange as it may sound to you, the nigger is going to help us get our property back. Our main tool and weapon is going to be a howling, murdering, Yankee-killing horde of rioting niggers . . ."

"Like the Jew was used in Germany," Steve said.

"I don't know what it's like, Steve. And believe me, Oman Hedgepath don't care. Believe me? You wanted a look at the master plan. There it is."

"Thank God you'll never be able to bring that about," he said.

"I just want you to know it ain't the nigger I'm against. It's the North I'm fighting. And it's not the nigger they're for either, it's the South they're against and they've used the nigger for an excuse to punish us all these years. Well, now the shoe is about to be put on the other foot, and by God, watch and see if we don't use this thing! See if we don't win!"

It was too much for Steve. He went to the door. "I'll see you," he said. "So long."

"Don't forget the funeral!" I hollered after him. I wasn't sure whether he heard me or not because he was already on the stairs, going down.

I locked the office and went down the outside stairs and up to Main Street, beside the bank. Main was wide and empty. I crossed the street to the City Cafe. Willie Joe Worth's wife, Flonnie, came to wait on me, a thin woman with long arms. She was slumped in the shoulders and pregnant, but smiling.

She had the same smile I notice on a lot of unhappy people. It's the way they hide their bitterness. It's always a quick smile, too quick to mean anything other than that they're hiding their unhappiness.

When she was back behind the lunch counter where she thought I couldn't see her, Flonnie's long face relaxed. A change came into it. If that look was unpleasant, at least it was the real Flonnie.

I thought well, overworked and underpaid, with her working days and Willie Joe working nights. If she sees him, I thought, when does she?

I could see them passing each other like automobiles do when they meet out on the highway. Sometimes one will flash its lights. I thought about Flonnie's children, kids without a chance in the world to amount to anything. That's the worst, Willie Joe and Flonnie having children they can't do for and don't want and me, getting to the age where I know I'll never have any kids of my own, getting to the age where realizing it hurts and never stops hurting.

I snapped out of it. Long as they were both employed, Flonnie and Willie Joe, then their children would be all right. Just because the children's father got tangled up with some nigger slut, was that any reason his name had to be blurted out in open court? Was that reason enough to ruin him and ruin the lives of his and Flonnie's children, just because some nigger had to *insist* on a divorce? Because if I can say one thing and be honest, when it comes down to brass tacks with me, blood is thicker than water. To me all coons look alike, I thought.

She poured my coffee. "Doing all right, Mr. Hedgepath?"

"Slowly dying, I reckon," I said. She smiled.

"How's your family, Flonnie?"

"Fine," she said, "except the nigger demonstrations are causing Willie Joe to have to work a double shift. That can't last forever though, can it? Haven't you all about got that taken care of?"

"I don't know, Flonnie," I said. "We tried four of 'em today."

"That's what I mean," she said. "Won't that stop them? Don't you think it will?"

"Let me say this," I said. "The North is going to have it a whole lot worse than we are. I don't claim this trial today will stop our niggers from ragtagging around, but we're going to keep this do-dah stuff in control down here. Up in the North it's going to be a different story. They're going to have trouble up there out of this world," I said.

"I sure hope you're right," Flonnie said. "That's exactly what they deserve, sending soldiers down on us."

"They'll have it all right," I said. "And they'll get sick of it. They'll have it up to their ears. Wait until they march on Washington."

"What about this march on Washington?"

"It'll cost the U. S. Treasury, that's you and me, about fifty million dollars just for hiring extra police to protect those Communist-front coons. Even so, it is bound to get out of hand. I hope it turns into the biggest nigger riot and massacre in the history of the world."

"Well, I sure hope so too. I sure hope you're right!"

"They're just liable as not to burn Washington, D.C., to the ground," I said. "It won't surprise me if they put it to the torch."

"I sure hope they do. It might learn somebody up there a lesson if they would burn it down," Flonnie said. "Get a big flock of niggers excited that way and anything's liable to happen."

"Sure," I said. "Why not?"

She went back and brought my dinner, meatloaf with vegetables, gelatine fruit salad on a leaf of wilted lettuce, and a couple of corn bread muffins. The muffins were burned black as gun metal on the bottoms.

"I know you couldn't pay me to be in Washington that day, or any other white woman with any sense. That's what nigger men really want, of course. It ain't gold enough at Fort Knox to pay me money enough to be in that city on that day," Flonnie said. "Is your supper all right, Mr. Hedgepath?"

"It's fine, honey," I said. "If I need anything I'll holler. I'm not bashful!" I laughed.

She laughed and went behind the lunch counter to her place beside the coffee urn. She didn't seem to be as unhappy as before. The nigger trouble had given her something, besides her own problems, to think about.

Hand it to the mothers in the South who've taught their children every generation since we lost that war how to hate and remember; just as the widows of the dead and the Daughters of the Confederacy hated, those women who raised the money (at a time when there wasn't any money to be had) to erect a stone monument to the Confederate Hero, high on a pedestal in every town in the South. Take the one in Price Park, and imagine niggers swarming past it, walking and running across that trimmed lawn in front of the monument, where whites never tread. The ground in front of the soldier is somehow sacred, as though to pass in front of those stone eyes were an affront outright. Still, across the street somebody built a shoe factory, I thought, when they should have left a white columned home on the ground. Since they didn't, at least they could give the stone soldier his lawn anyway, as a sort of apology for having stuck up a damned shoe factory in front of his nose. Industry and greed and the almighty Yankee dollar, Father, Son, and Holy Ghost of the South's downfall, and it's all taken place within my lifetime.

My mother, Miss Pearl Hedgepath, never admitted or realized there was any change coming, driving her old LaSalle, bumping into everything and everybody, gunning the engine and riding the clutch and scooting down the street like somebody steering a bump car at the carnival. Then one Saturday morning she finally drove her car slambang-tinkle into the back end of probably the biggest truck ever to roll into the South out of Chicago, up to that time. The truck was stopped for a traffic light when *thump*, Mother hit him from behind and the next thing the driver knew he was being called out of his cab and hailed for everything but a God-damned Christian gentleman by a little old frothing mad woman. When it came to him what was happening, that he was being blamed, he came down out of the cab like a deliberate, agile ape. I had already been called. I was just getting out of my car when he climbed down and snapped off a few cuss words at Miss Pearl like the expert he was. Having finished the prologue he was just drawing his second wind, getting into the meat of his argument when she screamed him down in her high shrill voice, so you could have heard it all the way down to Memphis (and at times I seem to hear it again) how she said: "You son of a bitch! Don't you know you're talking to a lady!"

Which is where any argument will end half the time, up in the air like a bird with no feet, like the truck driver's thick arms, a raised gesture replacing words, a look at the sky, Chicago style. Her outraged Southern voice having cut him down. He's discovered never-

never land then sure enough, when a ninety-pound woman in a black LaSalle will try to run over a Great Dane trailer, and failing that, will cuss out the driver and blame him for her defeat.

He turned to the crowd then, I remember, to the crowd of niggers and whites. "What is this — America?" he asked.

Nobody offered to answer or argue with him. Nobody told him it was The South. So he raised his arms again, that same way, got back in the cab and drove off.

"More coffee, Mr. Hedgepath?"

"No thanks, Flonnie," I said. She gave me my check. I followed her to the cash register and paid it. Then I crossed the street to City Hall and went upstairs. The courtroom was already half filled.

Cotton Turner, the Postmaster, greeted me, nervous as a bird dog bitch. Cotton pumps my hand and pushes me over to the speaker's table where there's a bucktoothed man who looks to be about seven feet tall. He has curly gray hair and wears thick glasses. "Dr. Burroughs," Cotton says, "meet Lawyer Oman Hedgepath."

It's like trying to shake hands with a tire tool. Dr. Burroughs says what a pleasure it is to meet me. I'm saying what an honor for us to have him in Somerton and thinking well God knows if this bastard doesn't break my hand maybe I'll be able to save my arm. Just when I'm about to give up and scream he lets go, swings around and grabs another victim. Something about his tic, the way his left cheek twitches, the jerky way he has of moving, reminds me of a rather obvious something, the Frankenstein movies.

"The black serf," Dr. Burroughs is saying in a deep voice, "always comes back to that, the nigger." I sat down. Cotton raises his hands for silence. Dr. Burroughs swings around like an automated trapeze and sits down. Cotton has us stand up for a prayer by Brother Windrow, the minister from the First Methodist Church. Then we sing "America the Beautiful" and salute the flags, the flag of the United States and the flag of the Old Confederacy. Then Cotton has us sit down again. He says:

"I was just talking to our honored guest, whom I will introduce in just a moment. And he was saying that if the United States could wipe out at one stroke half the unemployment, sixty per cent of the welfare rolls, eighty per cent of the illegitimate births and ninety per cent of the crimes of violence — yes, my friends, all that at one stroke, and solve the race problem at the same time, wouldn't that be a nice and wonderful thing?" The Postmaster warms up the crowd. I see them start to squirm. "But how?" he asks. They can hardly stand it. They swell, like a room full of balloons ready to pop. The Postmaster raises his arms. "Send the niggers back to Africa!" he shouts. They break into laughter and wild applause. "Take the fleet out of mothballs to transport 'em!" Murmurs of approval, right on cue. I speak up: "Amen!" They laugh.

"Let 'em have their own country like the Jews have Israel!"

Applause. That's how you can tell when they are warmed up.

I look them over, our Citizens — fathers, mothers, children, young people; sweethearts suffering the sweet pain of love; house painters and carpenters still wearing their overalls; tired clerks and businessmen; farmers and merchants, bankers; Templeton, the druggist; Toonker Burkette, the dentist; Lawyer Sears R. Buntin, young Dr. Asher.

Sears gives his sinuses a workout, between the bursts of applause, unconsciously advertising; anything to make somebody look around and say, "Well, Sears Buntin's here!" He'd break wind by God if he thought it would get him a client.

I look at Cotton, our young, handsome World War II Army veteran with dark wavy hair and strong white teeth. Cotton calls on honored guests and visitors from out of town, asking each one to stand and be recognized. The usual group from Jackson comes to their feet like it's a sort of drill they've practiced. They all wear black shirts. Each time they stand up that way at a meeting, I have to look at their belts to be sure they aren't carrying pistols. Maybe one day I'll look and the pistols will be there.

We have two visitors from Mississippi. They're in black business suits, like mourners, and finally, for dessert, we get to see an eighty-four-year-old man who has driven all the way to Somerton from Arkansas, just to hear Dr. Burroughs. The Arkansan gets a fine hand of applause. The Postmaster asks him to say a few words.

The old man's eyes look a little wild, but then the highway will do that to anybody, and what the highway doesn't do, Arkansas will finish.

"I just want you to know that the people of Arkansas are ready to march with you!"

Applause rolls in around the old man. He holds up his hands for silence, says he is eighty-four years old, as introduced, and will drive three hundred miles any day to attend a Citizens' meeting, rain or shine, sleet or snow. That gets even more applause.

"I'm just like the rest of you, just wanting to do anything that can be done about this thing to make it right, to keep Commonists from taking over this dear land I love, and handing it to the dad-blasted niggers!"

I didn't have a chance to sound the first "Amen!" It came from the back of the room. There stand Willie Joe Worth and Stanley Bumpas, the night police, their arms folded. Mr. Stanley's glasses glint in overhead lights. Willie Joe is smiling and enjoying himself, like a man without a worry in the world.

Then it was time for a three-minute break. Cotton announces that everybody will now introduce himself to the man on his right and the man on his left to make sure everybody knows who everybody else is. It's about the only way to catch some Communist son of a bitch from New York or Philadelphia, some God-damn spy from *Life* or *Time*, some pink, liberal one-worlder snooping through the South looking for lies to take home and print. His accent will betray him every time. I think now maybe I will take the opportunity to slip to the back of the room and have a word with Willie Joe, but then I think it might look funny. I think it will be better to see him alone. I think yes, alone will be better. It's been a long day. I feel myself slump and I remember poor Flonnie across at the cafe. By now she's closing up for the night. All around me they're talking. Almost before they've said anything I know what the next word will be. They all talk, all on one subject:

"*I call several niggers my friends, but . . .*"

"*We feed about fifty families of them from our one store on the Crossing, cash their welfare checks . . .*"

"*One needs a doctor I call the doctor and pay him myself out of my own pocket and if you don't think having nine families of them to look after on your place, well! I said nine families, I didn't stutter! Hell, it can break a man just to buy their medicine. They go in the drugstore and charge it to me. Sho! One gets in jail and you know who they call to come bail the somebitch out — my wife says why and I says well by God maybe I won't get it back out of the black somebitch but God damn, during ginning season now by God you take a*" *nigger's trained to work around your gin and by God you just see if you don't pay the bastard's bail!"*

"I got one comes to me every Saturday night and wants five dollars. He'll take that five dollars and stay drunk and get himself screwed constantly until Monday morning. By God, on five God-damn dollars. Oh me, that's one sick bastard on Monday but I stick him out there loading cabbage and oh God, if that ain't one sick nigger. I hear a nigger killed Mr. Jimmy. Wonder if it means anything?"

"Don't get me wrong. There are some good niggers, but —"

"This little bitch, she's about twenty I guess and her first husband got killed see, and she gets five thousand dollars insurance money! Hell yes, bought her a house, teevee, one thing and another and has her a government check every month. This nigger of mine took up with her and she's had a couple of little bastards by him. He stays up there with her — listen, she lives good let me tell you. Got that welfare check every month, drives a car, comes in the store and talks so fancy you can't half understand her. Wiggles that thing around. I mean she's strictly living high on the hog — a little old nigger, can you imagine?"

The Postmaster calls for order. Cotton introduces the speaker of the evening. Our honored guest has degrees from Harvard and Yale and Princeton and Oxford and Columbia University. He's a doctor of so many times you'd need an IBM machine to total them all. Otherwise somebody could say Dr. Burroughs wasn't educated. Whether he's human, that's the question bothering me when I look at him.

"And now here's a chance," says Cotton, "here's a chance to pass out these little cards if some of you will help me, in case you haven't had a chance to get one, which is a case of that I know some of us don't like to have to write checks out every month so this is a card you can sign and put the name of your bank on it and the amount you want to give — from two dollars for a regular member to five dollars, ten dollars, or some might want to give twenty-five dollars a month or more, just according to how they are blessed with this world's goods."

"I give ten dollars ever month!" the eighty-four-year-old man blurts out.

"And how much they love their country and want to do something about this thing," Cotton continues. "This way the bank will just automatically cash a check each month to the Citizens, signed by me. Each dollar goes into this fight. Part for your magazine that keeps us up-to-date on the latest progress, part for scientific studies of the nigger because it has got to be proved to some people scientifically that the nigger is the inferior race he is before we can either get the Supreme Court impeached or reversed. It don't matter which we do and we are going to do one or the other." The cards are all passed out now. The Postmaster clears his throat. "It's only a case if the white people in this land of ours will all join hands and march together, vote together, meet together, pray and worship together in this united effort. But folks, it takes money. Question?"

A man in the front row in painter's overalls has raised his hand. He's blond and his nose is pointed like a carrot. His blue eyes waver a little bit when he stands up. When he first opens his mouth no sound comes out, then he finds his voice. "Now if we have a local situation or happening," says the man in painter's overalls, "if we have one here, will the Citizens send in trained people to help us?"

The Postmaster frowns. He gets a bright idea. "Dr. Burroughs, can you answer that?"

Dr. Burroughs jumps like somebody has hit him between the legs with a broomstick. Then he gets to his feet very slowly, so they will get the full effect. He reminds me of an albino Globetrotter. The way his hair stands up only makes him seem taller.

"The question again?" His voice booms so you have to look at him twice to know if he really spoke or if somebody downstairs just got the volume up suddenly on an old radio.

The painter's blue eyes wag back and forth. "Does this money mean that if we have a local situation or happening here that the Citizens will send in trained people to help us?"

"I'm afraid I don't understand," Dr. Burroughs says. "Are you referring to states' rights or racial integrity? Can you narrow your question somewhat and define it?"

"What I mean is if they try to hire niggers into jobs or on jobs. Whereas, say if we had it to happen in Somerton that they tried to hire niggers for painters and carpenters and bricklayers — I mean, the niggers' organization will send in trained people to help them so will you send out trained people to help us in a fight?"

"I see," Dr. Burroughs says. "Now that word *fight* — now the Citizens' rule three is 'Avoid violence and the appearance of violence.' So when you say the word *fight* I have to say on a very strict basis of interpretation, no. Nobody's going to help anybody fight. If a fight comes the United States Army will do the fighting and it will help *our* side, evidence in Oxford just recently to the contrary. Don't worry about that one minute. Our Southern officers in the Army will take care of that. The fight is coming, by the way. Does that answer your question?" Dr. Burroughs lets off a bucktooth smile to charm the overalls off his questioner. "The extermination war is coming."

The painter's blue eyes move persistently back and forth. He draws a breath. Little murmurs go through the audience. "But say somebody tried to hire niggers on a job — say they just did. The nigger organizations have these trained people they send out. Will we get the same thing for this money? I mean people to help us?" he says.

Dr. Burroughs's face begins to twitch. He takes a breath deep enough to satisfy a West Florida pearl diver. "Ah," he says. "Now it's true that the Communists send out agents from the headquarters of these various Red Russian nigger organizations — trained agents, agitators, saboteurs, terrorists, what have you. But Citizens is not a Communist organization."

I begin to feel sorry for the painter. I think that if I had five million bucks and didn't need my law practice how nice it would be to cross-examine this famous Dr. Burroughs and find out just where the money really does go. But if you are in a profession to make money in Somerton you don't oppose the Citizens any more than you lay down on the railroad tracks in front of the two thirty-seven, so I sit there with my tongue in my mouth.

The painter tries to bore on in: "You won't send people to help us?"

"No," says Dr. Burroughs. "We are not like the Communists." Dr. Burroughs sits down like a praying mantis, his legs stuck straight out, his hands held up in front of his mouth. Whether caressing his teeth or hiding them, I can't be sure. Or maybe, I think, maybe he has caught a cockroach.

There is a strained silence. Moths flutter in through the open windows. Even the jury box is full. The Postmaster stands up nervously. The summer dark is pressing at the tall windows.

I look back at the crowd and see the house painter looking about him at the other workers, the painters, carpenters and brick masons who came in with him. Slowly these men all stand and walk out. There is a set of defiance to their shoulders. It is what you expect to see in the bearing of a tired elite corps. They walk like men who know they are going straight into combat. Those of us who sit still and watch them leave are like the men who are glad to be left in safety behind the front lines. Their women and children, also proud, but a little shamefaced, follow the men out. In the back of the courtroom a baby is crying. Into the seats emptied by the trade union men and their families come those who have been standing all this while — the latecomers — and the court is full again, more cards are quietly being passed out to these new people.

"I give ten dollars a month!" cries the eighty-four-year-old man from Arkansas.

"Now let's hear Dr. Burroughs!" says the Postmaster.

Dr. Burroughs snaps to standing attention and bows to the Postmaster. Is it my imagination? Does Burroughs really click his heels?

The eighty-four-year-old Arkansan has fallen comfortably asleep. The crying baby is quieted. I look towards the back of the room. Stanley Bumpas and Willie Joe Worth have gone.

Moments like this make you wonder why you came and what you are doing here. You wonder where it is all going to lead to someday.

The trouble is that you must finally take sides. In the end it is like the Civil War must have been, with people on both sides of the firing line wondering now and then about the essential rightness of all that is being done. The fight could not have been avoided.

There is no room any more for the moderate. Either you are for the South, or you are against her. If you are for the South, then you are for the Citizens and if it takes men like Burroughs to power the movement, then such men must be accepted. So here I sit.

Steve's trouble is he's trying to be a moderate when the time for moderation is past. Nowadays either you're with it and for it, or you're out of it and against it. At least I know where I stand.

As for Steve, he's yet to find out; as yet he hasn't learned his lesson. Nobody stands neutral any more. The times just won't allow it.

I relax my shoulders and wait for what Burroughs will have to say, knowing I'd just about as soon sit on the grass and be sprinkled with a hose as to hear him — but then you have to keep up appearances.

4

The Speech

He, the famous Dr. Burroughs.

With the old man from Arkansas dropped into a doze, only the children seem really awake as The Speech begins, describing a cannibal feast on the west coast of Africa.

The children sit like little sponges. They soak up every word and detail Dr. Burroughs chants in his hypnotic voice. They witness every scene he shapes with his arms and his twitching facial expressions. Like a witch doctor, he moves and shouts as though some demon were inside him jerking his nerves and sinews.

Dr. Burroughs begins with the pit full of stones, the wood fire burning to embers, the black orgy coming to its climax. Savage drums beat the pulse of that sensual rhythm. Palm wine is passed from lip to lip. The white traders drink with the black chieftain. Eight human victims are brought out and made to kneel before the fiery pit, then killed, each one, with a single sickening blow on the head.

The black human bodies are taken to the cook house. The women clean them, cutting off the heads first and skinning these delicacies for the witch doctors and their families, gutting the carcasses and stuffing them with breadfruit, and then bringing them back to be placed in the pit, wrapped in banana leaves, with the hot stones under them and on top of them. The stench of roasting human flesh reaches at the white traders from Boston. Faster and faster go the drums. The white Yankees take refuge in the primitive wine and steel themselves for what must follow.

Dr. Burroughs holds his nose. He retches. He clutches his stomach. He tells of the first shipload brought to Virginia. With a wave of his hand he shows us how blacks first began interbreeding with white indentured servants. We witness the dregs of England's slums and bordellos — white prisoners, whores, tosspots — and niggers, squirming in the corn shucks, trash mating with cannibals.

"Thus," chants Dr. Burroughs, "were brought forth the first of the New World's mulattoes, through the confluence of two sewers," he shouts, holding his nose again and evoking the stench of that charring, roasting flesh.

Stifling his nausea he relates the invention of the cotton gin. He tells the end of the slave trade and snaps his audience wide awake, for now comes the story of the breeding farms. He licks his lips. He describes the stud bucks and the mare women. He ties this in with John Brown's rapings and riotings and lynchings in the North. He quotes the law of 1705. Any nigger caught forty miles north of Albany, New York, shall be immediately executed, since any nigger that high in the world is trying to escape to Canada. This is an aside to show, before he leaves John Brown, what New York thought of niggers. (What New York thinks of them now!)

He chants of strong soaps and heavy perfumes white masters gave house servants to hide offensive, stinking body odors. He whipsaws back to New York City, in case anybody still thinks New York has any use for niggers, to tell about 1696 when they strip a nigger naked and whip him through the streets before dragging him around the city behind a cart; where in 1708 a nigger woman and an Indian man burn at the stake for slaughtering their white master, his wife, and five sweet, innocent white *children!*

With a shriek Dr. Burroughs pantomimes the modern Mau Mau, waves his long arm like a panga, and chants the New York City race riot of 1712, tells the score: nine whites dead but, praise God, twenty-two niggers executed! In New York City! One nigger hung up in chains to starve to death! In New York City! One broken on the wheel. In a meticulous demonstration of the wheel, Dr. Burroughs becomes the executioner, turns the wheel and makes popping noises with his tongue as the arms and legs of the nigger are each broken in two places with an iron rod. The bones pop like green sticks. Sure

— in New York City! The children turn pale and hide their faces against their mothers. The grown-ups squirm and smile. *Amen!*

Then hear about the Dred Scott Decision, faces dull again, but bright and alive when Dr. Burroughs chants the tale of the first American nigger-lover, Elijah Piersons *of New York City*, the first professional white integrationist, may hell fire burn him, who took part in nigger orgies, who raped his own daughter!

Now the Civil War, and 186,000 African cannibals fighting in the Union Army. Of these, 93,000 are former slaves, but such is the stench of the black man's ingratitude that he will attempt to cut off the white hands that have fed him, that he will drive bayonets into the hearts of those who led him out of savage darkness to Christ. As war ends, the rape and plunder of the white South merely increases until the Ku Klux Klan, mystic, strange, godsent cavalry of the night, rides down and strings up the niggers!

Laughter for the Ku Klux Klan, that bright spot! Laughter no sooner fades than the speaker chants the plot of 1905 when Communists organize the National Association for the Advancement of Colored People, shades of the ghoulish Elijah Piersons! Anxiety returns to the children's faces. The courtroom falls deathly quiet. Hear about the conspiracy to mix the blood of nigger and white in hospitals, to shoot nigger blood into innocent white veins under the guise of a necessary transfusion! Nigger blood is full of alien cells and little syphilis germs — nigger blood! Pig blood, monkey blood would be more pure!

Item: Washington, D.C., where of 854 cases of gonorrhea among school children in 1955, ninety-seven per cent were niggers; in our nation's capital niggers account for ninety-five per cent of those afflicted with venereal disease!

Dr. Burroughs chants slowly, like a guide conducting tourists through a decorated cave: "*Chancroid, lymphogranuloma venereum, granuloma inguinale,* and of course, our old friend *nigger syphilis,* the one great scientific contribution the nigger has given to Western civilization where little germs the shape of corkscrews swim through your blood, drill into your brain tissues and destroy it, eat it up! Then your brain's no better than nigger brains!"

His voice gets quieter and quieter. His audience leans forward to hear about Houston, Texas, in 1917 when nigger Army soldiers revolted, the score: thirteen niggers hanged, forty-one sent up for life! Yet Communists saw to it that niggers were allowed to stay in the Army even after that. Nigger soldiers overseas pass themselves off as American Indians and go to bed with innocent French women.

Sure, the audience knows what the nigger really wants, what he's really always wanted, chants Dr. Burroughs.

The next year, 1918, whites set fire to the nigger sections of East St. Louis and shoot them like rats when the black savages come running out of the fiery buildings. The slaughter continues, nigger blood coagulates in the gutters. The number killed is never officially counted, but see those niggers fleeing across the bridge back into St. Louis — ants leaving a burning log, bawling cattle! They stampede trying to get away! They trampled their old folks and the young children to death!

Laughter.

Yet this only begins it! Omaha, Nebraska, where white men had to burn down the courthouse the next year to get a nigger who raped a white girl! Chicago, Dr. Burroughs chants, the year: 1919, the score: twenty-three niggers killed, five hundred niggers injured, over a thousand nigger homes burnt to the ground. Whites killed: fifteen. "You ask why? Because niggers tried to swim at a white beach on Lake Michigan."

He shouts: "And now they want to wade into our swimming pools — in 1963! Didn't learn their lesson in 1919, did they? But they never learn, they can't learn!" *Amen's* from his audience, deep and loud as bullfrogs. "They don't have white brains!"

"Roosevelt!" he cries. "*Eleanor!*" He holds his nose. He indicates the stink of roasting flesh and tells how giving the niggers employment opportunities only led to the typical nigger form of gratitude illustrated in the Detroit riots where it took six thousand troops to restore order in 1943; the score: twenty-five niggers to nine whites killed. Our side wins again!

Father Divine and his young blond wife and the Communist Supreme Court and the niggers of the Ninety-second Division in Africa jumping up and running off like jack rabbits when they smelled the Germans. Laughter as Dr. Burroughs makes motions — a German shooting jack rabbits!

Little Rock and a thousand bayonets ordered there to mix the races.

The white do-gooders and one-worlders who are just like the old jungle witch doctors, always agitating while indifferent white people who ought to care and help are too rich and too busy getting drunk out at their private country clubs to pay any attention to the nigger threat which they will tell you doesn't exist at the very moment when American mulattoes are swarming off to Europe and passing as whites so they can marry innocent Italian girls and French women, so they can dip their foul pens in white ink.

But only consider the valiant Boers of South Africa, he chants, "Wresting civilization from virgin, uninhabited wilderness. Now in come the niggers wanting to take it all away from the brave Boers, but if they did take it, and exterminate the whites as is their practice and custom, my white friends, my fellow Citizens, I promise you that the lion would roar. In ten years fence lizards would frolic where once ran civilized streets, where stood cities before in South Africa. My friends *it would not take ten years for it to go back to the jungle* if the niggers got their wish and took South Africa over!" Applause.

Item: Washington, D.C. today where brawling, cursing niggers swagger into the most exclusive restaurants, sit down and order a watermelon and a bottle of gin, pour the gin on the watermelon and eat it, then pee on the door knobs! Yet only let the white restaurant owner complain and he's fined one thousand dollars and his license is taken away! The business this white man spent thirty years of his life to build, confiscated by the Federal Government!

"Is this what we want in America? Gin, watermelon and nigger urine?"

"No!"

"We want niggers in *our* cafes?"

"No!"

Case history: The poor Canadian white girl lured into marriage to the rich, lascivious nigger; her degradation as she submits to the filthy caresses of this nigger who bought her body. He befouls her at every opportunity. "Sometimes, my friends, as many as fifty times in a single day, even lending or selling her body to his black friends and cannibal relatives until at last, crushed, torn, and wasted beyond recognition this white girl dies, leaving behind her a brood of half-wit mulatto children destined to spend their whole lives on the welfare rolls. Wards of the public charity! Half-wits! We want *this* in America?"

[129]

"No!"

"No? My friends, consider Washington, D.C., named after George Washington, the slave-owning white Southerner recognized in every history book as the father of his country, the man whose engraved portrait is on the face of every last one of our inflated one-dollar bills. Yes, friends, in that city named for him there are 655 American white women raped by black African niggers every year. A white woman is raped by a black African nigger in Washington, D.C., on the average of one for every three days that pass. But will the Roman Catholic Communists and Jews who run the government do one thing to stop it? Will they lift a hand? Of course they won't, because this is exactly what they want. Sure, mix enough nigger blood with white blood and you'll destroy the white race in America, and when you destroy the white race, then, comrade, you have destroyed America! How many nigger signers of the Declaration of Independence?"

"*None!*"

"Name me one nigger genius! Of course you can't! But let me tell you about the nigger rapists. They produce plenty of them!"

Item: The ninety-pound white girl raped on Columbia Road in D.C. by the 250-pound nigger buck who rammed his fist down her throat and destroyed her esophagus.

Item: The 244 American white women raped by black African niggers last year in the City of St. Louis.

Item: The Communist U. S. Supreme Court will soon make it a violation of law *to label nigger blood as such* in hospital blood banks.

"What is this all about, where does it lead? To the complete submission of the white race to the raping blacks, to the creation of a national race the color of light chocolate! When that comes about my friends we will have a moronic mulatto population such as they have in mongrelized Brazil. The remaining whites will have to flee this continent to Australia, and please, whatever you do, *don't* say it *can't* happen!

"Before you say it *can't* happen pause to remember last October when the Federal Government sent 31,000 troops to Oxford, Mississippi, and killed two innocent white men just to force one crazy Communist nigger into the white university. Before you say it can't happen in America remember how this violent tyranny in Mississippi was bragged about all over the world by the United States Information

Agency. My friends, before you say it *can't* happen, *ask* yourselves, will it be them or us? Realize that unless our niggers can be peacefully forced to emigrate to Africa and places like South America where they can be accepted socially and have all the gin, all the watermelon, and all the women they want along with American foreign aid hand-outs — unless we can *rid* this country of them in *some* way, then the white race and the United States of America both are *doomed!*

"I'm asking you a simple question, will it be them, or us?"

"Them! Them!"

"*Them, or us?*"

"*Them! Them! Them!*"

"Will we stand and fight or will we turn over our women to be raped, our men to be killed, our children to be slaughtered and eaten? Do we want a nigger President? Well, listen, you already got one, a *white* nigger, and they're worse than the other kind! Is this what we want — a nigger *tyranny?*"

He begins the closing chant then, like the invitation to come forward, confess Christ, and be baptized. His voice drums out the words in a high monotone.

"*Them* or *us? Them* or *us?*"

"*Them!*" comes his reply.

"*Them* or *us!*"

"*Them! Them! Them!*"

They yell the word until it hardly makes sense any more. The speaker raises his arms for silence. "Then heed the sound, the clarion call of the bugle which harkened your grandfathers and your great-grandfathers to a holy war for the Confederacy and for states' rights, for states' rights and racial integrity! My friends, this time around we must *finish* the job!"

The applause comes then, like a spasm. It rushes all around him. They yell as he turns to salute the flag. They stomp and yell until it becomes like the chambered echo you will hear over and over again, long afterwards, after the courtroom has emptied and the trucks and the cars have rattled off into the countryside again, the roar will still remain with you, and the memory of that gaunt, hollow-eyed figure, standing like another fanatical Lincoln as he salutes and salutes and salutes again always the same flag, finally kneeling for the supreme gesture which raises a lump in every throat, kneeling to kiss the hem of

[131]

that flag, the battle flag of the Confederacy, implanting the kiss which brings the stomping roar suddenly down to respectful silence. The silence of Appomattox, broken only by the dismayed sobs of the children.

5

Oman Hedgepath

After the courtroom cleared I shook hands with Dr. Burroughs and stood by while the Postmaster counted the cards to see how many new members had signed up. The eighty-four-year-old man from Arkansas looked over the Postmaster's shoulder. "That was a good crowd," he said to me. "You always get that good a crowd?"

"Mostly," I said.

"We're in Birmingham tomorrow night, is that it, Charley?" said the eighty-four-year-old man.

"That's right, Birmingham tomorrow," Dr. Burroughs said. "Mining people, dynamiters. Non-violence is right up their alley." He smiled.

"Tomorrow I think I'll say I drove all the way from my home in Oxford, Mississippi," the eighty-four-year-old man said. "That ought to get a hand of applause. *Anytime* you say that you're bound to get a nice hand of applause, ain't that right, Charley?"

"That's right," Dr. Burroughs said.

"Where's your real home?" I asked the old man.

"Oh, I was borned near Cincinnati and raised close to Louisville, Kentucky," he said. "You might say I feel like I'm nearly from everywhere. Before I retired I was on the road several years selling shoes. For a while I worked out of St. Louis."

"Seventy-one," said the Postmaster. "That's pretty good."

"Every bit helps," said the eighty-four-year-old man.

Dr. Burroughs didn't say anything. Maybe he was thinking about the miles ahead of him, the next speech and the one after that. His

[133]

silence made me wonder again where it might end up some day, where it all might end up, the entire movement.

I had to think about getting in touch with Willie Joe Worth. It's the small things that worry you to death. Taking the time to make that extra little conscientious effort, going out of your way to do something not because there's any money in it for you, but simply because you happen to care about doing the right thing.

Responsibility is an anvil on your shoulder. It's the difference in a lawyer and an ambulance chaser. It's the difference, finally, between a man and a son of a bitch. A man will never put the anvil down. A son of a bitch will never pick it up.

"I got a pretty good hand of applause tonight," the old man said. "And Charley, I thought Charley did wonderful. For a minute it looked like they was going to tear down the building."

Dr. Burroughs smiled. The old man's flattery brought the speaker back to the present long enough to thank both me and the Postmaster again before he and the old man packed up their briefcases and left.

FOUR

1

Mrs. Osborn

A fat nigger man killed little Sonny Boy Mosby that never laid the finger of harm on nobody. Breathed no breath of sin. Tasted no lies in his mouth.

"Naw, Mrs. Osborn. Look here, Mrs. Osborn. See?"

Where they buried him or did they throw him away in the weeds? Burnt him on the dump like an old shoe after he's dead? The goddamns. Lavorn said Sonny Boy.

You goddamns.

When it's maybe Somerton maybe not. When it's maybe Tennessee maybe not or winter or ain't or dark daylight and the trees wear something under their dresses. Know something, keep it quiet. Who I said and Lavorn said Sonny Boy.

It comes out one on top the other fast as it can holler until finally she shut up and listen at her nose break. Hear the bone above her eye when it pop and bust and see the blue fire like a big flower when they hit between her eye and ear and that break. Until goddamns they breaking down the whole entire house in on her. "Hold her, don't let her bite."

Ain't nothing made to stand up and last any more. Everything made so cheap it break down in a hurry and you got to buy everything new and it break and break and they quit work on her head. They laid off now.

Now she thinking they over with it and her face all like mud and cotton mashed and mixed together. She haves the taste in her mouth

[137]

of broke off teeth and bit off tongue like something she can't swallow it and can't spit it out between her head and her face and she thinking living Jesus Christ.

Glass busting and then they push and twist, push and twist living Jesus Christ she went away. She now dead now. She dead now Jesus — push and twist can't yell no more.

"Mrs. Osborn? See who this is?"

No more she. Her gone away and she come back to life and go away. Little Sonny Boy Mosby swinging on a tire swing chained to the oak limb in the sun, in the shade, in the sun swinging back and forth, going in and out dead and live little Sonny Boy dear.

The goddamns got soft hearts. Send for Benny up to the L. B. Jones Funeral and say Mrs. Osborn done fell on her face, done tripped up and tore her britches out to the quarry ponds. Done went out there and down done the splits over a broke beer bottle and also down fell on her face a little. "We don't know, maybe she was dropped out of some airplane like they drop a bum," the little one said. They laughed.

Put a piano playing somebitch out of business cut off his fingers little Sonny Boy dear. Whore just the same way. Cut her goods and merchandise. Out where nothing but the dead can hear and listen. Spoil it so she can't sell it. No more. Like a big black bum — maybe they dropped her.

Doin the splits, trainin to get into vaudeville maybe. The great beer bottle act. They get to laughing. The big one drops his flashlight.

I said he killed Sonny Boy. Lavorn said and said.

And I said yes. Sonny Boy's gone and dead. He been gone since the last time I saw him yesterday Monday after he was up well, out in the tire swing and he couldn't hardly walk at first. I hear the chain. Screek and screek, screek and screek. Sun and shade. In and back out again like a teeny baby crying, got the colic. Screek and screek.

Make a sugar tit. Sonny Boy's dead. I said he never laid the first finger of harm on nobody.

Benny said. Then Lavorn said. Lavorn is crying. He is here.

"Sure, she know how to get there by herself. They pull soft ones for her. Likes a pig. It's about all she can eat. That's too much. Sonny Boy give her too much. Sonny Boy didn't need to give her all that. Take care of it now. Bring back the change. Now here — see what Sonny

Boy gave you? Try not to get so greasy this time. You going now?"

Lavorn said and said. Sonny Boy, he is here. I went. Over where they all live like friends together, across the road. They don't like rain, eating at the grass through the wire. Goat's the old granddaddy with eyes looking at me like marbles; dog he's brother. Has to smell everywhere and lick his dinkus under yonder and don't study nothing about work. Chickens are the children messing and pecking in the mud. Geese are the niggers. Having to make like they always busy or else brother he haves to bark. Then the pigeons fly. He is here. They don't like rain. The rain brought him here.

Down the whole way I went. They squawked good-bye after me, good-bye, good-bye, good-bye. The cars were out there still dying in the field. Busted and resting there waiting to die. Cucumber busted them. They put his eyes out and he busted them and they crippled him till he couldn't do nothing but crawl around like a possum, Lavorn said. Makes Cucumber no nevermind if it's day or night, or if maybe it's Somerton or someplace else, crawling under them at night, busting them in the shade of the moon. You can feel him under yonder when he goes in and out of them like a worm busting and breaking them down. Push and twist. The way he stay out there at night thieves and stealers stay away and don't rob him, Lavorn said. Eyes all the same at night, bright and the blind all alike, Lavorn said. He is here.

Daytimes he haves brother and the children and niggers and guinea hens watch so Cucumber can crawl himself in a hole if he want to have himself sleeps till his pets wake him and that's a customer come to buy something. Drink muddy water. Sleep in a holler tree. Take the chicken, the rat, the snake, they all dreads it, Lavorn said. Our Lord dreaded it. He didn't want to die. I dread it, Lavorn said.

It smelled hungry in my stomach. When I ate it quit.

Sad doves and locust trees fly down to drink. Black peoples cut that hole in the rock. Ducks come out the sky and light, settle that way like fine dust coming through the curtains. Ducks whisper down on the ponds like dust in the open eyes of dead peoples. So you know it's cold weather, that's why. They always looking up, two ponds, two eyes that don't close watch for the ducks. My daddy said.

He said and I said that's why it comes cold weather.

"Now look, I'm gonna explain it to you one time — one more time.

You gimme five dollars and I give you back the change for one barbecue, three dollars and — four dollars and seventy-five cents. Now you
got *me* confused. Just a minute. When I get a chance I'm gonna explain it to you."

I said. You God damn.

"You eat two barbecues because you got another one. You said I
didn't give you right change so I give you the whole entire five dollars
back. You got it in your purse. Look — look here in your purse, see it?
Five dollars. Mrs. Osborn? Here it is where you put it. You done forgot you put it there. Now you owe me fifty cents for two barbecues,
understand?"

"God damn you God damn nigger goose. Gimme back my money
God damn you nigger goose."

"Naw, Mrs. Osborn. That was the *change* I taken back. See? Wait
just a minute. All right. You paid me a nickel for your Grape. You
dranken one Grape and you had the nickel, right change. Then you
had a pig and you handed me the five dollars and said take the pig out
of it and when I give you the change, four seventy-five, you said it was
wrong so I gave you back the whole entire five dollars and you got it
there in your purse. I showed it to you. Remember?"

"My money back that's all, my money back, you God damn you."

"You ain't thinking right, Mrs. Osborn. You ate two pigs. You owe
me fifty cents."

*He went to the porch where it was cooking and I followed him into
the smoke of it cooking under the big tin lids like hats, smoke of hick-
ory and chunks of hot meat smoking slowly under the lids like eyes
already closed, him tearing the meat off the bones and throwing the
bones and the meat skin in the box on the floor.*

"What you do with that you throw away?"

"Throw it back in the hog pen."

"They eats their own kind."

"Well, they do. That's right. You thinking right now?"

"Thinking right, me."

"You know you owe me fifty cents?"

"I paid. I paid you in there. I paid you three times. You took my five
dollars Sonny Boy give me. The swing was going."

"Sonny Boy? Who?"

"Sonny Boy dear." Lavorn saw him. *He is here.*

"A great fat man? You seen a strange fat colored fella, Mrs. Osborn? Now listen. Tell me *where* you saw him at. It's important — hear?"

"A big fat nigger killed him. Lavorn and Benny saw him."

"Stay right there and let me wrap these sandwiches. I have to talk to you. It's real important."

"You know what they done to me, the God damns?"

"You told me all about it exactly about one million times. That ain't what you have to tell me. Just wait a minute. You said you saw a great fat colored man?"

"That's when I went away. They took a beer bottle and busted it . . ."

"Please don't talk and tell about that, Mrs. Osborn. Peoples don't wish to hear it. Now you say Lavorn saw him?"

He said and said at me. Who was it somebody I ain't saying if maybe even I knew, anyhow first they beat living Jesus Christ out of her out by the ponds where nothing but the dead couldn't hear it screek and screek until finally I folded down inside herself like a parasol under wings and listened to what I hear. He pulled the meat off the bones so quiet I couldn't hear him, little Sonny Boy dear.

"What she saw?"

"Nothing, she ain't seen nothing. She ain't in her right mind."

They said and said and the music made the night ink out the sun away from the window and Lavorn said *He is here* and said *He is here* and I smelled it and Lavorn got the dress and she took it and she said *He is here* and the dress was white like a shining white moth and the music downstairs made it darker on the window and Lavorn was gone and I smelled the green night and the bugs talked and said in it and talked and I smelled the green taste of all the bugs and the stars the same way, had the green smell through the window screen and when I looked up they were still there.

2

Lord Byron Jones

"Twist for the gentleman," said Lavorn.

Jelly dropped a quarter in the jukebox.

"Jelly can't bear shoes on her feet," Lavorn said, making change from the cash register.

The undertaker wondered what time it was. He turned to see his dim reflection in the mirror behind the bar — the tall black man, the gold-rimmed glasses on his nose, the white shirt, the dark suit. His Panama hat was like a soft mound of hemp on the bar beside his glass. He looked down at his glass. Lavorn was refilling it.

Looking up he saw only beer signs, electrical wheels and displays representing water tumbling in rainbow cascades, water rippling in mountain brooks. Everywhere above the bar he saw movements of light, illuminated photographs of snow flanked mountains and deep, crystal blue lakes — but not a clock anywhere.

He was conscious of the music, of its effect on his skin. The music made a tingling of nerves, like ripping fabric. With no hint of shame or self-consciousness Jelly was dancing, inching along on her heels, her legs spread wide, her body quivering under the yellow dress. She had forgotten this time to take off her hat. It dropped off like a white petal caught by the wind. Jelly danced with her eyes shut, her head turning from side to side with the rhythm, her chiseled features now in light, the next instant in darkness, like a pendulum. She began to move her arms in a slow arc. The undertaker groped for his glass. He drank it empty. The rum rolled past his tongue like oil. It spread into his body

like sweet wind fanning across a fire. The taste lingered. It was like a
voice saying, "Here, come this way." He began to sweat.

He knew he must phone Benny to come for him and take him
home. Then he must tell Benny that Lavorn was to have the first
Angel Chorus burial ever sold.

"Sweet black rum," Lavorn said, filling his glass.

"No." He tried to protest. She didn't hear him. He felt for the
watch in his pocket. I could show it to somebody and ask them what
time is it, he thought, that way I wouldn't have to look at it. Then I
might give it away to whoever told me the time, he thought, remembering Emma on their wedding night, saying, "So tiny sound I can't
hardly hear it. Take off everything else but not this. The rings too off
my fingers." "The rings too?" "Yes, leave the watch, just only that."

He hadn't wanted to take off her rings. That was bad, taking the
rings off, but he didn't tell her so.

He takes them off her fingers leaving only the platinum watch
studded with little diamonds, the watch he had given her for her wedding present, and kneeling down then into love like a man struck
blind by the sun, like a creature coming into daylight from under-
ground, Emma whispering a while later, Emma's breath flattened and
short, mingling with the sigh of his own breath. "So tiny sound I can't
hardly hear it," she whispers. "Listen —" putting the little watch to
his ear, his cheek against her warm breast. "Listen —" He listens. He
can't hear anything but her own pulse, the surging of his own heart.
He listens.

"Don't Jelly dance pretty — don't she? You like her?" Lavorn said.
"Don't you?"

He didn't answer. Jelly rocked back and forth like a piston on a
flywheel. He detected a taste in the rum now. He seemed to feel the
fluid rhythm of the rum taken up by his bloodstream, the rum pump-
ing and re-pumping through his whole system. Soon no place on his
body that he touched would feel like himself. Soon be drunk as a
goat, he thought, feeling the watch, thinking, Break the crystal and
feel the time. Let the deed be done; in the darkness of my pocket nobody will be the wiser. Break one and you break them all. Every
watch has a glass skull, every face a crystal bone protecting it from
the touch of life; every mind a secret movement working in darkness.
Feel the hour then; and know it.

"Now maybe Emma wouldn't want to cause you harm and evil, see. But now how can she help herself sometimes? She caught. She couldn't see the web before she got herself all entangled. Now she can't work herself out, that's all I'm saying. Maybe she wouldn't want to harm you, but maybe she can't help herself any more. So watch her — just watch her, don't you know? Don't go no place alone without you got somebody along with you for protection."

"Protection," he said. "Protection?"

"Nothing more frail than unprotected man," said Mama Lavorn.

"Take it you think I'm in danger? Take it you think I can't take care myself?" She reached forward with the bottle. "Perhaps I —" He'd had enough, couldn't she see that? Let her pour anyway. "Better call Benny," the undertaker said.

"Just set where you are," Mama Lavorn said. "Don't you know you need a bodyguard, somebody big and strong. A colored man can't go up against a white man alone, most of all not up against a police-man. Didn't you say yourself that Emma was making trouble? Why would she do that if it wasn't that policeman behind it?"

The room seemed to swing back and forth. He steadied himself. It took an instant to realize people were still dancing, twisting back and forth like a line of machines, like spindles in a mill. They went past him, thundering and careering, the faces seemingly wired, contrived here and there to smile, to show the occasional gold tooth. The juke-box battered on like a train, in ruthless mechanotony. The sounds jerk the bodies; yes, he thought.

The noise swirled around him like echoes in a cave. Then suddenly, as the music stopped, he saw Jelly across the room, slouched close to the pinball machine. The machine, sloping and four-legged, was like a horse. She looked up. She must have seen him. A smile, faint as the smell of lemons, appeared at the edges of her even mouth. Lavorn was holding his arm. "Come this way," she said. "Where it's more quiet. We can talk, see, back where there ain't all this noise"; though the noise had stopped. She held aside the curtain and led him down a hallway. "Here in the parlor," she said, gently guiding him. "Sit here, this here's the best chair, Mr. Jones. I want you to meet somebody."

Lavorn stood beside a stranger. She was saying here was somebody he might remember, Sonny Boy Mosby?

The stranger seemed to crowd the room. He bulged everywhere. His wet lower lip was swollen, rolled down to show the pink the way a black man's lip will sometimes do when he's been drinking. "Howdy do, Mr. Jones," Sonny Boy Mosby said.

"My boy that went away and left home some years ago," Lavorn said.

"I remember," said the undertaker. "Police beat him."

"That's me," Sonny Boy Mosby said. "Mama Lavorn say you needing a little protection? Say maybe the Man fixing to lean on you a little bit if you don't have somebody around to make him lay off, kinda? Maybe you wants somebody like me, because see that's kinda the business I'm in —"

"We want to do you a favor and let you have Sonny Boy keep close to you. Sonny Boy wants to guard your life and protect you," Lavorn said. "Don't you, Sonny Boy?"

Sonny Boy sat down on the sofa. He held a cigar box propped on his knee. "I'm gonna keep good guard on you," he said. "Where you go that's where I'll be, but don't nobody need to know. See? See because the best protection is what don't nobody know nothing about. Maybe you wouldn't say nothing to nobody. Not your wife, not to nobody but only explain to peoples working up to the funeral home that till the divorce come off why you got a man with you. But tell them they ain't to say nothing about him not to the police, not to nobody."

"You needing protection. Sonny Boy needing him a place to stay. The police too snoopy around here to keep Sonny Boy in this house." Lavorn smiled.

"I see," the undertaker said. "I think I see now." Sonny Boy Mosby's pink-lined lower lip was stuck out again.

"Known Sonny Boy every since he was a baby. When Sonny Boy born he had him a big wad of fat right on his forehead. Like a parpose? What's that fish?" Lavorn asked.

"Papoose," Sonny Boy Mosby said. "Indian baby."

"Porpoise," the undertaker said.

"*Ah-huck-ah*," Sonny Boy Mosby hiccupped.

"Otherwise where you at, Sonny Boy he gonna be there," Lavorn was saying. "What you done, hurt your thumb, Mr. Jones?"

The undertaker got out his handkerchief. "I have broken my watch crystal," he said.

Sonny Boy and Lavorn took him down the hall to a narrow room with a slanting ceiling where the stairway passed above it. There was a toilet and an iron daybed cot and a lavatory. The undertaker sat on the bed while Lavorn put iodine on his thumb and wrapped it with gauze and tape.

"Perhaps I'll lie down a moment," said the undertaker. The room was narrow like a cupboard. The walls were planks, painted yellow. There was no window. Newspapers and magazines were stacked on the floor against the wall, beside the lavatory. A bleached cloth curtain hid a makeshift clothes rack at the end of the room. Beneath the lower edge of the curtain he saw a tangle of high heel shoes, an empty cigarette carton, and a rumpled pink chemise which seemed to have slipped down from the midst of the clothes hanging above it. The slanting overhead shook as footsteps passed on the stairs just above.

"Sure, lay down a minute," Lavorn was saying. She helped him back on the pillow, Sonny Boy lifted the undertaker's legs and set them gently on the bed. "Sure," she was saying.

The next instant the undertaker was alone. The room seemed to close down over him like a lid. The cot seemed to float under him. Closing his eyes he saw a green flashing, phosphorescent vision. The cot seemed to spin slowly. Above him the stairs thundered. He felt his cheek. Tears or blood? His eyes weeping, his thumb bleeding? He couldn't tell.

The footsteps on the stairs tread mashed through him until he seemed undone and free like grain on a threshing floor. His gorge rose to a point of pain far back in his throat, causing his eyes to blur when he opened them. He groped about, feeling for anything to help him, anything to give him a grip on the spinning world. He rolled and the dark floor struck him, from above, so it seemed at first. Slowly he found his knees, drawing them under him he laid his cheek against the crooked drain pipe and stared stupidly at the edges of the newspapers and the ends of the stacked magazines. Leaning forward a little he saw the magazine on top. EBONY. Slickly fecal, a poisoned cockroach lay dying on its back just across the top of the E. The dark, crooked legs waved as slowly as stalks of sea grass swayed in the sea tides.

Turning away he slumped down on his belly. He groped for his glasses and found them, loose, but still clamped on his nose. The undertaker pulled the glasses off and raised up to put them in his vest pocket with the broken watch. Then he lay forward again with his cheek flat on the linoleum. Ahead he saw light and movement beyond the edge of the curtained doorway between the hall and the cafe barroom. He saw feet moving.

3

Willie Joe

Willie Joe rides the police car. His left hand is between his legs. His right hand fondles his pistol.

Sunk down in himself, buried in his night policeman's thoughts like a mole in the earth, Mr. Stanley Bumpas drives the police cruiser. His hands rest on the steering wheel like two soft pads. He has two styles of driving, slow as possible and fast as possible. The car barely moves along the street. Mr. Stanley lights a cigar. The smoke sucks out the window at his elbow.

The police radio breaks silence. "Yeah?" says Mr. Stanley, answering. Mr. Ike says: "On Dan Eddie, that nigger we got downstairs locked up?"

"Yeah?" Mr. Stanley answers again. He stops the patrol car beside the curb because he can't drive and talk both.

"That Willie Joe arrested?" Mr. Ike Murphy, an old man, broadcasts with his mouth so close to the microphone that coming out of the patrol car receiver, Mr. Ike's voice sounds like a bull trying to out-bellow a tornado.

"All right, now another nigger's done called. Says he's Dan Eddie's lodge brother. He wants Dan Eddie outta jail. Wants to know how much is the fine so he can get up the money. Says his name's Henry and he wants to get Dan Eddie out, so I told him whereas Mr. Worth was the arresting officer if he'd be waiting on the corner of Sycamore and Sixteenth — got that?"

"Sycamore and Sixteenth," says Mr. Stanley Bumpas.

"That you'll come by in the patrol car and talk to him about Dan Eddie. He said he'd be there."

"Okay, Mr. Ike. I gotcha," says Mr. Stanley. Mr. Ike goes off the air. Mr. Stanley looks at Willie Joe.

In the dash lights Mr. Stanley's skin looks like warm mashed potatoes. Mr. Stanley's foot stomps down hard on the accelerator. The car shoots forward in a series of jerks and screeches. Mr. Stanley is an expert at making a car roar and jump in a way that puts Willie Joe in mind of a bobcat. Under Mr. Stanley's control the patrol car is like some living, stalking thing. Mr. Stanley will brag: "This car's trained to track down, smell out, drag up and run in any nigger in Somerton the first minute that somebitch decides to step one inch out of line!"

Now that Mr. Stanley Bumpas has stomped the accelerator, the car whines like a buzz saw; the tires yelp like a runover dog. Sure enough, waiting on the corner of Sixteenth and Sycamore, not a block from the Crossing, there stands a nigger man. The patrol car stops at the curb. Willie Joe does the talking.

"Looking for me, nigger?"

"Please, yes sir. I wondering how much will be the fine of my friend name of Dan Eddie —"

"Say, you been drinking?"

"Naw sir, please sir."

"You look like you been drinking."

"Naw sir, I ain't been drinking. I don't drink."

"Disputing and denying my word, nigger?"

"Naw sir, but I don't —"

Willie Joe has swung open the door, gotten out and jerked open the door to the back seat. The nigger gets into the back seat. Willie Joe is right after him and suddenly all over him with the blackjack for being drunk, two licks; cursing an officer, seven-eight-nine licks while the nigger, too much surprised at first even to feel it, first saying: "Yes sir, please sir, naw sir!" Finally he knows what's happening and says: "Jesus, have mercy!"

Meanwhile Mr. Stanley has stomped the accelerator again. In what seems no time at all they've got the man delivered to the police station. Mr. Ike Murphy, who is nearing eighty, writes everything down in the log book, hardly changing expression. He writes: *Henry Parsons, nigger, age 35, weight 135, height 5-6, address 1740 Sycamore. Public drunk, resisting arrest, cursing officer.*

"Take him downstairs and lock him up," says Mr. Ike Murphy. Willie Joe hustles the nigger downstairs, locks him in one of the cagelike wire cells and goes back out to the patrol car.

Mr. Stanley Bumpas heads for the white end of town now, to the joints just south of City Hall around the mop factory. They go in and hear a little juke music at Jack's Place and get a couple of beers apiece on the house, but in a paper sack of course so as not to give anybody any wrong ideas about the police drinking on the job.

Taking the beers they go back to the patrol car to drink them. It's a hot night. The beer is cold. They've just about finished their second bottle, both of them, and Willie Joe is talking again, about his mama this time. His mama's been sick, down in the back, and he's been driving out in the country twice a day to see her. Willie Joe is just saying that when the screech-blah-screech of the radio signals another message from Mr. Ike. "His wife's waiting at Sycamore and Sixteenth."

Mr. Stanley hands his bottle to Willie Joe who takes all four empties back inside and sets them on the kitchen table behind the bar. Then he goes out again, gets in the car, and they are off, back across town to the Crossing and the same corner of Sycamore again where she's standing out in the open night waiting, wondering and afraid. So as not to scare her Mr. Stanley Bumpas eases the car up to the curb, very slowly and gently this time, but then, just as he is beside her, Mr. Stanley snaps on the red revolving light on the roof of the police cruiser. The little electric motor begins to whirr and the light starts flashing around and around. Mr. Stanley snaps the revolving light off. Willie Joe speaks up, very kind and understanding.

"Erleen Parsons?"

"Yes sir, please sir!"

"It's kinda embarrassing to talk to you this way. We wouldn't want folks to see you standing out in the open." Willie Joe eases his hand back very slowly and opens the back door. "Just get in the back seat, Erleen. We'll take you around the block."

"Is Henry all right? I got to get him out."

"Get in the back seat, Erleen."

She gets in the back seat. Mr. Stanley eases the cruiser away from the curb like the accelerator has an egg under it he doesn't want to break. Otherwise Erleen Parsons might flutter like a bird trapped on a summer screen porch. She must not notice. Willie Joe talks softly, soft as floating thistle down:

"Say you wanna get him out, Erleen?"

"Yes sir. Henry ain't never been in no trouble before. I can't understand it. See, he's got work over at the tanning factory. They be looking for him over yonder tomorrow. He need the work and if he doesn't show up they'll lay him right off. Another man will get Henry's job. I mean, you know, work is so scarce."

"I see," Willie Joe says. He is all kindness and understanding.

"The white man at the police station when I called, he said you could give me the details," Erleen said, "how to get him out because he didn't have nothing down to the station — only what was wrote down in the book."

Mr. Stanley picks up a little speed. It is just a matter of showing her how the rows are laid. She hasn't noticed so far, and when she does notice Willie Joe will almost be able to hear her heart fluttering. He hears her suck a breath when the police cruiser slows down for a four-way stop. The car eases on then, out the country road, across the railroad tracks south of town almost before she knows it. Willie Joe keeps talking and talking to her in that extra kind, soothing way, showing her bit by bit just how the rows are laid; that either she makes a certain decision for herself or else Henry Parsons might just lie in his cage downstairs under the police station until the tanning factory goes out of business, for all the law cares, or Willie Joe either, kind man though he is.

"Ain't that right, Mr. Bumpas?"

Mr. Stanley Bumpas nods.

"Comes down to a case," says Willie Joe, "of a man, of me, being asked and requested to rush things, to step in and manhandle sort of the due process of the law which has to be carried out step by step, whereas otherwise it ain't the law, understand me, Erleen? A man ain't just put in jail for fighting an officer and swearing at an officer and being drunk —"

"All right, yes sir. But Henry, he never drank, I mean he don't drink. He spit the taste of it out of his mouth forever with the help of prayer and his preacher. Henry, he —"

"He was," says Willie Joe, "reeling, staggering, stumbling down drunk — ain't that right, Mr. Bumpas?"

Mr. Stanley Bumpas nods, looking straight ahead down the road running beneath the headlights.

"Or else why would he of talked back to an officer of the law?" Willie Joe says. "Maybe you're talking back now, Erleen. Is that how it is? I'm trying and Mr. Bumpas is trying to be nice to you and explain it and you're talking back? Huh?"

She's silent. Willie Joe goes on saying now she can complain all she wants to about being taken out of town for example on a country road but after all didn't she appreciate what officers were trying to do for her — how much they were going out of their way not to let other people, which it wasn't none of their business, see her riding around in a police car? Wasn't they burning up good gasoline just to do her a favor? Well, wasn't they?"

"Yes sir, please sir," she says, taming down a little.

"Yes sir, please sir — hell!" Willie Joe shouts all of a sudden. "Do you want that God-damned nigger boy out of jail, or don't you? And if so what's it worth seeing you don't have one red cent of money? Nor nothing as I can tell but an awful terrible habit of running off at the mouth. Jawing all the time, ain't you? Giving some officer the lip!"

"Well, please sir —"

"So if you can't put your money where your lip is what are you aiming to put there — grass? Leaves maybe? Cotton hulls?"

"Wel-l, sir, please!"

"So you can't make up your mind, is that it?"

"Naw sir, please!"

"Well either you can make up your mind or you can't, ain't that right?"

"Yes, sir. That's right."

"So you can't make up your mind, is that it?"

"Yes sir, naw sir. Please sir!"

Mr. Stanley Bumpas clears his throat to signal Willie Joe it's time he, Mr. Stanley, spoke up and got into the act. Mr. Stanley has practiced it so many times it is almost like a musician will take up his banjo and tune it a little before he starts to pick it, Mr. Stanley, clearing his throat. It's going to be the same tune he always plays.

[152]

Willie Joe

Mr. Stanley Bumpas says: "I don't like it, Mr. Worth. Now, sir, tampering with the law and the due process. Since Erleen can't make up her mind I'm for taking her in and getting her name wrote down in Mr. Ike's book. Lock her up downstairs. Do it proper because it's the only way. Here I've done drove clean all the way out in the country trying to help her get her nigger boyfriend outta jail and she don't want to offer no cooperation. Let's take her in, Mr. Worth."

Mr. Stanley Bumpas slowly turns the car until it's crosswise of the road. Then he backs up, cuts the wheel, and they are headed back towards Somerton. Five miles ahead, across the flat bottoms, the lights of Somerton are like wheat sown into black velvet ground.

Because Mr. Bumpas is older, not way up in years like Mr. Ike Murphy on the night desk, but then an older man still and all, he knows how to say this so it sends a chill up anybody's back like smoke going up a flue pipe. When Mr. Bumpas talks it's like a fingernail scraping the inside of a rusty bait bucket. "We just have to go on and take her downstairs," he says, shifting at his glasses. He is a fat man who sits a certain way in the driver's seat like he just can't trust his whole weight to rest easy. Willie Joe offers to argue with him, and when he does, Mr. Stanley stops the car and cuts the engine, like he's thinking it over but yet not really convinced. Says Willie Joe to Stanley Bumpas, please, just let him get in the back seat a minute where he can talk to Erleen better and try to convince her of what's for her own good?

The police car sits stopped far out on the moonlit levee road, deep barrow pits on either side so that if Erleen decides to hop out and run she's got four directions to go — up the road, down the road, or into the barrow pits. The barrow pits would be all right too. Probably she can't swim. The most niggers can't. Mr. Stanley has stopped in a very exact spot just about five miles from everywhere. Not another car is anywhere in sight. Even if another car comes it will be five minutes coming after its headlights are first seen. Willie Joe gets in the back seat. Then it's quiet in the car and outside just frog sounds and bug sounds and water and muck and grass smells seeping through the car windows.

Mr. Stanley turns so he can see into the back seat, making piggy grunts, turning himself around so he can see how far Willie Joe has gotten with her. She has her chin down, maybe trying not to hear

[153]

anything from outside, only just her heart bouncing like a rabbit, smelling just the heat from between her breasts. She draws a deep breath. Willie Joe locks the doors on either side of her, moving real slow, like perhaps she is a wasp's nest. He is easing himself across the seat cushion. The seat takes his weight just beside her. She raises her chin the first time, maybe smells him too the way Mr. Stanley smells him — the sweatband smell of his hat, his white man's hair tonic, the tobacco and sweat smell of his body, sort of a sweetish odor. Willie Joe is saying:

"Course . . . now it's wrote in the book and I'd be taking a chance but then you say he's gotta get out and be back to work Monday morning and I admire a boy that has a job and wants to work as so many of them black, no count somebitches is always playing off and trying to rob their wages out of the boss they work for — but then take it this way, it's a chance for me that I'm taking, getting him off the book that way after it's already wrote . . . down —"

Willie Joe breathes like he's climbing the stairs. She isn't hardly breathing at all. He's breathing so much he can't hardly get his words out, breathing for the both of them, as Mr. Stanley has commented before about similar situations, that Willie Joe does all the breathing in a case like this.

Erleen's like somebody listening for something she's never going to hear. She is somebody hoping for something better than she has any right to expect, like maybe she expects to be treated like white folks for once. Willie Joe glances at Mr. Stanley. Mr. Stanley is wiping his glasses to get a better look. Mr. Stanley is like a big bird on a roost, taking it all in, watching and waiting. He slips his glasses on. The bright moon outside makes light in the car. It makes two dark pits of Mr. Stanley's eyes. Willie Joe sees Erleen raising her chin some more. She is venturing a look about, looking out the window at the moonlight as though she might be getting out of the car in a minute.

"Now — I want to help git, help you and help git this boy out from downstairs —"

Willie Joe touches her. She sucks her breath like she did once before. She's like a fish jerked fresh out of the water, trembling, just ready to flop. When she's undressed Willie Joe's white hand moves on her arm just above the elbow making a chill he can feel going all through her flesh like a breeze riffling the water. She's whispering: "Yes sir, please sir!"

"Ain't going to hurt you," Willie Joe goes on, consoling her. "Nothing you ain't done before plenty of times. God damn always asking favors you anyway till I wonder who the hell . . . nigger . . . thinks they are. You feel that? That's a pistol and God damn don't you think Willie Worth can't make this somebitch get up and dance and sing a tune you better believe God damn . . ."

From the front seat Mr. Stanley Bumpas draws a long, tremulous breath of satisfaction.

Willie Joe feels the flesh writhe under him an instant, twisting like a snake, but cornered, no place to run, the circle narrow and more narrow and turning in on itself, her teeth gritting, her head thrown back and turning side to side, whispering no, no, no until he hits center, the warm mark and her knees come slowly, slowly up. She is locked under him, hilted.

"Comes a car," says Mr. Stanley Bumpas.

"I don't need all God-damned night," says Willie Joe.

Mr. Bumpas turns anyway and starts the engine. He lets the car move slowly forward with the lights on until the strange car has whipped past. Then he parks again. The strange car is gone on shimmering and whispering away over its tires into Somerton, towards the rail crossing where Willie Joe can imagine the quick flash of its tail lights. The strange car is just gone and he comes out himself, shoots out of himself. He pulls back. The woman's knees come slowly, slowly down, trembling. Her teeth chatter a little, like she's freezing.

Willie Joe stands outside the car in the fresh clean moonlight and arranges himself, trousers and pistol belt. He reaches in the back seat for his hat. Erleen hasn't moved.

"Can I dress now?" she says. "Please, sir?"

"That's right. That's all for now. Mr. Bumpas don't indulge," says Willie Joe.

Mr. Bumpas shines his flashlight so she can manage her clothes.

"What about you, Mr. Stanley?" Willie Joe says.

"I wouldn't shag one of them sluts for four God-damned hundred dollars," says Mr. Stanley Bumpas.

"Just a watcher, that's Mr. Stanley."

"I don't mind watching. You just couldn't pay me, that's all. 'Damned if I would,' " says Mr. Stanley, quoting.

"Damned if you could nohow," Willie Joe says, all zipped and belted now. He opens the front door and gets in beside Mr. Stanley. "Damned if you could anyhow," he says.

The engine starts. Mr. Stanley flips on the headlights. Ahead to the left, the red aircraft warning lights on the radio tower blink slowly as a heartbeat. Across the road in front of the car little frogs leap. Their white bellies flash. Insects flutter in the car lights — moths and may-flies and green katydids dancing and swirling and smacking the wind-shield, leaving little blurs of tallow and grease. On and on they come, swarming out of the roadside grass. The car gathers speed. Willie Joe explains to Erleen Parsons in the back seat how the fact of her being cooperative has convinced him that the charge against Henry ought to be dismissed, but then the best the law can allow is a suspension of the charge, whereas it still hung over the nigger forever, as no charge serious as Henry's ever could be wiped entirely off the slate, didn't she understand? "In other words you just now made the down payment on the bill you owe me? Understand me what I'm saying?"

"Yes sir, please sir," she says.

Mr. Stanley Bumpas drives back through town, back to the corner of Sycamore and Sixteenth. He stops the car under an elm tree that makes a shade from the streetlight on the corner. Willie Joe is say-ing:

"You better be standing on this corner when I send word for you to be standing here not that you're anything to write home about but it's a case of me having to risk my job just to help you? And here's the only kind of payment you understand? Or if you ain't here just one time I'll be asking around after you and that nigger boy of yours to know why you ain't here whenever I sent word. Got it straight?"

"Yes sir, please sir." She gets out of the car, maybe a little wilted, like a wet pigeon. She stands there a minute before she crosses the street in front of the headlights. The car lights make her look bet-ter, more fine and slender and less frazzled.

Mr. Stanley Bumpas spins the wheel and stomps the accelerator at the same time. "No need to tell her everything you know," he says. The tires screech in the turn. They pass the ice house and the tin smithy and the freight office, then beyond the fruit sheds they pass the first white beer joint.

"Any complaints?" Willie Joe asks.

"If you just wouldn't talk so much and try to tell her everything you know is all. Shit, tell her one time. She'll be there. Shit — say it once."

"You complaining?" Willie Joe asks.

"No," says Mr. Stanley. "Your bidness is your bidness. Only you always tell everything you know. Give you time and you'll tell it all. Telling me every little bitty ass thing about the nigger undertaker's wife. Wearing your pistol in the bed with her. What her titties look like."

"Well, I never known you to stop up your God-damned ears," says Willie Joe pleasantly. "I just tell you, nobody else, on that."

"All right, but what do you tell her? Can't you just get shut of her and leave her alone? God knows ain't you got enough to take care of without hanging out with her all the time? Why don't you get shut of her?"

Willie Joe takes a minute to think about it. "I don't know," he says then. "Maybe I couldn't exactly explain it. She knows stuff. She says poems to me."

"Shit," says Mr. Stanley, turning right at the Lion station, off Hemlock into Twelfth. "Nigger poems."

"She went pretty far up in school," Willie Joe says. "She's got her college."

"Nigger college," says Mr. Stanley. "I bet by God you tell her everything you know. Shit on that kinda noise. I bet she knows your God-damned bidness better than you know it yourself, don't she?"

"You complaining? Because if you are —"

"No," Stanley Bumpas says, headed straight for City Hall now. "It's just no need for a man to tell everything he knows. I don't understand it. But then it's a lot I don't understand where anybody would put a piece of pussy ahead of a dollar and swap off his secrets for a nigger poem. Take an undertaker handles a corpse and then handles his wife and then you come along —"

"By God if you got a complaint on it let's hear what it is?" Willie Joe waits. Mr. Stanley clams up tight. "You don't think I tell her police bidness too, do you?"

Willie Joe waits for Mr. Stanley to accuse him of telling Emma about the two books Mr. Ike Murphy has on the night desk, about the first book which is a fake log where Mr. Ike can write in a prisoner's name just like he's booking him. Then if they can get cash out of him they can let him go and there's nothing in the city police records, not a sign on the official blotter that anybody could point to later and say the police were stealing fines. Or would Mr. Stanley accuse him, Willie Joe wondered, of telling Emma about the two receipt books? The one book for giving a man a full receipt for the amount of his fine and the other book for the official record of receipts, for the city records where the fines were cut down to something sensible for permanent recording? Where, in other words, did you take thirty-five dollars off a man, record five dollars in the official receipt book, and that left ten apiece for Willie Joe and Stanley Bumpas and Ike Murphy? Willie Joe waits, but Mr. Stanley doesn't raise any gripes or complaints. Instead he parks the car in front of the police station and opens the door, easing his feet down to the pavement. Willie Joe gets out on his side of the car. The dim globe lights on either side of the entrance to City Hall shine like a pair of full moons.

Willie Joe follows Mr. Stanley into the modern, brightly lit police station next door and smiles when he sees Oman Hedgepath.

The lawyer isn't smiling. He looks tired, he looks old and worn out, like the world has whipped him down. "See you a minute in private?" The lawyer asks this before Willie Joe can even speak.

"Sure thing, Mr. Hedgepath. Yes, sir!"

"Let's go in the conference room."

Willie Joe follows the lawyer, still smiling, for above everything else a policeman has to smile. He must be cheerful with the lawyers and the Mayor and the right people. All he has to do is remember to smile, and, once he gets the drift of what the other man wants him to say, to say it. Then he's got his job as long as he wants it. Like Mr. Stanley and Mr. Ike have told him maybe a thousand times: "By God, whatever you do grin and say yessir." Willie Joe remembers.

The lawyer shuts the door. "May as well sit down and be comfortable," he says. Both men sit down at the conference table. "What I have to say won't take long," the lawyer says. Willie Joe smiles across the table at him and pushes him the ashtray the Mayor used earlier, during the nigger trial. Although he's wondering what the hell it's all about, he manages to keep the grin fresh.

Oman Hedgepath lights a cigarette and puts it on the ashtray. He turns a folder of book matches in his hands, over and over. He looks at the matches instead of Willie Joe. Obviously something bothers him.

"L. B. Jones, the nigger undertaker, is a client of mine. Maybe you knew he wanted a divorce?"

"No sir, Mr. Hedgepath, I didn't know about it."

"Well, he wants a divorce. Although I didn't want to take the case there was some pressure on me to take it. So I took it. Now I've got to get him his divorce. It's ready to be heard Tuesday morning along with the uncontested divorce suits, something so routine I don't need to tell you about it. The witnesses just have a seat, the plaintiff takes the witness chair and tells his story, then the two witnesses testify. They corroborate the testimony of the plaintiff, and the judge grants the divorce. You've sat in court and seen it yourself."

"Yes sir, I have."

"All right. Now in this particular case the plaintiff's wife is accused of having relations with a white man, committing adultery with him. In order to make the divorce bill stand up in court it had to be put in pretty strong language. Still there was no need to name the white man — understand? Just indicating that he's white, that he works for the City of Somerton, that narrows it down enough for the judge. Now in an uncontested suit that's sufficient. Nobody cares who the white man is. So far so good?"

"Yes sir."

"Very well. In this case I plowed into a stump. Emma got herself a lawyer. She's petitioned the court to make us prove every point against her. This means that her lawyer can cross-examine my client's witnesses. In other words, instead of the white man's name going un- mentioned, the cross-examination is sure to bring his name out and whoever happens to be waiting in divorce court that day will hear it. Also the fact that the white man is a city policeman will be brought out if Emma goes on with this thing. Now I don't ask you how much you know about this, and I'd rather you didn't volunteer any- thing because what I know about the woman's relationship with the white man isn't going to help me or my client. You see what I mean?"

"Yes sir, Mr. Hedgepath."

"All right. Now I've talked to Emma's lawyer and he's being a son of a bitch about it. He knows he's got me in the bind. He knows I wouldn't want a white man's name to come out — I wouldn't want a policeman on our force to lose his job over something like this, although I'd naturally expect this to serve as a pretty God-damned severe warning to him that this kind of screwing around is particularly dangerous for somebody who's main duty in life is upholding the law. I shouldn't have to remind a policeman that cohabitation between white and colored in Tennessee is a felony. Shouldn't have to tell him that he can go to the state pen for cracking a nigger — should I?"

"No sir, you sure shouldn't, on that. That's right," Willie Joe says. He begins to feel a little hot and uncomfortable, maybe even a little sick, but still he keeps trying to smile. He feels his hands getting cold. The blood feels as though it is draining out of his face.

The lawyer takes a drag on his cigarette, puts it back on the ashtray, and takes up the book matches again. "I'm glad you agree with me there, Willie Joe. Now what has me bothered is why Emma would want to do anything that would expose the white man she's sleeping with and ruin him. See what I mean? Why does she show up here suddenly at the last minute and fight the very divorce she's promised L.B. all along she'd let him have uncontested, with no strings attached? Because as you know there has to be a reason behind everything. Further, as you may know, because Emma's not my client, I'm not privileged to talk to her myself. Understand?"

"I think so, yessir."

"Another man wouldn't be prevented from talking to her, and finding out why, and then proceeding to talk her out of this notion. All she has to do is tell her lawyer to withdraw her petition and then fire him. Wouldn't take her five minutes and our problems would be over. Otherwise, when L. B. Jones climbs into that witness chair Tuesday morning, if Emma's still stuck to what she aims to do now—pardon me, Willie Joe, but in that case your goose is cooked."

"Yes sir, it sure is," Willie Joe says.

"You knew nothing about Emma's fighting L. B.'s divorce?"

"No sir, not a word."

"Any notion why she'd suddenly decided to fight it?"

"No idea at all, sir."

"Do you want your name spoken in open court? You want to lose your job with the city? Shame your family?"

"Now, Mr. Oman, you know I don't want that to happen. Sir, you know that's something that just can't happen if I can do anything to stop it."

"I'm glad you feel that way, Willie Joe. Anybody can make a mistake, but it takes a man to admit to the world when he's wrong. Now you can see the situation's bad, but you can also see, I hope, that with a little finesse no one ever need know who the white man is. Just a little persuasion and I won't be embarrassed, the city won't be embarrassed, and you won't have this shame heaped upon you. It's up to you to handle it alone. Don't ask me what to do. Just be sure that sometime between now and Tuesday morning you have it fixed so your name won't have to be spoken in open court. Now isn't that clear enough?" The lawyer takes a final drag off his cigarette and stumps it out in the ashtray. He stands up and looks down at Willie Joe.

"That's plenty, Mr. Oman. You don't need to say another word. It'll be taken care of, sir. I can promise you that much on it. It will be taken care of, and I mean, sir, it will be done right," Willie Joe says. He stands up. He smiles. "Thank you sir, you done me a favor I will not ever forget."

"And taught you a lesson, I hope."

"Yes sir, taught me a good lesson."

"This conversation between us of course is secret. Neither of us will ever tell another person. It will be an eternal bond, a contract between us, won't it?"

"It sure will, Mr. Oman. I'll never forget it, what you done for me to tell me this. I know it taken bravery and guts and I know I done wrong and don't deserve no favor like this one. I —" Willie Joe looks at the green carpeted floor.

"It's all right," the lawyer says.

When Willie Joe looks up the lawyer has gone. He waits to give Oman Hedgepath time to get out of the building, then he goes out to the front desk where Mr. Ike and Mr. Stanley stand waiting to know what Lawyer Hedgepath had to say.

"What the hell was that all about?" Mr. Ike wants to know. "I bet he sat right there and waited an hour." Mr. Ike pulls out his watch with his palsied hand and looks at it. "By God, wait an hour he did. Lawyer Hedgepath waited one hour and seven minutes and wouldn't let me radio you nothing about it. Set right there and waited."

"It's about my mother's property, about her farm, and he had to talk to me private. That and a couple of other things. Nothing about you or us," says Willie Joe.

The two older men are impressed.

4

Mr. Ike

Running the night desk — one thing it was quiet. Mr. Ike had reached the age when quiet meant something to him. For another thing it was a writing job and Mr. Ike had been right smart of a scribe all his life. He could pen a beautiful hand even now that his fingers wanted to tremble when he steered the pen.

Finally it was a job of keeping books and records, and that was another thing he knew inside out, the business of records — especially the double-entry method, where the City of Somerton had one book and the night force had another separate one. This was the best double-entry system of any Mr. Ike knew.

Moreover he liked to question people. He liked having people under his power when he questioned them and he had a stock of funny questions and a store of funny remarks he could throw at them. He was best of anything else with niggers, since he really knew niggers.

For example Mr. Ike Murphy knew that the only way to faze a nigger is to kick him in the shins. He knew anything else you did wouldn't hurt a nigger, nothing at all until you got at his shins. Take a nigger's head. His head was so bony it was like the head of a garfish or in other words about the same as a cue ball. Work on a nigger's head all you wanted to and nevermind about getting to his brain. And of course Mr. Ike knew that a bluegum nigger's bite was just almost the same as getting struck by a rattlesnake, except worse, so when a nigger was hauled in Mr. Ike was always careful to look at the nigger's mouth and try to see the color of his gums before asking many funny questions. Mr. Ike was a prudent man and had a good notion that, poison as he was, a bluegum just might go wild and before a man knew it there Mr. Ike would be, bit by a bluegum and no power in the world to save him from laying down flat on the floor and dying the worst of all horrible deaths — his veins full of nigger venom.

It therefore distressed Mr. Ike that Willie Joe and Stanley Bumpas weren't more careful the way they tangled assholes with niggers like they did, just wading in on them and knocking them about like rabbits and arresting them and bringing them right on down to the station without ever once looking at their gums to see what they had, without even taking the simple precaution to make sure they hadn't laid hands on a bluegum.

Worse still, the two night police had ridden Mr. Ike pretty bad about his notion, so bad in fact that he had finally shut up talking about it at all any more. Still it irked him, and no sooner had Lawyer Hedgepath left than Willie Joe and Mr. Stanley took to winking and nodding at one another because they were about to bring up Henry Parsons to release him, and Henry was a full-blooded bluegum.

When they had brought Henry Parsons in earlier to book him, Mr. Ike had said: "Show your teeth, Henry. Let me see your teeth." He had shined his flashlight in the nigger's mouth and sure enough, his gums were blue as a razor blade. Mr. Ike had put the counter desk between himself and the nigger as quickly as possible. Then he had said: "Okay, Henry, close your mouth. We don't have to count your teeth and give you no receipt.

"Den-tal ins-pec-tion, te-eth, okay," Mr. Ike had said, writing down the information as he said it out loud. All the while Willie Joe and Mr. Stanley had stood by with grins on their faces, just as they stood by grinning now, enjoying Mr. Ike's nervousness.

"Reckon we dare go down and get him?" Willie Joe said.

Mr. Stanley laughed. "Haw-haw-haw-haw!" Mr. Stanley roared. Then he commenced to cough.

"All right," said Mr. Ike, "just wait till one bites you and then we'll see how loud you laugh. Couple of smart ass know-it-alls," he said aloud. To himself he thought, Sons of bitches that don't have nothing better to do than scare an old man; that can't respect the other fellow when he's done got old; that's a couple of pretty sons of bitches for you, he thought. "Yes," he said, "by God go on and laugh, and by God when that bluegum hauls off and fangs one of you hotshots in the settee, then I'll laugh, by God, because a laugh will help as much as anything else then. No medicine on earth will save you."

The two policemen went off downstairs after the nigger and Mr. Ike took his true murder mystery magazine from under the counter and settled down in his cane bottom rocking chair to read.

A nigger was like one of those little cups they put on the turpentine trees back in Mr. Ike's youth down in the South Georgia pine country. Once a tree was slashed the little cup was put there and a man went back from time to time and collected the resin.

Same with a nigger. Once you ever picked him up it was after that whatever you could bleed out of him from then on, unless of course some other white man had already done got to him first. But now one like Henry Parsons, a nigger with a factory job and no white man looking after him, from now on it would be just a case of picking Henry Parsons up and setting him down now and then. Ever so often Willie Joe and Mr. Stanley could pick him up and shake out his pockets, same as emptying a turpentine cup. Ditto for the nigger's wife.

Mr. Ike thumbed through the magazine towards his place where he had left off reading before all the night's interruptions had bothered him. He bought his magazines second hand, two for a nickel from Paul Frick, the quiet German-blooded fellow with a club foot who ran the bus station and collected magazines left behind on the bus. Mr. Ike thumbed past the one about the farmer in Iowa who ground his victims up and sold them for sausage (a man by God never knew what he might eat when he set his legs under the table in a cafe); about the couple in San Francisco that ran a nursing home and rat poisoned nineteen elderly senior citizens to death before the police caught on; about the plumber in Alabama that shoved his wife and mother-in-law through an airplane propeller; and the Canadian maniac who electrocuted his three girl friends on some bed springs which he had wired up just for that purpose. This one was wrote up very scientific, thought Mr. Ike, with pictures of the bed springs and the graves in the basement and a diagram on just how the maniac had wired the springs up to the house current.

Finally he found the story he'd been reading, about the musician in Mr. Ike's home state of Georgia who was a dope addict and was married to a lady acrobat night club performer who didn't have any idea that her husband, a bass violinist, was murdering entire families of people while he was gone off on trips alone by himself. Mr. Ike had just found his place when Willie Joe and Mr. Stanley came back upstairs with the bluegum.

Holding his thumb in the magazine Mr. Ike stood up to discharge the prisoner. "Henry Parsons? Well, are you Henry Parsons or down-stairs did you by God change your name?"

"Yes sir, please sir."

"Your name is Henry Parsons?"

"Yes sir, please sir."

"You gonna phone down here any more and ask questions of the law, Parsons?"

"Naw sir, never again, please sir."

"One of your friends gets in jail you gonna keep your black nose out of it, are you?"

"Yes sir, please sir."

"All right, that'll be thirty-five dollars cash money."

"Your honor?" Willie Joe Worth said.

"Yes, Officer Worth?"

"I'm gonna pay this nigger's fine, me and Officer Mr. Stanley both together, and Parsons is going to pay us back. Parsons has got a job, your honor, over at the tanning factory, and if he don't show up Monday he'll get laid off, so we already arranged it with him down-stairs, since he don't have the money, to pay it for him ourselves. Will that be all right, your Honor?"

Mr. Ike waits. "It's mighty irregular, goes against the regulations."

"Your Honor, sir," Willie Joe says. "Parsons has promised to pay us five dollars a week for twelve weeks."

Mr. Ike pauses to think about it. Willie Joe winks at him. "All right then, I'll suspend the charges, but they remain on the book still and all. The first week he fails to pay — Parsons, now I want you to understand this. You ain't to leave the City of Somerton except to go to and from your job. You pay these officers a five-dollar bill every payday for twelve paydays. If you miss one payday we'll have you

[166]

back down here and the governor of this state couldn't help you then because you'll have done broke your parole, understand?"

"Yes sir, please sir."

"And if you talk about this favor we're a-doing you tonight, against all regulations, then you can just give your soul to the Lord, because your ass will be mine. Now, Parsons, have I made all this clear?"

"Yes sir, I understand it all, please sir."

"Okay. Dismissed."

"I can go, please sir?"

"Get going," Willie Worth said.

The nigger turned and went out the door. Waiting for him to get gone Mr. Stanley Bumpas put Mr. Ike in mind of a big old indeterminate chicken, one that is neither rooster nor hen, like an undecided old chicken with cracked feet, that's how he stands watching the door where the nigger has gone out. Beside him Willie Worth is younger and stronger, but kind of going to fat himself and getting potbellied, like a dog that was once real active, but has taken his wolfish appetite into retirement and started swelling up, shaping out almost the same way a woman will when she's pregnant was how Willie Joe's bay window had begun to look, Mr. Ike decided.

When the police had given the nigger a minute to be gone they went on out themselves and got in the patrol car. The engine started and roared. The lights came on bright, and the car backed out into Main Street and moved on, going towards the Presbyterian Church.

Relieved to be rid of the bluegum, relieved to know the poisonous nigger was safely out of the building at last, Mr. Ike settled back down in his rocking chair, opened his magazine, and began to read:

" 'Is this blood darling,' Lydia inquired curiously when she noticed stains on Anton Groober's white buckskin shoes for the second time in six days and finally got up courage to ask him about the grisly marks.

" 'Ketchup,' her burly husband snarled, and struck her across the nose, savagely clubbing her with his heavy violin case. A dazed Lydia Groober screamed as blood spurted. Hot, scarlet liquid oozed over her filmy negligee. Fearfully she gazed into her husband's pinprick pupilled eyes, so shrunken by the horde of dope dammed up in his throbbing veins that she wondered if Anton were really normal. For an answer the huge bass violin case crashed into her ear."

5

Willie Joe

Willie Joe settles back against the car seat. Mr. Ike radios that there's a fight at Marvin's, the white beer joint, and Mr. Stanley takes his time about getting them there. Get there too quick, says Mr. Stanley, and you don't give things a chance to settle out. Take your time and if you have any luck the action will all be over, the decisions all made, and whoever has to be arrested will know it by the time the police car arrives and will be waiting along with everybody else. Best to have everybody waiting when police arrive. Then there can be something dignified about the whole thing; get there too quick and you might have to shoot somebody or hit somebody, something white people don't take too kindly. It's a philosophy Mr. Stanley has worked out over the years.

A nigger call on the other hand must be answered right away because in that case you never want niggers to be waiting when the police car arrives. Best for niggers to be fighting so you can see for yourself what it is and arrest the whole bunch. Get there when it's over and nobody knows anything; everybody able to walk has left and the only thing you find is the dead corpse if there happens to be one. A live nigger will never wait for the police, that's sure, says Mr. Stanley.

Willie Joe gets out of the car and walks into the beer joint. Sure enough it's all over. Marvin, the owner, who called in the complaint in the first place, has hit the other man on the head with a loaded broom handle, and the man is sitting on the floor beside the jukebox and bleeding pretty bad from a cut on his forehead where the broom handle caught him just over the left eye. The bleeding man says he works at the mop factory. Marvin offers to take him to the hospital to have his head sewn up. "I don't hold no grudge nor hard feelings if you don't, fellow," Marvin says to the man sitting on the floor.

"It's up to you, Marvin, if you want us to take him downtown," says Willie Joe to the owner of the joint, because in answering a call you always talk to the man who called in the complaint and offer to arrest the other fellow. That's what Willie Joe does. "We can take him downtown," Willie Joe says again.

"No need of it, I guess. I don't have no hard feelings," Marvin says.

"My head's broke," says the man on the floor.

"Well, God damn, didn't I tell you to shut up?" Marvin says, being very reasonable. "Didn't I tell you twice God damn it to hush? Wasn't you cussing and being very loud? I run a clean place here, fellow. You can go downtown with the man if you want to, now, but I don't bear no grudge."

"How about it?" Willie Joe asks the man on the floor.

"If Marvin wants to drive me to the hospital it's okay with me."

Marvin slips two cold beers in a sack for Willie Joe. Somebody drops money in the jukebox. It starts up like an electric churn. Two women get up from a booth and begin to dance. "Shake it!" Marvin yells. "I'll drive the somebitch to the hospital in my car," Marvin tells Willie Joe. "The mop factory carries insurance to get him sewed up. He ain't a bad boy, he's just mean," Marvin says. "I wouldn't want to send him downtown you know unless I had to do it." Marvin picks up a burnt out cigar from the counter and lights it, turning it over and over to get it started good.

"What's the good of being hard on a man unless you have to do it," Willie Joe says. He picks up the sack from the counter. "I don't want nobody to run it over me and I don't like to run it over nobody, unless I have to," he says.

"That's just the way I see it," Marvin agrees. "Long as you treat me like a white man that's how I'll treat you. Fair and square all around. It's all wrote in the Sermon on the Mount, you know that, by God? I'll live by that any day in the week. You take a man fol-

lows that and he's gonna be all right. 'Blessed are the meek,'"
says Marvin. He rolls up his shirt sleeves a couple of turns to hide
the blood stains and washes his hairy arms in the sink and dries
them with a bar cloth. "I'll spread some newspapers in the trunk of
my car and haul the somebitch up to the hospital directly," Marvin
says, taking up the cigar and turning it around and around the same
as he did when he lit it, while he puffs to get it going good again.
He takes the cigar out of his mouth. "Shake it!" he yells at the
women.

6

Steve Mundine

At the Somerton Golf and Country Club Steve Mundine sits at the green felt-covered table in the card room just off the bar, holding hands with his wife, Nella, and having a drink with the Price Burkhalters and the dentist and his wife.

The dentist is a quiet young man just out of the Army and his wife is a pretty girl with perfect teeth who smiles and winks at Nella now and then, trying to get Nella in the spirit of things, perhaps being even a little embarrassed for Nella's not enjoying Price Burkhalter's story about the Federal Marshal and the Negro demonstrators who descended on the park. Steve squeezes Nella's cold hand.

"Price Park," says Burkhalter for what seems the hundredth time. "My own mother's father." Because the hardware dealer is a little drunk his mind has begun to wander. "Didn't they used to call Somerton 'Chimneyville' because after the Yankee troops got through putting the city to the torch all you saw was chimneys standing alone? Took every horse, every hog, every cow. Slaves all jumped up and ran away, joined the Yankees. My Great-grandmother Price had her prize saddle horse confiscated, by God she just saddled the horse and got on it — her horses were all trained to kneel — and said: 'Take my horse, take me.' "

"Is that a fact?" said the dentist. "Trained to kneel?"

"I swear to God. 'Take my horse, take me.' Well, they took her to the Yankee colonel and he said: 'Madam, I cannot but match bravery such as yours with courtesy. Please keep your horse.' And my great-grandmother rode back home with her mare and into my store today walks this string bean son of a bitch . . ."

"Now Johnnie Price, you don't have to swear," says the hardware dealer's wife, "do you, honey?" She has a funny story of her own about the time a Negro girl tried to enter the University of Alabama when she was in school there, and she keeps interrupting Johnnie Price and beginning her story, but Johnnie Price has so far shouted her down every time.

"Excuse me, this God-damned son of a bitch," says Johnnie Price. "How's that?"

They all laugh, except Nella. Drunk though Johnnie Price is, Steve can see that the hardware dealer is becoming aware of Nella's silence. Steve laughs and squeezes his wife's hand to let her know she ought to laugh. He looks at her. Nella's beautiful face is very pale.

"I heard," says the dentist, trying to change the subject slightly, "did you hear that in the eleven Deep South states less than one half of one per cent of the niggers are going to school with whites? Yet the way the newspapers carry on you'd think integration of the schools was practically an accomplished fact, wouldn't you?"

"Hell," says Price Burkhalter. "I could tell them that much. The South will never surrender! We'll never surrender. You think anybody's really trying to help the niggers? Take what those Yankee agitators are doing in Birmingham. They don't make no attempt to help the niggers. All they do is just agitate them until they begin to tear up and burn down everything in sight, beginning with their own homes. Well what kind of help is that?"

"You all should have been at Tuscaloosa when this black bitch tried to enter the University," his wife begins.

"Hush a minute," Price Burkhalter says. "We all heard about that."

"We chanted, honey, I want you to know it was like the biggest pep rally you ever saw. '*Hey, hey! Ho! Ho! That God-damned nigger's gotta go.*' Well let me tell you all something, you can bet she wasn't around very long. Sick — it makes you sick. When Johnnie Price came home with those papers served on him, honey, I thought I'd faint. Well, I'm over it now and I told him, I said, 'Johnnie Price, fight the bastards right down to the line. Baby, your wife's with you!' Didn't I?"

"You sho' did," Johnnie Price says, suddenly so emotional he's almost choked up. He takes a sip of bourbon and water to hide his embarrassment. "She sho' said it, by God," he says.

"I heard," says the dentist, "maybe you heard the same thing, that this so-called biracial committee in Birmingham is patterned exactly on the Soviets, the Communist committees they set up in Russian cities back in 1917. Now the President's saying the United States Army is in the Birmingham vicinity to make sure the program of the biracial committee is carried out, whereas this biracial committee itself has no legal authority and has been revealed as a hoax by the City of Birmingham and the Governor of Alabama. So all the Communists need to take over any place is a biracial committee. Then the United States Army will come down and you've got a military occupation, just like they did it in Russia back in 1917."

"Somebody will kill that peckerwood. You watch and see if they don't," says Price Burkhalter.

"Who?" Steve says, squeezing Nella's hand.

"The President," says Price Burkhalter. "Some patriot will lay him low and I hope to live to shake the hand of the hero that does it. For two cents, by God —"

"Now, Johnnie Price," says his wife.

"Well, for two cents I would. So would any Southerner, or might I say any American. If somebody don't we'll have a military dictatorship run by the Pope at Rome with the full cooperation of the Kremlin. How about it, Nella, being from San Francisco, don't you agree that somebody ought to shoot him and save America?"

"I don't think Nella would quite —"

"I can speak for myself, Steve, thanks just the same," Nella says, taking her hand away.

"Nella," Steve says, "Johnnie Price is upset."

"Let Nella have her say-so, by God. I want to hear what Nella has to say," says Johnnie Price. "Steve, I'll ask you to let Nella alone so she can speak her piece like the rest of us, that is if you don't mind."

"I heard," says the dentist, "maybe you all didn't, I don't know, but I heard that —"

"Well, I can see one thing. I'm going over with Nella about like a turd in a punch bowl," says Johnnie Price. "Maybe I'm not such a damn big city gentleman Chattanooga lawyer like some others."

"Shut up, Johnnie Price. Don't you know how," says his wife. "Can't you shut up when you get tight?"

"I only wanted to hear what Nella thinks. Nella hasn't said one word all the whole evening. Steve has set right there and kept her gagged all night. Maybe Nella's ideas are different from my beliefs and ideas, does that mean I won't listen to what she's got to say on the subject? Ain't I pretty fair-minded in all your estimations?"

When nobody says anything Johnnie Price finishes his drink. "One more and I'm going home and hit the hay. Honey, you got a loud voice, holler at that nigger and tell him to bring us another round."

Obediently the hardware dealer's wife gets up and goes to the door of the card room and signals the bartender for another round, drawing a circle in the air with her finger instead of saying anything, as though there's someone asleep whom she doesn't dare wake up. She comes back to the table and sits down. "Anyone for bridge?" she says.

"Johnnie Price wants my opinion," Nella says. Her voice shakes. "I've sat here and listened to him paw and bellow all evening. Have I your permission, Steve, or should I phone Oman?"

"Don't phone Oman!" the dentist says. The dentist's wife shows her perfect teeth. The others laugh. The Negro bartender delivers the final round of drinks. Johnnie Price fends off the dentist and signs the tab. Only Steve and Nella have not laughed.

"Oman's true blue, and a damn fine lawyer. Best in this part of the state," says Johnnie Price Burkhalter, looking at Nella.

"Have I your permission, Steve?" Nella says.

"You know you don't have to have anyone's permission to say what you please," Steve says. Nella is suddenly crying.

"Nella, honey!" says Johnnie Price Burkhalter's wife. "Baby!"

The women try to comfort her. "Sweetie," says the dentist's wife, "are you pregnant? Are you keeping a secret?"

"Let me get some plain ice water. She doesn't need another drink," says the dentist. Getting up he goes into the bar.

"It's late," Steve says, standing up.

"Sure, we understand," says the hardware dealer. "My wife gets the same way sometimes. Don't you, honey?"

"For once, Johnnie Price Burkhalter, for once in your life, shut up?" says his wife. The dentist comes back with ice water. The wife's still telling the hardware dealer to shut up when Nella and Steve walk through the deserted bar and outdoors into the soft wind of the July night, beneath huge old oaks that seem to guard the club house, beneath high, rustling leaves. Steve and Nella walk each in a separate loneliness.

By the time they reach the car Nella's crying again. Steve tries to take her hand but she pulls away from him. He puts his arm about her shoulders. "Nella?"

"Don't," she says. "Please. God, I'm so homesick. I . . . I wanted to tell that boor a few things so much it made me sick. Steve, it's crushing me. No, don't touch me, please."

"But you're shivering," he said. "Nella, I love you."

"Maybe I'm just homesick. Steve, would you mind if I called Mother tomorrow? Maybe if I could just get back to San Francisco, even for a visit, if I could be myself for a little while? I can't breathe in this climate. I can't talk, I can't think. Either they're crazy or I'm crazy — and tonight, when you just sat there through it all, when you never raised your voice. Can you spend your whole life like this, Steve?"

He started the car and began the drive home, down to the highway between whitewashed tree trunks on either side, lining the golf course. There was a moon, there were drifting clouds. In San Francisco Steve had shown her, one night, how to tell if the moon were waxing or on the wane, by shaping the curve of one's hand to it. If the right hand fits, he thought, the moon is waxing. Drawn into herself Nella was weeping silently. The highway was like a pale, indecisive ribbon of silver and the dark flat fields brought a sweet smell of grass on the fluttering wind.

7

Nella

I began telling him to shut up, not to touch me. I said, "If it turns out that you have to pay the price of silence and conformity to have this dream of yours — the South, and Oman, and this great love of yours for the land —"

"Nella."

"Don't touch me," I told him. "I just wonder if the price isn't getting to be a little high."

"Nella."

"If the price," I told him, "is that high, if it means giving up and giving in, then I don't know if I'm going to be able to meet my payments."

Somehow we got home, to Glenraven. The sight of it started me crying again. It has moods that you don't think of a house as having. The architecture and the trees, the grounds, the integrity of the man who could frame Glenraven in his mind and build it.

As though he knew what must be passing in my mind as we sat there parked in the drive. I sat watching the shadows on the cypress porch, moon shadows and night shadows. I was not crying any longer — just watching. He said:

"The people who built these houses owned slaves but they didn't have any feeling of hate. You must believe that there are some of us still left."

"Then stand up and be counted," I said. "If you are really one of the survivors, isn't it time that you made your presence known?"

Finally we went inside. We went upstairs. When he touched me I knew without his having to say so that he had decided to stand up to them.

He was free again, the same Steve I had always known. The man I will always remember, saying, "Love, oh love!"

8

Willie Joe

While Mr. Stanley drives the police car slowly around and around the block of stores and little beer joints that make up the Crossing, Willie Joe sits beside the rolled down window.

"Get off the street," he says now and then. "Get on home now. Ain't anybody told you what time it is? What are you doing out this time of night, nigger?"

The sidewalks have been thick. The crowds now suddenly begin to disappear. Trucks and automobiles leave the Crossing square. One by one the nigger beer joints close. As an added precaution Mr. Stanley takes a turn up to Lavorn's Cafe and Tourist, but there the lights are already off, the doors already locked. Only a faint glow of light on the window shades upstairs gives any clue that the place is inhabited. The geese across the road in the blind nigger's auto junkyard set up a clutter. The patrol car turns around and heads back to the Crossing. "Cucumber's Automobile Graveyard," says the sign. "Used Parts."

Going over the tracks beside the dog food cannery, topping the railway embankment, the police see that the last car has left the parking area. Not a soul is on the streets. Thus the curfew is sealed.

"One minute to midnight," says Mr. Stanley, looking at his railroad watch and putting it back in his pocket. "Then it will be Sunday morning. Month's getting away. How about some coffee?"

As usual Mr. Stanley has it in mind to drive out to the truck stop on the Nashville highway. Velma, the night shift waitress, is the clos-

est thing to a girl friend Mr. Stanley's ever had. Midnight can't roll
around without Mr. Stanley having the itch to go see Velma even if
all he ever does is sit there and look at her like an old washer-
woman watching a pile of clothes. Velma puts sugar in his coffee
and does all the talking because she knows Mr. Stanley has saved four
cents of every nickel he's ever laid a hand to. He's got a farm
bought and paid for and Velma's getting up to where she must look
out for her old age. What a fine thing to have a nice farm, Velma
says. How she loves animals. What fun didn't she have at hog killing
time when she was a little girl back on the farm. Velma knows everything there is to know about a farm and what better manager can a
farm have than a thrifty woman not too proud to take hoe in hand
and chop weeds out of the cotton, nothing too fine but she's willing
to get out and dust cabbage when white butterflies appear? A
woman worth her salt can manage a fine flock of Rhode Island Red
hens and build a comfortable laying house. Hens will always lay better if they are made to feel comfortable, says Velma, if there's a
china nest egg in every nest and each good bird is dusted now and
then to remove her chicken mites. Who can make a good cow give
more milk than a good woman who becomes acquainted with cows
and calls them every one by name?

"They got machines nowadays for that," is the most Mr. Stanley
ever offers. But Velma knows that shy as Mr. Stanley is, even these
words are a compliment. Anything he says is meant well.

"How about some coffee?" says Mr. Stanley again.

"I tell you what," says Willie Joe. "Take me by Fort Hill and
leave me off and you go ahead out to the truck stop and have your
coffee."

"You mean now?" says Mr. Stanley. "You mean you have to go
see that nigger gal now when you just —"

"I just want to see my woman nigger a minute."

"Well, God damn," says Mr. Stanley Bumpas. "And then after that
you'll probably wanna go hop a couple of whores, I guess."

Mr. Stanley drives up to Fort Hill and turns into the alley behind
the undertaker's modern, ranch style house. Willie Joe gets out.
"Just come toot the horn for me after you've had your coffee," he
says.

Mr. Stanley nods, throws the Chevrolet in reverse and backs out so

[179]

fast he leaves a cloud of blue smoke standing in the alley, boiling in the last flash of the headlights, right where the car had been standing only an instant before. Mr. Stanley takes off down Fort Hill like a dive bomber. Willie Joe opens the gate in the neat white picket fence and walks through Emma's garden, past her blooming white roses, to the back door. He never knocks, but opens the door instead and walks right in the way any white man enters any nigger house, just the same as walking in a grocery store or a barn or anyplace else public.

The only difference is that Willie Joe comes in the back door, but then any man coming as regular as he does might cause talk if he used the front door. The back door connects Emma's flagstone patio with her den. The den is a big room paneled in cedar with a large framed picture of the white Lord Jesus hanging on the wall above a piano which she sometimes plays. In the picture Christ is in profile. The fireplace is flanked on either side with cages for Emma's lovebirds and her parakeets, the cages covered now with white cloths so the birds can sleep.

A small blue night lamp shines on top of the color television set in the corner opposite the white piano. Emma's white toy poodle, Ali Baba, lifts his head from his silk cushion on the sofa. Ali Baba's shrill bark scares Willie Joe. He is already nervous. He draws his pistol automatically. "Little son of a bitch," Willie Joe mutters. Ali Baba jumps off the sofa and prudently goes hiding under it. Willie Joe slips his .38 police special back in the holster and makes his way to the carpeted hall. The door to Emma's bedroom is closed. He tries the door and finds it locked. He slaps the panel several times with his open hand.

"Is it you?" says a voice inside.

"It's me," says Willie Joe. She unlocks the door.

"Come in, Sugarboy," says Emma. He walks into the bedroom and throws his hat on the little red velvet love seat. "Emma's been wondering when Sugarboy would come," she says. "Do you have to keep Emma guessing, Sugarboy? Emma grows to miss her swinging daddy, wondering when he's gonna come make it with her." She locks the door and turns around to him, smiling her superior smile. More and more she's got the upper hand now in a way she didn't have it once not so long ago. More and more she's having it her way, he thinks.

Willie Joe

Here she's even taken to picking a few dollars out of him now and then when it was just the other way in the beginning. She it was who used to give him money and what did she need any more money for anyway? Wasn't she rich, a nigger with all this, and him, a white man who owed on his house, owed on his car, owed on his furniture and appliances a dollar a week for this and a dollar a week for that until it looked like all a man ended up with in life were debts, and Willie Joe with his wife to think of and their two little girls? Not that he was a tightwad either, and not that Flonnie didn't waitress and dress the girls nice and do what she could with the debts, but neither was he somebody that squeezed a quarter hard and owned a farm and a used car lot like Mr. Stanley Bumpas. Money didn't mean so much to Willie Joe he had to worship it like it was God Almighty either, he thought. Still it was getting out of hand with this woman. Having sat him down on the velvet love seat, Emma has taken off her white silk shortie pajamas. She puts on silk stockings and a garter belt and touches behind her ears and dabs under her teats with perfume. She puts some very longhair music on her God-damn white Victrola, long as a casket, maybe a thousand dollars or more worth of hi-fi. Now she comes and sits on his lap. She curls her fingers in his hair just exactly like some whore in the Hollywood movies, movie magazines all over her bed and her white wastebasket full of beer cans. She's the only thing in the room black, only Emma and my damn shoes, he thinks. More and more, he thinks, she don't talk, she don't think, she don't act like a nigger at all but more like some sort of second wife that's got it in mind to run and control a man and pick a few dollars out of him now and then when he has other places he can put the money, four bill collectors for every buck he can hustle, yet here he sits, tame as a cat, and not a year ago it was Emma trying to break it off and not see him any more. Not a year ago he'd have walked through that door, he thinks, and slapped her around until she just about bounced off the walls and now, just in this little wink of time, she's got him trained another way entirely, like the God-damn lion, he thinks, that they pulled his teeth and jerked out his toenails and then by God laughed at him. Sucking me dry, he thinks, like a damned female spider working on a wrapped up bug.

"Bite me right there, Sugarboy," she whispers.

That's another habit she has, all the time biting a man different places and making him bite her, lately taking off his clothes like she's playing dolls with him. She has to have him take a shower and put on a white bathrobe before she wants to get down and really play house. Another time she draws a tub of hot water in that white bathtub and they have to play house in the tub. The tub will be so loaded with perfume that even Mr. Stanley comments on it, how sweet Willie Joe smells, by God. She's got fat gold guest towels big as a damned rug almost.

Her dark fingers unbutton his shirt. "Listen," he says. "By God."

"Something on Sugarboy's mind," she says. "Something bothering old Sugar. Just say it, baby."

"Just what the hell do you think you're trying to pull?"

"What?" She gets off his lap like a bee has stung her.

"I didn't stutter, by God," he says. "You wanna spill my guts, is that it?"

"Baby, I don't understand —"

He jumps up and grabs her. "Sugarboy, please!"

"Lawyers! Got to be like another big ass nigger I know and go whining to lawyers."

"Baby, you busting my arm. Sugarboy!"

He gives her arm an extra twist for good measure and shoves her backwards over the bed. She is up in an instant and already to the door, but too late. He is too fast for her. He catches her hair, coarse as old wool. He jerks her backwards. "Lawyers," he says. "Been getting fancy and seeing lawyers?"

"Sugarboy, let me explain to you. Darling, please let me explain?" She is down now, hugging his knees, wiping her face on him. Next thing, he thinks, she's done tore my britches. "Listen, let . . . let me tell you, hon."

"You nigger," he says.

"Don't call me that, please!"

"You black stack of —"

"Please! Listen a minute."

"I'm listening, by God. You think they wouldn't come warn a white man? You think a nigger can spill a white man's guts in this town and him not be warned? I seen some fools, but you take the God-damn prize. I oughtta blow your God-damned brains out!"

He snatches out the pistol. "How would it be if I blew that black nut off from between your God-damn shoulders? How would it be?"

"You wouldn't," she says.

"I wouldn't?" He reaches down with his left hand and slaps her.

She stands up, wiping her eyes. "You wouldn't. You might beat up a woman, that's your style all right — women and children, that's your big, swinging style. I don't feature you for a triggerman though. You aren't framed up for it. I see you for a lightweight. Beat up on a woman, that's your style. I knew that the first time, the first whiff of your hair tonic. Sure, the big man, the law."

"Try me," he says.

"I thought you wanted to talk about lawyers. You want to shoot me? All right." She turns around. "My back's turned, big man. Go ahead! Shoot!"

"Aw hell," Willie Joe says.

She turns back around. He puts up the gun. She goes in the bathroom to rinse her face. She comes out and primps her hair back into shape. She wears it sort of casual. He gives her that much, she sure as hell knows how to fix herself up.

"If you had it this good, would you want to give it all up?" she says.

"I thought you said before —"

"But nevermind that, just answer me. Say if you had it made like I do? Okay, so I'm making it with you and old Lord Byron Lovernuts wants his freedom. Worried out of his mind. Says take the house, take your car — but, Sugarboy, it also takes money. Do you have the money, Sugarboy? Do I have the money?"

"Oman Hedgepath says if you don't back out —"

"Listen, honey. Let me ask you. Who does have the money?"

"L. B.'s got it. Did I ever say that black bastard didn't have it? But what you ain't taking into account is I'm on the police force. I'm married. I need this job. Listen, you know I like this job? And you're gonna spill my guts? Either you back out or L. B. backs out or they spill my guts. So where does that leave me?"

"That's right, Sugarboy," Emma says. "I can see you don't need it to be explained no further than you already have it."

"Okay then, call Sears Buntin and tell him you've changed your mind."

[183]

"Sugarboy, big man, don't you know Emma better than that by now?"

She sits on the bed and opens a movie magazine.

"You won't call him," he said. "I can shoot your black brains out, but you won't even lift up the telephone."

"Honey, if you want this case stopped, maybe you better talk to L. B. Maybe L. B. might listen to reason if you talked to him right straight."

"So it's put off on me," Willie Joe said. "It's no way out, by God. It's no God-damn way in the world out of it and that's just how it's all planned, ain't it?" He sat down. He was tired, like an old man, and only thirty-five years old and he was tired as if he'd been all day in the fields plowing. "God damn it, what if he won't listen to reason?"

"I know, Sugarboy. I been thinking the same thing myself. I been think what if L. B. won't listen to reason. Something's going to have to give somewhere. I thought the same thing myself."

"But why'd you have to do it? When you said, you said! Said it once you said it a thousand times, laying right there in that bed. What did you care if he divorced you, you said."

"Just say I changed my mind. Just say I like things just like they are, Sugarboy. Women have the privilege to change their minds, don't they? You feeling sick? Want some milk of magnesia? Maybe an aspirin?"

"Shut up," he said. "God damn you to hell!"

"Come here and lie down a minute, Sugarboy. Your mind's all worried."

"Caught," he said. "Caught, by God." He was sweating. He felt like a large dry cockroach was trying to walk down his throat.

"Did I hear Mr. Stanley toot the horn?" Emma said. She got up and turned down the volume on the hi-fi. "Didn't he toot for you?"

9

Lord Byron Jones

Benny and the other man, Mosby, were helping him. They helped the undertaker outside the cafe, and put him in the car between them. Benny drove. The undertaker told them: "I have nothing — no reason to go home, you understand?"

"Don't worry about it," said the fat man, Mosby.

"What's the time?" said the undertaker.

"It's pretty late. Everything's shut up," Benny said. "You fell asleep. Mosby gonna bodyguard you. Don't you worry, hear?"

"I'm not worried," he said. The car turned up Fort Hill past the lighted porch of the funeral home, past the illuminated clock above the porch. He couldn't see the hands on the blue face and realized his glasses were gone. Too late, he found them in the breast pocket of his suit. He put them on his nose, but by then they had passed the funeral home. By then Benny had turned down the side street in front of the undertaker's house.

"Pull it on in the carport," L. B. Jones said, "beside Emma's car."

Benny obeyed. When he touched the brake he hit it too hard. The car lurched, and Benny fell against the horn. "Power brake messed me up," Benny apologized. He cut the ignition.

They got out. The undertaker walked on ahead without assistance now, going around the house to enter the back door. The front door was never used except when Emma had company. She never had company any more. They were all three in the house before the undertaker saw the white man.

"Hold it right there!" The cop, Willie Joe Worth, stood in a defensive crouch, his pistol drawn.

"It's only me," said the undertaker. "Jones."

"You and who else?"

"Just friends. They work for me. You know Benny."

"Well, you better watch, by God, the way you walk in a house without knocking," the policeman said. "I don't like nobody sneaking up on me."

"We didn't see no police patrol car. We didn't know you was here, sir," Benny said.

Willie Joe Worth put the pistol back in its holster and snapped the holder strap around it. "You're up mighty late."

"The dead don't keep regular hours though. Neither can we," said the undertaker.

"I heard a horn toot. Is Bumpas out there?"

"We didn't see nobody when we come in," Benny said.

The policeman went past them to the window, looking out on the patio and into Emma's garden and the alley beyond. Everything was dark out where he was looking, everything black as though the other side of the glass had been painted with stove paint, as though whatever was beyond the glass might be solid, like a seam of coal. The glass reflected the room, the little lamp on the television set, the figures of the three black men standing behind the white policeman. "Thought I heard a horn," Willie Worth said.

Nobody volunteered to tell him Benny had hit the horn accidentally. The white cop turned back to face them, rubbing his hand over his abdomen and heisting his trousers. His hand went straying between the crotch of his trousers and his pistol belt. He was saying: "Some people you can't reason with, no, by God, they ain't got no reason power in them, no common sense. You couldn't beat sense into some people. They build their own trap and walk into it. You boys get on with it now, hear me? I got something private between me and Jones."

"Yes sir, just a minute then," the undertaker said. He turned to Benny, speaking quietly: "Take Mosby to my room and let him turn in. Show him the bed next to mine. Leave by the front door."

"Yes, sir. All right, sir," Benny said. He motioned to Mosby. Benny and the fat man went into the hallway. Mosby seemed to fill the doorframe. He passed through it like a bear entering a cave, big and shuffling.

"You want to talk to me?" the undertaker said. The white man seemed wrought up and preoccupied. The undertaker had guessed what it was. "You wanted to see me?"

"I tried to reason with your God-damn wife. I like to be reasonable. No telling how many God-damn favors I done for people. Me, Willie Joe Worth! A favor here and a favor there, see what I mean? What do I expect to get in return? All right, a fellow's either a Christian or he ain't? Am I right? Okay! I wanna live and let live, see what I mean? So a fellow says to me, well God damn, Willie Joe, and I say to him, all right, let's talk about it. Now ain't that fair?"

The undertaker nodded. He took a cigarette from the gold case in his breast pocket. The rum had left his mouth dry. He tasted bile. His senses were slowly coming clear again. He lit the cigarette. "Go on," he said. "I'm listening."

"I don't like nobody pushing me into no corner. I'm this way, that as long as nobody don't push me, then I'm friends with everybody, black or white. Ask anybody. They'll tell you. You think a man's color makes any difference to me? I played with niggers when I was a kid, growed up with 'em out in the country. Sure, I got nigger friends, just like you got white friends. But listen, I don't like to get pushed into no corner and you take lawyers, now they don't care. It's just a day's work with them, but I got the job of enforcing the law around here and it's different with me. Let a few of the right people get the wrong idea about me and I'm out of a God-damned job, see what I'm telling you?"

"I think I do, Mr. Worth."

"So I wouldn't want to see nobody walk into something blind and get hisself hurt, if you know what I mean. I don't care who he is, by God, I think he deserves a little warning. I never thought it was no bad idea to give a man a second chance if he done something and never down thought it out just what he was doing or how it might go against the other fellow and hurt him, see? Why hurt him? Why cost him his respectability? Jones, why would I want to hurt you, or turn it around, why would you want to do something to hurt me? You got anything against me? Any complaint you want to make? Because if you do, by God, then you can take it up with the Chief of

Police. It don't have to go no further than that. In fact, by God, we could phone the Chief right now and get him up out of bed if you've got some complaint you want to make against me. I like anybody to come straight out and say what's on his mind, I don't care who he is. You got a complaint?"

"It might not be quite as simple as that," the undertaker replied.

"Not when you go dragging a bunch of God-damn lawyers into it, no, it ain't. That's what always messes a man up, taking everything to lawyers. For instance, take if a colored man's wife was to fool around on him a little and he got tired of it, take if the other white man was reasonable, why wouldn't he agree to leave her alone if he was straight out asked to do it in a nice way? Then it wouldn't be no call for the colored man to come out and divorce his wife, would it? What does a colored man need with a divorce anyway? Did you ever stop and think about that? So if a colored man was to tell his lawyer he had done changed his mind and didn't want no divorce, why everybody could rest easy and forget about it. Couldn't they?"

"Could they?" said the undertaker. Car lights appeared in the alley above Emma's rose garden. The horn sounded.

The policeman looked around nervously, staring intently at the glass again. He turned back to face the undertaker. "If I get word by noon Monday that will be soon enough. If Mr. Hedgepath notifies me by then, it'll be all right. If he just phones me or sends me word by noon that it's been called off — I don't mean postponed. Called off. I wouldn't want there to be no misunderstanding on it. Hear me?"

"Yes, Mr. Worth." The horn sounded three times, impatient now.

"If a man didn't get no word by noon then he'd know the other fellow meant to go on through with it, and wasn't going to listen to reason."

"I understand, Mr. Worth."

With a curt nod the white man turned and went through the door, seemingly swallowed by the outside night. The car lights moved out of the alley. The undertaker was alone. For a moment he watched the slender silhouette of himself in the glass, the barely perceptible movement of the cigarette smoke.

He went to his bedroom (past Emma's doorway with the usual slit of light showing at the bottom, the reminder that Emma was there, but no longer his). Beyond the windows of his pitch dark room, moonlight was deflected on the white roof of the carport, the light diffused by clouds, and the glow so faint, and uncertain, as to suggest fog.

The patrol car passed in the street below like a deep sea fish, at a snail's pace, deep down the hill, the tail lights like dull, drowned, incurious eyes. On the other bed Mosby wheezed in his sleep, his breath coming steady, like the pulse of a factory, like the other night sounds the undertaker had lived with — throb of the cotton gins, crash of the canning factory, murmurous whirr of the icing machines in strawberry season.

He had lain with Emma, sometimes half awake beside her in that other room, drifting with her, night after night, in what seemed to be an endless dream of life, possessed of and possessing the only woman he loved. The work sounds from below the hill beside the tracks had been lulling and murmurous. They had been pattern, rhythm, fabric and definition of his contentment. Just as he imagined the sea must have a meaning for lovers who dream beside it in each other's arms, just so those factory sounds below had been like memories of the womb's cradle, the bone bed, the live dish of the mother sea that rocked mankind and taught man love before he knew the word that tolled him into life.

Now he never lay down that he did not lie down into sorrow. It was like stretching out prone in the midst of a field of grass, closed in on all sides, from every direction but from above. Gazing in that direction towards the blind, the dead, the cold infinity of unbeautiful, eternal sky, he knew he would not be the last man to envy the dead, nor the last to inhale with his next breath the misting fear of death, thinking: It is nothing to fear because it is nothing. Because neither thought nor word can know or say what it is. Beyond says it best.

His mother had said: "Teach yourself not to want anything." When she had gotten quite old she had said: "I have taught myself not to want anything. I don't let myself want things. The more you can do without, the less you can want, the better."

After he had put off his glasses, undressed, and lain down he got up again. He took two sleeping pills from the envelope the doctor had given him. He swallowed both capsules in the wash of his own spit and lay down again to wait for the tincture of faint, poisoned dizziness; to wait, and hope that when the chemical invitation came he could accept it; he, who had been wise in all things but one and thus lay down a cuckold, shared a roof in common with an adulteress, and allowed a murderer to sleep beside him.

FIVE

1

Oman Hedgepath

Black or white what does it matter except that the God I always saw as a child had a thick brown beard and leaves around his middle, and he was strong and white, like a German.

I turned into the driveway and parked behind the house under the carport and went in across the back porch and through the kitchen. I got a new fifth of Irish whiskey from the pantry and sat down and unrolled the evening paper. Irish whiskey tastes like Tennessee moonshine because it's all made the same, in a pot still. The taste of the two whiskies is both hot and soft and raw, all at the same time, always a shock, it was like pleasant indecision, the kind that can happen only when two or three things converge to make you happy all at once. I was happy.

I began to feel better and I read the newspaper. A nigger integration leader defined non-violence: "If the white man shoots at the Negro," quoth he, "the Negro will shoot back," putting it on the basis that the straightest shooter will win, in which case the nigger's lost before he begins. The white man's gun always has been truest.

Except for the embarrassments at first Manassas (when both sides fought and ran) it was cold turkey. One white man in six marched to war. The South was intent on protecting a two-billion-dollar investment in slaves. The Yankees were drafted and driven to it, but still they went walking into death (call it gallantry on both sides), white Anglo-Saxons shooting it out, one in three going down at Cemetery Ridge; pinning names and addresses on their backs before walking into the cannons at Cold Harbor. By Appomattox nearly a million lay fallen. The words for that war are all noble words.

Sitting at the kitchen table I declaimed it aloud:

"It was not on the battlefields of Austerlitz or Waterloo where Napoleon won, and was conquered, nor at Gettysburg where the greatest struggle of modern warfare was witnessed . . ." I was fourteen when I memorized it. It's the kind of stuff Southern gentlemen are raised up to believe. I entered my first high school declamation contest and declaimed that the greatest battles are fought within the human heart, that the greatest of all battle standards conflict had on it: *I conquer myself.* I believed it — back then.

The whiskey was just taking hold when I heard the screen door slam on the back porch. In Henry walked like a damned old black ghost. He stood there, buttoning his white shirt.

"You all right?" he says. "You call me?"

"I was only practicing my speech," I says. I gave him the first line and watched Austerlitz and Waterloo and the rest slide over him, as beyond the reach of his mind as anything imaginable. It was almost the same as quoting the Lord's Prayer to a dog. "How do you like that?"

"Hit sound all right to me," he says. "But you sho' got to watch Mr. Sears Buntin when he git down on his knees."

"I might get down on *my* knees, though," I says. "Have you considered that?"

"You will. Dat's what I'm talkin' about you *will* ef you don't cork up dat bottle. Next you gonner be playing the pianer and trying to sing or running up the long distance bill. Next you gonner be on the phone ef you ain't keerful. Ain't you sleepy?"

"Go to bed," I told him.

"Old mens don't need much rest, but young mens in they prime, like you, needs his rest."

"I'll get it," I says. "The biggest night of all is on the way. The long night. The final, non-violent integration."

"You know I ain't going nowhere," he says. "Is that what's got you? You think I'm gonner go to Washington, Oman?"

"Mr. Hedgepath, please."

"Well, sometime I fergit. You was Oman first."

"Not since I turned twelve years old," I says. "How does it feel to be an old nigger and have wool growing on your head instead of hair?"

He considered it a minute. "Well," he says. "Hit about the same I guess as another white man if he had hair on his head instead of wool." He passed his hand over his head. "Nap," he says. "Same as a sheared sheep, but you sho' don't have to comb it. What make you ask me that? You think I'm going on that march, don't you?"

"Sure, you want to see the women. That's why you bastards go to church. Always looking to trade and swap women. Just one word, that's all you have in your head — cabbage."

That got him. "Shame!" he yelled, laughing. "Shame!"

"Hell yes, let a carload of niggers break down on the road. Two minutes later you got another carload stopped in behind them helping them. You said so yourself — just to see the other nigger's women, that's why you stop. Anything to get more."

"I would like to see that march," he says. "They gonner fry fish too, ain't they?"

I picked up the newspaper and pretended to read it. "There will be free fish and barbecue and the Black Midnight Choir from the Washington African Baptist Church will sing 'Do, Lawd.' "

"Listen at that!" he says.

"Artemis D. Gangbang, excuse me, the Reverend Doctor Artemis D. Gangbang, pastor of the African Baptist Church, will hold hands with the President and the Attorney General and pray for watermelon, gin, and integration."

"Do it say that?"

"Right here," I says. "Read it for yourself."

"You know I can't read. Do it say that?"

"Sho' do," I says. "Artemis D. Gangbang, president of sixty-nine different nigger organizations and choirs and street minstrel shows. Sure, he's the head knocker nigger. The President of the United States is gonner shake hands with him."

"Now I know that ain't right."

"Why," I says.

"The President. He ain't gonner shake hands with no nigger. You got to be kidding now. Ain't you?"

He was right. I was kidding myself. "Sit down," I says.

"Sah?"

"Pull up a chair and sit down."

"You want me to, Mr. Oman?"

"I told you to."

"Well, sah. All right."

He sat down at the table. "Now tell me, what do you hear from your head?" I says.

"Sah?"

"Just tell me what your head's saying."

"Well, sah. Hit ain't saying nothing much. Naw, sah. Sometimes I wants to sing hymns."

"Well, sing one," I says. "Sing 'Do, Lawd.' "

"Mr. Oman . . ."

"God damn it, sing 'Do, Lawd!' "

So he sang it. Henry sang in his cracked, quavering old voice, thumping his right hand self-consciously on the table, not looking at me but over my shoulder. I got up and got a glass out of the pantry and poured him a shot of whiskey. He didn't look at it but went on singing "Do, Lawd" like perhaps singing it would give him courage. He looked low on courage. That bony old black hand kept coming down on the table. He was trying to grin and sing at the same time, his rotten, broken, old man's teeth showing now and then, and him still looking past me, beyond me, even after he had sung the last verse and chorus. At the end he let it die like the groan of a bagpipe, ". . . do remember me, 'way, beyo-ond, de blue!"

"Have a drink," I says.

"Well, sah."

"Go on. Have a drink."

He held it in his mouth a long time as though to remember it well. Then finally he swallowed it. He let that short little nigger sigh they all make when you give them a drink. He bowed, nodded somehow, and touched his forehead as though to pull the forelock that wasn't there, giving the old sign of thanks so instinctive that it's automatic, like the hound turning a circle before he lies down. I poured him another one. "Now old nigger," I says, "in a minute I want you to dance for me."

"Yessah, yes, sah."

"Because every last one of you black somebitches *can* dance, can't you?"

"Yes, sah. That's right. You right about that, Mr. Oman."

"Dancing and singing, that's all you're good for."

"Yessah, you right there, Mr. Oman."

"Because the nigger don't have the brains the white man's got."

"That's right. You sho' right there, Mr. Oman. You right every time. Yes, sah!"

"He's just a strong back."

"That's all he is, Mr. Oman!"

When you've made a man say his mother's a slut and his sisters are all whores and gotten it from him he doesn't know who his father is, then you can still make the old bastard dance; that is, if he can still walk you can make him. After three shots or so you can make him get up and jig and waltz like a chimpanzee.

My grandfather was more original. I never saw it but they say he used to get drunk. They tell it on him that my grandfather used to get drunk and take an ax out and make one climb a tree and say he was a coon and make another one chop the tree down, the wonder of it being that my grandfather never killed a single one that way, but then they were all drinking. And maybe that's why nobody ever got killed.

2

The Funeral

Steve and Nella were in time to sign the register and speak a word of condolence to the grocer's widow and look on the face of the dead man before the funeral was to be preached. The widow took them to the head of the casket herself.

"His face was tore up beyond the sight of recognition. You'll have to say they done a good job, won't you?"

Nella said yes. Steve Mundine nodded. The corpse looked like a department store dummy wearing glasses.

As though she had guessed what must be on his mind, Steve heard the widow saying, "Without his glasses he didn't look natural. Not like himself. That's his old pair, the others was tore up by whoever it was killed him. This way anybody would recognize him to remember him. Looks just like him, don't it?"

"Yes," Steve said. Nella nodded this time. They neither of them had ever seen the grocer alive, but Oman had phoned that morning before they left for church to tell them to be sure to attend the funeral.

"He sure thought the world of Oman Hedgepath," the widow said. It was a sort of accusation, Steve thought, but after two years in Somerton he was accustomed to it. It was these people's way to compare him thus, indirectly, to his uncle, thus to let him know that his own, and Nella's own, generation would never, in these people's opinion, live up to Oman Hedgepath. Neither for goodness nor strength nor steadfastness nor friendship nor sure knowledge of the law.

Oman appeared now as if by magic, shaking hands constantly as he made his way through the crowd, his face stern, even cold, his expression in keeping with his bearing and dignity and the solemn occasion of death and ceremony. First, on reaching the casket, Oman took the widow's hand, though she didn't offer it but held back, plainly unaccustomed to being touched. Yet she seemed pleased, even so, even perhaps triumphant. "He's with God," Oman said again, quite loud enough for everyone in sight to hear him say it. The widow only nodded, and then, almost convulsively, her pale forehead touched the sleeve of Oman's coat. He gave her his handkerchief, and led her then out into the little folding-chairs chapel, and seated her in the front row with her kinspeople. Then he returned and sat in the back row with Steve and Nella. The hymn was called and Oman sang "Nearer, My God, to Thee" in that same firm voice, almost leading the others. The reedy, transistorized tones of the electric organ poured out a flood of music. The sounds were flaccid as the warm flowery wind from the inevitable, throbbing, impotent window air-conditioners. The chapel was hot. Steve began to sweat.

Nella removed her gloves. She accepted a cardboard Sunday school fan from the fat funeral director. Steve felt the gentle wind from Nella's fan. On the heels of the hymn the preacher, wearing glasses almost identical to those Steve had just seen on the corpse, called for prayer. He expressed the steady conviction, over and patiently over again, that the grocer was, indeed, with God. The preacher called down blessings on the heads of the congregation here present. In the name of Christ Jesus, he sounded the *Amen,* and began, without pausing, to make what he could out of the life and meager existence of a man who had apparently never done anything, within the memory of anyone present, but mind a niggertown grocery store.

Mind that store he had, honestly, courageously, constantly, faithfully and fruitfully until, by the inexplicable Grace of that Power which knoweth all things before they happen, the grocer had met his reward for all those years of steadfastness. A man had walked into his store and robbed him and beaten him to death, this good grocer, who had loved the Lord all his days.

Was not man then tempted in this hour to question God, and ask why the good must suffer? Yet was not this very hour one in which to reaffirm faith in God? For God knew, didn't He, what more terrible fates and heartaches this man had been spared? Might not this death have been merciful after all? Might not Mr. Bivens have lain abed eaten up with cancer? Was he not, indeed, better off to be at peace in Glory? Taken, yes, taken he had been from the midst of a busy life. Missed, yes, missed he would be, but only have faith, the preacher went on, reprimanding and reminding his listeners by turns, only have faith, he said, "And all shall meet again on the Other Side."

Another hymn, another prayer, and, mercifully, the service was over.

"Are you all going to the graveside?" Oman whispered.

"Should we?" Steve asked, as they stood up.

"Isn't really necessary," Oman said. "By the way, I talked to Willie Worth last night."

"You *told* him?"

"Had a little man-to-man talk with him and set him wise," Oman said in a swift monotone. "It was the only right thing to do. Not for his sake of course, but for my client's. Better slip out now if you aren't going to the graveside."

"Drop by to see us later, if you can," Steve said.

"I will," Oman replied, standing back for the casket to roll past. "Excuse me," he said then and stepped past Nella into the casket's wake. Oman was a pallbearer as usual. Steve stood with Nella and watched Oman help take the casket from the cart and down the front steps of the funeral home. Oman helped place it in the waiting hearse.

Oman paused then, respectfully again, as the rear door of the hearse was closed for the beginning of that final, wending journey. Everyone seemed to be watching Oman, and Oman alone, as though what happened next somehow depended on him, as though, no matter what, they knew Oman Hedgepath would always be there when needed. The prototype of the Southern man who will stand hitched, Steve Mundine thought. He made a mental note to pass the remark on to Nella at the first opportunity.

On the way to the car, crossing the hot side street, so hot that the asphalt gave a little under his shoes, Steve said it.

Nella smiled. "Yes," she said. And after a pause: "I find it frightening."

"He isn't acting. He's real, he means it," Steve said, helping her into the car. Little beads of perspiration stood on her upper lip.

"I know," Nella said. "It doesn't get any better, does it?"

Steve went around to the driver's side. He started the car and drove slowly down the hot street. People crossing from the funeral home stood aside for the car to pass.

"He told the policeman," Steve said. "Last night."

"He what?" She touched her mouth. "But Steve, you talked him out of it! Told him! Steve, why?"

He wondered if he should have mentioned it to her, after telling her only last night that it was all settled. He had believed Oman wouldn't do it, yet he had felt an uneasiness about it. He had told Nella that Oman wouldn't go to the policeman in order to get her mind off her homesickness, to make Nella look in some direction other than in the direction of her shock and her despair, to show her, if possible, the direction of progress and hope. He had wanted to make Nella see, and had wanted, perhaps, to convince himself, that Oman would protect his Negro client.

Suddenly the whole thing was fallen a-shambles, beginning with Oman's phone call, before church, insisting that they attend the funeral of a perfect stranger. "It would look well," Oman had said. "No need to let on you and Nella didn't know him."

"Oman won't be changed. You'll never change him, Steve," Nella was saying. "What will this cop do?"

"Obviously Oman believes Willie Joe Worth will hush the scandal somehow to save his job. Put pressure on the Negro's wife, perhaps. Or intimidate the Negro himself."

"Whatever it takes."

"Whatever it takes," Steve said. "That's it, I'm afraid."

"And yet he breathes the same air we do, lives in the same world — Oman can actually stand up and complain with a straight face about monsters who believe the end justifies the means! He can . . . he can . . ."

"We pushed him into taking the case," Steve reminded her. "I'm wondering if Oman wants to show us how wrong we are. I am wondering if secretly, deep down, Oman wouldn't be pleased, cost what it might, if this whole thing blew up in our faces. What wouldn't he give to be able to say, 'I tried to tell you. I told you so. You wouldn't listen.' I can hear him."

"Keep driving," Nella said. "If we go home now, I'll cry like a helpless little bitch. He's trying to castrate you. He's so castrated himself he wants that feeling for everybody. Then *you* can sit by the way *he* can and no sort of atrocity will make any difference, no sort of injustice will move you! Steve, I'm sorry. *I hate the South!*"

Steve drove on past the deep lawn. The columns of Glenraven shone like alabaster, green shutters sturdy and serene beside every window, everything open and gracious, as though somehow purified by Saturday's rain.

Nella had run through the tall empty rooms ignoring the litter about her feet and admiring the grace of the high ceilings. Saying our house, because there would be no little stuffy apartments, none of the shuffling and moving around she had known as a Navy wife; our house, and he had thought at the time that Scarlett O'Hara couldn't have been more proud of Tara than was Nella Mundine of Glenraven.

As a sentimental gesture that year, on their third anniversary, Steve had given her a copy of *Gone with the Wind*. They had sat up some late evenings reading it to each other.

In terms of hard cash it had taken fifteen thousand dollars to buy the place and forty thousand more to restore it. The place had been more than anything else a sort of ghost, a shell of the old, bygone, planter class elegance. Our house, its imported marble fireplaces and mantelpieces long since stolen, rain beating through broken windows, balustrades ripped away for kindling by tramps building fires for a night's warmth by one of its broken hearths.

For a while the restoration beguiled her. Oman seemed always in the midst of it, buying back what remained of the original furniture, bringing pieces from the old family place, hiring masons and house painters and going up on the roof himself to lend, with the magic of his presence, new spirit to the work. Oman knew how to spend money. Steve gave him that much. Oman could be unselfish and charming. Oman had been so proud to have his nephew, his heir, not merely move to Somerton, but settle there. Now suddenly it began to unravel. It was coming all undone.

"Oman means well," Steve heard himself saying, "I asked him to drop by this afternoon."

"Did he *tell* the Negro? Did he do him the courtesy to tell him he thought more of protecting a philandering white cop than he did protecting his own client? Didn't you just say yourself, only last night, that telling that cop might be the same thing as signing the Negro's death warrant?"

"Maybe I was exaggerating. Nella, I asked Oman to drop by. I can talk to him. What else can I do? It isn't even my case. We can both talk to him."

"I've got to get out of Somerton," Nella said. "Steve, I don't want to see him — ever; you've got to listen to me, Steve!"

"I'm listening," he said. "I'll see him about it. It could be that Oman's right. It's his town. He got the boy his job."

"Who?"

"The policeman. Oman doesn't want to see the man lose his job. He wants to do the right thing, Nella."

She was shaking her head. "I'll phone Mother. I'm going to San Francisco, Steve."

"Nella —"

"*Will* you drive me to Memphis?"

"Yes," he said, struggling to shake off an inner desolation. "Of course."

"If I can just get away from this swamp, this miserable . . ." She was crying. "If I could only do something, Steve, if I could only put one of those signs around my own neck and stand out there with them and say, *This is wrong!* If I could only have an opinion of my own. Steve. Steve."

"I know," he said. "I feel the same way. What can I do, though?"

"Steve, life is too short." She tried to get ahold of herself. "It . . . it's too short to be lived where an entire society is setting out deliberately to castrate the man you love. Fear, Steve, they make nets of it and once you begin to be entangled then it's too late to struggle."

"I could warn the Negro," he said. "It would be meddling. Oman would take it as meddling. I could warn him anyway. Not that I'm in any way involved. Not that I'm responsible."

"You wouldn't have said that two years ago, Steve. You'd have said we're all involved, all responsible."

"Would I? I suppose perhaps I would," he admitted. If he warned the Negro perhaps Nella would stay, if Nella herself became involved. But if she did involve herself, then what? Either way, whether Nella remained or went home to San Francisco, either way she was committed. If she remained in Somerton, Nella *would* speak up now. He thought: *She has run away from her last argument. From here on out Nella will speak her mind, and to hell with Oman, to hell with the law partnership.*

"If we stood and fought, if we stayed and decided to see it through," he said, then, thinking aloud.

"I could stand it better than this," she said. "I can't stand this. Steve, *this is wrong.* If we believe it's wrong and we don't say so, if we remain silent, then *we* become a party to this injustice. If we sit on our hands, *then we're guilty by default.* Who isn't against this thing is for it. Am I thinking, Steve, or is it just emotional?"

"You're thinking," he said.

"Then they're wrong, they're insane."

"They'll never admit it, though," he said.

"Then we'll cram it down their God-damned throats," she said. "We'll rub their pious Bible Belt noses in it. We'll wear signs, if that's what it takes. Carry placards and get thrown in jail with the others. We'll beat the bigoted, self-righteous bastards because they're wrong and they *know* they're wrong. Find the Negro and warn him, Steve!"

"Now?" he said. "Just like that?"

"Isn't it now or never?"

Steve turned the car west and drove to Fort Hill, up the broad street beside the Negro funeral home, past the crest of the hill and back to the right. He parked in front of the undertaker's modern ranch style home.

"Want to wait in the car?"

"No," she said. "I'll come with you. I'm involved too, remember?"

He helped her out of the car. The heat held a heavy scent of roses. He felt the sun on his left cheek like a warm hand. The young maple trees on the undertaker's lawn seemed still as bronze. Steve Mundine hadn't imagined, before now, that it required courage to tell another man his life was in danger. Merely lifting the brass door-knocker and letting it fall was like a formal farewell, such, he thought, as a snake might bid to its shed skin. He raised the knocker and let it fall again.

3

Lord Byron Jones

He was marveling inwardly. He had never met or imagined anyone like Mosby, sitting opposite him at the round breakfast table.

The fat man ate with a dreaming sort of preoccupation, intent on his food, but relaxed. He took everything from the container straight off to his mouth without bothering about a plate or glasses, or utensils. Milk out of the carton, crackers and bread from the box, canned goods from the can. All he used was a pocket knife and his fingers.

The undertaker rarely ate anything more than a little lean meat, or a dry piece of toast, and black coffee. He rarely wanted food. Apparently Mosby wanted nothing else.

Mosby seemed now to be almost finished. Using the pocket knife he was buttering whole slices of light bread and putting them in his mouth and washing this down with a swig or two of milk. The chair creaked under him.

Mosby didn't seem to see the undertaker as long as his jaws continued to move. Mosby stopped eating, pushed back from the table, and got the last bent cigarette from the package beside the cigar box. He lit the cigarette and sat smoking quietly. The white smoke curled about his thick, fat fingers.

Emma came from the den with her coffee cup and put it in the sink, on the other side of the room divider. She ran water in the cup and got a bottle of red mouthwash from the shelf above the sink and began rinsing her mouth, spitting in the sink. From where he sat the undertaker could see her naked buttocks when she leaned forward.

Her shorty coat rode upward. She didn't have any shame about her, no more than a cow or a field slut, he thought. She said something.

"What?" he answered.

"White people to see you," she said.

"Where?"

"Setting in the front room."

"You answered the front door like that?" He stood up.

"If I wanna go like this in my own house do you know of a reason why I can't?" She turned around. "Do I have to walk around ashamed all the damn time to make you happy? Say, Old Lovernuts?"

Mosby stumped his cigarette out in an empty tuna fish can. He closed the blade of the pocket knife. "Want me to come with you?" he said.

"Just stay here," the undertaker said.

"Yeah, Fat Ass. Eat another loaf of sandwich bread," Emma said.

"I might have to knock and slap some of that shit out of her if she was mine," Mosby said.

"Shut up, Fat Ass," Emma said. "Quit letting flies out of your mouth. White people waiting on you, Mr. Nuts."

"She wants you to slap her, don't she?" Mosby said. "She begging for it."

"Maybe that's why Mr. Nuts has to bring a lardy old bum home with him. Mr. Nuts can't do his own fighting himself. Mr. Nuts has to have help. He says, 'Somebody help me, 'cause I can't help myself.'" Emma laughed.

"Please lower your voice, at least," said the undertaker.

"You telling me to shut up?" she asked.

"Just please lower your voice."

"Because if you tell me to shut up I'll slap you back into last Thursday. I'll lay a plank upside your head. Your days are numbered anyhow." She turned back to the sink. "Your days are numbered, Mr. Nuts."

The undertaker sighed and went through the pantry. He pushed open the door to the white dining room where the walls, the draperies and the furniture were white, and the carpet underfoot was mauve brown. Fear stopped him a moment. He had never known anything like it before. For the first time in his life, instead of waking from a nightmare, he woke to one.

He wiped his sweating hands on his coat lapels and opened the door to the living room. The white man stood. The undertaker recognized Steve Mundine. "You wanted to see me?" he said. Then he saw the girl.

"My wife, Mrs. Mundine. Mr. Jones," said the young man.

"How do you do," said the undertaker. "My wife didn't tell me right away. I'm sorry if you've been waiting —"

"Don't apologize," she said. "We understand. We want to help."

Steve Mundine drew a deep breath. "I know that my uncle, Oman Hedgepath — your lawyer — saw Willie Joe Worth last night. He explained to Willie Joe what would happen in divorce court Tuesday unless either you or your wife decide to drop the case. Quite frankly, I think you're in danger. My wife and I decided that you had better be warned."

"Mr. Worth spoke to me last night," said the undertaker.

"Then you know already," Steve Mundine said.

"I had figured as much, yes."

"Will your wife withdraw her cross-bill?"

"I don't think there's a chance of it, Mr. Mundine."

"Couldn't you talk to her?"

"I couldn't, no."

"Then perhaps I could persuade her."

"No, you couldn't help." The undertaker paused a moment. "You don't understand. She is not a woman to be persuaded of anything."

"Then what about you — are you going through with it?" the young man asked.

"I don't know." The undertaker looked from one of them to the other. Their faces were tense. The young woman made as though to speak and then stopped herself. Obviously she was having difficulty controlling her own feelings. She looked at her husband. The undertaker smiled. His face felt stiff. "You see," he went on slowly, "Mr. Worth delivered me an ultimatum. He gave me until noon tomorrow to withdraw the suit."

"Then he threatened you? Did he?" the young lawyer asked.

The undertaker nodded. "I believe it would be fair to say he threatened me — yes."

"Have you told the police?"

The undertaker smiled again. "The police, Mr. Mundine?"

"My God — you can't call them, because . . . because . . ."

"You can't help me, Mr. Mundine," said the undertaker.

"I can go to the District Attorney," Steve Mundine said. "The law isn't powerless. Yet all we have is Willie Joe Worth's word against your own."

"And what would happen when the District Attorney called the police?" said the undertaker, observing the young man closely, seeing how for the first time Oman Hedgepath's nephew had come to grips with the true intricacy of a thing which he had, until now, believed to be preposterously simple. "Because as you can see," the undertaker went on, "there is really no way out. I'm hemmed in by a perfect circle."

"The Grand Jury," Steve Mundine said, groping.

"Controlled by white men, honest, well-meaning white men, but men dedicated all the same to a structure which, in some situations, calls for silence. I've thought through all the angles, Mr. Mundine. I've had time to think them through — months."

"The months my uncle put you off," Steve Mundine said. "I insisted that he take your case. Did you know that?"

"I didn't know it," the undertaker replied. "I've wondered what brought him to change his mind. Perhaps I didn't want him to take it. Perhaps I knew that he was the one man who wouldn't take the case because he would understand immediately what was involved — black and white."

"Then it may be I didn't do you such a favor after all," Steve Mundine said.

"You did me a great favor. I've been brought down to where every man should be brought, to that line — I'm not sure I know how to say it. But in every man there is a determining point, or there should be. A man says to himself he won't take any more. Past a certain point he will act, one way or another, for better or worse. In other words, you can push him only so far! I think I have discovered how far I could be pushed."

"Then you're going to act? But how?"

"I have acted," said the undertaker. "I've demanded a divorce. I have appealed to the law. For a man in my circumstances this, by itself, is enough. Merely to stand up for my rights — this suffices. Still, I must decide . . ."

"Perhaps," Steve Mundine said, "if I spoke to your wife. Sometimes a stranger can be more persuasive than a husband."

"Sometimes," said the undertaker drily. "In this instance however you couldn't help, and as for trying to talk to her, I'd rather you didn't."

"As you wish," Steve Mundine said. "Do you really not trust the District Attorney or the Grand Jury? You would not trust the District Attorney?"

"You are forcing me to say it, Mr. Mundine."

"Well then, say it! Good God, look, I'm trying to be of some help. You're in trouble!"

"I don't trust him, no, not in this situation."

The young man apparently took the remark as an assault on his profession. He reddened. "You can't be serious!" he said.

"How long have you lived in Somerton?" the undertaker asked. "Two, three years? I've lived in this county all my life."

"I have never run into anything so damned incredible! A policeman threatening a man — all right, you've lived here all your life. Then what's to be done?"

"I have no idea. Nothing probably," the undertaker said.

"How can I —" the young man glanced at his wife. "How can we help you?"

"You cannot help me."

"You mean to say we would only make it worse, don't you? Isn't that what you mean?" The young man reddened again, and then, as though to himself: "We'll see about this!"

"Without wanting to seem rude —"

"Rude?" said Steve Mundine, like someone shocked out of his reverie.

"I don't think that you can help at all," said the undertaker. "I think you very possibly might make things worse than they are already." He sighed. "The fact is that I have a decision to make. It's really very simple — either I back out or I stand up and demand my rights. I have to do it on my own. It's my decision to live with. To back down, or to take the risk. Nobody can protect me. You are both very kind to call on me, though."

"But why?" said the lawyer's wife, speaking up, breaking the fabric of her silence. "Why can't we help you? Why can't we defend you? Look — we're offering you help."

"Our worlds are not the same, Mrs. Mundine."

"Nella, he's right," Steve Mundine said.

"It can be difficult sometimes. I don't think it is ever pleasant to remind a white person that you yourself are a Negro, and that this, by and large, makes a difference. It is not something pleasant or easy to talk about, or think about. But it is true," said the undertaker.

"Truth is always unpopular," Steve Mundine said. He stood up abruptly.

"You're welcome to stay," said the undertaker. "Would you like coffee?"

The young woman had also stood up to leave. They seemed more than merely angry. They seemed also hurt and affronted. "Coffee?" the undertaker repeated.

"Another time, thank you," said the blonde young woman. She was, thought the undertaker, quite beautiful and quite determined — strong willed, very proud, and foreign to Somerton. The white couple started for the door. Lord Byron Jones was ahead of them. He opened it.

"I thank you for your concern," said the undertaker.

"Of course," said Steve Mundine. "Good-bye."

"Good-bye," said the undertaker. Obviously they had expected another kind of reception. Like expectant heroes they had come sure of finding a helpless, terrified suppliant. They left looking curiously insulted. Their generous white charity had been rejected, their white concern rebuffed.

The young lawyer's car whirled into the driveway and backed out fast, turning. Steve Mundine drove away like an angry man, like a wild kid who can never express himself otherwise so foolishly, nor yet so well, as behind the wheel of a car. The undertaker closed the front door. He went back to the kitchen.

"Your days are numbered, old Mr. Nuts, numbered I say," Emma said, chanting, taunting him. "You're no damn good, Mr. Nuts!"

"Can't you shut her face up," Mosby said. "She like a radio turned up loud as can be."

"If you're ready, we'll go now," the undertaker said.

"I'm ready," Mosby said.

"Where are you all going?" Emma said.

She followed them through the den and out to the patio. "Where you going?"

The undertaker and Mosby got in the convertible.

4

Mosby

His landlady in Kansas City, Isabel Kay Pasco, she would sure miss him and would take her key maybe and unlock the door to his empty furnished room where he was gone out of it and she wouldn't bother anything, wouldn't touch anything. Isabel Kay would merely look into the room and remember and think of him and wonder when he would be home again because she was a long, lean woman with a good heart and she would be missing her man, Mosby, who left her so satisfied.

Thus now and then he was homesick. Wearing overalls and work shoes he drove Benny's old car out of town, a fishing pole stuck in one of the windows, the cigar box beside him on the front seat. Headed for the Somerton Lake, all alone, he thought of Isabel Kay Pasco because that morning Emma Jones had walked around in front of him wearing a shorty coat that didn't hide nothing but only showed herself off all the more.

Afterwards, at the funeral home where Benny had given Mosby the old clothes and the fishing pole and the key to this old green Plymouth, the undertaker, L. B. Jones, had said: "You can't protect me. I appreciate what you want to do, but nobody can protect me."

"Well I can try," Mosby had said, trying to get his mind off Emma's nakedness.

"We can all try," Benny had said.

"The decision has to be mine and mine alone," the undertaker had said. "Still you can stay with me, Sonny Boy. I don't mind having you stay with me. Maybe I can be some help to you, but you don't have to worry about protecting me."

"He ain't worried," Benny had said. "Sonny Boy ain't worried about nothing. Are you, Sonny Boy?"

"Nothing but fishing," Mosby had said, and Benny, taking this for a signal, had walked with him out to the car, leaving the undertaker behind in the funeral parlor.

"You gonna find Bumpas out there because it's Sunday and he's gonna be there," Benny had said. "So maybe this will be your chance. I know Bumpas will be there."

"Maybe this time I'll just scout him. I don't know," Mosby had said, because he was feeling uncomfortable. He didn't want to admit it to Benny but he was feeling uncomfortable about killing the cop and it wasn't merely because he was afraid to do it. Not that a bit, because he *was* afraid and any man *would be* afraid. It was more than fear too, and he couldn't lay his finger on what it was unless it was just the feeling he had, now the grocer was dead, that killing a man was a wrong and a terrible thing. It was all the more wrong and terrible if you set out aiming to do it, much worse than if you just blew up and did it without aiming to do it, like it was when he laid it on Bivens. So he had told Benny: "Maybe this time I'll just scout him."

Down the side of a hill the road passed out of town into the countryside, curving and dark red and winding between cotton fields and pastures before it dipped down and crossed a concrete bridge. The road lay flat then crossing a bottom divided by ditches and levees. Any direction you took out of Somerton there was the swamp and the low ground and the bridges that humped over the creeks and the ditches and the cypresses moving in close on either side of the brassy red road and marching back again to thin, distant lines far away and as flat as Kansas until one tree in particular stood alone, and that was a tall dead cypress far ahead and to the left side of the road with limbs on its sides like spikes or thorns.

He watched two dark specks on one of the thornlike limbs. When the tree was about seventy yards ahead of him the birds flew, two crows, slow in flight. So Mama Lavorn claimed, did a man's body lie above ground unburied or was he hanged and left hanging as a warning to others not to steal and murder (and once long ago they did it that way here in this country, so she claimed), then the crows would get to the body and eat his eyes and have his sight; eat his tongue and have his speech. But the worst yet, did they eat his brain, then they had his memory and his thought and would fly then into houses before Death arrived and beat their tar-black wings against the walls and speak with the voice of the dead. They would light on the shoulder of the person old man Death had chosen next.

Did they eat the body of a murdered man, so Mama Lavorn claimed, then they would fly straight to the dead man's relatives and speak the name of his murderer so the dead man's kinfolks could plot their revenge.

"And that," Mama Lavorn had told Sonny Boy, "that is why we buries the dead — so they can't pass on no juju to the crows."

"But Mama Lavorn? Why wouldn't it be a nice thing to have the crows tell all old Death's plans? Don't peoples want the crows to have no juju, Mama Lavorn?"

"Child hush! Don't you know the only thing worse than old Death is to know when he's coming right down to the hour and minute?"

"But can't you stop him if you know when he's coming?"

"Can't nothing stop old Death because he carries a railroad watch in his vest pocket and he's always on time to the tick. He's always on the job and he never takes no rest. He rides the black paddyroll wagon day and night, and when you hear it thunder, that's him, crossing a bridge somewhere!"

Thus it had seemed to him sometimes that he saw the black paddy-roll wagon in the firelight shadows from the coal grate in his room, flickering and riding and rolling along the ceiling sometimes at night when the Devil blew his breath on the grate and made the banked fire suddenly burn. Death's railroad watch ticked in the fire, ticked in the wallpaper, ticked in the icy floor while the paddyroll wagon licked and licked the ceiling. Thus had he lain, a small boy, half waked up and afraid to move and holding his breath and afraid to cry until his fright finally burst and he called out and his mouth and tongue then had the taste of blood.

When he screamed Ponselle always came to his room and banked the fire again, putting on fresh coal from the scuttle and piling on fresh white ashes until the tarry smell of the fresh banked fire would fill the room and comfort him and let him breathe once more between sobs. Then sometimes Ponselle even came to bed with him if she wasn't busy back in her own room with a man. She sometimes came to bed with him and warmed his feet between her thighs and laid his head against her bosom and warmed his ears and told him someday after the harvest, when the last grain of earth's wheat and corn was threshed and every crop was laid by, then he would be an angel and the boss of the angels would send for him.

"Where must I go when he send after me, Ponselle?"

"Go straight to the Tabernickel, Sonny Boy, because everybody going to leave from there."

"What about the bad peoples?"

"God will burn them in the fire like thorns, Sonny Boy. He will snatch up and set fire to every thorn tree on earth and fling all that flaming trash and all them bad peoples right straight down into the Bad Place!"

"How about the wheat?"

"He will take that up to heaven for to feed his angels, Sonny Boy."

Then the grate shadows became wings on the ceiling and the fire popped and talked to itself deep under its ashes while gently Ponselle's hand sought between his legs, holding and nursing him there and stroking his little goober to make him sleep, and she always promised him that when he got twelve she would give him his first breeding. When he got twelve he would be coming a man and Frankie would give him some too. Frankie would breed him.

"But not Mama Lavorn."

"No, Sonny Boy, because she your mama and that can't be in the plan."

"Will us get married, Ponselle?"

"Naw, baby. Married peoples only fights and try to kill one another. Don't never get married, Sonny Boy. Hear?"

"Yes'm." A warmth like feathers would spread over him before he slept.

The warm air fluttered like wings through the side window vent of the car, tugging the rolled up sleeve of his work shirt. The road rose and crooked out of the bottom between red clay banks gullied until they looked like a long row of skinny old bearded men. Beyond the clay banks he saw the orange Tennessee Game and Fish Commission sign just where Benny had promised him he would see it, the sign on the right side of the road and then on the road's left, when the clay banks fell away, Mosby saw the hatchery ponds and the long grassy slope of the earth dam.

He turned off the pavement into the chert gravel access road between fencerows buried in honeysuckle vines. The road bent through a gap in the vine thickets and the lake lay revealed. It was bounded by the long straight reach of the dam at the end, and a wide sheet of flat, green water went stretching back from the dam into woods and coves.

Mosby parked the Plymouth beside the last car in a row of them standing on the gravel lot. He got out, taking the cane pole, and walked slowly with the cane on his shoulder to the counter. The man behind the counter was in the shade of the wooden building. The counter was higher than Mosby's waist. He stopped, looking only at the white hands and down then at his own shoes, past the expanse of his belly in overalls. His belly was tingling and unguarded for the lack of a belt, his black belly wanting nothing so much as to feel a belt's sure bite about the body's midsection.

"You want something, boy?" the white man said.

"Yessir."

"You want to fish?"

"Yessir."

"Got your license?"

"Naw, sir."

"Then you need a one-day permit. That's fifty cents. Your permission to fish this lake is seventy-five cents. Makes a dollar and a quarter. Okay?"

"Yessir, that's okay."

The hands took up a pencil. "Name?"

"Adam."

"Adams?"

"Yessir."

"Adams who?"

"Thomas Adams."

"Where you live, boy?"

"Somerton."

"Okay — can you sign your name here?"

"Naw sir, I can't steer no pencil."

"Okay, put your mark here and here."

The hands pushed both permits at him. Mosby made an "X" on

both permits, where the finger directed. "Now, that's a dollar and a quarter," said the white man.

Crossing the dam he saw the hatchery ponds. They were bright squares of water reflecting the sky. Grass stood tall about the ponds' edges like green wheat.

"For His angels because He don't feed them nothing but light bread, Sonny Boy."

Across the dam a path led between thistle and jimsonweed, purple bobwhite peas and yellow daisies. Half hidden against the ground lavender maypop blossoms made a heavy perfume. Little gray butterflies fluttered. Grasshoppers lurched and flew from one bending weed stalk to the next. Bream roiled the shore shallows, leaving their beds and fleeing to deep water at his approach. He left the path and passed into the woods, through a stand of thick-leafed chinkapin oaks.

> *Humble, rumble, bumble bee,*
> *Built him a cabin in a chinkapin tree;*
> *Tripped on a keg, broke his leg,*
> *Couldn't work no more,*
> *So he had to beg!*
> *Flew to the east, flew to the west,*
> *Stayed all night in the screech owl's nest!*

He had put the evening sun behind him. Beyond the oak thicket a stand of straight pines made a corridor. In the windless silence of the pines he felt his blood beating. Thrushes stirred the leaves under the chinkapin oaks, little mock-buck thrush birds Benny called them. Such birds mocked the footsteps of deer.

Mosby stopped and put down the fishing cane beside a holly bush. Miles away in the woods a logger's chain saw whined. He walked on. He saw a fence and a field.

He had put his hand on a fence post to climb over the barbed wire when he saw a tractor. Not a hundred paces off, the tractor stood hitched to a hay bailer. Beside the tractor, working on it, stood Stanley Bumpas.

Mosby stepped back into the pines and sat down. With his back against the rough bark of a tree, he watched, shivering.

Like a big bear the policeman climbed into the driver's seat and started the tractor. Behind it the steel tines of the baler gnashed. The machine clanked impatiently. The engine quit and Stanley Bumpas climbed down again. He walked back to the hay baler. He was soon bent over it, wiring it here and there and striking it with a hammer.

If at night he was something else, a policeman, here he was a farmer bothering nobody, going about his work out in the hot, silent sun. What kind of man would walk up on him this way when he was working so hard to get his hay crop made? Mosby wondered. Walk up on him now and lay it on him before he might know what it was after him? Mosby thinking: Him, that once beat up and nearly killed a little thirteen-year-old nigger boy, that was me. Yet pain carries no memory, he thought.

The hammer sounded steel upon steel. Mosby took the Webley out of the cigar box. He cocked it, uncocked it, and put it back in the box. The hammer continued — steel upon steel.

What's the difference now? Mosby thought. It was a long time ago, so what's the difference now? With something happened so long ago, it ain't the same no more.

He could crawl under the barbed wire and be on top of him in five minutes. It didn't seem hardly worth it any more.

He put the pistol back in the box and got up and walked back to the lake. It lay smooth and flat as ice. The sun was burning above it like a flat ball beyond full green trees on the opposite shore. Above at the shallow end crows were passing, on the way to roost, silently. He thought of the fishing pole and went back for it. He found it where he had left it, by the holly tree. Carrying it like a spear he walked back to the lakeside, feeling inside of himself like a king because he was free now and didn't have to kill nobody, because it didn't matter and besides, what happened was a long time ago and Isabel Kay Pasco would be waiting for him in Kansas and wondering where he had been all this long time, her good man.

The decision and his freedom came together in him like a new power. In his belly it was strong as hunger. Suddenly he remembered how Benny had said if they turned a man loose in the woods how he would go wild like a hog and his hair would grow long and he'd forget his speech and live by what came to his hand, on bugs and berries. He would sleep with his ear to the ground and his nose to the wind, the way slaves did back in slavery times when they ran away to the swamps and went wild, just so they did, and so would a man, even today, was how Benny told it.

Drink muddy water; sleep in a hollow log.

5

Oman Hedgepath

They prepared to put him in the ground. It was one of those country cemeteries. The unfortunate thing was the rain. I thought well now Earl's casket will get the test for waterproof. The grave was half full of water. Brother Dodson, the preacher, took me aside and said did I think they ought to try to fill it up so the casket would not be lowered into water.

I said well ask the funeral director — ask Earl — if it will float. I said you can't fill that hole with dirt — not gumbo mud like this — and dry it out; you'll have to go get a pump somewhere because look it's already half full of water and throwing dirt — black gumbo mud — in would only raise the water level, wouldn't it?

"Well, I don't know," Brother Dodson said. He called the funeral director who was standing by the hearse down on the dirt road. "Earl?"

Earl left the hearse and came over. "Why don't they try to find high ground," Earl said. He wasn't really asking. He was only commenting. It was like something said about the world in general, not specifically about a grave half full of water.

"Well, it's had to have happened before," I said.

"Oh, it's happened," Earl said. "God, I reckon it's probably happened a thousand times. When they dug it it was dry though so I figured it wouldn't have time to get that full before we got here. I had 'em dig it just a little while ago. I mean they just finished maybe an hour ago. If we don't hurry and get him in it maybe it might over-flow, like a damn artesian well."

"What can we do?" Brother Dodson said. "I don't like the idea of lowering a casket into water. It won't sound right. It will go splash."

"Let me find the niggers. Go stay with the widow and let me find the niggers," Earl said. "We try to keep them out of sight, but I see the truck yonder so they are probably hiding. You want to keep them out of sight. Nobody likes to see them. It's too grim. I don't want a bunch of spades with shovels hanging around, you know?"

"I'll go with Earl," I told Brother Dodson. He nodded and went to-wards the road, to stay with the widow and keep the others in the cars. Earl and I went on across the cemetery. The truck was pulled in beside a pine thicket.

"You wouldn't think it was this wet," I said.

"Shit," Earl said. "When you're in sight of cypress trees it's always wet. You can't go six feet down and find nothing dry if you're in sight of cypress trees. Even the God-damned Indians knew that much, that there wasn't nothing dry. So they made burial mounds so at least they wouldn't have to drop theirs in a pool of water. Some of the Indians buried their dead in churns. Sure, churns." Maybe he thought I didn't believe him.

"Hot as it is and dry as the ground is on top you wouldn't ex-pect it," I said.

"It's hot all right," Earl agreed, "by God."

When we got to the truck we could see the grave diggers sitting in the shade of the thicket right where Earl knew they would be. They wore overalls and ditching boots. There were three of them.

Earl didn't even look at them. "Run bail that God-damned grave out," he said.

They got up and took five-gallon oil buckets out of the back of the truck.

"I told you it would fill up," one said to another.

"Hurry," Earl said. "Nobody can't get out of the cars till you get that hole dry."

They trotted off across the cemetery. Two jumped in the hole. The big one reached down for the buckets and emptied them on the ground. Earl and I went to the grave where the niggers were working. The chairs were lined up under the tent awning.

[222]

"Okay," Earl said after a minute. "Oman, if you don't mind get the pallbearers out and you all get a grip on the casket. When I wave my handkerchief get them out of the cars and you and Brother Dodson bring the casket and come right on — I'll wave my handkerchief."

I went back down to the hearse and motioned to the other pallbearers. They got out of the cars. I could hear the water chunk and splash, chunk and splash. We opened the hearse and slid the casket out a little way. Earl waved his handkerchief and we started for the grave. I could see the niggers running for the thicket with their five-gallon buckets and Earl by the grave wiping his face. The sweat dripped down my cheeks from my sideburns. Earl and the ambulance driver had it ready. We squished through the mud and put the casket in place over the grave. Then we sat down.

"Shall we have prayer?" Brother Dodson asked. It was short and sweet. One psalm and a final prayer and Earl and the ambulance driver let the casket down. I heard it gush and gurgle. I looked at Earl. He was already beside me and already had the widow's arm, leading her back to the car.

"Let's start the procession back to town," I said. "It's hot out here. Somebody might faint."

The others nodded. We went back to the cars.

It was pretty low ground for a cemetery all right. I'd always heard they put them on a hill to be closer to God. Live and learn, I thought, remembering how it sounded, like a boat being put in the water, that chunk — splash.

I got in the car with Brother Dodson. His feet were muddy too, like mine. We sat together on the back seat with Johnnie Price Burkhalter between us. Nobody said anything because it was too hot. The line of cars went back towards town, slowly again.

6

Mama Lavorn

She sat Mrs. Osborn down at the table and opened her a beer and gave her a Goody's Headache Powder, tearing the end off the envelope and dumping the powder on Mrs. Osborn's tongue, then handing her the beer so she could wash the powder down. "God damn," Mrs. Osborn said quietly, her voice hoarse from squealing. Sunday always made Mrs. Osborn nervous. Maybe it was the quiet in the streets. Somehow she knew it was different. It always frightened her.

Lavorn stepped outside the cafe and stood a moment feeling the sun on her thin arms, the heat bearing in on her and burning. There was no pain any more. Just the feeling of lightness was all she had, the feeling of her bones getting light. Time had been when she could not stand up for long at a time without the weight of her body bearing down so on her feet that they hurt. Now she was more comfortable standing up than lying down, more comfortable walking than sitting. Once she had sat on her high seat behind the cash register of the Look and See, in her telephone operator's chair, like a queen on her throne, wearing rings and ear bobs and purple dresses and laughing until her whole full body shook. She had been fat and full of the moisture of life, but now that moisture was nearly all dried out of her, and when the last bit of it was gone she would rise — straight up to the sun and beyond it, she would float away. Lavorn knew.

She went slowly around beside the house and propped her hand against the rough trunk of the oak tree where Sonny Boy's tire swing had hung, once upon a time. Beyond the railroad tracks where the old post road slanted and curved in from the northwest she saw the funeral procession returning. She heard the front door screen slam and looked back. Jelly and Coreen, dressed like twins in red blouses and black slacks, went down the road, high breasted girls with hips that pumped and flowed like water as they went, a temptation to all mankind. The girls carried their laundry bags. They were on their way to the coin laundry. No more black wash pots boiling in the yards, Lavorn thought.

She went slowly back to her garden. The sun on the corn gave a smell. She pulled a red tomato from the rough green vine and chewed the pulp and spat it out juice and all. She needed only the warm taste and feel of it in her mouth, that was enough. She didn't care to swallow. She chewed the pulp slowly, walking down towards the stink of the cabbage rows, her mouth wet by the blood-warm juice. Beside the twisted bean vines she looked down into the weeds for the melons. She crouched and saw the melons where they grew, each hidden by its own vine's secret shade. She squatted to feel the smoothness of one young melon and then another, running her tired, thin hands over the smooth, warm skin. From the cafe Mrs. Osborn screamed, and screamed again, always the same impatient sound, jagged as broken glass. Across the road Cucumber's geese answered her.

Mama Lavorn closed her eyes. Soon the melons must be ripe. Soon, she thought. Soon.

7

The D.A.

The District Attorney was Arnold Burkette, the dentist's, Toonker Burkette's, little brother. He had been the District Attorney for a year and would someday be the Circuit Judge if the succession continued as it had in the past.

The Circuit Judge retired, the District Attorney moved up to the judge's bench, and a nice young lawyer from a good family was made District Attorney.

Like his brother, Dr. Toonker Burkette, Arnold Burkette was a careful young man. He depended on his wife to select his clothes. Everything he wore came from Janus Galeburg's in Memphis. Galeburg's was famous for its line of name brand suits. Arnold belonged to Rotary. Arnold was a member of the First Baptist Church. Arnold did his banking at the Farmers and Merchants.

He had responded to Steve Mundine's call with the natural alacrity of the man who realizes certain facts. Fact One: Oman Hedgepath was largely responsible for Arnold's getting appointed District Attorney. Fact Two: Steve Mundine was Oman's nephew and law partner. Fact Three: Steve wouldn't want to see him, Arnold, on Sunday, unless it involved Oman in some way.

Thus Arnold had brushed his teeth, combed his hair, and put on his Galeburg's Panama straw hat, kissed Dotty, his wife, and reluctantly walked one block to Steve Mundine's place, over the warm, shady, buckled sidewalk, up the shaded drive, across the cypress-decked front porch and into the high ceilinged house, without knocking, of course. It was rather impolite to knock. Steve was expecting him. Steve appeared in the hallway sure enough. He asked Arnold to come on back to the library.

Nella was there. She'd been crying. It passed through Arnold Burkette's mind that he might, inadvertently, be getting into something domestic and therefore dangerous. He had his first little vibration of misgiving. He said: "Bourbon and water, that would be lovely," and sat down while Steve fetched him a drink. Arnold had been lying down most of the afternoon watching television and reading through the *Commercial Appeal*. He didn't want a drink really. Actually he didn't like whiskey, but it was one of the amenities. Steve Mundine returned with the drinks.

"Hot weather we're having, isn't it? Typical July," Arnold Burkette said. Since Nella hadn't offered to take Arnold's hat he dropped it inconspicuously on the floor beside his chair. He sipped the bourbon.

"Arnold, we're at a loss," Nella said. She smiled. "Arnold, we need help." For a Yankee she could be very charming, Arnold thought. He smiled.

"You know me," Arnold replied smoothly. "I'll help you anyway I can." He smiled again. "What's the trouble?" He looked from Nella to Steve.

"Well, it's Oman," Steve said. "We've gotten into something. Oman's sort of gone off the deep end. Do you know Lord Byron Jones?"

"You mean the nigger?" Arnold said. "Sure I know him. Is he giving you trouble?" Arnold could fix that quick enough.

"Well, not exactly. You see Oman's getting L. B. Jones a divorce," Steve said.

"Oh, me. Nigger divorce suits," Arnold said. "How did Oman get caught up in something like that? Lawd, Lawd. There's no money in 'em. They're more trouble than they're worth. You have my sympathy!" Arnold laughed politely.

Nella and Steve looked strange. "Is there something in this I don't know about? Y'all look kinda funny —" Arnold said.

"It's a little complicated," Steve said. "You see Lord Byron's wife is demanding strict proof."

"Sure," Arnold said. "She wants L. B.'s money, so she's gonna make it hard on him."

[227]

"But it's more than that. Because the man the Negro's wife is accused of sleeping with is a white man," Steve said.

"Lawd, help us. You don't mean there's a white man involved? And Oman took this case? I can't believe Oman would take a case like this if he was in his right mind," Arnold said.

"Why do you say that?" Nella asked.

"Well," Arnold said, "don't get me wrong. I'm not one to criticize Oman Hedgepath. He's as fine a lawyer as I know and if he took a case like this one I know Oman had to have a good reason. But anything that's nigger versus white in this sorta context is poison. I mean it's almost the first thing you learn when you get out of law school, isn't it?" Arnold Burkette appealed to Steve. "Maybe Oman was forced to take it. Don't let me stop you before you tell me what the problem is, though. I've got a terrible habit of buttin' in with my opinions!" Arnold laughed politely again. "So she demanded strict proof? Then what?"

"It so happens that the white man is a Somerton policeman."

"Oh, Gawd," Arnold said.

"So in order to get one of them to back out of the case, either L. B.'s wife or L. B. himself, Oman went to the cop last night and told him that if something wasn't done the whole thing would be dragged out in open court Tuesday morning at the hearing."

"Sure," Arnold said, nodding. "Here Oman's got a white man, a city employee, and if his name is dragged into it then the white man loses his job. I see what Oman's trying to do. He's bringing pressure on either the nigger's wife or the nigger himself. It really doesn't matter which, and the cop's in a position to apply all the pressure anybody needs to keep a scandal from breaking out in the open over it. I'd probably do the same thing, wouldn't you?"

"You would?" Nella said. "You'd warn the policeman?"

"I would, I think. Wouldn't you, Steve? I mean where a man's job is involved, and you take all the uproar and the scandal, a nigger woman and a white policeman. It can't help anything to have that sort of mess come out in the open."

"But what if L. B. Jones is put in jeopardy, Arnold?" Nella said.

Arnold laughed. "He's in plenty of jeopardy all right! But then he's the one that came to Oman wanting a divorce, isn't he? Oman didn't go to him, did he?"

"Let's get this straight, Arnold. In your opinion, if L. B. Jones is in danger, then it's his, L. B. Jones's, own doing?" Nella said. "Because I want to get it straight."

"What Nella means, Arnold," Steve said, "what she's wondering about and what's got me a little worried, is who's going to protect L. B. Jones?"

Arnold smiled. "Well," he said, "not the police, obviously. Not when one of their own men has his job and his reputation endangered. Who is the policeman anyway?"

"Willie Joe Worth. He's on the night force," Steve said.

"Kind of a young guy? Rides with Mr. Stanley Bumpas? I know him," Arnold said. "He's a nice fellow. He stopped me once for speeding. I was coming home from the country club. Nice fellow. Be a shame to see him lose his job. Hasn't he got a family?"

"Yes," Nella said. "And he's a white man."

"There's that old Yankee insistence! Don't I detect a little of that, Nella? But we're white men too. I imagine Mr. Worth has some children, doesn't he?"

"Yes," Steve said.

"Then all you can do is hush it up."

"But if it were a white divorce case, what then?" Nella said.

"It wouldn't be so bad then. Wouldn't be any problem," Arnold said. "I know it looks bad, but that's just the way it has to operate. There isn't any other way really."

"Can you, as District Attorney, protect L. B. Jones?" Nella asked.

"Can I? Sure, if he comes to me and can show me he needs protection, I can protect him. You mean to say he's coming to me?"

"No," Nella said. "He isn't. We went to see him and tried to tell him he should come to you."

"Oh," Arnold said. "Now I see. You and Steve went to him. Today?"

"Yes," Steve said.

"Does Oman know this, Steve?"

"No," Steve said.

Arnold stood up and put his half empty glass down on the coffee table beside the magazines. He remembered his hat and reached for it. "I tell you what, Steve. I mean, and Nella too. Talk to Oman, and whatever Oman wants to do in this matter, then I'll go along with it.

I'll cooperate in any way I can. Whatever Oman says. I'd trust Oman's judgment implicitly, of course, and so would you. Or if L. B. wanted to come to me himself, I'd talk to him, of course. But if no crime's been committed —" Arnold paused.

"Arnold, can you protect him?" Nella said.

"Well," Arnold said, "I'm just the District Attorney. If the Grand Jury decides there's been a crime then of course you've got an indictment there. That's different. But where there's really nothing to lay your finger on — you talk to Oman, that's my advice, Nella. I can see you're both pretty well shaken up over this thing."

"We are," Steve said. "We damn well are."

"Dotty's not feeling very well this afternoon and I better be getting back home," Arnold said. "Come to see us. Thanks for the drink." He waved at them and walked out of the library into the hall and straight out the front door, back into the oven stillness of the outdoors without waiting for Steve to show him out or for Nella to dismiss him.

If they thought they were going to get him crossed up with Oman over a nigger, then they were badly mistaken, Arnold decided. "Badly mistaken," he muttered, thinking how embarrassed Oman Hedgepath would be to know his own nephew, not to mention that Steve was also his law partner, was meddling with Oman's clients and not even telling him about it.

"What was it Steve wanted, honey?" Dotty asked, when Arnold was settled at last, back in his comfortable chair with the television glowing unobtrusively before him again, the images flickering and the sounds flowing so a man didn't have to think. Arnold could forget his troubles and doze in the room's twilight while the heat outdoors raged on, for the heat raged; oh, yes. Arnold had never thought of it any other way than that it raged. Summer was a storm. Winter was a long sleep. Only the brief days of early spring and the waning interim of Indian summer were worth anything. The rest was lost because the country was so extreme and the seasons were extreme and the land was a rough land hardly fit for human habitation unless a man learned how to relax and doze, how to push cares and worries aside and let life pulse on inside him as it would. Taken that way a man could exist a long while.

"Something about a nigger," Arnold Burkette said. He closed his eyes.

SIX

1

Oman Hedgepath

I was no sooner home and had changed my shoes and thought I'd
drop by to see Steve and Nella, than Henry walked in on me. He was
wearing his best clothes, having been all afternoon at church, as usual.

"They git the man buried?" he says. He picked up my muddy shoes.
"I just shined them slippers yesterday."

"He's buried," I said. "Six feet under the gumbo. And nobody
knows yet who killed him."

"You got a little time to spare me, Mr. Oman?"

"What?" I felt it coming the way you sometimes feel before you
answer the phone when bad news is calling. You reach your hand out
for the phone and it's like little spiders are walking up and down on
the nerves inside your fingers. "Time?"

"Well, we — our church — has a problem," he says. "If you would
be kind enough to talk to the peoples."

"Where?" I said.

"In the kitchen," he said. "Reverend Burnley axed me personally ef
I would take the matter in hand fer him. Hit won't take but a minute."

"On Sunday?" I said.

"Well, the ox in the ditch. I say git the bull calf in a ditch you gotta
git him out soon as you can. He going back to college tomorrow. So it
has to be today and the Reverend Burnley axed and requested me. It
wasn't none of my idea. Ef the answer must be no then that's what
I'll tell 'em."

"That's all right," I said. He followed me down the service stairs carrying the shoes. There were five other niggers in the kitchen. The only one I knew was Georgine Beggs. Reverend Burnley introduced himself and wanted to shake hands with me.

"Everybody take a seat," I said.

"We got some troubles, Lawyer Hedgepath," Georgine said. "You nice to take your time with us on this day."

"We appreciate your interest in our affairs, Lawyer Hedgepath," the Reverend Burnley said in his best preaching voice. They sat in a polite semicircle. I sat on the kitchen stool, facing them.

"This my daughter, Maxine," said Georgine, touching the girl. Maxine ducked her head. "That's Reverend Burnley who you already know him, and beside him my husband, Major." Major grinned and nodded. "Next to Major, that's Thomas Houston Fly." Thomas Houston Fly was a young man. I pegged him right away for a nigger college student. He wouldn't look at me.

"All right," I said. "Skeet your pizen."

"Shall I tell it, Lawyer Hedgepath?" Georgine said.

"That's usually the best," I said. "Henry," I said. "Open everybody a Coca-Cola but me. You know what I want."

They laughed, Henry loudest of all. He fixed me a drink first and then opened a Coke for each of the others. Everybody drank their Cokes but Thomas Houston Fly. He held the bottle propped against his leg. He wore a spiffy black suit, loafers, gray socks and a long narrow gray tie. His long legs were stuck out in front of him like prise poles. The others sat prim and stiff.

"Shall I tell it now, Lawyer Hedgepath?" Georgine said politely.

"Tell it," I said.

"Well, Maxine is my youngest child. Lawyer Hedgepath, I raised her with all the strength I had in my hand to raise her right, to teach her the difference between what is right and what is wrong."

Maxine hung her head.

"Didn't I, Reverend Burnley?"

"In-deed," said Reverend Burnley. "I been having the whole family in my church. They been regular. Brother Major is a farming man. Sister Georgine is a fine woman. Henry will tell you, Lawyer Hedgepath."

"Amen," Henry said. "Amen."

Georgine cleared her throat. "Everything went along all right until Maxine went in high school. Everything went all right until the night of that senior prong. That's when the trouble started, at that senior prong, didn't it, Reverend Burnley."

"Yes, yes," Reverend Burnley said. "That's surely and certainly right where it began."

"The what?" I said. "The senior — "

"You know, Lawyer Hedgepath. That high school dance. The senior prong?" Georgine said.

I nearly choked in my bourbon. "Go on, Georgine," I told her.

"Well, Lawyer Hedgepath. Maxine has commenced to gain weight since Thomas Houston Fly taken her to that prong."

"You're the father?" I asked the young nigger. "The daddy?"

He nodded, still not looking at me.

"Whose boy are you?" I asked him.

"You mean who is my father?" he said, in a precise monotone, maybe tinged with mockery, I couldn't tell.

"He Dock Fly's boy," the Reverend Burnley said. "You know Dock Fly, don't you, Lawyer Hedgepath? Didn't Dock used to farm for your daddy?"

"Yes," I said. "All right, Thomas Houston. You got this gal pregnant. What you got to say for yourself?"

"Nothing," he said. He was sullen.

"Lawyer Hedgepath, all we asking Thomas Houston to do is marry her and give the baby a name," Georgine said. "He can leave her tomorrow if he'll just marry her today. We just want our baby to have a name. We just want Maxine to be able to call herself Mrs. Fly. We ain't asking him one thing more than that."

"We done taken out the license and got everything ready," said Reverend Burnley. "We done axed him twice yesterday and twice today. Everytime Thomas Houston done spoke out and said no. Whereas a month ago, Lawyer Hedgepath, he agreed when he come home this weekend that he would give Maxine's baby a name."

"How about it, Thomas Houston?" I said.

"I won't do it," the boy said. "And you can't make me do it."

"It won't cost you anything," I said.

"I won't do it," he said, staring straight ahead. "And you can't make me. I'm free, and you can't make me."

[235]

"If she just hadn't of went to that senior prong. Now look at us!" Georgine said.

"How old is she, Georgine?" I asked.

"Fifteen. She fifteen and he won't ever have to see her again," Georgine said.

"First you said you would marry her. Now you say you won't. Thomas Houston, Georgine's gal is below the age of consent. You've committed a crime. You know that?"

"I'm eighteen," he said. "You can't make me marry her and you can't touch me. Because I'm free."

"Who told you that?" I said.

"Don't you worry about it," Thomas Houston Fly said. "It ain't bothering me."

"Listen, boy, watch it!" Georgine's husband said. Major took Thomas Houston's arm.

"Lemme go," Thomas Houston said. "Lay your damn hands off me!"

"Now see what I mean, Lawyer Hedgepath?" said Georgine. "Taken her to that senior prong. Got her messed up, and now listen to him!"

"Where you going to school, Thomas Houston?" I said.

"Fisk University," he said.

"Stand up," I said. "Stand up!"

He did so slowly. Standing, he was taller than he looked to be sitting down. Maybe he was more frightened than he seemed. It came to me maybe this staring straight ahead business was something the nonviolent demonstrators had taught him. Thomas Houston was a different breed of nigger all right.

"Now let the gal stand up beside him," I said. "Stand the gal up beside him, Georgine."

When she stood up her belly showed. She stood by the boy.

"All right, preacher," I said.

"You mean marry them now?" said Reverend Burnley.

"Right now," I said.

"But Lawyer Hedgepath what if he won't say — "

"He'll say," I said. I walked out of the kitchen and up the hall to the closet under the front stairway. I switched the light on in the closet and took a gun off the rack, the biggest one there. It was a ten-gauge double barrel, my father's goose gun. I got two magnum shells from the bottom drawer of the gun cabinet, switched off the light, broke the gun open, and walked back to the kitchen.

"He won't say," Reverend Burnley said.

I loaded both chambers, closed the breech and cocked both hammers, one at a time. "Come hold this gun, Georgine," I said.

Georgine took the gun.

"I do," Thomas Houston said. "I do!"

"I will, say that first," Reverend Burnley corrected him.

"I will," said Thomas Houston. I could barely hear him.

"And will you, Maxine, take this man, Thomas Houston, to be your lawful wedded husband, to love him, cherish him, honor and obey him as long as the both of you shall live, in health and sickness, good times and hard times, for rich or for poor, and keep yourself only for him, so help you God?"

"Yessir."

"Say, I will."

"I will. That's what I meant, I will," Maxine said.

"Shut up and just say what you told to say," said Georgine. "Ain't you caused enough hooraw? Senior prong, I hope you don't come after me no more about no senior prongs!"

"Hush, baby. Let Reverend Burnley do his do," Major said gently.

"Repeat right after me," said Reverend Burnley, "I Thomas Houston Fly . . ."

"Say it loud, I wanna hear it up loud, Mr. Prong," Georgine said, holding the gun right on him.

"I-THOMAS-HOUSTON-FLY . . ." His hand shook so much he spilled the Coca-Cola.

"Now we gettin somewhere," Georgine said. "We grindin corn now."

"Unload the gun and put it away when you're through with it," I said.

"Want me to clean it?" Henry said. "Mr. Oman?"

"If it's been fired," I said, "yes, clean it. And be sure to mop up the blood. And clean my shoes."

". . . TAKE-THEE-MAXINE-TO-BE-MY . . ."

I could hear Thomas Houston Fly all the way out to the carport, that precise college nigger accent of his popping the words off at full volume, at the top of his black lungs. Somebody had told him he wouldn't have to marry her, that if he stared straight ahead long enough nobody could make him do anything, that all it took was the guts to say no over and over again and he'd get what he wanted, his freedom; somebody had told him that he had a perfect right not to marry the girl if he didn't want to; so it boiled down to that, to a test of his own freedom.

Driving back to town I thought of my father, who never had any doubts, how they tested him too at times and how he had replied to one test before the nigger could get over the barnlot fence. I had ridden behind him that day and beside one of the ponds there had been signs, lumps of weed and green moss drying on the bank where drag seines had been emptied, clear evidence that the pond had been seined against my father's specific orders that it should not be seined, that no pond on our place was to be seined.

We had ridden then to the barnlot. The nigger responsible for the seining had been just taking the harness off his mules, pulling off their collars, and when my father, Ernest Hedgepath, politely inquired about the pond and the seining the nigger had said: "I don't see no hahm in mens dragging a seine after catfish anytime they wants to," whereupon my father jumped down fom the horse, already running it seemed when he hit the ground, the little hawkbill knife already out. He caught the nigger at the fence just as the nigger started to scale it, the nigger going up the fence and then quivering and falling back into the barnlot like a stricken fly, his whole body quivering like a fly's wings before he dropped. He uttered what I thought to be his death yell, and I thought: "Dad has killed a nigger." The scream went down to my vitals. I sat there on my little pillion holding to the back of the saddle watching my father fold the knife and put it back in his pocket. He looked at me with an expression that said, better than words: "Of course that's how you handle a nigger — quickly." My father had to get a doctor then and have the man sewn up from shoulder to buttock. The times were such that nobody questioned the thing, because my father had only done his duty. Nor was the nigger fired off the place. The nigger stayed the same as ever. Once he got well he worked the same as ever and the same nigger's son, Dock, had worked for my father, and now Dock's son, Thomas Houston, stood up to be married in my kitchen with my father's goose gun held on him and, perhaps, in Thomas Houston's memory, either his conscious or his unconscious memory, there was the knife scar on his grandfather's back.

My father always said: "To faze a nigger, Oman, kick him in the shins." My father would not have gotten the gun. Ernest Hedgepath would have kicked Thomas Houston Fly in the shins and made him jump over a broomstick and would have called him married and then dared him to dispute it. Such was the simple beauty of another age.

"To faze him kick him in the shins," my father always said. His father, my grandfather, wrote a book entitled: *At Last, the Mystery Is Solved: The Negro Has a Soul!* He rode the train to Memphis and had his book published at his own expense. He sent copies to all his friends, there being considerable argument in his time as to whether there could be a black soul, and again, whether seventeen families of them living on our land could be human. My father reduced the number to thirteen families before he died, and the tractor and the cotton picker brought it down to seven families the last time I counted. Seven, that is, if one hasn't picked up Saturday and headed north without telling Henry.

The road began a long leisurely curve up what couldn't be termed a hill except in flat country such as this, in this loveliest section of all, passing between cotton fields purple-green and ready to bloom. Far down from the road in a dead oak tree the old hawk sat motionless as stone in his usual place, his great speckled breast plainly visible across the intervening distance. I always feel his ominous majesty, as though by right of prior claim the bird really owns the hill and the broad thriving fields he overlooks. Beyond the timber tract on my left, on the other side of the gentle slope, I passed my property line. Here the whole aspect changed for the worse, from the rundown fence to the small landowner's house, the house neat enough itself, but the tenant shack down from him on the same road stood unpainted. It was almost falling down, a white man's house no nigger of mine would call fit for habitation, lacking even a well in the yard so that hapless, ragged, white tenant children had to walk two miles to the landowner's house to fetch water in buckets.

The tenant family seemed to live and especially to wash and dress themselves on the porch in plain sight of the road.

Nearly every morning there was a grown, half dressed female or two in a ragged pink slip or less, leaning towards the broken mirror on the porch wall. Fine enough in July, but what would become of them in cold weather?

[239]

They were sitting on the porch in Sunday dresses and overalls. They waved and I waved. There was, sure enough, on the side porch where they dressed, a towheaded girl standing barefoot in her slip. For all her surroundings her face, which was turned towards the road, had a serene expression. She was washing up, getting ready for her date, the swain in the $150 automobile. I could almost see him.

At the intersection I turned directly north. I could see Somerton now in the distance, the fertilizer plant on the left, chuffing red smoke into the air, even on Sunday, and the swatch of green on the right, the cemetery. The road crossed what had been a marsh before it was drained. Cattails lined the barrow pits under the road bank. The great flat fields, flat as a lake bottom (which they had once been), lay fallow for miles on either side of the road, this drained land. It lay fallow because it flooded some winters anyway. The roiling government ditches sometimes broke out of their levees. For this reason the land was in the Federal Land Bank. Thus flood or drouth, these land owners had their government rental checks. They left out of cultivation lands which Federal money had caused to be drained and put into cultivation in the first place at a cost of God knows how many millions. First the government drained it; now the government rents it.

The Government — a calculated insanity. I had to hiss through my teeth at that fallow land covered in wild grass. Here and there was a sprinkling of yellow field daisies. Almost no life except the occasional kingfisher on the phone wires. Vagrant flocks of starlings went slanting down the sky here and there. It was nothing like the land I remembered, before the marsh was drained, nothing to compare with the coots and the wilson's snipe, the bitterns, green herons, grebes, cormorants and snowy egrets. The wood ibis had been here. So had the Canada geese and the snow geese, the mallards, the blackjacks and the gadwalls, the baldpates and the redheads, the ringneck teal and the canvasbacks. Now only the ghosts of that cacophony, only the dead whisper like dust in the memory, strange cries from the winter's twilight of my childhood, sounds of the last pink glow of a winter sundown.

Back then the road had been thick impassable mud through the winter. We made a long detour down to the west and then north over the high ground to the Memphis highway before we could reach Somerton from this direction. I had stood on the south edge of these marshes with my father, both of us in thick clothes and rubber boots, both watching the ducks crowding down to roost. Down they came by the multiplied thousands. But never again, I thought, crossing the railroad tracks and entering the city limits. On my left behind neat lawns the look-alike brick dwellings of the "white" Federal housing project, and on my right the rarely painted wooden frame houses, structural calamities where the independent white man prefers to live in lust and clutter rather than submit to the drained, measured and subsidized Federal orderliness of the "project." He prefers instead his own mellifluous stagnation of shacks and sheds, preferring that which the poor everywhere seem to prefer, a house with an undefinable poetic ugliness of its own — the rusty tub, the tractor tire painted silver and filled with dirt and planted with geraniums in its center, ferns growing in blue striped lard buckets hung on wires from the eaves of the porch. It's his farm, no matter how small. Besides his garden he has chickens, rabbit hutches and pigeon cotes. Everything is tucked and folded everywhere and somewhere in the midst of it, half dead, you see his inevitable hound. Chained to the kennel, his mute Lazarus, starving and mangy, licking his sores, eating dirt and wondering, perhaps, if hunting season will ever come again.

If it was wrong anyway it was life, if it was disorganized anyway it was more reasonable than any dozen God-damned nigger marches on Washington. I thought what a fine thing if the march would get out of hand like a high pressure firehose and run wild. It would serve them right and us right; them for believing they can whip North America to her knees with marches and stunts and newsprint, us for letting them believe it.

What they deserve in Washington, where it is all promises before an election and all excuses afterwards, is exactly two million screaming, kicking, drum-dancing African jigaboos to razor the cods off every back-peddling Federal leech they can catch, catching them all, cutting them, and flinging their parts into the Potomac in one last gigantic orgy until nothing in the way of white men but eunuchs could be found, from the Pentagon to the White House to the Washington Monument. It would serve them right, I thought.

For the way they are running it now, with promises and excuses, they will get the entire nation down on the nigger. The nigger will be outlawed the way the Indian was, until finally we will wipe every last nigger off the face of the North American earth. Some scientist would think to collect and preserve the last one, to embalm the last nigger and stand his corpse in the Smithsonian Institution beside the Passenger Pigeon and the White Unreconstructed Southerner.

I swerved to miss a dog in the street — a damned cocker spaniel. I missed him and suddenly thought of Mrs. Clyde's dog, Benjamin, and of Mrs. Clyde's insistence that Benjamin and Cassie liked me. The parrot could say my name: "Oman? Oman?"

Mrs. Clyde's New England accent had made the parrot sound foreign when he called me, mocking my landlady's high clear voice long after she had left for the summer. I was alone in my room with my lawbooks, the parrot calling me, Benjamin barking downstairs, sparrows chirruping in the Spanish eaves outside my windows. I smoked a pipe then, very much the young student about Nashville, the lawyer-to-be, sometimes writing Miss Mary twice a day and getting, sometimes, two or three letters from her in one delivery, the off-white perfumed stationery and the small, clear, feminine handwriting which said how Miss Mary missed me, dreamed last night we were married, wondered what we should call our first child, whether Oman, or Mary, depending of course. It was settled, we would live at my home and keep house for my father. She drove out to see him. She and her mother invited him frequently for Sunday dinner. Mary almost slipped and called him Father, instead of Mr. Hedgepath or Mr. Ernest. She and her mother had been to Memphis, buying her trousseau, and there were always a couple of lines of crosses at the bottom of the page, a whole cemetery of them it seemed, one for each kiss, and sometimes, reluctantly, she wrote: *Goodnight, my sweet Oman, my dear love.*

Mrs. Clyde was away no more than two weeks before there was intimacy between myself and the nigger, Cassie, nothing physical as yet but sexual tension was in every look between us, nonetheless, the covert admission that I kept trying not to see. I kept telling myself she was just a nigger until she said she didn't know but thought maybe she was in a family way, saying: "Maybe you'd just look. You could tell, couldn't you?" "By looking?" I asked. The parrot climbed his cage with that patient beak and claw persistence that would keep him alive for a century; he was so deliberate in everything, which is what I liked about him. "Maybe you'd just come up in the attic and look," Cassie said.

I got up and knocked over my coffee cup trying to leave the table. She was ahead of me going up the service stairs. I could smell her. Benjamin's claws clicked along behind me. I heard the parrot: "Oman? Oman?" Mrs. Clyde's voice, as though the parrot understood the whole thing, and the cocker spaniel coming along behind, very businesslike, that was Benjamin, and we were in the attic and the smell seemed stronger there maybe because it was hot. She was pulling up the dress and pulling the switch cord on the big unfrosted light to make sure I could see because the outdoor light coming in the attic windows was weak. I kept thinking, *She is doing this in all innocence out of some mysterious belief in me*, thinking in such a tone of high seriousness when I already knew I had already asked her by just looking at her. She had already said yes without the subject ever being mentioned, just a glance and a smile, the way she turned her head and I had known; and it was time now either to run away or sit down. I sat on the covered arm of one of Mrs. Clyde's overstuffed chairs stored properly, the New England way, with a sheet draped over it and me thinking Cassie didn't want me to do what I was going to do and therefore I must not do what I was going to do because it was, and is, against Tennessee law, yet I deliberately waited for the denied, shut away and disciplined man in me to weaken. I waited. The less disciplined beast in me took hold. When it was too late I thought to look down at my own deliberate loneliness, to witness the wonderment, the uncontrol, the almost madness. Then it was too late. The overstuffed sofa, companion in exile to the chair, served. It served again and served every morning after that regardless of anything, except for weekends when I visited Somerton. Benjamin got so accustomed to the morning's ritual that he would be ahead of Cassie, first to the door leading to the attic stairs, first up the stairs with Cassie after him, and then me.

Once Cassie said: "I thought you was a doctor." I said: "No, a lawyer." And she: "What's the difference. It don't make any difference." This by the summer's end. She knew then. She said the child was stirring. Mrs. Clyde came home.

"Oman? Oman?" I had gotten used to the parrot. Nobody had taught him to say it.

So it only remained for me to ignore the call, for Mrs. Clyde who ordinarily woke about eight o'clock every morning to be waked early that one time, not by the parrot but by Benjamin's whimpering. The dog had been sleeping on Mrs. Clyde's bed and Cassie had shut the attic door after us. Benjamin had whimpered at the door, a sort of squalling, the sound he made anytime he was shut out or shut in, Mrs. Clyde had waked and come upstairs. "Oman? Oman?"

Mrs. Clyde opened the attic door and Benjamin slipped past me, up the stairs.

"Oman?" said Mrs. Clyde. Because when she opened the door she was seeing more of me than she had ever seen before. I was wearing socks, that's all, having come down to let Benjamin in and having no sooner reached for the door than it opened. "Oman?"

I said, "Excuse me," and closed the door.

"Oman?"

"Yes," I said, talking through the door. "Yes, ma'am?"

"Is Cassie up there?"

"Yes, ma'am, I'm afraid so," I said.

I heard her sigh. "I want to be calm and sensible, Oman. No silly emotion. It's gone on all summer, has it?"

"Yes, ma'am, I'm afraid so."

"Is the child yours?" Her voice was trembling.

"No — well I don't know. I — we think it may be her husband's."

"Would both of you please get dressed and come down?"

"Yes, of course," I said.

"Tell Cassie not to be afraid. Tell her I don't blame her."

"Yes, I'll tell her," I said.

Mrs. Clyde went away, back downstairs. I went back to the attic.

"I heard her what all she said." Cassie had slipped her dress on. There was never anything to put on under it. I passed my hands over her. We both knew it was the last time. "I'm sorry," I said. She was weeping, using the hem of the dress to wipe her eyes. Her belly was pushed out high with the first child of hers, ripe as wheat, and neither of us knew if it were by me or the nigger she had married. "Trouble all the time," she said. She kept sighing.

I got dressed. "I'm sorry," I said. "What if it's mine?"

She turned away from me, lonely and small, her arms folded. "It ain't. It's mine and nobody else's."

"But what if I'm the daddy?"

"I married the daddy," she said. "Marrying, that's the trouble. Marrying ain't nothing but trouble. Married peoples! Married shit!"

"What will he do if . . . if it's too white?"

"It won't be," she said. "Nothing can't get too white. Not to suit me. It can't get too white. You don't have to worry."

I had a twenty-dollar bill, emergency money. I took it out of my wallet. "Probably you'll need this," I said.

"You gave me trouble. Don't give me money. I don't want no money."

"Twenty dollars," I said. "For the baby. Take it," I said.

She looked at me. "The baby ain't for sale," she said. "It ain't yours nor his nor hers," she nodded at the floor, "down yonder. It's mine."

"All right," I said. I put the bill back in my wallet. "I'm sorry."

"What's the difference? Leas' I don't have to wonder no more. You all the peoples that haves to wonder because it's mine and can't nobody buy it off me. You ain't lookin at no hoe."

"That isn't what I meant," I said. But it didn't carry any conviction because until then I'd never considered that it would ever be over, that it would ever end, that it ever could end. Youth has a way of making everything look eternal. Everything is a mountain then, out of time because it will always be there. You don't see it any other way until what you thought would be forever suddenly crumbles and disappears. It hurts your feelings every time as though God took it on Himself to trick you and then laugh.

"Ef you have to spend yo' money take it to a hoe house," she was saying, "it's plenty hoes be glad to take yo' money."

It was over. "I'm sorry," I said. It was all I could say, and I was sorry, sorry it was over, not sorry for anything else, just hurt and exposed and shamed and afraid because there was so much more of the same thing ahead of me and I was learning for the first time what it would be like, how it felt to lose and lose and lose, how you suddenly fill up with emptiness. You feel overfull of your own night, your own inner darkness. Your heart gets lost in it.

"Let's go then," she said. "Benjamin done let the cat outta the bag, didn't you, Ben?" She reached down and rubbed the dog's ear. "Sorry little old son of a bitch, you," she said. "Had to tell on us, didn't you? Couldn't mind you own business and leave other folksies alone? Huh, Ben? Huh?"

Benjamin wagged his fat rump back and forth. He was a quivering, leaping frenzy of love for this woman, this nigger who was taking it better than I ever could, and she was only nineteen. "Let's go then," she said. She stood up and smoothed down the dress. I went on ahead of her, downstairs to the high-beamed sunken sitting room with its pale stone fireplace and wrought-iron doors at one end, barred affairs which Mrs. Clyde had locked at night before she had me in the house. They led to her bedroom and bath and another sitting room. Now she'll lock herself in again at night, I thought.

"Sit down, Oman," said Mrs. Clyde.

"I'll stand," I said.

"No foolishness now, no hysterics."

"All right." I took a chair.

Mrs. Clyde motioned to Cassie. "You too, Cassie," she said.

"Ma'am?"

"Sit down. If you can go to bed with him you can sit down in the same room with him, can't you?"

"Yes'm. That's the truth," Cassie said. "That's right." She sat on a massive brown wooden chair, very Swiss and baroque, like a throne. It was very becoming to the thin pink dress and the slender, dark arms folded across her middle.

"It never occurred to me somehow that this could happen," Mrs. Clyde said. Her voice trembled. "Oman? Oman?" the parrot called from the kitchen. "But then it did, it has, and the blame is at least partly mine. I should have known two young people couldn't . . . yet Cassie was married. All summer long, you say?"

"Yes, ma'am," I said.

Perhaps Mrs. Clyde was wondering how to be calm and New England and sensible. There was a long silence. I saw Cassie's pulse beating in her neck. I heard the French china clock ticking on the mantelpiece. Cardinals were twitting outside in the shrubbery. On rainy days they clicked against the glass doors of the library, attacking their own reflections. I had made love to Cassie on the floor of the library. The red birds had clicked like Death tapping against the doors, the fireplace had smelled of cold soot. Yellow patterns in the rug had made Cassie all the more beautiful. Undressed she was like an Arabian Indian, anything but what she was. Naked she became human, the Word becoming flesh, I thought, remembering what had made her seem a person to me, and I saw the pulse beating in her neck where I had kissed and I thought she didn't belong on such a throne, but on rugs instead and naked and the musk and animal scent, the woman scent; it was like feeling the edge of a knife in the dark, feeling the sharp edge all blind and without knowing if you've been cut; it's that sharp and you can't say, you can't think the word, *love*, because God you're lost; God, you can only feel the humiliation, feel God laughing because He knew it was forbidden in the first place, to begin with, and being older than the world He knew its impermanence.

"Oh, dear," Mrs. Clyde was saying. Poor lady, it hurt her too, having to tell us to leave in that tone of stern reluctance that children hear sometimes, the voice of God speaking, pronouncing sentence, reproving. "If only you hadn't deceived me," she said. I knew then she had known it would happen, if she had only been able to admit it herself, she had known all along it would happen and that she would have to ask us to leave. It would leave me with a lifetime in which to think it over and consider those wrought-iron doors and the long evenings over conversation and tea, the inviting, not quite motherly kiss good night, the imploring look, Mrs. Clyde saying how safe she felt, how there was no need now, with a man in the house, to lock those gates. Now they would be locked forever against me, I thought, marveling at the pale smoothness of her skin, now, when it was already too late to do anything but marvel. Mrs. Clyde blushed.

There had been no way to know that Mrs. Clyde's New England conscience would make her write Miss Mary. "*Oman? Oman?*" The parrot was so wise and deliberate, back there with his seeds and his lusts and his little secret betrayals. Why, I don't know, Mrs. Clyde had named him Pan; maybe for the same reason the dog was Benjamin and the house was Spanish Colonial architecture and every piece in it selected so carefully I could almost feel where her eyes had lingered on a lamp or a bowl or a figurine, taking possession even before she paid for it. "Dear me, this hurts," Mrs. Clyde had said. "You'll neither of you ever appreciate just how much!"

I can only suppose that she somehow accidentally saw the announcement of Mary's engagement. I was already in Somerton by then, in law practice. I got the clipping from the *Nashville Banner* with a note from Mrs. Clyde which tendered veiled congratulations. "Cassie has a son, a baby boy. I've seen him," she wrote at the end. "Mrs. C."

Because she was even then waiting, struggling with that conscience of hers the way the sea must eternally struggle against those cold, rocky New England coastlines. In retrospect I can see her start the letter a dozen times and fold it away. I see Benjamin asleep on the floor beside her feet. She must have carefully chosen her words and chosen her time more carefully still, because the first I knew that anything was wrong was in the back room at the Somerton First Methodist Church when the music somehow didn't start and my father kept pulling out his watch. We already suspected what nobody wanted to admit, least of all Miss Mary's mother, Miss Louise, and the preacher, of course.

So it was over, quick as a snail draws in his horns. Miss Mary married a Memphis bank clerk and phoned me that same night so I could wish her happiness. With tears in her voice that I could feel on my own cheeks, Miss Mary said: "Oh yes, Oman," almost like an afterthought, "I finally heard from Mrs. Clyde." Then she had put the bank clerk groom on the wire. He giggled and apologized for stealing my girl, promising though that he'd take good care of her. They were at the Memphis train station just about to get on the Pullman for New Orleans and he wanted me to know by God that he was going to take good care of Mary. I wouldn't have to worry about Miss Mary, because by God he was going to take good care of her and wouldn't I have to agree that in all such cases it was a question of may the best man win? He must have repeated himself sixteen times: "May the best man win!"

When I had finally gotten Mary back on the wire it was no use trying to tell her I was sorry, no more than it had been any use trying to tell Cassie.

And my father, without knowing any more about it than the preacher or Mary's mother, Miss Louise, had only said: "Well, that's life. That's women."

Even if he couldn't know he was, by God, *he was* exactly *right*.

"Oman? Oman?" It was Nella Mundine standing beside the car where I sat in it, parked in her driveway. I'd been sitting there God knows how long.

"Hello," I said. "Hello, Nella."

"We heard you drive up. I kept thinking you'd come inside. Will you? *Oman?* Is something wrong?"

"I'm all right," I said. "I'm just coming in. Steve, is Steve here? It was a pretty sad funeral," I said, getting out of the car.

"I kept looking out," she said. She took my arm. "You sat so still for so long. I was beginning to wonder if you were all right."

I looked down at the tapering beauty of her arms, long and small and golden. I saw her hair, soft as sunlight, pulled back in a tight French roll. I smelled how beautiful she was and felt the nearness of her long, slender body. So much beauty, and the touch of her, brought back everything I had known and everything I had not known; it brought back everything I had gained and the sense of everything I had lost and I knew then that it was only my entire life I had frittered away, living it so long without love, so automatically, that nothing but the touch of beauty could bring it back to me when the years and the breath begin to come a little short. This is how it will come to you, it will come to you that it is too late, that it has been too late for a long, long time.

"There he is," Steve said from the porch. "What kept you so long?"

Nella held my arm all the way inside. "You've got to do something for me, Oman," she said.

"I will," I said. "You know I will if I possibly can."

Steve handed me a bourbon and water. The house was so cool and the library was so dark it took me a minute to get used to it.

"Oman," she was saying in that pleasantly foreign California accent, "this really has a meaning, a significance for me and Steve that you somehow fail to appreciate. This whole thing — Oman?"

"Go on," I said. "I'm listening."

I wasn't listening though. It seemed somehow that I had never seen her so clearly before, little Abolitionist bitch though she was and as foreign to me as anyone could be, with those deep brown eyes and that exquisite profile turning aside now and then as she spoke. I could see everything I lost. She was turning the cigarette in fingers that were as tapered and beautiful as her arms, and her voice going on and on in that compulsive way she had of talking around a point to coax and drive it home like cows in the summer's evening, driven from pasture to barn.

"Are you listening to me? *Oman?*"

"Of course," I said. And I thought: You would fall in love with your own nephew's wife. Given half a chance you would fall in love with her. She sits there and talks. She can't realize anything of what goes on inside an old man. She knows nothing of an old man's starving desolation. She talks and she smokes and she smiles and Steve sits and hardly pays any notice because he doesn't half realize what he has, that he owns this angel woman. Steve speaks up only now and then. They talk about the nigger and then about Willie Worth and the nigger again.

It began to dawn on me what it was she wanted. It slowly came to me that she was asking for the one thing in the world I couldn't do for her. It would (I knew even before she asked me) come down to a request for the single thing I couldn't do even if the world were to change somehow and put Steve out of the picture, even if time were to back up and let me have my youth again. You would have to look, did you ever see that part of her, to make sure she has a navel because she looks like nothing born, I thought, she's too perfect. And I thought, she's about to begin hating my God-damned guts.

"My dear," I said, "what you're asking me to do is utterly out of the question. I think you've built this thing up in your mind. It's gotten out of all proportion. You'll never know how hard it is to refuse you anything you ask — but the answer is no."

She looked at me, cold and pale at first, then suddenly red, burning with anger and her eyes unmistakably filled, brimming with hatred, and all of it just for me.

I knew it was the end of the line when I looked at Steve. He was trembling with it. It was obviously all he could do to control himself, to keep from springing at me then and there. The mask of Mars had entered his gentle features. His fine nostrils flared. His big fingers folded into fists. I might just as well have slapped her in his presence.

Refusing her now, in this instance — it was too much for them. All our pretenses came tumbling down then, like the walls of Jericho. The masque was ended and we were caught fast in the bitterness of hard reality.

2

Nella

I fled upstairs. They would fight now. Fists and chairs and breaking furniture. My heart rose. Blood went beating in my throat.

In the upstairs hall I stopped and held my breath to listen and the wonder of it came to me. They were still talking even though I had felt that Steve would move, I had seen the movement working in him, and Oman, calm as ever, and waiting for the attack — two strong men about to go at each other.

They were still talking. Steve's voice was thick and strange, filled with such utter rage. The sounds had blood in them.

Oman's voice was the same, but full of the same wisdom and guile, and unafraid. Neither feared the other. Neither would yield a point or back down.

I stood shaking and felt a fool for running. I went to my bed and lay down. In my room the voices were faint, like a vibration, an occasional lofting sound in the hallway and I had thought surely Steve would hit him, I had thought now my man will hit him, Steve's going to hit him.

It had seemed very important to get upstairs before the first blow was struck. I had thought to stay out of it until one of them had gone down and couldn't get up again, and I hadn't been sure who would lose, my Steve, or Oman Hedgepath.

I lay for a long time and I knew then that they wouldn't fight. That Steve had too much respect for him and Oman too much self-control, that whatever rage there was between them would form into words, those vibrations rising, wisping in the hall like smoke — deciding nothing at all.

Brilliant, beautiful me, thinking all along I could convert Oman Hedgepath, when all along he had been waiting for the perfect opening so he could knock me flat on my can.

I cried. It came to me that it is not losing that hurts so much, as it is the humiliation.

And Oman saw it plainly, his eyes saying: "Chicky doll, I hate to do this, but I'm going to kick you in the mouth. I'm going to knock hell out of you because you've been asking for it, and the time is now."

All the while I was saying back: "No, you can't do it because you're a Southern gentleman and all I'm asking you to do is one little old cotton picking favor. I'm radiating five thousand kilowatts of pure blonde sex and you can't do it to me, Oman, you know you aren't that strong. I'm asking you to drool and pant and lie down and roll over and play dead just this once. I'm asking you straight from between my breasts, to lower your gaze and murmur, 'Of course, my dear, I'd be delighted.'"

He paid no attention. He did it like a surgeon, with a quick, clean, antiseptic sentence.

Just when you think you've discovered what the power is that woman has over man, you meet an Oman Hedgepath who makes you lie down in cold rage and weep in cold anger and you know what it must be like to be raped then, to be jerked out of a car and knocked down and have that part of him stab in like a knife, to be crushed and smothered, to be numbed and reminded in the most humiliating, the most unthinkable way, that when all is said and done you're still only a woman.

You can think and read and win diplomas and wear a man tailored suit sometimes, but you've only to overreach yourself once and Oman Hedgepath is ready. He will trim you down to size and when it's over you'll feel like you never were, from birth, anything but a stupid, helpless, powerless gash.

Fair game.

3

Willie Joe

His mother. He was her youngest. Willie Joe was the baby and God knows she loved him. She called him "plum pretty."

"Little Willie, he's plum pretty even if I do say so myself."

Willie Joe's daddy died whenever Willie Joe was just a baby. His daddy come down of an evening with a bellyache and Willie Joe was just a breast baby, not even to his second summer whenever his daddy come down of an evening with the bellyache.

Ed Worth was a farmer his whole life. Ed Worth never done nothing but to farm. He managed niggers and mules. Knew them both like the palm of his hand. Knew dirt the same way. Could pick it up and feel when it was time to plant so he rarely ever had to re-plant unless of course he got rained and drowned out which can happen to any man now and then if he stays with the ground long enough. Re-planting is what makes the growing of cotton expensive on everybody, it matters not who he is.

He come in after dinner-time maybe about three of the evening. He was a lean man with strong square hands and bright blue eyes and he never said much but what he said he meant it. He complained of an ache in his stomach which would not go away and consulted with a neighbor friend who was right smart of a man to read and know of remedies and he, the neighbor man, told Ed Worth probably what he needed to do was drink a pint of whiskey and six ounces of castor oil and go to bed as that would cure nearly anything about the belly and guts, whereas the oil, anybody knew what the oil did, cleaned them

[253]

guts out, and the whiskey drew out the pain so the oil could work and the whiskey flushed on along with the oil and shined up and cleaned up where the oil had been so a man was clean as a bird barrel the next morning when he got up from his bed. Were it possible to squint through his insides they would be as clean in there as any bird barrel on any shotgun ever cleaned by the careful hand of the careful hunter.

Ed Worth drank six ounces of castor oil and a pint of whiskey and went to bed and his wife covered him up with quilts and put hot bricks wrapped up in rags under the covers to make him sweat and when it come about eight o'clock and the sun was down Ed Worth commenced to feel sicker, he said, and he said the pain was not gone but was only worse and so bad he did not think he could stand it much longer if something didn't happen to make him get easy.

About nine o'clock Ruby, his wife, rang the bell out in the yard and the niggers come and loaded Ed Worth into the wagon with shucks under him and quilts on top of him and Ruby got in with the baby, carrying the baby too, and though it was only six miles to Jackson they drove twelve miles to Somerton to the Dr. Dillworth Clinic because somebody said Dr. Dillworth was the only man in the world to do anything about a bad bellyache, and Dr. Dillworth would give Ed something to make him easy so that in the morning his insides would be clean as a bird barrel. The road was rough and the night was black and they did not spare the mules.

Ed Worth had commenced to moan whenever the road was too rough and it was the first Ruby knew of that he was sicker than anybody had suspected before that, because he was not a man to let himself go that way and make any sound no matter how much he hurt. He had been kicked and had his leg broke and his shoulder strained and lost two fingers in a corn grinder and never once uttered the first sound to say that he was hurting only to remark on it that he was. Never no groan ever come out of him before, that she knew of, until where the road was rough as it was and it wasn't any light so she could see and the baby got fretful and cried and didn't want to let the nigger hold him, the nigger that was driving and couldn't of held the baby anyway. She finally laid the baby down and taken Ed Worth's head on her lap, but Ed Worth wouldn't even have that; he was hurting too much. He didn't want nothing but to be made easy and it was that way until they got to the Dr. Dillworth Clinic. And it was deep in the night then.

Dr. Dillworth could not be found at first but was located at the Somerton Golf and Country Club where he was out there in a drunken condition playing cards and had to be throwed in a tub of ice water and dosed with strong coffee before he was in any kind of condition to look at Ed Worth, but after this happened Dr. Dillworth's hands were as steady as oak wood and he poked Ed's stomach one time and said it was appendicitis and why didn't they take him to Jackson if it was closer as the difference of six miles might make a lot of difference in the long run, swoll up as Ed Worth was and already ruptured and Dr. Dillworth said several things about country experts that drenched a white man with whiskey and castor oil like he was a sick cow and then sent him in when it was already too late to be operated on when if a doctor had gotten to him early it would be a better chance. He said: "Have I got your legal permission to operate, Mr. Worth?" And Ed Worth said: "Yes."

He never even woke up from under the spell of the ether. "Yes," that was the last word he uttered in life. Ruby kissed Ed Worth and he kissed the baby and the nigger come in and said good-bye to him before ever Dr. Dillworth wheeled him off into the room and put him under the knife. He never made no charge for the operation, Dr. Dillworth. He just said God damn it he did all he could. They say he was blinking back tears. All the Worth connections from everywhere come down to the clinic and set around on the steps and talked low and visited and done what they could for Ruby and helt the baby for her. Dr. Dillworth was a terrible man to blackguard whenever he got mad and disappointed and he come out blinking back his tears and had the young doctor with him, Dr. Ocie Pentecost, who helped him do the operation, and Ed Worth never woke up from the spell of the ether. Dr. Ocie Pentecost took Dr. Dillworth back to the country club and Dr. Dillworth got so drunk he could not stand up and said God damn it he done all he could do and he cried and said it was a sad comeup when some wise country son of a bitch would drench a white man like he was a God-damned cow and then send him into Somerton to die too proud by God even to borrow a truck and speed it up, no by God, haul and drag him in town behind a pair of mule fannies twelve miles.

Willie never down knowed his daddy.

Ruby hadn't nothing left but the baby. The others was all growed up and had their own famblies to mind after, not that they didn't help her. The girls helped her and their men was some comfort but the baby took up the empty slack in Ruby's heart so she couldn't never do too much for him.

Willie Joe loved her back and she grieved that it wasn't nothing she could do to get Willie his start in the world. He was the last and the youngest and hadn't no daddy to fend for and provide for him. Uncles he had, and brothers, but they are not the same as a daddy who can prize the boy's head between the barn doors and whip him when he needs it to keep the state penitentiary from having to do it later is the reason and can't nobody serve a boy that way but his rightful daddy, or say when he gets in small trouble: "Boy, go out and cut a goodly size branch, a limb, for by God I want you to whip me with it as I have not done of my duty by you for you to be in no trouble like this, for by God it was my duty to raise you different or you would not of did what you done." Until the boy can say: "Paw, I never thought." For it will give that boy the lowly feeling of his own meanness and his sin to have his own daddy say: "Boy, go out and cut a goodly size branch, a limb." It is only his daddy can say it and words such as that cannot be spoke by woman, nor reach from beyond the grave. Woman has but prayer. She has no fist hard enough to guide and curb her baby and her boy when he is coming a man.

Ruby grieved. Willie was hardly on with the county to drive the school bus than he was married and he taken to drink and the bus run off in the ditch and it was trouble about it and he couldn't drive no more as they taken away his license so he could only ride, and his wife, Flonnie, taken to waitressing; she wasn't nothing to begin with, had nothing, come from nothing, worked her toils on him, roped and lassoed him before Willie hardly knowed. He had no daddy to explain to him and warn him of how trashy women are always out to rope a man, how her legs give her away everytime what she is that she don't have nothing else she can offer, no dower nor nothing but tough brothers and her mean old squint-eyed daddy saying by God anybody good enough to crack Flonnie by God better be good enough to marry her and by God stay with her and look out for her or by God there was one place where any sly, slick-head son of a bitch would stand hitched and stay where he was put, in a house six feet long and six feet deep. So long as any woman had brothers enough and daddy enough how much more dower did she by God need? They was drinking men and whiskey makers and jailbirds and give Willie the very devilish drink that was the downfall of his job with the Sligo County Board of Education — driving the bus.

It was then Willie commenced to helping on the beer truck and never listened when Ruby tried to tell him it would be better to farm and keep his path away from Somerton. He would not listen. His beer job failed him and he taken to setting about the Crossing all day in his shirt sleeves like a nigger and laying down drunk on white whiskey.

There come a rash on his flesh and he was sick and nothing Ruby could do for him though he was her baby and all she had. Her girls could not comfort her. Her boys were gone to Hammond, Indiana, and something like a knot, like a closed fist taken hold under her breast bone until she could not collect eggs nor pick a peach without she saw the sorrow of her baby laying in the filth of his own destruction like a nigger, without she saw how he had fell so low niggers would look down on him and be sorry for him and buy him whiskey and go up to Templeton's and buy him a little bottle of paregoric so what he drank would stay with him. And Willie lain in his own corruption like a hog instead of a white man and Ruby could not stand the sight of milk nor churn butter and she thought to lose her mind and go plumb mad if there was not some relief.

Her girls had to take turns, one this week and another the next, to live with her. They fed her with a spoon and kept a close watch on her for otherwise she would drink vinegar if they didn't watch, until they knew she was very like to go out of her head or do herself some damage to her vital organs. She hadn't no interest in anything.

Until her oldest girl that knowed the Griggs woman that worked for Oman Hedgepath said Ruby should go see Oman Hedgepath and talk to him because he was one man who would listen to whatever anybody said and then tell his advice and help if he could because he was that kind of man, that his word was his bond and for any kind of trouble he was the best there was, it didn't matter what.

She hadn't no hope it would do any good, but Ruby went and seen him and a little while after that Oman Hedgepath got Willie on

with the police which was an idea nobody had never thought of before
that Willie was cut out for a policeman. Oman Hedgepath said when
a man was cut out for one thing and you set him to do another he'd
go sour on that other job just like milk spoils because he wasn't cut
out for it and there was a Plan (Oman Hedgepath said God was in
it), a Plan by which each man was called to do a certain thing and if
he done that thing then life would shape about for him into har-
mony, with his own self, and his fellowmen on earth.

Ruby loved her baby and he loved her back, and when Willie had
time he would dust out to her place in the country for a basket of
peaches or a few dozen eggs, or some butter. Anything she had. She
made him corn bread in the oven like he liked but never had at
home on account of his wife that waitressed and hadn't no idea
how to cook anyway. By her legs alone that much was plain, that his
wife wasn't no use in the kitchen. When Ruby had money that her
boys sent her and her girls give her she saved it till it was enough to be
of some pleasure to Willie, whereupon she give it to Willie for it
seemed to make him less fretful to have money in his pocket now
and then, burdened down as he was with a wife that couldn't have
nothing but little daughters and griped about her feet was sore and
pulled down ten dollars a week and tips and couldn't save nothing,
couldn't put nothing back so it was all on Willie until he couldn't
stand it no more sometimes and he would drink to ease his sorrow a
little, with his wife working days and him working nights until he
sometimes said it looked like there wasn't nothing else but work in the
world. It had commenced to grind on him he said.

"I tell you," Ruby said. "Little Willie is plum pretty. If I do say so
myself."

It come Monday.

All of Sunday Willie Joe had been sick with his feeling of worry.
And because he hated his house because it smelled wrong and it
looked wrong and the linoleum in the living room was cracked and
he hated his wife, he slapped her. He popped her a couple of good
ones, and felt sorry for his little girls because he had never wanted
them in the first place and there they were looking at him like they
knew it. They would put their little arms about his neck, Wanda and
Lana, and they would kiss him. They didn't care for their mother

nearly as much as they liked him because he felt sorry for them and couldn't deny them anything they asked for if he could get it for them.

His wife sat in the easy chair holding a washrag to the bump on her forehead where she had run into the wall when he popped her, holding her head. Her hair was like so much string, her eyes red, her big feet bare with the corns showing, and her housecoat wrapped around her. Hot though it was, hot enough to boil blood, she was shivering.

If she wasn't such a damned old ninny I could stand her better, he thought.

"You feel better, Daddy?" Wanda said. She was the oldest. She was seven. Lana was four and had to be taken to Mrs. Whitelaw's every day. Mrs. Whitelaw had taught Lana to call her Mammy and Lana kept saying she wanted to see Mammy. Sunday was the worst day of all days. Down in hell it's probably Sunday everyday, Willie thought.

The little girls climbed in his lap. Soon there would be another one and it would be a girl and Mrs. Whitelaw would teach it to call her Mammy. Mrs. Whitelaw would have Lana and the baby and it would make three daughters. He never wanted the first one.

I'll get myself cut, he thought. "I want Mammy," Lana said. She looked at her mother and started to cry.

Wanda told her to hush and Daddy would let them play with the rabbits if Lana was a good girl and wouldn't cry. *I'll get myself cut.*

The old lady started crying.

"What's your damn pain now?" he demanded.

She shook her head. His old lady was such a ninny she never made any noise when she cried. Flonnie was like a damned box turtle, she just hissed. She made him sick.

"I'll give you something to cry about," he said. "What's eating you now?"

"R-r-rabbit mess. They'll g-g-get rabbit mess all over my floors. I'll h-h-have to clean it up."

"If the rabbits mess on the floor Lana and Wanda will clean it up. Won't you?"

"Oh sure," said his old lady. "They'll clean it up."

"You shut your God-damned mouth," he said. "Hear me?"

"Don't get mad, Daddy," Lana said, kissing him.

He got up and carried the girls out to the backyard to the rabbit hutch. He put them down gently. "Now let's see," he said. "First we better feed and water them."

Wanda ran to the back porch and brought back half a coffee can of feed. Willie Joe put the dark green pellets on the floor inside the hutch. The rabbits began to eat. The doe was black. The children had named her Nigger. The buck was a white rabbit with pink eyes. The girls called him David, the old lady's idea perhaps. If Lana had been a boy the old lady had talked about naming him David because it was a name she liked. Probably she had been screwed one time by some traveling salesman son of a bitch named David, Willie Joe figured. He'd be damned, he had told the old lady, if a son of his would ever walk around in broad daylight with a pissy name like David.

So the white rabbit got stuck with it. Sometimes Nigger would bite, but David was gentle. Willie Joe got water from the hydrant and Lana brought the pasteboard box from the living room and he put the rabbits in the box and carried them in the house with the little girls following him. He put the box down in the center of the linoleum rug.

Of course the old lady didn't really mind the rabbits. When Willie backed off and sat down the old lady was ahead of the girls to the box and got David and cuddled him on her lap. Lana put toilet paper in a shoe box to make a bed for Nigger so Nigger could take her nap.

For some reason the rabbits helped get his mind off his worry. Willie Joe could feel the pain of his worry ease a little just watching the rabbits and listening to the cute things Lana said, listening to her "baby talk." Nothing was nearly so hateful any more and he didn't know why.

"You love Mama, David?" the old lady said.

There sat his old lady getting ready to drop another girl anytime now in a month or two and that would be more doctor bills and she would probably miss two weeks off work. Wanda and Lana weren't paid for yet. Ocie Pentecost got forty dollars for girl babies but you could pay him anytime or never. It was the Catholic hospital that screwed the dog and had to have fifty dollars cash on the God-damn line before they'd let a dying man have an aspirin. Willie Joe had felt like spitting in their Catholic faces both times. Stanley Bumpas

said half of that fifty bucks had to be sent straight to the Pope in
Rome, overseas. The Mayor, who had the real dope on it, had said
hell it was probably closer to thirty-five dollars for the Pope every
time a Protestant woman had to go in to have her baby, and if that
wasn't enough, said the Mayor, they had a hospital rule, although you
couldn't make the doctors admit it, that if it come down to a matter
of saving either the mother or the baby the Somerton doctors were
under strict contract and a bond of five thousand dollars to let the
mother die and save the baby so the priest and the Sisters could
sprinkle holy water on it and adopt it by force and have it raised up a
Catholic.

"Sure," the Mayor said, whenever the hospital was mentioned around
City Hall. "We pay for the Pope's whiskey. You ask any whore in Memphis if her best customers ain't Catholic priests and if Father don't tip
them fifty dollars just like you or me would act with a dime. If it
wasn't for the sick laying in there helpless somebody ought to burn
that God-damn hospital to the ground!"

You couldn't beat the Mayor for a man. Nobody could beat him.
Nobody pulled the wool over his eyes and got away with it because
he was sharp as a tack, a thousand one hundred per cent true blue and
never lacked for a smile and something cheerful to say.

"You love Mama, David?"

I'm going to have myself cut.

A couple of the boys on the day force had had it done. They said
it wasn't nothing to it. You went to the doctor and signed a paper
and handed him twenty-five dollars. You had to sign a paper because
once you were cut you couldn't have no more children, couldn't never
again knock nobody up which was the general idea but a doctor didn't
want some undecided son of a bitch coming back afterwards saying he
wasn't satisfied and wanted to be hooked up again because that
couldn't be done no more than you could unring a bell. What was
guaranteed was that a man would never know any difference and
could do it just as good or even better than ever afterwards. Screw all
you damn please.

The boys that had had it said it wasn't no limit to the women that
followed them around wanting a little, women that nobody would
ever suspect, ladies they couldn't name and didn't down dare even mention, like the fellow says, that once they heard a fellow was cut

they wanted some so bad they'd call him out of bed at night and beg him. A man would God damn come near to putting his phone on the secret unlisted, they said.

"Lay down, Nigger! Stay in your bed."

Worst part was the doctor shot you in the cods with a needle to deaden the pain. About like a mosquito bite, one boy said. Then he made a slit in your bag and took a pair of pliers and lifted up two little old cords and just crushed the hell out of them. Didn't take a jiffy and a man might be uncomfortable for a couple of days, but after that he was home free.

. . . myself cut.

It came to him that he hadn't wanted any of it. Not the old lady, not Wanda and Lana nor the one on the way inside the old lady's belly kicking and tumbling, not even the rabbits, really, though he hadn't nothing against the rabbits. But he was thinking that every problem in the world could probably be worked out and solved if a man that didn't want it this way would just be cut before any of it happened to him because with poor people it wasn't nothing in it for them but work anyway. In his whole life maybe a man might not ever be happy but a dozen times and half of them would have been when he was laid out drunk and couldn't down remember it. Maybe six times in his whole life a man would feel free. All the rest of it he was no better off than a nigger except he had white problems which a nigger could never imagine, he had worries a nigger never heard about.

The world could feel sorry for a nigger where it could never pity a white man. Niggers could lay on their bottoms and take government relief where a white man couldn't do it and still hold up his head in the daytime.

Because a nigger, he don't have nothing he has to prove.

It was time to put on his uniform. Not the old lady nor the girls, nobody noticed him leave the room. Back where he slept it smelled like the old lady, her sour stockings and her shoes. She never threw anything away. Her rags and shoes and uniforms were everywhere like a load on his back. He almost couldn't step or move without touching something in the bedroom that was hers and had her smell on it. Before he could dress he had to light a cigarette and breathe smoke to get the taste of her out of his system.

When he stepped in the bathroom to brush his teeth there were Wanda's and Lana's little toothbrushes on the lavatory and Lana's plastic duck she played with in the bathtub and his holster, belt and pistol hanging right where he always left it, on a nail over the commode. When he pissed, always the last thing before he left the house, he could zip up his pants and put on his gun. Then, by God, he was ready. He put on his hat.

Stanley Bumpas was in the car waiting when he walked out and they were off then without a word between them, down to the station to check in and read the bulletin board and the notices about wanted men and lost automobiles before they signed the duty list. Then it was nothing at all, the whole evening quiet while they sat parked at the Crossing where niggers milled around and strolled back and forth after church for a while, until about ten o'clock when the crowd petered out to just a single person now and then, now and then an old automobile muttering and bumbling across the railroad tracks and droning and sputtering up Fort Hill.

Mr. Stanley drove one block up to the Gulf station to take a crap. He had the dribbles, he said. He felt bloated any more, he said, after his meals. He'd been out to his farm cutting hay. "I hadn't hardly eat nothing a-tall, today. Hardly a bite." He was awful gassy just here lately, he said.

"Maybe you're wormy," Willie Joe said.

Far from smiling, Mr. Stanley considered it seriously. "No," he said finally, before he got out of the car. "I think it's something else besides worms. I don't know, I wonder if I ought to see a doctor."

Years before, Mr. Stanley's brother, Mr. Pharaoh Bumpas, had died of cancer, and every so often ever since Mr. Stanley himself seemed like he tried to have it. Mr. Pharaoh had been a Constable. He'd been in the bad habit of eating baking soda. Took it by the tablespoon for his stomach, so Mr. Stanley said, and it gave him cancer of the lungs.

Without being told the nigger gas station attendant cleaned the windshield and checked the tires, the oil and the water. Then he polished the headlights. Moths fell dying from the lights above the gas pumps.

When Mr. Stanley finally returned he looked pale and drained.

He got back in the car. "God," he said. "I don't know what's wrong with me. God dog if I can figure it." He took out his watch. "Well," he said. "It's Monday."

It come Monday.

4

Emma

Flip on the television. Listen to the radio. Read the Sears catalog, drink beer out of a pop-top can and paint her toenails Ivory Glow or Luster Pearl. Anything.

She might cut her hair off, wear it African instead of having all the time to have it straightened, pressed and yanked and set, sprayed until it felt like a dried paintbrush. She got the headache once a week on account of what she had to go through with her hair. It always took at least one Goody's powder and two aspirin to do her any good. She might be the first colored in Somerton to wear it African like the secretaries in New York City, the girls in *Ebony* magazine. She thought: Lord, anything.

Finally though it was too fuzzy-wuzzy. They looked like boys instead of women. Maybe a man wouldn't like it. Maybe it would be his printed invitation whereas he would think here I got me something so poor I can lean on her anytime it pleases me. She can't holler because she's so fuzzy-wuzzy.

Willie Worth opened her bedroom door. He walked right in. He looked better than yesterday, she thought, not so shook up. He didn't say anything.

He was pretty and soft and white. He looked hard but he was really a warm skinned man. Hair all over him growing black the way it did on his pale skin made him look rough, but he wasn't. He was smooth.

His peculiarity was his gun belt, wearing it the way he did so he wouldn't be without it else, as he said, he wouldn't feel safe. He undressed and walked around the room. He liked the rug. He liked to admire himself in the mirror on the bathroom door. He admired himself full length naked with the pistol slung on his hip. He might stand maybe thirty minutes sometimes and draw the gun and crouch and draw it. Like a kid.

She watched him. Like a kid in front of the mirror, like there was nobody else in the world as long as he was standing there, only him and the gun. When he got tired of the mirror he got him a beer out of the ice chest by the bed. He bent his elbow three times and the can was empty. Then he stretched out on the bed.

"I missed two periods. I'm gaining weight," she said.

"Lying," he said.

"Ask the doctor, he can tell you. I've had it and you gave it to me. I got a living child in me. If you don't believe and respect my word ask the doctor because it's true — a baby. Your baby, see what I mean?"

"His," he said. "You let that nigger knock you up."

"No," she said. "I don't need to lie and swear falsely."

"Then that's why — that's why."

"What do I want for myself?" she said. "But you can't take it away from a baby. My baby has to have what's his. I can't let anybody rob my baby. He can't amount to something if his mammy's divorced and hasn't got anything. He's got to have something. I can't have him come in the world without a dime, can I?"

"Mine," he said.

"Your baby. He will be almost as white as you. He's gonna be something and nobody isn't about to rob him now, before he's ever had his chance."

"So," he said. He left her side. "So." He walked like an old man. He looked like a man that has seen his doom, looked it in the face, lifted the white veil and kissed that bride on her dead teeth. He laid off the pistol belt and put on his trousers.

"Listen," he said at last, "I know a man, he's practically a doctor. You won't hardly feel nothing. He gets a sorta tube from the drugstore and runs it up there and it stays there a couple or three days. Then you bleed a little and then you just piss him out, see? Then you don't have no more problems. He comes right in your house and lives. I can phone him and he'll be here in a hour. You won't have no more reason to fight the divorce. Take a baby's got no daddy, see what I mean, you don't want him! He is bound to be half nigger! It won't take this guy hardly an hour to get here. He uses big words like the best doctor you ever saw. If I was sick I wouldn't want nobody else to look at me but him —"

"No," she said. "I never had anything before. I didn't know it. I went all my life and never had anything until it happened, whenever it was you knocked me up and didn't even mean to do it then. But you did. Then I had something. Now I got somebody that will love me, honor me. You can't take him. Can't anybody take him. I have and own something now that will cherish me. Once somebody knows what that's like you can't make them turn it loose. See what I mean, Sugarboy? I didn't even know what I was doing. I just wanted something different. You gave me that. Then I wanted you to quit. I found out you can't always stop what you can start. You wouldn't let me go. So I learned something."

"So," he said. "You're gonna have it when I could have a man, I mean a real expert here? He'd be here in less than an hour. If I called Oscar now he'd be here in forty-five minutes. You wouldn't hardly feel nothing. You wouldn't, but you won't. You have to *take*, don't you? You *wanted* it, didn't you? Something else white you can own because everything you have has to be white? He stays in a roadhouse. He's got half the motel rooms."

"No," she said. "Don't say any more about it."

"I seen him operate! It is this tube. It looks like a fishing worm. He runs it up a certain distance up yonder, he knows just how far. Then he tapes it the end of it to your leg and a couple of days later or three days maybe, see? It won't cost much," he was saying.

His hair lay on his forehead like moss. She watched him. The belly, the gut, the beginning of what he would become, the kind of man that would go to stomach until his stomach would own him. Just his appetite and his gun, she thought, that's all that will be left to him in the world, just only that. I had to love him.

"White," he was saying. "Bed, rug, wall, me." He had never noticed it before. "Me," he said, looking around.

"You," she said. "I had to love you."

"I don't know if he would operate on a nigger," he said. "Probably though he would if I asked him to do it special for me."

"Nevermind," she said. "You won't have to ask him."

He looked like he might hit her. She waited. Her heart skipped. She got ready for it.

There wasn't time to scream before his open hand cracked across her face like a pistol shot. He slapped her three times. He worked like a mechanic. The last blow started the blood from her nose. Her scream died in a low moan. She watched him back away. More as an afterthought than anything else, he stepped back towards her and chopped a blow to her solar plexus — the finishing touch by the master mechanic.

He stood back again, pushing at his dark hair. Tangled and curly, it fell like a dark shadow across his forehead. "And here it is Monday," he said reflectively. "And you never told me anything, never said nothing. You knew it but you didn't tell me."

"Keep a little something to yourself my mama always told me," she said. It hurt her to breathe. For an instant he looked as though he might work her over again. Then he seemed to change his mind.

"God," he said. He began putting his uniform on — the slacks, the short sleeve shirt, the hat. "God knows," he said.

Without another word he left. He closed the door. She moved. She limped across the room and bolted the door and went back to the bed. She tried to lie very still. That way it didn't hurt quite so much.

Yet no matter how still she lay little blooms and bursts and blood beats of sensation broke and grew like flower blossoms. When she closed her eyes they kept coming at her, starting with a dark spot, black like a seed and then swelling, coming at her head with one no sooner gone than another was there growing the same way, shaping and shaping her pain. She felt as though she were lying on a brick.

She cupped her palms above her navel and lay tasting her bitten tongue, saliva and blood pooling for long intervals until she was forced to swallow. She drank the black substance of her humiliation, blood and spit and pride and the shape of pain, the doom flowers, the bursting petals. She swallowed.

She dreamed.

A knocking at the door woke her. She got up and unlocked the door and staggered wearily back to the bed.

The undertaker came in. "Are you all right?" he said at last.

"I'm all right," she said.

"I heard sounds — fighting."

"You heard sounds," she mumbled. "Ain't that something? The big nigger man heard sounds in his own house."

"He beat you, didn't he?" He sighed. "Don't you even want to cover yourself? Do you lie here naked all the time? Did I hear you scream?"

She was too tired to answer. He drew the sheet over her. "Blood," he said. "He did something, didn't he? Is that what you want to live with the rest of your life?"

He was in the bathroom. He was bustling around. Picking up and straightening up like an old woman. Should have been, she thought, a woman. She swallowed. The taste of blood was not so heavy now.

"Keep on with him," he said. "He will finally kill you."

"I'm not worried," she mumbled.

"Do you need anything?"

"Open me a beer," she said. "Put it in my hand. Pop the top. Maybe you might not know how to pop the top. You get that off the teevee. It ain't in no books. Can you pop the top, big man? Say, Mr. Nuts?"

She put her hand out and closed her eyes. "Turn the radio just loud enough so I can hear it," she said.

He put the cold beer can into her palm. She gripped it. She felt weakness in her fingers. The radio snapped on:

"Rollin, bowlin and trollin the whole night through with your all night swinging beat of the most popular melodies brought to you each and every evening and all night every night. Have you tried the new drink everbody squawling and bawling about, Mister Twister in the peppermint bottle, the wine that is fine? What is the good word? Mister Twister. Who drinks the most? Colored folks! Yes, frens, Mister Twister. Put some in the ice box and have it ready for Freddie and Teddie, pour some for Eddie, and here's little Valentine Dulake with her hottest new recording of 'Please Me, Baby, Please Me!'"

The music poured out, a low-groaning, melancholy piano blues, a sobbing voice not quite man, not quite woman. The piano tromped its straight fourbeat. The disc jockey coming in over the music: *"Yeah, baby. Yeah, yeah, ohhhhhhh!"*

Like dust from the dusty road little Valentine Dulake's voice settled over Emma's eyelids until Emma saw the dust of home again, recalling how it had settled on the teacher lady's car, and the car so fine and

[269]

white and beautiful that little Emma Lee Lessenbery who was only five, and her sisters and brothers who had other ages, twirled and danced in the yard and made little dog squeaks like puppies. *Yipe!* and *yipe!* they squeaked. Little Emma Lee twirled until she fell down drunk from whirling and the yard rose and rocked under her at a slant. She saw chickens bathing in the dust under the house, the red lady hens rustling their feathers. *Yipe-yipe!* Emma Lee squeaked. All the children squeaked. Then Army, the oldest brother, drew a bucket of cool water from the well and rinsed the dipper so the teacher lady, who sat on the porch visiting Emma Lee's mama and papa, could drink. The teacher took the dipper and sipped only a few tiny swallows, like a bird.

"Such cold, delicious water," she said. All the children heard her. *Such cold, delicious water!* "Thank you, Army, I've had an ample sufficiency." They heard her. *An ample sufficiency!* The rest of the water was poured on Mama's zinnias because nobody else drank for being too shy. Nobody else could have swallowed for shyness. *Yipe!* and *yipe!* they shrieked and danced and fell twirling again and then listened to hear every word Papa said, Papa saying *"Three* might be too young. *Eight* might be too old." Emma Lee's papa, thin as Mama was fat, sitting with his legs crossed and smoking his pipe, something he always did on important occasions. He studied his thumbs in his lap like he was talking to white men, although the teacher lady was colored. But though black she wore a white dress like an angel. Papa's thumbs, the one thumb rubbing the dark bowl of the pipe and the other thumb cocked up and still like it was glad to be resting, like it was also listening to hear every word spoken, Papa saying: "Emma Lee, come here, baby girl," and Mama saying: "Emma Lee!" The children shrieking: *"Emma Lee! Emma Lee! Emma Lee!"* until Emma Lee was almost dizzy, ready to faint for being called to the porch. She went. She saw Mama, how Mama held the baby sleeping against her arm so cuddled up there and fat and dead to the world back of his little fists.

"On the porch where Miss Ethel can see you, baby girl," Papa said.

Army's strong hands took her. She was lifted straight up on the porch. "Here, child," Papa said, taking her on his lap. "Say howdy-do to Miss Ethel, to the teacher lady?"

"Howdy-do," Emma Lee whispered.

"Do you want to come live with me and go to school?" said Miss Ethel. Her teeth were pretty and white. Miss Ethel was pretty with her black hair pressed straight and severe and pulled back tight against her smooth head.

"Say, 'Yes, ma'am, thank you, Miss Ethel,' " Papa told her.

"Yes, ma'am," Emma Lee whispered, looking across at the sleeping baby. Emma Lee folded her own thumbs like Papa's.

The other children, all but Army, had skimmed away into the meadow like birds. They were pulling wildflowers from the deep grass that grew down below the yard in the fields. They were bringing the yellow flowers and making a circle with them in the dust, all about the shining white car.

Only Army stood very still and tall, just where he was, because he was sixteen and could carry Emma on his strong shoulders and be her horse. Around the well he had carried her and down to the laying house, beside the barn lot, to the pen where the mother sow lived with all her little pink-white children. Army could call crows with his mouth and whistle through his fingers so loud he could stop wild rabbits still in their tracks. He could fling a stone clean out of sight, he could clear the fence in a running leap and make dolls from corncobs. He made little fairy wagons out of empty thread spools and soda boxes and hitched bugs so they pulled the wagons like mules. Army stood very still.

"It will be better if we bring her. I will bring her to you," Papa told the teacher lady.

"Yes, that will be better," Mama said.

"We will explain it to her," Papa said.

"I'll wash her clothes," Mama said.

Army looked at his feet.

"Good," said the teacher lady. She went down to the car then. Papa followed her carrying Emma Lee in his arms. Mama came with the baby. The teacher lady admired the circle of flowers in the dust like something pretty and magical about her car; she hated to drive over it she said, and so when she got in to start the engine the children broke the flower circle so the car could pass and not drive over and crush the flowers. Army ran ahead of the car to open the gates, fast as a deer he seemed, running and running ahead to open the gates and the children dancing and singing, chanting: "*Teacher lady, teacher lady!*"

"Someday," Papa was saying, "you'll be like the teacher lady. You'll be a teacher. You'll go to school, baby girl."

"*School, school, school!*" the children sang. "*School! School!*"

Army came running back, closing all the gates as he came. Back Army came, almost out of breath. "She going to take Emma Lee?"

"Yes," Papa said. "She going to take her. Emma Lee going to school."

"*School! School! School!*"

Such a feeling as Emma Lee had never known came over her. Papa put her down. She could not dance any more. Emma Lee stood still and the children wrapped the blossom chain about her, around and around.

"*School-school-school!*"

Only Army did not sing. He ran away to the woods and did not come home until supper-time. Papa had to whip him. Papa had to strap Army for running off when there was work to be done. Army didn't cry. Army was so quiet the strap made a sound heard through the whole house, passing out into the yard, *whap-and-whap-and-whap*.

It was a strange thing, passing into the yard and into the woods, the sound of the strap without Army crying. Mama said finally quit. "Quit." "He won't cry," Papa said. "He being rebellious." "No," Mama said. "He grieving. You don't understand. Army grieving." "What he have to grieve about?" Papa wanted to know. "You don't understand," Mama said. "You have to quit and cease."

Papa quit. He put the strap on the wall beside his bed and sat down then in his own chair and pondered a sadness in his own heart. It was night and the children lay on their pallets. The owl talked in the woods. The baby woke and fussed. Mama rocked the baby and her chair went *squeak* and *squeak* on the floor and the wind stirred and brought a smell of cypress balls and clover and trees blooming in darkness. All the cattle were quiet. Only the owl talked and told himself woods business like an old man scolding with himself in the midst of his dotage, talking and scolding like three persons instead of one alone until day hushed him, cool daylight when the covers and quilts came damp and the children were cold and the roosters crowed and Mama put kindling in the stove until it roared in the kitchen. The children dragged the puppy out of the ashes where he had slept and took the

kittens out of the woodbox and played with them on the floor and
made the baby laugh. They had "crumble-in." Mama crumbled corn
bread in the milk still warm from the barn and the children ate and
Papa and Army washed up on the porch and had crumble-in and Papa
read the Bible verse and a psalm and prayed:

"Let the child learn and attend her lessons and please the teacher
lady, Lord. We thank Thee for that Emma Lee was chosen to go live
with the teacher lady. Amen."

One last time Army took her riding on his shoulders. One last time
she told the old sow good-bye. One last time she kissed Army, she
kissed her sisters and brothers, she kissed Mama and the baby and
then got in the wagon, up on the seat beside Papa who was wearing
his hat and his black coat and the wagon moved. Army trotted ahead
of it to open the gates. At each gate he waved. The children followed
too, chanting and chanting: *"School-school-school!"*

In her heart Emma Lee was fearful.

Papa spoke to the mules.

See the fences and the fields end on end the white butterflies and
the sunblind tearblind heat and morning's death of going away forever
and forever she knew it, of going away and the wheels said it in dust
of forever goingaway and the leaves by the road so dark green and
dusted yellow nodded with the sorrow of it, of going and going,
the mules and their ears listening for it first forward and then behind,
listening to hear it, the chains a-jingle with goingaway so she could
not look at the white sky waking and the clouds lonely and shaping
turkeys and old ladies and men with beards like God, all the things
Army could see and show her, Army who lay down and looked up and
showed Emma Lee how the clouds made chickens and dogs and the
shape of heaven and death and boats in the ocean. One day, so
Army had said, if he lived, one day he longed to see the ocean and
have a bottle of water from it, before he died he longed to see it if
only once. So it might be that when he got up a very old man and if
he had not seen it by then he would find Emma Lee wherever she
was and they would go to the ocean together even if so it turned out
they had to walk, they would go there and see it, he said. It had salt in
it. Mountains too, tall as the sky. Army longed to see mountains
someday. A single stone from a mountain, to carry in his pocket.
That would be better than money, he said. If a man had seen the

ocean and looked on a mountain then he would be rich all his life, said Army, he had said, "Because can't nobody take that away from you."

Papa was saying: "What you get in school, can't nobody take that from you. They can take everything else — land, house, money. But what's in your head, they can't take that. Because that's yours. One thing they can't take, one thing that will be yours. Once you get that then you finally got something. Don't grieve, baby girl. You fixing to have something now. Something none of your other kin will ever have. Don't grieve. Mama put ribbons in your hair, see? To make you brave. Anybody with ribbons on them, then can't nobody make them be anything *but* brave."

So she sat straight. Brave was to sit straight and not look at people. Brave ribbons. Let Papa raise his hat. Brave was to be quiet and straight sitting on the wagon seat with her shoes together side by side and her ankles touching and holding her hands in her lap with her thumbs folded just so, like Papa folded and looked at his. She drew brave deep breaths and didn't look at Papa when he kissed her the last time and set her down, but went straight in the house with the teacher lady and sat on the bench beside her while the teacher lady played the piano and said: "See here, this is middle C?"

The piano had strange teeth, some black and some yellow. It smelled ugly.

"Middle C. Can you play middle C for me?"

She would call the teacher lady "Miss Ethel." "Not Mother, not Mama, because I'm not your Mama or your Mother. I don't want you to get a wrong idea. I'll call you Emma. We'll take off the Lee. A new name for a new home, a new life. Emma?"

"Yes, ma'am."

The teacher lady took her to see the bathroom. "Here we have the bathroom indoors instead of out in the yard. You'll get used to it."

It was as Miss Ethel said. She had gotten used to it. Because it was best that she not see her own people, because it would have only made her sorrowful and homesick, Miss Ethel waited five years before she took Emma to the country to see her people. Emma had remembered Army most of all and had looked forward to seeing Army, as though he would be there to open the gates in front of Miss Ethel's car.

He was not there. Another boy instead opened the gates. There were flies on the porch Emma had never noticed before. Army? When she asked Papa told her Army had worked as a logger and somehow had cut his leg with a chain saw and bled to death in the woods, so deep was he cut and nobody being about to help him or hear him holler. There was a dangerous thing, said the old man (hardly the Papa she remembered), a chain saw. It made such a dangerous whine and bucked so when a man tried to hold it, like a thing with a mind of its own. A crosscut saw, said the old man, now there was the better thing, but a chain saw, hadn't he allowed it was dangerous?

With their grief so long buried and the knowledge of Army's death so long ripened in their memories how could Papa and Mama appreciate what Emma felt? Miss Ethel had changed the subject. One of the small children had offered to take Emma and show her where Army was buried. Papa had lost the sight of one eye, he said. The eye had clouded over, gone milky. For a while it had been, looking with the one eye, like peering into a hallway filled with smoke, the old man said.

Mama, who looked young as ever, held a baby on her lap. When Emma looked at her Mama looked away, avoiding Emma's eyes.

"Cataract," Miss Ethel said, folding her white dress about her knees. "Perhaps."

"I sees very good with the one that the Lord left me," Papa said. "It does very well. I said I wondered if milk caused it. I used to drink milk."

"When his eye began to fail and started to going out he quit milk," Mama said. "He laid off of milk and that saved the sight in the other one."

Miss Ethel looked at Emma and said nothing. Later, she said, on the way back to town: "I wanted you to see what you came from, what you were taken out of, because that way you can know what your opportunities and advantages are. Now you see, don't you?"

"Yes, ma'am." She had been thinking only of Army, thinking: Where is he? Seeing the woods, hearing the cruel whine of the saw, like the screech of a cat, and suddenly it bit his leg and let the blood out of him. Had he lain very still and thought about the ocean to get his mind off of it? Death? "Where is Army?"

"Who? Your brother? In heaven," Miss Ethel had said. "Didn't you want to see his grave?"

It was as though she had gone back to see her people and had found only strangers living in a dirty house on a miserable little patch of ground: thinking afterwards, "Emma Lee is dead and gone too."

Miss Ethel suffered from angina. Miss Ethel suffered a stroke and died. Emma, by then already eighteen, played the organ at her funeral because it was what Miss Ethel would have wanted. The undertaker had come to call on Emma afterwards to compliment her, to help, he said, in any way he could. Miss Ethel's money and her property went to relations in St. Louis and Oklahoma.

The undertaker, L. B. Jones, would send Emma to Nashville, he said. Miss Ethel would have wanted her to be educated for a schoolteacher. Meanwhile she could play for funerals and earn her keep when she wasn't off at school, he had said.

She had thought since: *If I had married him then.*

Then L. B. Jones had seemed a little like God. Because she hadn't known anything. She hadn't known anything of the pool hustlers and the black and tan clubs, the men. She hadn't been told. Miss Ethel had raised her in a tower of purity. Emma hadn't had any way to know, hadn't had any experience but the experience of trust and obedience so that she had gone away pure, dumb as a chicken right up to the moment it had dawned on her one Thursday night in the front seat of a Buick that she and the girl on the back seat (already engaged and growling like an animal) had been speaking a different language.

The man had drawn something smooth and silken all the way down her legs and off her feet before it had come to her that she had said *yes* without even knowing she had said it so that she no sooner corrected it, saying *no!* than his hand had cracked across her face backhanded like a pistol shot. He was in her like a charge of electricity, before she could catch her breath, the car doors open and the blood-tasting swell of her mouth, the blooming pain flashing back of her eyes and then the cold glow of the stars, her head back then, just off the edge of the seat and stars seeming to stare back at her across the frozen distance.

It had made her cautious. She had healed, and done it next for love, and when that proved false for caprice, then for viciousness, and finally only to see what it was like; a few times she had endured it for money which lay in her hand like slime until she spent it.

Then she graduated. Then she came home and married him, who had some notion, some creeping worminess about him that wanted nothing but the dark and long old man's sighings as though each time he must gather courage sufficient to survive the grand ordeal of self-giving, all of which might have been as wonderful as he imagined it was had she married him before.

If I had married him back then.

"Is that all you want then?" he was saying. She opened her eyes and looked at him, his pajamas, his red silk robe, the pince-nez glasses. Poor son of a bitch, she thought, poor hopeless son of a bitch. "I've been afraid you'd drop the beer and spill it. Probably that one's warm now. You've been holding it so long. Want me to open you a cold one?"

"Can't you sleep?" she said. "What's wrong with you?"

"I heard the sounds, the scuffle. Him beating you. It worried me."

"You mean you care? About me?"

"You know I do," he said. "Emma, I can't help it. If I were a man of violence." He didn't finish it.

"If you were a man of violence, what?"

"I'd have killed him just now. He wouldn't have walked out of this house alive. Mosby offered me his gun. I . . . I couldn't accept it."

She smiled. "That's all right," she said. "A gun — that's not your style anyway. The fat boy has a gun, huh?"

"Yes."

"The fat boy's supposed to protect you. Is that it?"

"He needed a place to sleep."

"Who is he?"

"Just a man."

"Just a man," she repeated. "He's no ordinary man. I know that. Somebody sent him to you for protection, didn't they? You think a fat boy like that can help you?"

"Emma, if you'd just listen. If you'd just be reasonable. I could forgive a lot; I could forget a whole lot. I'm not a man of violence, you know that. But I'm a man of strong will. If you'd make me a promise —"

"No promises," she cut in, "you know better than to ask for promises. Promises, from me? Have you gone crazy?"

"Emma —"

"Either take me like I am and live with me —"

"That I won't do," he said.

"All right, then. Do I have a right to fight you in court?"

"Yes," he said. "We both have our rights. At least you understand that. And you know if I insist on my right to equal treatment before the law . . . you know."

"Something might happen," she said. "I know. You might break your leg — or your neck. But then that's your problem, isn't it?"

"I suppose it is," he said.

"Sure," she said, almost tenderly. She struggled to sit up and swung her legs down, sitting on the edge of the bed. She sipped the beer. He averted his gaze. "Sure, if just once —"

"You're all right then?" He opened the door to the hallway.

"I can manage," she said.

He went out and closed the door. She sat looking at it, the gleaming knob of gold, the framed white expanse of the panels.

The beer leaked. It dripped from her chin into the valley between her breasts. She watched it make a dark line across her stomach, slanting, questing off to the left. It went down and was lost.

5

T. K. Morehouse

Well it will end up they will have every man, woman and child into court before it is over.

It were noon before I reached Somerton with a new batch of papers. It was not raining.

I pulled into Alf's and got water in the radiator and air in the tires and bought three dollars of regular and a Coca-Cola. I says well at least it is not raining.

"No," says Alf, "but it is hot enough to burn the tee-tee off a brass bulldog."

I stepped inside the station. "Do you know the Mayor?" Alf says.

"Howdy," I says. The light of recognition did not come into his eyes. I seen he was too drunk. He sat on the sofa like somebody had shot him and throwed him at it.

"Greetings, greetings, greetings," says the Mayor. He lifted his finger.

"They got that nigger that killed Mr. Thingamabod," says Alf. "You hear about it?"

"They did?" I says. "Then it *was* a nigger."

"Sure," Alf says. "I guess he'll get the hot seat. They caught him over about Chickasaw. He claims to be innocent but they got the goods on him."

"They all claim to be innocent," I says. "But they're every last one guilty. What was the name of the fellow he killed, the groceryman?"

Alf snaps his fingers. "Aw, Thingamabod," he says. "Who was it, Mayor?"

"Bivens," says the Mayor.

"That's it, Bivens," Alf says. "They caught this nigger last night over about Chickasaw. He was driving a Dodge automobile. The Sheriff brought him over this morning and him and Mayor went down to the store and took him inside where the crime was committed at and he confessed. Signed a written confession, didn't he, Mayor?"

"Always," says the Mayor, "always take him back to the scene of the crime. That will break him down, every time."

"Was he a great fat nigger like they said?" I asked.

"Stripped down you could see ever bone this nigger had in his body," says the Mayor. "All that fat nigger stuff was just a damn rumor. This was the skinniest nigger to be alive that I ever had to look at; where he had his knee joints looked like a couple of mock oranges. Took him in the store and showed him the very blood of his dead victim there behind the counter and he confessed. We found a tire tool in the Dodge and when the blood on it is compared to Mr. Bivens's blood I believe I'm sure it will show up as the same blood and the tool that done the damage. This nigger's a dope fiend and he was in there lookin for dope and when Mr. Bivens didn't have no dope to give him he went wild and climbed all over Mr. Bivens with that tire tool. I was able to scrape a little blood off of the tire iron with the help of the Sheriff."

"So he wasn't fat," I says.

"Shit naw," says the Mayor. "Have I seen you somewhere before?"

"Morehouse," I says. "T. K. Morehouse."

"Sure," he says. I knowed he was too drunk to move. I seen him trying to think. His face screwed up in a knot. It didn't help him none, though. He couldn't think. Of course he couldn't. "Glad to see you again," he says, finally. He had to give it up. "Open me a Coke, Washington," he told the nigger.

"I'll have to unlock the machine," says Alf. "Washington ain't much of a hand with keys. About like a monkey."

"Well, he can open a Coca-Cola, can't he?" says the Mayor.

"If you hand one to him right-side up he can, most of the time," says Alf. He opened the machine and got a cold one and handed it to Washington. The nigger reached in the pocket of his overalls and took out an opener and opened the Coke. Then he handed it to the

Mayor. I never seen a nigger move quite so slow. He went back then and leaned against the edge of the counter where he always stayed at. I says: "Well, I better go. I have to call on Dr. Templeton. Reckon he's at the drugstore?"

"Never knew him to be no place else," says Alf.

"That's the store on the corner acrost from the bank, ain't it?" I says.

"Ohhhhh," says the Mayor. "Now I remember. You got one for Doc too? What's he done?"

"One what?" says Alf.

"I expect he told his tenants to git off his farm if they wanted to vote. Fired 'em," I says. "That's the reason for the most of it, you know. They git restless and want to sign up and register and vote."

"What?" says Alf.

"He's that Fedral shitbird that's serving all them God-damned papers on everybody," says the Mayor. "Stirring up nigger trouble."

"It's my job," I says. "As a United States Depedy Marshal."

"You got one for me?" Alf says. "What if I tell Washington he can't vote?"

"Then you'll probably git one if they must to find out about it," I says. "They're gonna give everybody one afore hit's over."

"Don't worry, Alf. They'll get you by and by," says the Mayor. "Just thinking about it gives me the Fedral shits. I thought I knew you from someplace," he says, looking at me.

"That's right," I says.

"Washington, you son of a bitch, you can't vote," Alf says. "I forbid your ass ever to *think* about voting. You hear?"

Washington nodded.

"Now do I get one?" Alf says.

"If the right man hears about it you will," I says.

"Can't you take my name? Ain't you the law?"

"Look, Alf," says the Mayor. "I'll turn you in, if it means that much to you."

"Well," Alf says. "I don't mean to make no Fedral case out of it, but I wouldn't want people to think I was some kinda nigger-loving chickenshit. If everybody else gets a paper, I guess I ought to have one too. Who else has got 'em?"

"Ohhhh," says the Mayor. "Let's see. Chief Fly, Oman Hedgepath, me of course, Junior Burkhalter. I couldn't name them all. Dr. Templeton."

"I'd sure be much obliged if you would turn my name in," Alf says.

"Washington might have to sign the complaint too," the Mayor says. "Hell, they have to have all kinda proof. The FBI has to come talk to every last bastard concerned, don't they?"

"That's right," I says. "It's a right smart involved in gettin a paper. A fellow just don't snap his fingers and have one right now."

"Well by God, I *want* one," Alf says. "I can guarantee Washington will sign anything I put under his nose. You have it wrote up and by God I'll have Washington sign the son of a bitch."

"I'll do that very thing for you, Alf," says the Mayor. "I'm damned if I won't." He picked up the half-pint on the floor beside the sofa and took a drink. "Drink?" he says to me.

"No thanks," I says. "I better go give Dr. Templeton his papers. Is he a man given to temper and rash fits?"

"Nice a white man as you'd want to meet," says Alf. "You can tell him I said so."

I got in my car and drove up Main Street and got a parking place in the front of the Bargain Store acrost the street from Templeton's and plugged a nickel in the parking meter and walked across the street and on in the store. They was laying tile.

"What's happened here?" I says.

"Had to jerk out my soda fountain," says the man. He was pale and gray like a drugstore doctor. "Had to jerk it out or otherwise, you know the kind of unpleasantness that goes on nowadays, otherwise."

"Are you Dr. George Bethpaige Templeton?" I says.

He looked at me kind of funny.

"Why, yes," he says.

"T. K. Morehouse," I introduced myself. We shaken hands.

SEVEN

1

Lord Byron Jones

Embalming a child that began a tiny fish swimming and ended a bird flown, just so, a dead child, like the cage where there used to be a finch or a canary. It was like a sad empty cage, a dead child, that handled so easily one man could do the job alone without help. Since Benny was invited to eat supper with Lavorn and Mosby, L. B. Jones had told Benny: "Go on, I will do it alone."

A child is everything the same as a man but smaller. The head took work to draw off the swelling. He must draw that off with a needle. The job needed wax and paint so that the father would never believe he had hit his son, had struck him down in anger and stomped him with angry feet, so nobody would believe, or hardly believe, that the cage ever had been emptied in the first place. The art, he thought, contemplating the art. He made an incision in the neck and opened the carotid artery, deftly, gently. If the spleen had been ruptured there would be blood pooling and heavy in the lower cavity, blood to be drawn off; the circulation pump must be set going first.

He went about sponging the little body, adjusting the head clamp for the child beaten to death by his own father, the little head all lumpy and swollen, the little rib cage broken.

The child, a little man in every particular with delicate fingers and sweet curving eyelashes.

With a quick movement the undertaker clamped on the rubber tubes from the embalming machine and set the pump working.

L. B. Jones tightened the belt of his white half-sleeve smock, slipped off the black rubber apron, and stepped out into the hallway for a smoke. The dead child's father was there seated in a white chair beside one of the tall gilt-framed mirrors, his face frozen in the impassive ashen mold of guilt and sorrow, the shock of what he, the father, had done, as it were almost engraved in his forehead, wrinkling from the down-looking eyes. The man had been crying again.

"I killed my baby," he said. "Somebody oughtta kill me." Saying it to nobody, telling the silence, the walls. The woman, the child's mother, sat farther down from him, young and slight and afraid. She stood up. The undertaker lit a cigarette. She approached him, her voice fierce from fright, saying:

"Henry Parsons would been better off to kill me because me I'm the one; he hates me, you understand? Henry have to pay the police every week. Money every week? Got himself in trouble; I got myself in trouble. You wouldn't understand. Rich mens like you don't know the trouble of poor peoples like us. What the poor has to put up with, what the cops will do. So Henry killed his baby. But listen, Mr. Jones! Maybe you can't believe it, but Henry love this baby. If you could believe . . ."

"I believe it," said the undertaker.

"Then maybe I can stand it," she said fiercely. "See, Henry hate himself. Can I tell it all to you?"

"Yes," the undertaker said.

"I has to help pay the fine too, so they'll keep it quiet? Because we can't go to jail. They got the papers on me and they got the papers on Henry. So if the man says to you either do it or go to jail, if the man says either let him do it or by God he will put Henry in jail or something worse! What then? I told Henry. I said, 'Honey, I have to do it. Honey, I can't stand it if they take you away from me, because, baby, you all I got in this world.' But see, Henry he don't understand. See, it's really me! But he had to hit the baby boy. Will God forgive him, Mr. Jones?"

"Forgive?"

"Will God forgive him, mister?"

"Yes," said the undertaker.

"Someday we have to stand up," Henry Parsons, the father, said. "Some one of these days."

"Hush," she said.

"Some one of these days," he repeated. "You think they even gonna put me in jail? They ain't. I only kicked the breath out of my own little man. It ain't bad enough to suit them. They won't even lock me up!"

"Baby, Henry, hush," she said.

"Somebody got to stand up someday," he said. He was crying.

"Will they lock him up, Mr. Jones?"

"No," said the undertaker. "The doctor reports it to the Grand Jury, that's all. Henry didn't mean to do it."

"How do they know that?" said Henry Parsons. "What I meant?"

The undertaker turned away because it wouldn't help to tell them that some crimes were so awful nobody had the heart to bring them up for prosecution. It wouldn't help to attempt to show them that there was nothing gained sometimes. A woman strangled her baby. A father slew his son. A male nurse in a home for the feebleminded killed an old black man, drowned him or smothered him because he hollered and kept the other inmates awake at night. Best to bury all such dead. Sit still and say nothing, thought the undertaker, thinking: That's what you tell yourself. Nothing's perfect, you say.

The law can do only so much, go only so far. The rest is up to the heart. Finally it is a decision inside man himself, what he will do in any given situation, how he will choose to live or to die. He has to live. He has to die. He might as well have a choice long as he's about it. Someday, somebody must make a stand.

"Somebody got to stand up. That's what they saying," Henry Parsons said.

If the spleen had ruptured there would be blood in the lower cavity, the undertaker remembered, blood to be drawn off, and the body must be checked, tested for hardness. "Excuse me," he told the mother. He stepped back into the embalming room and closed the door.

Handling the child was easy. He folded back the delicate little lips and took two sutures, drawing the black thread tight before tying the stitches off and folding the lips down for the effect of a quiet and pleasant smile. The sutures changed the whole appearance of the sad small mask. The undertaker tested the flesh of the cadaver here and there.

Carefully he drew off the intestinal gases and put in fluid.

He shut off the machine, unhooked it, and rolled it over next to the wall, and closed the neck incision. Then he painted the calm little face, beginning with the eyelids. While the paint dried he rolled the casket into place and dressed the body. Finally he loosened the head clamp and laid the little boy in the casket. He stepped back to consider the hands, whether to fold them or lay them at the sides. As he took the little hands and brought them forward the phone rang. He folded the hands and shucked off his rubber gloves before he picked up the receiver. "Yes, hello?"

The wires hummed. There was a click and then the buzz of the dial tone broke into the wordless void. He put the phone down. It rang again. Again he answered. Again nothing. The third time he let the phone ring a dozen times before he answered, and after he had said hello he heard the other's breathing, as though constricted, brought short with pain. "If you have something to tell me, go on and say it. I know you're there," said the undertaker. "Whatever it is, say it."

When there was no answer he hung up and went on about his work, arranging the body in the casket, and waiting for the phone now, thinking that perhaps they had only wanted to make sure where he was. Since he hadn't left town and hadn't called Oman Hedgepath to call off the divorce hearing they would be forced to act now, forced to do whatever it was they felt they must do. Now he would face the test, he thought, standing back. The child looked at peace. He closed the lid. *Somebody must . . .*

He opened the door and rolled the casket out into the hallway. Both parents stood up and followed him to the small visiting parlor on the south side of the hall. He positioned the casket. He opened it and trained a soft light on the child's serene face. Then he draped a scrim of cheesecloth over the opening. The cloth gave a little more separation and distance, and made the features softer. If a person were not careful it would seem that the child were only asleep and might stir any instant, open its little eyes, and smile.

In a distant part of the funeral home the phone was ringing. "Now," said the undertaker. "He's ready." He stood back. "See for yourself."

"He looks real pretty," said the mother. "See here, Henry Parsons? Don't he look pretty?"

The man was fearful, yet when he looked in the casket his face lost its frozen quality. Tears began to loose themselves on his face. He sat down on a folding chair. The tears kept coming.

"He grieving," she said. "He finally grieving now." She sat beside her man, she, who endured everything for love of him, who sacrificed anything to protect him. It was too private a moment to watch. The undertaker quietly stepped out into the hall. The phone was like a tingling nerve. He removed his glasses and walked slowly into his office and sat down and put his hand on the white telephone, feeling the vibration of each ring. He answered it then. The voice was Benny's.

". . . downtown at the jail," Benny was saying. "They picked up me and a white boy that come in the cafe looking for Sonny Boy. They need sixty-seven-fifty in cash. You'll have to bring it but . . ."

"I'll bring it," said the undertaker.

"But maybe you better not. If you're busy and can't leave, like you say. Maybe you could get somebody else."

"I didn't say I was busy. I'll bring it. I'm not afraid."

"You finish the child?"

"Yes."

"Then if you coming right away they won't take me downstairs." There was a pause. The new voice was a white man's, very slow and drawling. "This Mr. Ike. If you come on right now we won't put him downstairs, whereas otherwise we have to take him on down there and lock him up. You coming right now, L. B.?"

"Yes sir," the undertaker replied. "Right now."

"Well, I don't mind doing anybody a favor," said Mr. Ike. "They brought in a white boy with him, a God-damned Yankee agitator. He's going downstairs, I'll tell you. But Benny's one nigger we never had no trouble out of and you being a good nigger yourself. Well, bring sixty-seven-fifty in cash and come right on."

"Yes sir, right away."

The undertaker hung up the phone. He got up slowly from the desk and walked to the window and opened the venetian blinds. Beyond the impotent glow of the street lights the sky to the west was still red. It was streaked with the long dark clouds of a summer twilight. A truckload of cabbage went past, headed slowly down the hill towards the packing sheds.

He turned from the window and went back down the hall to the little parlor. The man and woman sat side by side, holding each other and whispering. "Excuse me," said the undertaker. "I have to leave, but you can send for your kinfolks and friends when you're ready for them. Someone will be here to help you."

"You won't be back, Mr. Jones?" said the woman.

"No. I won't be back."

"Then, we thank you, Mr. Jones, for what you done," she said. "You made him so pretty I said we didn't hardly know him."

"You're welcome," said the undertaker. "Good-bye."

"Good-bye, Mr. Jones," said the man, speaking at last.

The undertaker stepped into the bathroom off the hall on the opposite side and washed his hands, slipping his glasses off to rinse his face and dry it. The water was only faintly cool. He wiped his glasses with his handkerchief, put them back on, and went back to the embalming room. There wouldn't be time now to clean it up. Now would mark the first time he had ever left this room to disorder. It was a rule never broken, that the room must not be left this way with the paints and the syringes and the scalpels unwashed and out, the empty fluid bottles not thrown away. He slipped off the white smock and hung it carefully on an empty hanger and put it on the clothes bar. Then he took his black coat and put it on, careful not to bruise the pale carnation pinned to the lapel.

Out he went then to the garage, feeling his way in the dark past the two hearses and the body wagon to the seven-passenger Cadillac sedan. Before he married he had always driven the sedan or taken a hearse. The cars all needed driving or the batteries would go down. Emma had insisted he buy the convertible so the two of them, man and wife, could drive cars as alike as twins. He got in the sedan and started the engine and backed out slowly into the street.

They could have done it, he thought, in the garage. They had the chance.

Except for the sedan the street was empty. The Crossing, below the hill, was silent, Monday evening under the street lamps, Monday evening over the empty tracks where the elk and the buffalo had grazed and wandered before the coming of the black men and the whites who owned them. A bat circled into the light of a street lamp. He put the car in forward drive and went slowly down the hill. There was no sign of anything wrong.

The dead son and the living father, the parents sitting by and whispering out the words of their grief, the downtrodden poor, he thought. It happened to them and they accepted it and said only: "Someday we have to stand up."

Run? The undertaker smiled. The hushed wind from the dark street fluttered at the window beside him. No, the nigger wouldn't; wouldn't run. *I won't.*

The police cruiser came quickly from behind him without showing lights. He was forced suddenly into the curb. The headlights of the police car flashed on once, then off again. Almost as soon as he had touched the brakes the door beside the undertaker opened. A quiet constricted voice said: "Cut the engine, leave your keys in the switch. Come on! Cut your headlights."

The undertaker obeyed. A hand gripped him firmly above the elbow. He got out of the car. The policeman pushed him to the police cruiser. The back door was open. He got in the back seat. The white man got in beside him. The police car moved, heading straight for City Hall, up the wide street, but then it turned right suddenly. The car lurched forward again.

"What's the charge," the undertaker heard himself saying. "What have I done?"

In the front seat Stanley Bumpas gave a strangled laugh.

"If you're arresting me there must be some charge."

"Reckless living," said Willie Joe Worth beside him.

"That's good," Stanley Bumpas said. The car was passing down a dirt street, slamming into potholes, splashing into puddles. Stanley Bumpas coughed.

"Mr. Oman never down called me," Willie Joe Worth said. "Nobody never down phoned me all day long. I waited to hear if somebody would give me the news that the divorce was called off, but nobody called."

"I told you, didn't I?" Stanley Bumpas said.

"You didn't forget to call Mr. Oman, did you, nigger?" Willie Joe asked.

"No," said the undertaker.

"Now you see?" Mr. Stanley said from the front seat.

"For the last time, you *ain't* gonna call him?" Willie Joe said. "You didn't mess up and forget?"

"No," said the undertaker in a voice he hardly recognized as his, sounding as though he had run a long distance already. He was trembling. He sat bent forward like an old man. Something prodded his side. "You didn't forget?" He caught at the thing to push it away and felt the pistol. Then something stung him on the head, a numbing lick like a yellowjacket sting. He no sooner put his hands up to shield his head than the pistol was jabbed against his ribs, striking his side like a wedge. His arms came suddenly down. The blackjack caught him again, above the ear, again on the cross swing above the eye before he could duck. The blows landed with cold, surgical precision. The gun hammered piston-like against his ribs. The welts rose on his head. Each lick and gouge found its mark. There was no lost motion.

"Pop him, Willie Joe, lay it on him!"

"Try to grab . . . my . . . pistol . . . will you!"

The undertaker felt a hot saline surge rising from his belly into his swollen throat, pouring and pouring. In his arms, into the pit and marrow of his legs it poured; at the same time he was thinking: Only be calm. Be still. Don't be a fool. Take it. Take it. Beat them that way. God, help me. Help me beat them that way.

But the flowing, dripping agony, he found, had a will of its own; his body had a deeper mind, a spinal intelligence that knew its own will and its own fear so that suddenly, in spite of his calm reasoning, this other stronger spirit took him over. The undertaker began to move and thrash. His hand groped out and caught the door handle. In the same instant that the door opened he was out with it in a long lunging somersault leap above the road hearing the tires already skidding in the muddy gravel before he struck and rolled and found his feet and ran in the direction he faced when he stood, straight across in front of the headlights and through the tall horseweeds to the fence, grabbing the rusty, gritty mesh, going up and over the barbed wire strands that crowned it, his clothes ripping as he dropped to the ground inside.

Behind him, on looking back, he saw the cruiser's spotlight jerk crazily at the sky and stab down then, sweeping the fence above the weeds. Running straight on he dodged behind a bulky shape and smelled grease. He felt the twisted, broken outlines of a wrecked automobile and knew then, for the first time, where he was. Holding his breath he heard the wild outcry of Cucumber's geese and the muffled barking of the blind man's dog.

Over the top of the wreck he saw the second-story windows of the Look and See Cafe and Tourist. The cherrytop light on the police car began flashing. The cruiser moved up the road and stopped in front of the cafe. With ruby red turns the light splayed the street and swept the sides of the cafe. Girls appeared at the upstairs windows. The screen door slammed. The rotating light made the other wrecks in the junkyard seem to leap into existence each time it touched them. With each pass the light repeated the revelation of mechanical carnage. The light licked and licked again, like a burning tongue of blood.

"Police," said a voice; flat, clear, matter of fact. "Police!" A tattoo of blows, wood on metal. They battered the door to Cucumber's shack. The dull, disembodied echo drifted across the junkyard like river sounds. The knocking ceased. The undertaker heard a mumbling voice, Cucumber's, then the louder one. "Police," it said. "Police."

The blind man mumbled again, the whining voice of the blind cripple who dissected metal carcasses by feel and touch. The gate to the junkyard squeaked.

"This away, gentlemens," said the whining voice.

Their flashlights revealed him, a black man in rags, creeping like a wounded animal on the ground, dragging himself through the gate. "This way, gentlemens."

They stopped. The flashlight beams trembled along the edges of the fence.

"Make it easy on yourself," Willie Joe Worth called. "Come out! We got you anyway!"

"Look all you please, gentlemens!"

The geese were quiet a moment. The dog barked monotonously.

"Unchain the dog!" Willie Joe Worth called. "Come out! The dog's gonna find you!"

"Stay still where you're at, gentlemens. I'll fetch the dog!"

"Sure, didn't I tell you?" Stanley Bumpas said.

"Shut up," said Willie Joe. "Let him get the dog."

"Didn't you ever hear of handcuffs? He could be to the south city limits of St. Louis by now. What made you leave off the bracelets?"

"Will you shut up?" Willie Joe said.

"The dog, gentlemens!"

"Give me the chain," Mr. Stanley Bumpas said.

"Careful, gentlemens!"

"*God* damn," said Mr. Stanley.

"Bite you?" Willie Joe asked.

"Bit me," said Mr. Stanley. "The son of a bitch. Look at him, lay-ing on his back."

"Stan, Stanley! Hey!"

The shot cracked close to earth, like a breaking stick.

"Did you have to do that?"

"He bit me," Stanley Bumpas said. "See how it's done? Right in the head."

"Gentlemens! Gentlemens?" The geese began whooping again.

The undertaker walked into the open. "Here!" he called.

The flashlights found him. "Hands on your head! Walk this way!"

Both men were on him. They bent his arms behind and handcuffed him.

"Wait, here," said Mr. Stanley. He took something from his pocket. "Here," he repeated.

"Tape?" Willie Joe said.

"Paste his mouth shut," said Mr. Stanley.

Willie Joe peeled a strip from the roll of adhesive tape, tore it off, and stuck it across the undertaker's mouth.

"Takes three strips," Mr. Stanley said. The tape smelled fresh and clean.

"What about his eyes?" Willie Joe asked.

"They can't holler," said Mr. Stanley. He turned to the blind man. "You know who I am, nigger?"

"Police?"

"We never been here, understand me?"

"Yes sir, gentlemens!"

"You can get another dog."

"That's right, gentlemens!"

"Let's go," Stanley Bumpas said.

At the road they kicked him. His knees hit the rear of the car. He fell. They opened the trunk, lifted him, and threw him in on top of tow sacks and tire tools and a coil of forgelink chain. The flashlights snapped off. The trunk lid closed, leaving in his mind's eye the last image, cruel faces under uniform caps, faces lit by the glow of the red taillights.

The engine started. He smelled exhaust fumes. He heard gasoline sloshing in the tank. The tires eased, after a time, out onto smooth pavement. The car gained speed. West, he thought, out the Memphis highway. He rested his head against the spare tire, thinking: Let it come. Lord, let it come swiftly.

His scalp burned where he had been hit. The swollen places felt like wet cotton. Moving his hands he felt the rough tow sacks and the links of unyielding chain.

I had only to be willing, he thought, instead of unwilling, to have had the best the black man's world can offer.

Peace, beyond understanding.

He thought: Forget the could-have-beens.

Be with you now, and forever more.

Came down from heaven and was made man.

The dead child: He will not come back to me, but I will go to him.

The darkness roared like a torrent. He seemed hurled downward, between walls of night.

Then quiet. A dew-garden stillness silent as tar; silence, swooping in concentric rings. The automobile had stopped.

In the stillness, inwardly, he prayed. Not for strength, not for life. Only peace, the swift-coming deliverance. Amen.

The trunk lid opened, he opened his eyes and saw the faces, the cruel red fire of them. The breath of the men was on him. They lifted him, straining and heaving. They seemed to move in a sort of fire. The night air touched him. They raised him up and he walked. Gently now, they led him, whispering to themselves. Trees were about. Damp grass was underfoot. Out of the grass insects sang the green smell of life swollen, swelling to burst like a swarming of gnats everywhere and everywhere all about him as though to make him heartsick for all the loss of everything past, the heart's exile, fleeing, running and running away. Lunging, running alone, headlong.

"*Kneel.*"

All silently, his knees buried themselves in grass. Something kicked.

Kicking him down into scarlet and viridian marshes, mashing him to earth. Kicked with a flash, an echo so it seemed then, slowly and slowly and secretly like the growth of flowers. The blow was over him and he, under it, seemed to flow out of himself like oil, in warm secrecy towards a single pinpoint of fading, plummeting fire.

2

Steve Mundine

The phone was ringing. Steve held doggedly to the paper, the conservative afternoon daily that gave Oman so much solace with its David Lawrence columns and Old South editorials.

Nella came downstairs calling him. Steve pretended not to hear.

She came in the library. "You're wanted on the phone," she said. She wore white shorts and a white blouse and white canvas shoes.

"Who is it?"

"The police station," she said. "Shall I say you're not here?"

He laid the newspaper aside. She could be so cool. The Nordic calm, the ice, he thought, inherited from her Norwegian father. "I'm sorry," he said.

"It's all right. Will you take the call?"

"Yes."

He picked up the phone. "This is Steve Mundine," he said.

"Lawyer Mundine?"

"Yes," Steve said.

"Police station, Mr. Ike Murphy. We got a little situation here," said the voice.

"Go on," Steve said. There was a silence.

"Hate to call anybody at home on nothing like this but the boys brought in a white fellow who claims some nigger at Fisk up in Nashville give him your name. He says you belong to the In-Double-A-Cee-Pee which of course I know the somebitch has got to be lying about that. But he had your name and we have to let him have one phone call so this is it. The Mayor has handed down the verdict that this is the law on it, one phone call, like the little boy says." The old man's voice was quavery.

"I see." Another silence. "Go on."

"Somehow he got your name," said old Mr. Ike Murphy, pausing, reaching as it were into the depths of a kind of reluctance, not believing what he really knew already.

"I see," Steve said.

"Somehow he got your name. I tell you now, Lawyer Mundine, these somebitches is getting smart. Here he comes a stranger to Somerton and knows the name of a respectable white lawyer. Getting smart like the little boy says. Tells me he's got the right to make this call. Soon as ever the boys get back we're gonna work his settee over though to where he will by God think twict before he sets down in another nigger restaurant again."

"He sat down in a Negro restaurant?"

"Look 'n See Cafe and Tourist, Mama Lavorn's whorehouse," said Mr. Ike. "Next thing I guess he would of went upstairs and bought himself a slice of the dark meat, only the boys went in and caught him red-handed setting down. Had done ordered a meal."

"He's a white man?"

"What I'd call a gosh-damned white nigger," said Mr. Ike. "Whereas, like the little boy says, if you wanted to hang up now and then leave your phone off the hook so when he dials your number he'll get the busy signal, then that's it. It's perfectly legal then on orders from the Mayor that if he gets the busy signal for his one call then we can take him downstairs, see what I mean? You wanna hang up now?"

"Just a minute," Steve said. "Who is he?"

"Now it's entirely up to you on how you want to handle it. He's standing right here. He's got a beard like Jesus Christ and in about fifteen minutes when the boy get back he's gonna wish to thunder he was by God crucified. They'll stick an electric cattle prodder to his you know what. So if you wanna hang up and then leave your receiver off the hook, on that, like the little boy says. He can't call nothing else but this one number he's requested which is your phone there at home. So just give the orders, whatever you wanna do, Lawyer Mundine. I know what Oman Hedgepath would do, by God."

[298]

"I'll tell you what you do, Mr. Ike. You put the prisoner on the phone, right now," Steve said.

"That's your decision? You wanna *talk* to the somebitch? Lawyer Mundine?"

"Yes. You put him on the phone. Right now."

"You don't have to talk to him," said Mr. Ike.

"Put him on the phone."

Mr. Ike sighed. "All right. If you won't listen to good advice."

The receiver at the other end sounded as though it were being rubbed, the old man stroking it, caught in his indecision, between two fears, the immediate fear of Steve Mundine and the continuing fear of his job. The policies of the Mayor and Oman Hedgepath, of Sligo County, Somerton, Tennessee. The South.

Then a new voice, a young voice.

"Mr. Mundine?"

"I'll be down to get you," Steve said. "But listen carefully. I'm going to drive right down. I won't be five minutes. But to make sure they don't hustle you downstairs you keep talking on the phone. Give information as though I were asking for it. Your father's name and address. Your school, if you're a student. Where you were born. *Anything*, see?"

"I understand."

"All right, keep talking. I'll be right there."

"I was born in Connecticut . . ." the young voice began.

Steve put down the phone. He called upstairs to Nella.

"They've got a white boy at the jail, arrested for sitting down and ordering a meal in a colored restaurant. I'm on the way to get him."

She was coming down the stairs. "I'm going with you," she said.

"Like that?"

"Like this," she said.

They stepped into the warm night, the quiet brooding heat.

"I'm going to break the speed limit," he said.

"Go ahead. We need to break something. A white boy?"

"With a beard," Steve said, starting the car, putting it in gear.

"Oh, God," Nella was saying. "A beatnik."

"Probably," Steve said.

Without stopping at Main Street he swung around the corner and hit sixty before he touched the brakes, passing the Presbyterian

Church. He touched the brake again in front of the picture show advertising its Elvis Presley movie. The light at Fourteenth was red. He ran it, hit the brakes one time just front of the Somerton Hotel, and U-turned, parking against the curb in front of the police station.

The bearded boy was still on the phone. Mr. Ike stood a few feet away. Both were visible through the plate glass windows of the station.

Nella didn't offer to wait. She got out on his side, sliding under the steering wheel. He opened the glass front door, with "Somerton Police Department" on it in gold leaf. Nella went ahead of him. Steve saw the groping expression on Ike Murphy's pale face. The old man's mouth opened and closed like a trap when he saw Nella, and then Steve coming behind her. The bearded boy was still talking into the phone.

"Ah," said Mr. Ike.

"How much is the fine?"

Mr. Ike walked behind his counter and steadied himself, his face turning a deep red.

"The fine?" Steve Mundine said.

"Sixty-seven-fifty will make his appearance bond," said Mr. Ike. "Cash."

Steve wrote a check.

"Where are you from?" Nella was saying.

"Connecticut," the bearded boy said.

"Talking to the prisoner not allowed before he is freed," said Mr. Ike. "On that, like the little boy says."

"Are you a student?" Nella said.

"Yes," said the boy.

Steve Mundine pushed the check across the counter to Mr. Ike.

"I can't take a personal check," Mr. Ike said, his hands trembling, "Cash."

"You know my check is good," Steve said. "Make out a receipt."

"I was through here a few days ago on the train," said the boy.

"Shut up," Mr. Ike said. "The rule is no talking."

"Are you speaking to me?" Nella said.

"No ma'am," said Mr. Ike. He wrote out the receipt. He took the check, pretending to study it, and then pushed the receipt slowly across the counter to Steve. "He's free to leave now. Court meets to-morrow at ten-thirty."

"They also arrested a Negro, Benny Smith. He's in a room back there," said the boy. "Nobody's come for him. He was talking to me when the police walked in and grabbed us both."

"You have a Negro here named Benny Smith?" Steve said.

"I do," said Mr. Ike.

"What is the amount of his fine?"

"Appearance bond is sixty-seven-fifty," Mr. Ike said. "Cash."

Steve Mundine wrote another check. This time Mr. Ike had the receipt ready for him. "I'll get your nigger," said Mr. Ike. He walked into the back hallway, opened the door to the booking room and hollered. "Okay, Smith, somebody's done bought you."

Benny Smith came up the hallway to the counter. Mr. Ike walked behind the counter, jerked his cane bottom chair a few feet back and sat down. He opened a magazine.

Nella took Steve's hand.

"I'm much obliged," Benny Smith was saying. "They called Mr. Jones but he hasn't come."

"I'll take you home," Steve said.

"Just back to the cafe, please sir, if you will, Mr. Mundine. They called Mr. Jones, that's who I works for, but something must of happened to him."

They were on the sidewalk now in front of the station.

"Who?" Steve said.

"L. B. Jones," said the tall Negro. "Lord Byron Jones. I works for him."

The bearded boy and the Negro got in the back seat.

"Are you the witness?" Steve said.

"At the divorce tomorrow, yes sir, that's right," said the Negro. "Me and my sister, Lavorn Smith."

"They just walked in and grabbed us," the boy was saying.

"He come to town looking for Sonny Boy. Him and Sonny Boy Mosby, that's Lavorn's adopted child — him and Sonny Boy met and had a conversation while coming on the train from Memphis. He seen Lavorn's from the train window. So he come looking for Sonny Boy and was hongry. Lavorn said well for him to set down and she would feed him because he was hongry so I set down to talk to him and wasn't thinking nothing about it."

"They grabbed us," the boy said. "They twisted my arm. It's lucky I had your name. In Nashville when I said I was coming to Somerton they gave me your name. Otherwise I wouldn't have known who to call. I'd heard about police brutality. Now I know what it is at first hand."

"That's possible," Nella said. "Is your arm hurt much?"

"In the shoulder, but not much. Only a little, I think."

"Tomorrer when it going to hurt," Benny Smith said. "That shoulder will speak to you tomorrer."

Steve drove up the dirt street by the railroad track and stopped to let Benny Smith out at the Look and See Cafe and Tourist. "Much oblige to you," the Negro said. "I'll get your money to you."

"I'll get out here," said the boy, opening the door.

"Come with us," Steve said. "You won't be safe here."

"So this is segregation," the boy said. He got back in the car and closed the door. "So this is how it is. It says tourists, doesn't it?"

"It's a whorehouse. They keep girls upstairs."

"So what?"

"We're doing you a favor," Nella said. "Isn't one arrest a night enough for you?"

"I'm only going by what the sign says," the boy insisted. "So the girls are prostitutes."

"Yes," Steve said.

"Where are you taking me?"

"Home with us," Steve said.

"That's best," said Benny.

A Negro woman came out of the cafe to the car. A fat Negro man in a brown suit came out behind her. They stood by the car.

"L.B. didn't show up," Benny said. "This here's Lawyer Mundine. He come and got us, me and the boy."

"Thank you, Lawyer Mundine," said the woman.

"This here Lavorn, my sister," Benny said.

"Will you get out and come in?" Lavorn said. "Would you like some beers? This here is Sonny Boy, Lawyer Mundine, Sonny Boy Mosby. He's my baby."

"Let's go in," Nella said. "Why don't we?"

"Not now," Steve said quietly. Then to Mama Lavorn: "We can't this evening, Mama Lavorn. We have to take this boy out of harm's way. Another time we'll come visit you."

"I understand," Lavorn said. "This your wife, Lawyer Mundine?"

"Yes."

"She's awful pretty."

"Thank you, Mama Lavorn."

"Was the other man they caught down there at the jail?" Sonny Boy said.

"I didn't see no other man," Benny Smith said. "Only me and this white boy. I phoned L. B. but he never came."

"They caught a man in Cucumber's junkyard and throwed him in the trunk of their car and hauled him off," Sonny Boy Mosby said. "We stood right here and watched them do it."

"Hush," said Mama Lavorn.

"A man?" Steve Mundine asked. "A Negro?"

"He was a Negro," said Sonny Boy Mosby. "We stood by and watched them do it. Never opened our faces. They shot Cucumber's dog."

"The police?"

"That's right," said Sonny Boy. "Killed a blind man's dog. Cucumber out there in the darkness burying his dog now. They throwed that man in the trunk like he was a sack of cow feed. We all just stood acrost the road here and watched."

"Hush, Sonny Boy," said Mama Lavorn. "Hush!"

Two girls wearing black slacks and red blouses came out of the cafe.

"This is Lawyer Mundine and his wife, girls," said Mama Lavorn. "This is Jelly and Coreen. Say hello to Lawyer Mundine. He got Benny and the white boy out of jail."

"How do, Lawyer Mundine?" said one of the girls. They looked like twins, both spare and slender, exotic and pretty. The other girl was silent. They leaned forward, looking in the car and smiling.

"They didn't see no other man at the station," Sonny Boy Mosby said. "The one we saw them catch and pitch into the trunk of their car? They didn't see no trace of him."

"Maybe they brought him in the back door and put him downstairs," Benny said. "Maybe he could be downstairs and that's how we

[303]

didn't see him. They left us off and went out on another call. I talked to L. B. He said he was coming but he never arrived. He's got a child up there though. His mind's all worried. He had that child to fix up and embalm. You can't blame him."

"Could you find out about the man they caught, Lawyer?" said Sonny Boy Mosby.

"Unless somebody phoned me about him, either the police or the man himself, it wouldn't be any of my business," Steve Mundine said. "Tomorrow I'll inquire about it though. Maybe the man was drunk, sleeping it off in the junkyard."

"That has to be what it was," said Mama Lavorn. "Won't you come inside?"

"My husband won't let me," Nella said. "Another time though . . ."

Steve put the car in gear. "Come again!" Mama Lavorn called.

" 'Bye!" said the girls, Coreen and Jelly, waving.

When they reached the corner and turned towards the Crossing the boy spoke from the back seat. "What a night," he was saying. "What if I hadn't had your name?"

"They would have taken you downstairs," Steve said.

"And used the cattle prod, like the old man told you on the phone?"

"Yes, probably," Steve said.

"Couldn't you sue them?" the boy asked. "Isn't that torture? And I thought he was kidding."

"Electricity doesn't leave any marks," Steve said. "Besides, you have to have witnesses. You have to prove they did it. An accusation isn't enough. No grand jury in this part of the world would render a true bill on a report like that. Your word against theirs."

"So the people here approve the practice. Putting a cattle prodder to a man's testicles."

"That's right," Steve said. "If you're an integrationist, then they approve of it."

"Yes," Nella said. "Nobody's kidding you."

They passed into Main Street. The police car was parked in front of City Hall. The night police were standing at the desk talking to Mr. Ike Murphy.

"There they are," said the boy. "The bastards."

"It has to be experienced to be believed, doesn't it?" Nella said. She put her hand on Steve's leg. "To be believed. You see I'm from San Francisco, but I married a Southerner. Steve's from Chattanooga."

"Are they this way in Chattanooga?" the boy was asking. Steve turned in the driveway. He smelled mown grass wet down by sprinklers turning and humming in the darkness.

They took the boy to the library and fixed him a Scotch and water. Nella and Steve had a bourbon while the boy told about his travels, sipping his drink and rubbing at the sole of his shoe, having sat back and crossed his legs as though to bring the tennis shoe within reach so as to rub it while he spoke, always questioning, questioning himself, Steve observed, probing his Yankee's motives for coming into the South as a student stranger, a vagrant tourist. Young men, Steve thought, young men went to Mexico in the same spirit of questing, wanting to know how that foreign country was, wanting to see and to know that which they were not supposed to see and know. The boy, like the rest of his serious kind, sought truth. It was a passion with him. Truth in everything (rubbing the shoe sole, stroking his beard, sipping his Scotch very slowly). Obviously the boy was well bred. He was educated and mannerly. Even charming, as he began, now and then, to smile. Nella carried the other end of the conversation. She gradually told him of her own and Steve's commitment, and mentioned the undertaker, L. B. Jones.

"So much terror," said the boy.

"Yes," Nella said. "I wonder if we can really stay here, Steve and I. You see we promised each other we would. There's the practical thing. Steve's a lawyer. How can he practice here once people understand that he isn't for segregation and electric cattle prods? Merchants, doctors, teachers — others can hide their beliefs, but can a lawyer? Not and be honest about it. On the question of the law there can be no doubt, regardless of how one feels, one way or another, segregation is now against the law in the United States of America."

"But aren't more laws needed?" the boy asked.

"Not since the Supreme Court has ruled as it has," Steve said. "Laws enough are on the books now. Enforcing them would bring about complete and immediate reform. Every lawyer, North and South, realizes this, but no politician in either part of the country will admit it. In the North they call for more laws. In the South they fight the idea. It's a mock battle over a mock issue. The demagogues want the votes and will say anything to get them. The answer, as President Kennedy has said, lies in the hearts of men, not in the laws. Law can go only so far."

"What do you people think of the President?" the boy asked. "I mean as Southerners."

"Honest men believe he is probably the one man who can pull us through this crisis peacefully. I believe Kennedy to be a godsend."

"Why?"

"Because he's honest," Steve said. "Even when it hurts him."

"What about your segregationists?"

"They hate him, that's true. But even if they hate him, still they respect him. They know how he stands. They know he's not a turn-coat. Secretly most of them, even the ones that howl about him the most, admire and respect him for what he is," Steve said. "If any man can pull us through this, Kennedy can."

"I believe in him too," the boy said. "He may be too honest for his own good though. Sometimes I wonder if America is really ready to be told the truth, if lies aren't really what this nation wants. So you people plan to stay here, in the South?"

"I can't really answer that," Steve said. "The choice is between some sort of unhealthy compromise and going into the streets and joining the sit-ins ourselves. We might do more to stay here and fight it where we can. In the end it might be more meaningful than taking the extreme course."

"Direct action, non-violent protest. That's all I heard in Nashville. There at least you can sit down to a meal with Negroes. You can talk to them. But not here. Here you can't even talk to them, can you?"

"As you've seen, associating with them presents its difficulties," Nella said drily.

The boy began yawning. He declined another drink and politely said he wasn't hungry, though he might take a glass of milk. Nella took him to the kitchen. Steve followed. The boy drank two glasses of milk and then went upstairs with them and was shown to his room, protesting that he could stay in a motel, but thanking them at the same time for their hospitality.

In their own room Steve and Nella lay abed, awake, and talking.

"We did something," Nella kept saying. "We finally *did* something." The feeling was very fine and encouraging, like the end of a day spent hiking. Steve lay with his conscience washed clear, his mind smooth and unworried.

"We struck a blow for freedom," Nella whispered close to his ear.

3

Mosby

We stood there and didn't do nothing and we *knew* who it was, that it wasn't no sack of cow feed and wasn't no drunk man and we stood there just like we stood back when they come in and took Benny and the white kid with the Jesus beard. We didn't say nothing. It scared us so bad.

The little young lawyer Mundine brung Benny back and took away the white kid with the beard like Jesus and Mrs. Osborn says: "They taken Jesus," because she saw it, that ain't got any sense only what's left after they beat it out of her poor old brains but she saw what he was like. "Jesus," she says. And screamed.

But Benny and Mama Lavorn didn't say nothing. Only opened Mrs. Osborn a headache powder and poured a beer down her. "Where you going?" Mama Lavorn said.

"I'll be back," I said. "Only acrost the road. I'll be back."

"Why go over there, Sonny Boy?"

"You know what it was. We all know what it was. Who we trying to kid?"

Didn't nobody answer or say nothing. I went out the screen door and crossed the road. It wasn't no lights burning because of him blind. I called him.

"Over here," he says.

My eyes got used to it. I could see him like a shape of something there behind his house bent over in his garden, all squatted down. He was digging.

"They leaned on your dog," I said.

"I can get another dog."

"Who was it?" I said.

"Who what?"

"That the cops got him. Who was he?"

"Do I know you?"

"Sonny Boy Mosby."

"Come back — back home? But you don't sound like no little boy. They shot the dog. I don't know which one. My dog bit the cop."

"Wasn't it the big one?"

"I don't know, Sonny Boy. Where you been at?"

"We stood acrost the road. We watched it. The fuzz throwed him in the trunk of the automobile and didn't nobody move a pin to say nothing. They took him off."

"Who?" Cucumber said, his face down in the earth, digging his dog's grave hole.

"Was it him?" I said. "You known me from since I was a little boy. Was it him?"

"Was he who? You know I can't see. It were just a man!"

"Come on," I said. "Didn't he say nothing?"

"He come out from hiding and give himself up. They didn't have to go get him. He give himself up."

"Wasn't it him?" I said. "Can't you tell me?"

"You mean the undertaker?"

"L. B. Jones," I said.

"It was. I smelled him," Cucumber said. "They shot the dog and I smelled that and he come up then and they put the steel bracelets on him. Flowers and that other; death the way you smell dead peoples at a funeral. I knew it *was* him."

He put his dog in the hole and commenced covering him up.

"So did I. I knew it too and so did everybody else. They know it over at the cafe, that that's who it was. The fuzz come and got Benny because they knew Benny would phone him and Benny did. They got the white kid just because they happened to see him. They come after Benny because they knew he'd call the undertaker to come get him out. We all knew what it was and we didn't any of us do nothing. Just stood there like wheat. Wheat. Can't nobody walk, can't nobody talk and speak up?"

"True," he said. "But you can't fight them and do any good, can you?"

"They got me the same way," I said. "Only they just beat the shit out of me. Now they taken him."

"What's he to you?"

"I promised him I wouldn't let them take him."

"I can get another dog, cheap. Somebody will give me one," he said. "I'm making a little hump here. If I get lonesome I can come out and find where he is. I can lay my hand to it. He thought they meant to harm me so he bit the man. The man shot him. He wanted to be good protection and all it did, it got him his death. A hump will mark it. I feel bad, you know? It's hurting me because I had him since he was a little puppy. He wasn't no old dog."

"It was the undertaker," I said.

"It was him, but he done it to himself. Because he didn't choose wisely. A woman has to be picked wisely or else it will be too bad sometimes."

"You ought to know," I said. When I was little he had told me maybe a thousand times about his wife. She had lye boiling on the stove when Cucumber come in drunk. He said something crossways to her and she taken the lye and flung it in Cucumber's face. That's when it all went dark on him. Blind as fourteen bats, crippled up like Cooter Brown's grandmaw. But alive. His dog was buried. He went crawling back to his house. "Come in?" he says.

"Naw," I says. "I knew. I just had to make sure."

"If you know anything forget it. You gonna stay around?"

"Not long enough to raise no green moss," I said. "Why don't anybody ever do anything?"

"They can't win, that's why. You know that. Ain't you had enough that other time?"

"That other time I was small."

"So now you made a big man."

"Something like it," I said.

He thought about it. He was quiet, crouched on the door sill to his tin-sided house.

"Then I hope you luck," he said. "Maybe I'll see you beyond somewhere. The blind supposed to have their sight back when we get over on the other side. I take a great portion of comfort from that. I can get another dog."

"Yeah, you can do that," I said.

"Come in?"

"Naw. I better go."

"You sick over it?"

"You could say that."

"Did you know him?"

"I knew him," I said. "And he was all right. He wasn't scared of them. They didn't take no points off of him, you know? He never give them the pleasure. Now he's gone."

"How do you know? Maybe they just got him locked up."

"He's gone," I said. "I can feel it when somebody's gone."

"Where do you feel it?"

"Behind my belt," I said. "Somewhere back of my belt is how I know. Maybe I better go lay down or something, till this passes. I was supposed to look out for him but I went and ate supper instead and after that I just stood there like a knot and watched them take him like I didn't even know who it was or why they had him." I turned away to leave.

"Good-bye then, Sonny Boy."

"Good-bye," I said. I went through the gate and closed it. The geese didn't say anything. I smelled them, feathers and goose shit and sour feed on the ground, and the goat, I smelled the goat. I smelled him where I couldn't see him. Maybe they miss the dog; maybe they know, I thought.

I stood a minute under the trees in front of the cafe. It was a moon now and I stood out of its shining, under the trees a minute, and let myself breathe before I went back in the cafe.

It was quiet. Just a few was drinking beers and nobody saying nothing. The jukebox wasn't playing. Jelly wasn't on the pinball machine but her hat and white gloves was on it. She come around the counter barefooted. "Was it?" she says.

"You knew it was," I says. "Same as me. Same as everybody."

"Jesus!" Mrs. Osborn hollered from the backroom.

"You hongry?" Jelly said. "Mama Lavorn said feed you because you bound to be hongry."

"I ain't hongry," I said. "I'm sick. I'm tired right down into my legs."

"Why don't you come lay down then?" She gave a little grin. "Free on the house. Then maybe you can be hongry and eat."

"You knew it was him, didn't you?" I said. "The same as me. Emma done it to him. That bitch done it to him and hadn't no reason to do it. Where's Benny?"

"To the funeral home, looking for L. B."

"He won't find him. He knows he won't find him."

"Maybe you like mens and don't care for women. You think Mama Lavorn gonna care?"

"Quit trying to prove something," I said. "I just need to lay down awhile. Maybe I'm sick. I don't feel good."

"Come on then, you can lay down in my room."

"I can find it. I used to live here."

"I'll show you," she said. She went upstairs in front of me and put the light out in her room and raised the shades. "Not much breeze. I got a fan." She plugged it in and stood where the light from the hall was on her. I took off my coat and laid down. The bed squeaked. The pillow was damp like the wind rain had blowed over it. The breeze from the fan was on my face and my neck. She stood right where she was.

"Don't try to prove anything on me," I said. "Just let me lay here awhile."

"But before wasn't you always hongry?"

"That was before," I said.

She passed her hand over my face, gentle as cobwebs. I thought about the light going around on top of the police car and the fuzz dragging and hauling and shoving him and he fell and they jerked him up and then like a sack of cow feed they throwed him in the trunk and the lid come down, *click-snap*, and they put the light off and rode away with him in there in the dark and never one of us made a sound, only Mrs. Osborn, yelling after they went off. She was there watching when they come and got the white boy and me telling him good God why did he ever come looking for me, didn't he have no more better sense than to come looking for some nigger he just met by accident on the train? Or didn't he know and hadn't I already told and explained it to him where this was, down here, how it was different, and Benny showing off to be nice to him and setting at the table with him and Lavorn going to feed him when the cops come through the door.

"Let me wash and bathe off your temples," Jelly said. She wet a cloth in the lavatory and wiped my face. She undid my shirt buttons. Her hands smelled good. I felt better.

"Business is knocked up," she said. "Everybody gone home. All got the hell scared out of them."

"They all know," I said. "Don't nobody have to explain and tell it to them. They know."

"Benny come," she said. "Benny found the car, the big sedan. It was on the street by the curb with the keys in it. Benny took it to the funeral home. I told him it was L. B. they taken out of the junkyard. I told him you knew it was L. B. Jones. He didn't believe me. He went to see Emma. She said she hadn't seen no sign of him since early this morning, so I said: 'Benny, call the police, why don't you?' He didn't say nothing."

"It was L. B. Jones," I said. She untied my shoes and taken them off, and my socks and washed my feet. I laid with my eyes closed.

"You mind if I lie down here?" she said.

"I don't mind," I said.

Jelly got next to me. She got herself comfortable with her arm across me and her leg across. "I could sleep with Coreen but this here feel safer," she said.

She wasn't trying to prove nothing, so it was okay. I laid there and it run through my mind how times used to be, how it was. Presently she went asleep. Maybe life can pass from the dead into the living. One person can be another person until you never lose them what they really are but only like a snail when you find his shell in the woods all white as flour and the snail, he is gone. He is somewhere else. Later on maybe you find him under a log, alive, so maybe he passed. They say man can pass. Can come back a dog or a goat or a lion, or a woman either, she can come back too and maybe one night lay beside you. She ain't really dead but only passed and come back to you this way. Which if that how it is that would be very fine. I wasn't hongry. I couldn't of eat nothing or drank nothing. Because when the time come I hadn't did nothing, after I promised him. After I promised him that couldn't nothing touch him long as he had me around. Yet the time come and I only stood and looked off in another direction like maybe I never known who he was.

Chunk they pitched him in and *chunk* and *click* closed the lid on him and the car growled off with him and I standing there and smelling burnt gasoline and never moved a twitch until too late to of done nothing about it.

She jerked in her dreams. I put my hand on her until she commenced dreaming easy again. I couldn't sleep, no more than the owl, my eyes open, drinking darkness.

4

Mr. Ike

He said to them when they finally came back, he said:

"Where all the hell you all been? Little Lawyer Mundine come and paid out the two you dragged in here. Where all you been?"

They looked at him. Mr. Stanley Bumpas cleared his throat. "We had to kill a nigger," he said. "You can't accomplish nothing like that in five minutes you know."

Willie Joe Worth looked maybe a little peakid, thought Mr. Ike.

"Well kill all the somebitches for what all I care, but at least let me know where you are."

Willie Joe went to the bathroom.

"What's wrong with him?" Mr. Ike said.

Mr. Stanley smiled. "He's puking. He never done nothing like it before and it's give him the pukes."

"Like what?"

"Killing a God-damned nigger," said Mr. Stanley.

"You missed seeing little Lawyer Mundine's wife. She come in here half naked," said Mr. Ike. "Is he really puking?"

"Go see for yourself. I been expecting him to bring up hair."

Mr. Ike walked around to the bathroom door. Sure enough, Willie Joe was retching.

"He's puking," said Mr. Ike. "Did you kill any nigger in particular? Should I phone up the Mayor?"

"You keep your God-damned old shaky hands off the phone," said Mr. Stanley.

"Well, but killing. That's sorta important. The Mayor might want to be notified."

"If you mean to live and do well you better keep your God-damned old toothless mouth closed," said Mr. Stanley, not being unpleasant at all, just matter-of-fact.

"But it's just a nigger, ain't it? Or why else would you tell me?"

"Because you butted in and asked me," said Mr. Stanley, "when it wasn't much of your God-damned business. So I told you. We killed a nigger."

"Well. Well I'll be damned," said Mr. Ike, really believing him now. "Why and by God who and what about it?"

"This nigger had Willie Joe over a barrel. It was either him or Willie. This nigger undertaker, Jones. Know him?"

Mr. Ike thought he knew him. He nodded. "Well, well!" he said. "Killed him, did you?"

Mr. Stanley smiled. "Had him kneel down. Willie Joe plugged him. Then we tied him up to a tree to make it look good and I taken this little pocket knife." Mr. Stanley took out his knife and opened the large blade. It was honed down to a fine edge, Mr. Stanley being known for a careful man who kept his knife sharp. "Taken this very blade," said Mr. Stanley. That's when Willie Joe puked the first time. Willie was holding the flashlight. But like I explained to him, you got to make anything like that look good. Like another nigger done it, out of nigger revenge? So I altered him and taken his shoe strings like a nigger does when he wants others to know that here is one corpse that will not shag *his* wife ever again."

"Ah," said Mr. Ike, swallowing his spit. "Ah, oh me!"

"Just keep it quiet. When they find it we'll pick up some suspects. That will be all there will be to it." Mr. Stanley closed the knife and put it back in his pocket. Willie Joe Worth opened the bathroom door and walked out.

"Maybe I could use a drink," Willie Joe said.

"Maybe so could I," said Mr. Ike. He had saved one half-pint by hiding it from the Mayor behind the typewriter under a folded newspaper. He opened the bottle and handed it to Willie Joe. The young man killed half of it before he handed it back.

Mr. Ike had a couple of sips. "Stanley?" he said. "Drink?"

"No thanks," said Mr. Stanley. "I had some beer earlier. Whiskey somehow don't agree with me no way. My stomach's tore up as it is."

"What's wrong?" said Mr. Ike.

"He's got the dribbles," Willie Joe said. He tried to laugh. Instead he hacked a few times and cleared his throat and looked from one man to another. His eyes were all red and queer. Thought Mr. Ike, Mighty strange looking.

"I'd as soon have the dribbles as the pukes," Mr. Stanley observed. "Some I could name get the pukes awful easy!"

"I couldn't see doing that," Willie Joe Worth said. "Shooting is one thing but that other, that's something else. What if it was you? It hurts me down here in my own privacy just to think of it. Stanley cut him though, and never blinked a God-damned eye. Did he tell you?"

"Oh, I'll say he told me!" said Mr. Ike. "Reckin when somebody will find it?"

"Anytime tomorrow," said Mr. Stanley. He had his pocket knife out again. He was paring his fingernails and cleaning them. "I'd like to see anybody's face when they do find it," he said. "God knows, wouldn't you all like to be there!"

Neither Mr. Ike nor Willie Joe could think of anything to say to that. Mr. Ike looked out the glassed window. There was nothing to see in Main Street but bugs circling and swarming the street lamps and little bats slicing through the swarms, catching their dinner.

5

Emma

Just to tell her he'd done it. That was Willie Joe's only reason for coming. He hadn't anything else on his mind except his own private vision of the thing, as though he really couldn't tell her all of it, simply saying: "Well, by God, it's done."

"That's fine," Emma said. He was drunk, she saw.

"Fine for you," he said thickly, "by God."

"Fine for you *and* me," she corrected him. "Your job's safe."

He was drunk, not listening. He drank a beer and then another.

"You coming to bed? Say, Killer?"

Instead of answering he walked out, maybe a little unsteady on his feet. He left her all alone in the house. The police car scratched off in the street outside.

"Well," she said. Emma confronted herself in the full-length mirror. She saw youth and beauty, wearing a white negligee, little white mules, white lipstick, white fingernail polish. She smiled. "I got an idea," she said. "I got an idea that's the last I'll see of him."

What to do with her freedom? Reflectively both hands passed over her belly. *Mine, my child, my baby.* Only a teeny-tiny not very noticeable little swelling.

First came the funeral. She saw it. A Memphis choir, Memphis organist, two preachers, a bank of white Memphis orchids back of the white casket and everything splendid so people would say later, would tell the boy when he grew up, would say to her son, "We saw your daddy's funeral. Wasn't anything like it ever before in Somerton."

She folded her arms across her breasts. The ecstasy of her plans began prickling her scalp and running over her body like little ants.

Victor. The name came at her. Victor Jones.

"Victor Jones," she said aloud, testing the sound. "The son of Mrs. Lord Byron Jones. It is a boy," she said, to reassure herself, "but if it isn't I'll name her Victoria."

The room was too quiet. She locked her door and turned on the little white radio. She got a gospel message. The hypnotic, singsong rhythm of the preacher's words was soothing as a deep hot bath.

She drifted, feeling again and again the prickling ecstasy of her plans.

6

Oman Hedgepath

When it turns out that you are supposed to know everything anyway, the very moment it happens, it will sometimes turn out that you
are the last one to get the word. I saw that Steve's office was unoc-
cupied. Miss Griggs was at her desk, my enduring, my menopausal, my
efficient Miss Griggs. She barely nodded. I'm used to that too. When
they get her age you can mark it down that to expect anything
other than the expected from them is to be sure of a surprise. I
thought, Well, God damn. A nice day for billy goats.

"Call the Mayor," she says.

"At home?" I says.

"At his office."

I thought, Well, he's downtown mighty early. The thing was of
course that she already knew. She thought I knew of course.

I slammed the office door and phoned City Hall. It wasn't even
seven-thirty. It rang about a dozen times. Finally the Mayor himself
answered.

"Well, how is it going," I says. "This is Oman."

"Good," says the Mayor. "We got them both."

"Got who?" I says.

"Emma and Benny."

I didn't say anything.

"The one with the most to gain, was how I figured it," says the
Mayor. "It had to be a nigger. That narrowed it down, because no-

body but a nigger would have cut him that way after he was already dead. Dr. Pentecost and me went out there and Doc said it was practically certain he was already dead whenever they cut him, you know, whoever done it. Who stood to gain but his widow? Then again she would of had to have help. We got them both downstairs, charged with murder in the first by God degree."

Something began to dawn on me. "Who —" I says. "Murdered who?"

"Lord Byron Jones, who do you think?"

"Somebody killed him?"

"You mean nobody phoned you?" he says. "Sure, he was killed last night. Shot to death. A logger found him around daylight just as he was going into the woods. And nobody called you? We got Emma and Benny downstairs. They're already booked. I'll have to say this, she couldn't of done it all alone. We picked Benny up last night and would have had him all night if somebody hadn't come down and got him out of jail. Chief Fly would not want me to say it but I'm going to say it. That whoever done that set the stage for this whole God-damned thing."

"Who got Benny out of jail?" I says.

"Steve," he says. "And more besides. He come down and paid out a white boy, a God-damned agitator with a beard and everything. The white boy knew to call Steve! Had his name from some nigger outfit in Nashville as the man to call. Pardon my French, Oman, but your nephew is spitting in the soup. You know what I mean?"

I didn't say anything.

"He's cooperating with the Communists mighty heavy. I can't help it if he is your nephew, he's a Bolshevik, Oman. You're just going to have to face up to it. It's a lot of talk about him that's been going on behind your back."

"Maybe you better tell me all of it," I says.

He did. He told it all. Bumpas and Willie Joe Worth walking into Mama Lavorn's and there sits Benny at the table with this white boy, the kind that bums the roads nowadays through the South with his head crammed full of non-violence and nonsense about the "white power structure." They get him to the station with Benny, and they are about to take them both downstairs when the white kid demands his phone call. It so happens that the name he has is Steve Mundine.

"As a result of that we lost one of the best niggers this town ever had last night," the Mayor says.

"You're sure Benny was in on it?" I says.

"I got both confessions here on my desk, sealed, signed and delivered."

"Did you use force to get them?"

"I wasn't present for that part of it," the Mayor says.

"Just so it wasn't beat out of them, is all."

That gave him a moment of pause. For the first time he hesitated. "All right, well, maybe you better talk to the prisoners yourself. In my opinion we've got a case that will hold water with the Grand Jury. I'm ready to let the District Attorney have it today, right this morning."

"That's mighty fast," I says. "Maybe I better talk to the niggers first."

"You're City Attorney," he says. "I'm just a country mayor, but by God I'll tell you this much. Maybe you don't need to be reminded, but people expect a murderer to be caught! Don't make any mistake about that."

"I'll tell you what," I says. "You stay away from Alf's this morning. I might just accidentally need you sober."

"Coffee," he says. "That's all I'm drinking."

"Just stay on this side of Main Street," I says. "I have a couple of things to clear up — a divorce hearing for one thing."

"Divorce? What divorce?"

"L. B. Jones was quietly divorcing Emma. The hearing was set for this morning."

"Would that have any bearing on this killing?"

"That's what we have to consider. I want you to sit still and hold your horses for a while. Don't say anything. Don't talk to anybody. Understand?"

"Ah," he says. "You know something. You think it wasn't them . . ."

"I think it wasn't Benny," I says. "Benny was one of L. B.'s witnesses for the divorce hearing this morning. He was too loyal."

"But it was Emma?"

"We'll see about that. For right now I want you to paste your lips together and stay off the telephone."

"All right — but they've both confessed. I can't understand why nobody called you, Oman. I'm sorry about that. Chief Fly or some of the boys must of slipped up and forgot. I thought they had talked to you."

"That's all right," I says. "Probably everybody in Somerton knew about it before me, but it's all right. The main thing now is just not to be too hasty. The world is full of headlong bastards that want to pick up the ball and run with it before they even know which direction the goal posts are in. That's my point."

I looked up. Steve had come in.

"Just sit still then, and I'll be in touch," I says. I hung up the phone.

"Hello, Steve."

"Is that all you can say? You got what you wanted, didn't you?" he says. A cold kind of early morning anger had whitened out his face. His hair looked rumpled, like he had washed it just before he went to bed. He was nervous and glittery. He looked hard as glass.

"I'm rather busy right now," I says.

"I'll bet you are busy. Covering tracks, fabricating lies? Do you know who they've arrested for the murder of the man you had killed?"

"Wait a minute," I says. "The man's dead — but the killer, that's a matter for the courts."

"Don't hand me that crap! You know who killed L. B. Jones! More than that, you know you're implicated."

"I know nothing of the kind," I says. "I do know that a certain group in Nashville has your name. I know you got a racial agitator out of jail last night. I'm wondering if what people are saying about you can be the truth. How did they get your name, Steve?"

"I belong to the NAACP."

"You admit it? You's not kidding?"

"I'm damned proud of it! It's you I'm ashamed of — to think that Nella asked you — hell, begged you to protect that man. And you said he *was* protected. Nobody would dare lay a finger on a client of yours, you said. Sure, L. B. Jones was safe! 'I have him in the hollow of my hand,' you said."

"Maybe I did say that. I thought I did have him in my hand, Steve. It was a matter of doing the right thing as I saw it. Maybe I am responsible — indirectly."

"Indirectly! Oman, why couldn't you listen to me?"

"Because things just don't work that way in Somerton, Steve. There's a right way to do things and a wrong way. You don't raise miscegenation like a flag and fly it from the rooftops. You don't smear people and ruin people."

"Oman, a man is dead!"

"All right, God damn it! So he's dead. All he had to do was show a little common sense and he'd still be alive. I didn't kill him. Hell, how many hours did I waste trying to talk the black son of a bitch out of filing for a divorce in the first place? How many times did I tell him I didn't want this God-damned case? How many times did I tell you I didn't want to take it — that it stank! Eh?"

"This is what I was afraid of," he says. "From the first. I've been afraid something would happen to make us — all of us — have to choose sides. So long as nobody had to choose sides, there was a chance it could be worked out fairly and peacefully. Now —"

"Well, which side have you chosen?" I asked him. As though it were any use, now, as though anything could save him now. Steve was right about one thing. The lines were drawn. If by dying he hadn't accomplished another thing, Lord Byron Jones, by his death, had defined the issues for us.

"I made that choice a long time ago," he said. "I'm on the side of freedom and equality for everyone. Equal treatment before the law; equal protection under the law."

"Ideals and abstractions, Steve?"

"A man is dead," he replied. "Can't you realize it? How abstract is that?"

"I hate it worse than anything in the world."

"But if you had it to do again, would you have handled this case the very same way?"

"I wouldn't have taken this case."

"But if you had taken it, Oman?"

I drew a deep breath. "I'd have handled it exactly the same. The undertaker had his choices to make. I had mine. Neither of us forged the system of the society under which we must live here in the South. Both of us have had to come to terms with it day by day, all our whole lives. Steve, that nigger knew what he was doing."

"And you, Oman?"

"All right — I knew."

"What will you do now?"

"The right thing," I says. "I'll always do the right thing as I see it."

He turned away then. It was that sort of moment between two people that is always hard for the both of them to believe. It was that sort of moment when nothing avails. We had both known from the first, I suppose, that our beliefs at this one point, at least, were poles apart. It was the sheer desire to make the partnership work that had brought us this far. Now those efforts to dissemble, those masks, those polite lies and evasions that had always served in the past lay back of us like the rubble of war. He would never see it my way; I could never see it his. Even that shallow sort of agreement, founded in sand, the so-called "agreement to disagree," couldn't hold us anymore.

"Why couldn't you listen to me?" he muttered, more to himself than anyone else. Then he left. He went out and shut the door behind him. The essential truth of the defeat we both shared turned my insides to gravel. My tongue felt as though I had licked a slate.

And still you move. Still you act. I went downstairs and past the hotel to the police station. It was like getting out of bed when you have fever. Nothing was quite right. The glare from the sky hurt my eyes. I thought it will be August and harvest soon and collections will pick up; things will begin to ripen now, as though by some act of sacrifice the wheels of this season could turn at last, oiled with blood. Do we get a sort of pagan satisfaction, must we have Death, must we want it sometimes for the sense of relief, as though a tight cord were unwound from the heart — that's the feeling. There's no shame, only tingling and satisfaction, and a light-headed sort of relief, now, when it's all over.

Chief Fly held his paper cup of coffee. I smelled it in his breath when he opened the security door and took me downstairs to the cages. One contained the emaciated black accused of killing Mr. Bivens. He lay like a bundle of rags and sticks, like something you see in famine pictures from India. He couldn't have mustered the strength, I thought; not in a thousand years could he have mustered the strength to beat Mr. Jimmy Bivens to death. He was the perfect sacrificial victim though. A sick, black dope addict.

The Chief's coffee had a fresh-hopeful smell of morning. The cages smelled like cooped up night. You forget from one time till the next what it is like "downstairs." What you smell isn't so much the stopped up toilets or the unwashed bodies. What you smell is all the pain beyond pain, the hopelessness that burns like the glare of an unfrosted light bulb. What you smell is the fear of living and the fear of death; the dread of it all.

"Here, nigger," says Chief Fly, kicking the heavy wire door to one of the cages.

I saw Benny sit up. "Sah?"

"Mr. Oman wants to talk to you, nigger."

Benny came to the cage door.

"Nevermind about the confession," I says. "Did you do it?"

He looked at Chief Fly. "I signed it. I confessed," he says.

I turned to the Chief. "Wait upstairs a minute, would you, Chief?"

"Yes sir!" He went off quick march up the stairs.

"Did you do it?"

I saw tears on his face. "How could I, Mr. Oman?" he whispered.

"But did you?"

"Naw, sir. You know I couldn't. I didn't."

"Did she?" I pointed to Emma's cage.

"She's only the cause of it."

She had come to the door of her cage. Her eyes were puffy. Her face was a little swollen, like a half risen biscuit.

"If you don't get us out of here how are we going to bury him?" she says.

There she was, with her fanny practically in the electric chair, and all she could think of was his funeral. That's a nigger for you, one hundred per cent.

"Did you kill him, Emma?"

"That's what they said. I'm a lot of things, but I'm no murderer."

"You a whore, that's what," Benny said. "He knows what you are. You don't have to try to hide nothing from him."

"All right, you tell me then, how are we going to have the funeral?

Locked up like this?" She wiped her forehead on the back of her hand. "Can you get us out of here?"

"Sears Buntin is your lawyer — not me."

"Listen, white man, don't play with me, hear?" she says. "If you don't mind? I've had about all I can take. Benny and I didn't do it."

"We'll see," I said.

I went up the skeletal wooden stairs. The treads were worn and rundown like the heels on old shoes. I knocked on the security door. Chief Fly unlocked it.

"Let's step in the booking room," I says.

"Anything wrong, Mr. Oman?"

When I had closed the door so no one would overhear us I looked him straight in the eye. "How did you get the confessions?"

"Cattle prod," he says, bright as a bird and twice as proud. "Socked her with it once. Had to lay it on Benny three times. That's all it taken, just four electric charges in all."

"Just for curiosity," I says. "Where do you lay it on a woman?"

"The tits," he says. "Rarely do you have to sock one in the ass with it. Now a man . . ."

"I know about that," I says.

"Yes, sir. Was there anything else?"

"No," I said. "No thanks."

True to his promise the Mayor was in his office when I got there. He was still drinking coffee. "I just thought," he says. "Nobody's up at the funeral home to embalm him. Willie here, ah, Willie has something on his mind," says the Mayor.

He and Willie Joe Worth had been talking, just the two of them in his office. When I walked in they had both stood up. "Just laying up there at the funeral home with nobody to embalm him," says the Mayor, repeating himself. He went to the window. Willie Joe had begun looking at the Mayor's photographs framed and hanging on the wall. There were pictures of B-26 bombers. The Mayor had been a gunner in the Army Air Force.

"Willie?" says the Mayor, still looking out the window, with his back to me. "You might as well go on and tell him what you told me."

"I killed him," Willie Joe Worth says. He was still looking at the pictures.

"You killed who," I says.

"The undertaker — that nigger."

I could see where his uniform shirt was wet at both armpits. He held his cap, turning it nervously in one hand.

"Alf might get a heart attack if I don't show up over there pretty quick," says the Mayor. "Maybe I oughtta get over there and see how Alf's doing this morning."

"Maybe you better stay here," I says.

"Willie Joe said he wanted to turn himself in to me. I said we already had the guilty parties. I said besides I wasn't the one he should turn himself in to because you were probably the man he ought to turn himself in to if he was determined on doing it."

Willie Joe turned away from the pictures and put his hat on a chair. He unstrapped his gun belt and handed it to me. "I done it. I'm turning myself in to you," he says. He tried to smile. "That was a good thing, that you thought enough of me to come and tell me the danger I was in and got me to — to do what I could about it. So, what I mean is, Benny didn't do it. Neither did that woman nigger, Emma. Because I did it."

"Single-handed, you did it?" I asked him. The gun belt was unexpectedly heavy. I laid it on the Mayor's desk.

"No sir, Mr. Stanley Bumpas helped me. I know now I ought not to have done it. But it was either the nigger or me. I had to kill the son of a bitch."

"Self-defense, that's what I'd call it," the Mayor says. "I told him we had the guilty parties. I already tried to talk to him. He won't listen to reason."

"Can you prove you did it?" I says.

"My gun there will prove it," he says. "I just handed you the proof."

"Don't you realize you're an officer of the law?" I says.

"That's what I said — my exact words to him," says the Mayor.

"Take me in yonder and have them book me. Lock me up," Willie Joe says.

"I can tell you I don't want it on my desk," the Mayor says. "Don't lay this God-damned thing on my desk, if you don't mind. Because I'm going to tell you both, like I'd tell a friend, by God, I don't want any part of this God-damned business. Nigger and white? Don't try to bring me in on it!"

"He's told you all about it then?" I says. "Willie told you?"

"Far more than I ever wanted to know," says the Mayor. "If you'll just be so good as to excuse me, I haven't heard one word that was spoken here in this office today. Some things a fellow don't want to know about. This is sure as hell one of 'em."

"Sit down," I says. "Both of you."

"I'd rather stand up, by God," says the Mayor. He sat down. "I hate to see that God-damned gun on my desk. I'd rather have my old mother's dead body laid out there, much as I love her, bless her heart, as to see that God-damned pistol laying there where it is."

"Just take me in yonder and book me, that's all in the world I'm asking of either one of you," Willie Joe says. He had sat down on the Mayor's green sofa. Sweat rolled off his face, down his neck, and into the open collar of his shirt. "I killed that nigger," he says.

"But you couldn't have," I says. I was hoping against hope. "Describe him. How was he found."

"Don't worry, he did it, Oman," says the Mayor.

"A nut in either hand, his shoe strings gone — to make it look like niggers done it," Willie Joe Worth was saying. "That was Mr. Stanley's idea—to make it look like niggers."

"Satisfied?" says the Mayor. "Want him to draw you a picture?"

"Just book me! I done it!"

"Will you God damn it please shut up a minute?" says the Mayor. "You want us all to be stuck up salt creek with you? What kinda city do you think people will imagine we're running where a police officer gets caught out for sleeping with a confounded nigger? If you could just explain to me why, in the first place. Ain't there white pussy enough to go around to keep the Somerton Police Department satisfied? If you were trying to change your luck I'll tell you one damn thing, you succeeded, and you changed my luck too, and Oman's luck, by God you changed his. Until I woke up this morning my life was pretty smooth and happy. Here I was until this morning, Mayor of a clean, decent little city. Nobody getting rich, but nobody in the poorhouse either. Not all the industry we could use; but some industry. Not dry as the dries would want it and not wet as the wets would like it, but just damp — so a man can get a drink. By God, I'm *needing* a drink, I can tell you. Somerton, Tennessee — ruined, the very name dragged in the dust and the mire of miscegenationous . . . miscegenationous pricking around by a cock hungry bunch of bastards in police uniforms!"

"Mr. Mayor, I'm awful sorry. Just book me."

"Book you, hell. Book you, my grandmaw! I'll not book you! I don't even want to look at you," says the Mayor. "I wish now by God I'd never *seen* you."

"Both of you wait here for me. I'll be back directly," I says.

"All right," says the Mayor. "The Apostle Paul couldn't be re-elected with something as terrible as this on his record. And here I was planning some day to run for governor. I'll be lucky if they'll let me drive the garbage truck."

"I'm awfully sorry," says Willie Joe.

The thing about it, I thought, on the way to my office, was he really was sorry. He really was a boy with a lot of good in him, a boy with a lot of hopes pinned on him by a mother who loved him as much as my own mother loved me. Someway, though, he was off on the wrong foot. Somehow, perhaps, all of us were. But you get so far along, you get so deep in a thing, and the time to look back and take the measure of your doubts is past. Past a certain point, for better or for worse, you've got to act.

Steve came out when I walked in, like a bass rising to a casting plug. He trailed me the same way, straight into my office.

"You need something?" I says.

"I have to know what you're going to do."

"About what?"

"This murder."

He stood there representing the other side. The FBI and the process servers. The do-gooders and the meddlers. He was in a righteous rage. As usual all he could see was the surface — the depths, the further implications, all that, I knew, would be lost on him.

"Innocent people are downstairs in that jail," he was saying. "And what will you do? What will anybody do?"

"Steve —"

"Anything?"

"Steve, I wouldn't have had this happen for the world."

He didn't believe me. He couldn't. So this, I thought, this is how it has to be played. You're wrong no matter what you do or how you do it. To the other side everything you do will be wrong and you will lose anyhow, you'll lose him any way you play it and you'll never convince him of your sincerity. He will never believe that here was a man doing his best, doing the right thing as he saw it and understood it. You'll never get it over to him, I thought. I wanted to grab him and hold him and say to him, son, if you ever believed in me —

It was too late even for that. The other side had him and he would never come back to me. He would forget me but I would never forget him.

"Steve," I began.

"Skip it," he said. "After all, what's the use?"

He was right, of course. "I'm sorry, boy," I said.

He took out his handkerchief and wiped his hands on it. "Is Somerton typical?" he asked.

"Yes," I said. For a moment hope flared in me. Might he have survived his baptism of truth? I thought: If only he can accept it.

He shook his head sadly. He turned and walked slowly out of my office. I called after him. He didn't answer.

That's the other side. I thought: Either fight them back on their own terms or they'll tear you to shreds — no, they'll tear you to shreds anyway. So play the game by their rules, I thought, tit for tat.

I opened my desk drawer and got my pistol and put it in my coat pocket. It felt heavy as a brick bat. When I went back out Steve was packing his law books. Miss Griggs was crying, sitting there with a deed rolled in her typewriter, weeping into a little handkerchief. Before I could get out of the office Nella walked in and walked straight over to Steve and kissed him. She picked up a cardboard box and began helping him pack.

There was nothing I could say. When I stepped out on the sidewalk the sun fell on me like a blanket. I saw the Mayor looking out his window, staring across at Alf's service station when I passed. I walked in by the Mayor's private entrance and shut the door. Willie Joe was looking at the airplane pictures again.

"Excuse me a minute," I said. I went into the Mayor's lavatory to wash my hands. I soaped them twice and rinsed them in cold water. I dried them slowly to get off the last of whatever it was, perhaps grease from the pistol, but then again, something I have felt since occasionally, like maybe I've just shaken hands with a nigger.

They had sat down again. I could see part of the Mayor's chair and his crossed legs, with blond hair showing between his socks and his trouser cuffs. The gun belt was just where I had laid it, still on the Mayor's desk.

Neither of them looked at me. They both looked straight ahead, waiting. I closed the door to the lavatory quietly. Because they had handed it all over to me they were thinking that all that remained now was for Willie Joe to be punished and the Mayor absolved. I thought yes, the whole world would lay it on my doorstep if it could. As if I could help it. As if I had anything to do with it in the first place. Let a man be the grandson of slave owners and that is how it will follow him, tied about his neck, thrown across his shoulders, an eternal burden of dead guilt to be dragged and toted all his natural life. Something he can pass on to his sons, if he happens to be lucky. Then they can struggle with it. It's like toting a corpse.

It came to me that here we had brought the whole thing straight off the land, direct from the plantation into town, the whole structure of the feudal organization, centuries of it, dedicated to the notion of landowner, overseer, and serf.

A serf was dead. The overseers were waiting to see what I would do about it. They would accept anything, just so long as I did it. For their part, they had nothing to offer except that one of them wanted his punishment pretty badly.

"So you killed him," I says finally. "Well, nothing we do, any of us, will bring him back to life, will it?"

"No, sir," says Willie Joe.

"It's already done, by God," says the Mayor.

I took Willie Joe's bright, shiny .38 special out of the holster. He sat watching me like a hypnotized bird. He couldn't have been more concerned if I had laid my hands on one of his children. His arms came up from his lap. He laid one of them on the arm rest of the sofa. The other he put down at his side.

"With this gun?"

He nodded, still watching me. The Mayor nodded too. I opened the gun. The cylinders were loaded. I emptied the cartridges into my hand and looked through the barrel. It was shiny, clean as a bird gun, bright as new money. A paraffin test would pick up powder traces on his hands, though. That, with the death slug and Willie Joe's confession, would get him two years on a charge of manslaughter, with the right lawyer, before the right jury; this regardless of how hard the state might push for a first-degree conviction. And all the filthy aspects of the case would be dragged straight into the newspapers.

All for what?

Because a nigger wouldn't listen to reason, but instead had to stand up and beg for death; and not some nigger from the North, from Chicago, not some young kid without good sense. Hell no, he was home grown. He was fully mature and raised to know better. Me telling him, his wife telling him, Willie Joe telling him — he had been one nigger that would not listen to anybody. I put the pistol and the cartridges on the desk.

"Did you try to talk sense to him?"

"He wouldn't listen! I tried everything in the world. I give him time to think it over. I went out of my way to be nice to him and he walked off from me with his neck stiff as a Chevrolet crankshaft and never down even thanked me." He paused. "But I never in my life hated nothing I ever done before as bad as this. Coming right down to it, by God, I sho' hated having it to do."

"But it's done and were there to be nothing more said about it the whole thing would blow away like smoke and disappear. Wouldn't it?"

"Sure it would," says the Mayor.

"Yes, sir. It might. Nothing wouldn't change what I done, though, would it? Just get the case airtight against me. Let the law lay it on me. Otherwise I know I'll never be able to lay down and sleep again. Maybe after that, maybe then I can get right with God. That — what I done last night — that showed me how far I have strayed from the path . . . I wasn't cut out to be a man killer. I ain't hardened down to it like Bumpas. I couldn't down hardly make myself shoot a dog. If you want me to do it I'll lie and say I made Mr. Stanley go along. I'll clear him. Okay, Mr. Oman?"

Why feed the God-damned Communist cause if you don't have to do it? I thought. Fight them with their own weapons.

"Willie Joe," I says. "Let's consider the cold facts. Your decision has to be your decision. And, son — I wouldn't have you do anything hasty that you would be sorry for later." I stepped over and let my hand rest on his shoulder for a moment. He nodded. I circled back towards the desk and got the pistol again.

"The facts," I says. "First consider your mother. You come from proud stock, son; I know you love that dear mother enough to die for her a thousand times. Those tender hands that nursed and cared for you through childhood illnesses — they conveyed the love that only a mother can give her son. Man knows such love from two sources only — the woman that bore him and his country, the land that gave him shelter and sustenance." He was looking at me. When he looked away, shamed, I struck.

"Would you break that dear Southern lady's heart now? When her hours, perhaps even her minutes are numbered even as God numbers the hair on the head of a child — a dear little daughter? Must you plunge your own flesh into an early grave? Son, I want you to try to look at me."

He couldn't do it, of course. He couldn't let me see his tears.

"And that dear, brave wife, Flonnie? The noble mother of brave children? Flesh of your flesh, bone of your bone? Are they worth standing up for? Aren't these worth a bit of inner struggle and heartache if it will protect them? Have you guts enough to shelter them from ruin?"

"He's a brave boy, Oman. I know he's got the guts," says the Mayor.

"I guess," says Willie Joe. "I guess!"

"You *know*," I says. "You wear the badge of the City of Somerton just as our fathers, a hundred years ago, wore another uniform — the Confederate gray. They gave their lives to defend the women and children of the South from nigger rape and ruin, from the devastation of racial mixing. They died, Willie Joe, so your daughters would not have to grow up and marry niggers. Will you defend their honor this same way?

"So maybe you have made a little mistake. At least now you've learned your lesson. More than one man has slipped off the straight and narrow when he wasn't thinking."

"That he has," says the Mayor. "Many a man has done that and lived to get over it."

"I'd say you've killed a man in the line of duty. Is that so bad for a police officer? Doing your duty as you saw it? Must we book you and bring you to trial and heap shame down upon your loved ones for this? Would you ask us to do that? Hurt and aggrieve your mama, break your dear wife's heart, cripple the reputations of your children and destroy their happiness before it has had a chance even to bloom?

"My son — and that's how I feel toward you —"

"Me too," says the Mayor.

"My son, when you lay that belt on this desk and say you want to turn yourself in, this is what you're asking us to do. And for what? To feed the weakness of your false guilt? So you blew one sorry nigger jackass to hell, that's one less to go prancing and tooling around in his big black Cadillac! Do you drive a Cadillac? Do I? Does the Mayor? Son, it's your decision, but if I were you, *I'd go on just like nothing happened.*"

"But we got Emma and Benny downstairs," Willie Joe says.

"Son, would you be willing to swap promises with us? Do you feel you can trust me?"

"Everybody trusts Oman Hedgepath. You know that," Willie Joe says.

"If we can promise you that Emma and Benny will go free, can you promise us, on your word of honor as a son of the Confederacy, that you'll never breathe a word about this, that you'll put down and forget this false guilt, that you will hold your head up henceforth and from now on like the Christian police officer you are?"

"And that you will quit cracking that nigger, put that in there too," says the Mayor. "I want that stopped."

"You'll get them out of jail — aloose?"

"I give you my word of honor on it."

"It's gonna be hard," he says.

"Sure, it's going to be tough, but you can do it," I says.

"I promise," he says.

It was like somebody had lifted a manhole cover off my chest. Willie Joe wiped the corners of his eyes.

"That's all we need," I says. "A Southern man's word is his bond." I put down Willie Joe's pistol and took my pistol from my coat pocket. "We'll swap guns," I says, "you and me."

I put my pistol in his holster. "Take care of it. It belonged to my father. When the City issues you another pistol give this one back to me if you don't mind. Only take your time. Wait a year and then report your pistol as stolen."

The boy looked downright sick.

"And take today off and get yourself some rest," says the Mayor. "Maybe I might arrange it so you and the wife could take your kids on a little vacation. Maybe next fall you'd like to drive them over to the Smoky Mountains for a few days and have yourself a vacation with pay. A man can't work a double shift forever without it will finally begin to grind down on him, no matter how much man he is."

"Willie Joe's a lot of man," I said. "Go on home now, son."

That served to square his shoulders a little. The boy stood up and strapped on his gunbelt. I put my hand on his shoulder. I gentled him out the door and closed it after him.

"That was beautiful as anything I ever saw," the Mayor says. I put Willie Joe's pistol in my coat pocket. "I just don't know how we can keep our promise and turn those niggers aloose though. I wouldn't know what to tell Chief Fly."

"Confessions gotten with a cattle prod?" I says. "I don't know about you, but I don't want the FBI walking in behind me every time I try to go to the toilet. Do you have any idea what they can do if we get nailed with another civil rights suit? This little hearing about desegregating the city park won't hold a candle to what could happen if they nailed us for cattle prodding a couple of prisoners. What would we do then? Have you got any idea?"

Of course he didn't have the first idea. He nodded. "Yeah, when you put it in that light. If they slapped another God-damned civil rights suit on us."

"You'd need their permission to sneeze," I says. "But now it's up to you."

"Why hell, Oman, I feel like you do." He caught the spirit of the notion. "What do we need with a God-damned busload of Federal agents underfoot? Do we want to be stumbling over some God-damned FBI son of a bitch every time we open a door? What would you do?"

"Tear up those confessions and release the prisoners for lack of evidence."

"Then Benny can go ahead and get to embalming that nigger," he says. "And she can get on with her plans for his funeral." He paused a minute. "And then I can go on over to Alf's, can't I?"

"Why not?" I says.

That struck him as funny. He grabbed my arm and slapped it. He phoned Chief Fly and told him to get somebody to take Benny and Emma to the funeral home, to turn them loose, giving him a dozen reasons why the FBI would come in otherwise, telling him to tear up the confessions, and laughing into the phone like he had never had a worry in his life. He hung up the phone. "You coming over to Alf's?"

"You drink mine," I says. He laughed again. He went ahead of me out into the hall, shouting and waving to people. Traffic in Main Street stopped for him like he was God, letting him get across to Alf's where the cares and problems that bother the rest of us would never find him.

There was just time, by then, to walk upstairs where the Divorce Court was convening. Mine was the first case called. Sears Buntin was nowhere in sight.

Judge Hatton looked up from the bench and I stepped forward. I was more conscious now than ever of the heavy, swinging awkwardness of the pistol weighting down my coat pocket.

"All right, Mr. Hedgepath?"

"If the court please," I said. "Comes the solicitor for complainant and moves that the bill filed in this cause by the complainant be dismissed on the grounds that complainant is deceased."

Burke Hatton nodded. He looked at the Clerk. "Dismissed upon the payment of costs in this cause, upon the motion of solicitor for the complainant, George Gordon Lord Byron Jones. Thank you, Mr. Hedgepath." Long ago we had played football together for Somerton. I played center, Burke Hatton was a guard. Looking at him it came to me that he was an old man — lean, stern and honest.

He looked at me over his glasses and nodded. I turned away and went on back downstairs. Sweat was forming between my shoulder blades. With the pistol still heavy in my pocket, and the whole business still heavy in my mind, I walked around to where my car was parked behind the bank. First I considered the river, but it would be my luck for some fisherman to drag it up. It would be just my million to one bad luck that some sorry bastard would find it in the river.

So I took the road for home, down the asphalt, between the marshes and the field flowers, and up the gravel, then, to my driveway. As I turned in the drive quail scooted out of the shrubbery and crossed in front of the car. Instead of turning into the carport I drove on up beside the white fence, towards the barn.

I got out into the hot July silence, going through the thick grass until I came to the wooden well cover. Painted navy gray, it rested in the grass like an outsized Roman coin. I raised it, rending spider webs. A black widow flashed her scarlet hourglass pattern at me, set like a jewel in her burnished, jetty abdomen. The dry corpse of her mate hung close beside her. Slowly the black legs moved her to the wood where she crouched, as though waiting. I took out the pistol and dropped it. With my pulse pounding and sweat edging out of my hairline, I listened. I heard it strike, splash, and reverberate. The spider waved her legs in a gentle spasm of ecstasy. Just as gently, so as not to bother her more than was necessary, I lowered the well cover back into place. Then I straightened up and headed for the cool sanctuary of the house.

Henry had the radio going in the kitchen.

"You heard it?" he says.

"What?"

"About the Mr. Lord Byron Jones funeral? Hit's day after tomorrow and de public invited. They 'nouncing hit ever fifteen minutes. Ain't we going?"

"We?"

"Well you waited on him, didn't you?"

"You God-damned old savage," I said. All he lacked was a spear, a drum, and a chicken bone.

"Ain't we going?" I nodded. He grinned. "I said you wouldn't want us to miss it. Hot damn, I can't hardly wait!" He got up and began snapping his fingers and shuffling around the table.

EIGHT

1

The Funeral

EMMA

From the moment he arrived from Memphis, Luther X had hardly left her side. He was big shouldered and dark, with an Indian type nose. He smiled in a mysterious way when he spoke. Maybe she was a little scared of him, not that he gave her any outward reasons for fear, with his dark suits, his spiffy shoes, and his light, snap brim straw hats. Except for the strange quality of his smile he might have been another insurance salesman, a Negro rent collector, or yet, one of those black men who always seem to have money, to wear good clothes and drive sharp automobiles, without ever giving any sign or clue as to where this prosperity springs from. Luther X was waiting for her at the funeral home when she was taken there from jail. Mr. Stanley Bumpas gave Emma and Benny a ride home in the police car since he was on the way to his farm anyway, he said, since now, with the weather finally right and so much hay to get in, he was busy every day at his farm he said — cutting and baling. Mr. Stanley had let them out in front of the L. B. Jones Funeral Parlor for Colored. Benny had gone straight on inside to take care of the undertaker's body. Just inside the front door, in the white painted hallway with the rose carpet, Luther X had stood waiting for Emma.

For two days and nights since he had stayed with her. Luther X helped her so she hardly had to think. He was the sort of man who thought of everything first. With his help Emma saw to the finishing touches. Her white shoes and the white maternity dress, the white gloves and the white hat and white veil were all his notion.

"Fine and beautiful like a bride," said Luther X to all this, when he had dressed her. He had seen to it that the big chapel room at the funeral parlor was properly arranged with reserved seats down front for blood relations and pallbearers, and reserved seats at the back of the auditorium for white friends of the deceased. Fixed on the curtain behind the pulpit was a big moon and star emblem of the Nation of Islam surrounded by four words in a language Emma didn't understand.

"Those read 'Justice, Freedom, Equality' and 'Islam,'" Luther X said. He smiled. "Islam?" He smiled handsomely again, in response to her question. "That means peace. We are peaceful," he explained.

Emma stood back while Luther X issued last minute instructions. "Chief mourner, Benny, that's you, sits here?" Benny nodded. He sat down obediently and adjusted his teevee tray. The tray contained a stack of telegrams from friends of the deceased to be read during the funeral service. Beside the telegrams were the greeting cards from the floral sprays, telling who sent the flowers and how much they cost. These too would be read aloud, as was customary, and a grand total, citing the cost of the flowers and the telegrams taken together, would be announced at the end of the service.

Next to the greeting cards was a stack of white linen handkerchiefs. Benny would soil these one by one, as the service progressed, and drop them on the floor at his feet, in his capacity as chief mourner.

Emma's chair was down front next to his. In addition to a stack of handkerchiefs, her teevee tray had on it a small silver pitcher of water with a silver goblet beside it.

"All right, Benny here," Luther X was saying. "Let's seat the Gospel Beale Ramblers yonder, to the right of the pulpit?" The Memphis choir came down single file, resplendent in their white robes, and took their places on the platform. At a signal from their leader, a fat yellow woman with a noticeable goiter, the Gospel Beale Ramblers sat down.

Luther X had a word with the Gospel Beale Ramblers, saying: "We all know of the eminence and the importance of the deceased." He pointed to the magnificent white casket, already in place in front of the pulpit. "That is the reason why you were notified, why my people, the Nation of Islam, was notified, why all of us are here today because here lying dead and murdered by somebody, we don't know who, is one of the most wealthy and outstanding and important black men in the entire State of Tennessee, and when I say that I'm taking in North Mississippi."

"*Amen,*" said the choir.

"I'm taking in East Arkansas."

"*Amen.*"

"Southern Missouri."

"*Amen.*"

"And Southwest Kentucky."

"*Amen.*"

"George Gordon Lord Byron Jones, may he forever rest in peace."

"*Amen.*"

"So let's put on a show everybody's going to remember. Let's match all these lovely flowers and long telegrams with some singing that will never be forgotten. Let's be worthy of that white casket and the smiling face of the man lying in it. That man's happy because he knows that he was not murdered and killed in vain. We going to see to that."

"*Amen.*"

Apparently satisfied that the choir was warmed up, Luther X turned. He looked at Emma with that special style he had. It made her shiver. He came close to her and took her arms above the elbows, above the reach of her white gloves. He looked deep into her eyes. "You made out the check, didn't you?"

She nodded. "Two thousand dollars to the Nation of Islam," she said softly.

"I'll take it now, then," he said. "Otherwise we might not get together after the service. Being gone as long as I have I must get back to Memphis very soon now."

She raised her veil and got the folded check from the bosom of her white maternity dress and put it in his hand. "This is just a down payment," she said. "When will you get back up this way?"

"Very soon," said Luther X. "Positively be sure that I'll be back very soon. Important work is to be done here in Somerton." He turned and regarded the casket for an instant. "I like that smile on his features. That's real good," he said. "He was a distinguished man and he had style, didn't he? Those little gold glasses show it. He had some real style about him. You wonder who would want to kill a man like that, don't you? From the number of books he owned, your husband must have been a real gentleman."

"He was," Emma said. "He was a real big gentleman all his life."

Luther X looked at his wristwatch. "All right," he said in a loud voice. "Let the organist come and sit down and start playing. Something soft for the peoples to march inside by when the doors are opened. Let's also have the local ministers from the Somerton Tabernickel have their seats on the platform. Please, gentlemen, let's move because it is nearly time to open the doors. Step right along." He looked at Emma and smiled again. It was almost like the comfort of his big hand, moving slowly across her belly late at night, like his tongue and his breath reaching her all at once. His smile came as a promise.

He came back to her side. "Now you can be seated," he said, taking her arm. "As I have told you, don't expect me to dig very deep into explanations up there on the platform because with whites in the audience it can't help nothing to blow our secrets. We don't need to let the cat out of the bag to Whitey. See what I mean?" She nodded and sat down, hardly listening to what he said. She kept watching his eyes. She felt his smile linger over her body like a quick breeze touching a pond surface, making little riffs of purling excitement. She would, she knew, do anything he asked and believe anything he said. No matter what, she belonged to him now.

"I'm grateful," Emma said. She pressed his hand to let him know she loved him.

"You won't be sorry," he said.

The music began. Luther X went to the platform and took his stance behind the pulpit with the local preachers sitting just back of him. Benny gave a deep, muffled groan beside her.

"That's good," Luther X said in a loud, steady voice. "Let the ushers open the doors to the auditorium now." Seated facing Benny, with her profile to the audience, Emma saw them entering from the rear of the chapel. First came the Negro pallbearers followed by a crowd of white people who found seats in the reserved sections to the rear. The pallbearers marched to the front and sat down. Still the crowd came. The seats were quickly taken. Negroes and whites together crowded in and stood by the windows. They pushed about the walls until the chapel was jammed. The ushers put folding chairs in the aisle. The Gospel Beale Ramblers stood up and began singing.

It was, Emma observed, as L. B. himself would have wished. Beyond a doubt it was the biggest funeral, black or white, ever seen in Somerton. Luther X smiled, triumphant behind the pulpit. She heard Benny mourning and remembered to take a handkerchief. She lifted her veil and touched the corners of her eyes.

The child, Victor, kicked. Probably it was the music, she decided. Maybe he heard it inside there, in the dark. Maybe he heard it and it made him want to dance under her heart.

MOSBY

Everybody comes to his funeral but before, when he needed us, nobody moved. We all just stood there and me also like the others. So I got up early and taken Benny's car and the fishing pole and the cigar box. The cop was out there baling hay. What they found when the white ambulance went out there, Benny said, had to be collected and put in a plastic bag. "Just a rake and a plastic bag," Benny said. "They didn't have no use for no stretcher," he said. "When you finally fixed him you sure fixed him, Sonny Boy," Benny said.

"God damn the rest of them too," I said. "I'll fix the rest of them. I'll fix all of them. Maybe I'll make a lifetime job out of it."

He asked why and I said: "Because killing never made sense to me before they killed him. But when they killed him, that's when I got off the fence. I woke up when they killed him. They beat me and beat her, Mrs. Osborn, but when they gave it to him that way I couldn't take no more. That made up my mind where it was not made up before."

"You sure fixed Mr. Stanley," Benny said. "He's sure fixed now."

I got up and did it early so I'd be back on time for the funeral. She has her nerve to dress like a white angel and sit out front for the world to see her crying when she never cared shit about him and everybody knows it. I reached and took Mama Lavorn's hand, so little and shrunk up like a paw. She looking real good. Benny brought back her gold dress and she put on gold shoes. On the other side of her Jelly taken her other hand.

MAMA LAVORN

When he was little and tiny he used to like to hear about Noah and the Ark.

STEVE MUNDINE

Never again will I stand aside, defer to age and bigotry. We'll take it into the streets. They have to recognize it then. It's the only kind of language they understand. They won't fight out in the open. The open fight is the one thing they want to avoid at all costs, so that's where we'll make them fight it, in the very place where they don't care to confront it. In the public streets.

NELLA

Except for this he might *never* have moved, my husband. Horrible as it is, perhaps this death has served a greater purpose. Through it Steve has come to a final realization. Otherwise he might never have come to it. Otherwise I might have been dragged along with him, punished for the rest of my life.

If I think about him long enough maybe Steve will turn his head and look at me. Maybe he will think about me for a moment and get this other business off his mind, just long enough to think of me.

To think anyone would kill, yes, sacrifice a man in cold blood. To think anyone could live with himself as a murderer. To think anyone could cover it up and protect whoever did it. To think any society anywhere would have that much power and would use it in such an evil fashion.

It is all so unthinkable. Yet there it lies, the mute testimony that screams louder than sirens. All he demanded was justice. That's all he insisted upon. He didn't want charity or mercy. Just what was his, by rights. He wasn't even trying to vote. He wasn't so much as marching on the sidewalk with a sign. He didn't picket. He made no public outcry. He wasn't just another black ham doing it for money or notoriety or some idea about what God wants.

He was just a man like any other man. All he did was ask for a divorce. I hope Oman is satisfied. I hope his widow is satisfied, raising that veil to wipe her crocodile tears, flaunting her pregnancy, already flirting before they can get him decently in the ground.

Negroes are barbaric.

MOSBY

Jesus, he blew up quick. He just blew up. I thought, Jesus. He never even had a chance to holler. I thought, Jesus, would you look at that.

WILLIE JOE

The tractor was still running in the sunshine and the baler was still champing and the tractor was standing still. Because you can put it out of gear so the tractor, it won't roll ahead. But when the drive shaft is connected to the baler you can't, nobody can't, throw it out of gear. You have to shut off the engine, and Stanley Bumpas, he had sense enough to know the engine has got to be shut off. But he didn't shut it off. Instead he got down off the tractor with the engine still turning. And again, if he had took a stick, but no he must have used his arm, his own hand, his own flesh and substance and bone. And when he reached for that tree limb the baler had to of grabbed him and eat him, chopped him up, and his blood must have went, shot off everywhere as it was on the hay and on the machine and on the ground. He made two bales, part of him in one and part in another. He made two and a little bit more that the machine didn't know what to do with, and I thought: Probably God done it to him for when he taken that knife to that nigger's privates and cut him. God made me see it as my punishment, as part of mine.

That I should see it, the cutting of that nigger, and that I should see Stanley cut and made into two bales, and now see that what it was all along is that she, Emma, is knocked up, as a portion of my punishment at the hands of God. That's why she changed her mind, because I knocked her up when if I'd of gone ahead a long time ago and had myself cut, then wouldn't none of this have happened nor come to pass. That she would get knocked up and then for that reason change her mind about the divorce and have to fight it; that I would get caught in the middle between either laying it on her or letting this nigger laid out here, letting him down, whereas neither one of them would listen to sense. Each had reasons of their own and wouldn't nobody back down.

When Mr. Stanley reached for it then *it* grabbed him whereas when you reach to grab something maybe you will sometimes grab something else like the wrong thing, or else you will think you are grabbing something only it will turn out that *it* is getting a hold on *you*. By the time you or him either knows what is happening, by that time it is too God-damned late to do nothing to stop it. He was done chopped up. Probably he yelled, but wasn't anybody nowheres around to hear. He yelled before his blood shot off but nobody heard it and *chop* and *chop-chop* and mash and cram it wrapped him and tied him and cut him off in two bales, the first one part hay and part him and the second one mostly just him, as neat as nothing I never saw, blood slung everywhere and the engine still running *pack-pack-packa-pack-pack* in the sunshine of this morning in the field, *pack-pack-pack*, in front of where it had left behind and dropped bale after bale after bale by the dozens until it run up on the tree limb. Bumpas he climbed down and never thought to shut off the engine, only throwed the tractor out of gear in a hurry to get his hay to the barn, the hay mowed and laying so nice and dried and green where it had stood before, straight as wheat, laying nice and dried and green and the bales green and Bumpas, he never thought, neverthinking Bumpas he got off and reached for the tree limb and when he grabbed it the baler grabbed him. When I got there going after him to get him and remind him about the funeral which he said he didn't want to miss, when I got there the baler's arms were still thrashing *ah-crash-ah; ah-crash-ah; ah-crash-ah* in the sunshine and the tractor parked still so it would of run there parked all day until it give out of gasoline, just so it *would,* have run on and still been a-running had not I found it still running and cut the ignition switch.

A tree limb.

Still green.

A tree limb.

Still with the leaves on it barely wilted. How would an oak limb, how would it get clear out in the middle of a hayfield away from all the other trees and be laying there to jam his tractor, a red oak tree still with the leaves barely wilted? Bloody leaves, but barely wilted, where it had been tore off some tree four and five hundred yards off in the woods and laid right in the path where he would run over it is the mystery to me. The leaves hardly down wilted. Probably someway somehow he done it himself and never down thought what he did.

Reached for it with his hand. His blood shot off and *ah-crash-ah-pack-packa-pack* until whenever I cut the switch.

Whereas if I had only had myself cut. Whereas if I had only taken twenty-five bucks to Doc and told him: "Cut me."

THE MAYOR

That's one way to do it, by God. Trip and fall into your own God-damn hay baler.

Alf drove me and Oman out there in his car. Alf's face yellowed out until he looked like a piece of stale corn bread. When he saw it he said: "God knows."

The ambulance came a little while after we got there. It didn't look much like a man. It looked more like where a fast shitting freight train had run over and ground up a God-damned seven-hundred-pound cow. Piece here and a chunk there. It was no trick for them to find it all. Most of it was baled.

Even Alf took a drink, which Alf seldom does. "Could *you* tell who it was, that it was Mr. Stanley?" he says in a low voice. They were putting it in plastic bags. It stank pretty awful. Willie Joe had the pukes over in front of the tractor. I took a drink. It was hot as fourteen Birmingham whores, standing there in that blind open sunlight.

"In a mashed up sort of way," I says. "No doubt by God but that's him. Wouldn't you say, Oman?"

"It's him," Oman said.

"I seen a corn sheller one time strip a white man's arm of flesh clean down to the bone from the shoulder," Alf said. "But I never seen nothing the match of this before. By God, that's some awful sight, ain't it?"

Oman said he had to get back and pick up his nigger to take him to the funeral, so we left. On the way back to town I mentioned to Oman that if he could tell me who shot L. B. Jones I'd buy him a Coca-Cola, for nobody, said I, had a reason, and without no reason you got no excuse and without no excuse you got no case against anybody. I said it for Alf's benefit. Oman just nodded.

"Frankly, Alf," I says, "I think that nigger committed suicide."

"That's my verdict on it too," Alf says, looking at the road, watching where he was going. "Nobody had a hard on for L. B. Not a soul that I ever heard of."

I turned and winked at Oman.

Yes sir, he was one rich black son of a bitch. I liked him and I never wished him any harm and if he'd have kept his place he'd still be rich and alive today. I was never one to begrudge a nigger getting ahead and making all the money he's capable of making, getting all the education he can learn, and wearing just as nice clothes and driving just as nice a car, or better, as me or any other white man.

They had some kind of nigger lodge emblem stuck up on the curtain behind the pulpit. She was the thing to look at though, more than the casket. When she lifted the veil I could see what it was that Willie Joe went off the deep end about because she has got the looks. I could almost use some of that myself, but you take in my position I'd be a fool to want to risk my good name and reputation, no matter how good looking she is.

I leaned close to Oman's ear. "Is she pregnant or is it my imagination?" I says. Benny was passing up some of the telegrams to be read.

"You're right!" Oman whispers. "By God, *that's* it."

"That's what?" I says.

Oman didn't say. He has a way of clamming up sometimes that if you didn't know him you might take it amiss. After a while Oman leaned over again.

"How about that for a black widow?" he says.

I had to agree with him that she was all right. Nobody could of ever accused old L. B. that he didn't know what he was doing when he latched on to that piece of tail. Take Emma Jones and Nella Mundine and that would give you probably the two prettiest women in Sligo County, or maybe farther away than that even.

Steve never hardly even seems to notice her. I guess a man can get used to anything after a while, but in his case it's hard to see how.

I'll be God damned if on the other side of me Alf hadn't wet his cheeks crying and had to use his handkerchief. I knew what it was doing it. I knew it was that nigger music. It will hit many a white man where he lives.

OMAN HEDGEPATH

You can take a nigger out of Africa, but you can't take Africa out of the nigger.

My old savage sat down there clapping and hollering in the midst of the pall bearers. Somehow Henry bulled his way in among them and now what he came for in the first place was starting — the reading of the telegrams and the flower prices and the *amen*'s falling like tom-toms.

It takes a nigger to read names like Oatha and Barnesse and Tooley from a card on a floral spray and tell the cost of it, and make it all sound like a sort of native poetry. The sheer rhythm of it is enough to make a dead man want to pat his foot and clap his hands to keep time.

They hum along with it. It was like being in a log canoe somewhere in the Congo. That humming sound, the shouts and the rocking back and forth. The old bastard was getting what he came for; Henry was down in front drinking in the voice of his cannibal ancestors. Say what you please, but they'd all run wild again if they were given just half a chance. You don't have to scratch them to see the savage in them.

That's why any considerable number of them will scare the average white man who isn't used to them in numbers, why it will scare the average Yankee to death. They can smell fear, a nigger can, just like a dog, and it works on them the same way blood affects a school of sharks. They close in on the white man when he's half scared out of his pants, and there you have your riots in the North, whereas if they had any notion up there how to handle the nigger, they'd never have one minute's trouble. Their trouble is they don't know the nigger and they aren't ever going to take the trouble to know him. All they know to do is run when one moves in next door. To scream if the bus takes their kid to a nigger school.

They see neither his good points nor his bad points. They've got nothing for him; they've got less than nothing against him. Truth to tell, they never even see him. He doesn't exist for them except as a poor downtrodden abstraction several hundred miles away in the almost forgotten South. He's an abstraction they were taught about in school, like Infinity and Pi.

[351]

Consequently, though they've rarely ever even seen him, the Southern Negro, they know all about him. They understand his needs and his problems, his hopes, his fears, and his aspirations better than anybody below the Mason and Dixon Line. The white Yankee really feels that he knows more about what the Negro wants than the Negro himself. Consequently he's always wanting things for the Negro that the Negro hardly cares about and rarely thinks about. He wants a job for a Negro who would rather not work in the first place. He wants the vote for a Negro who would sell his vote for a shot of whiskey and would really rather not be bothered in the first place.

He is like a man, the Yankee is, who wants to put socks on all the roosters in the world because he imagines that they are tired of going barefooted; a man who is willing, moreover, to vote for any politician who will promise to do this. He will contribute heavily to any organization which will tell him that it can and should be done.

I was thinking along this line when it dawned on me that the preacher had said something. I had been watching Emma. Now I looked at him, really for the first time.

"Not the white man's heaven, but in paradise! George Gordon Lord Byron X is in paradise, the black paradise of Islam which is a better heaven than our white brothers will ever know. It is a heaven the white man cannot know. It is a proud, black heaven!"

"*Amen!*"

"I say to Lord Byron X, I say sleep my brother, for you have earned your rest. I am here all the way from Memphis to say to him justice, freedom, equality and Islam go with you and abide with you for you were a good and faithful servant, *proud* to be black!"

"*Amen!*"

"His widow, Miss Emma, she promised me last night that she would henceforth be a witness for Islam. She asks now to be known as Emma X. She tells me that she has no wish for anything that is the white man's, but prefers to be a witness for the Muslim cause and a black woman of the Nation of Islam. Call her Sister Emma X. She tells me that she and Mr. Benny will continue to see to it that the L. B. X Funeral Parlor for Colored is carried on like the fine business it has always been. She will not *let* her people down!"

"*Amen!*"

"Down deep in her sorrow, down beneath it, there is a secret joy. She carries a child. The child she carries, she has told me, will be named Victor X. That child will be raised in the Muslim faith, separate from the white man, apart from the white man's world, as our people, black and white, here in *this* part of the country, *prefer* it. Emma X has never been a part of that white world. She realizes it now. It took the death of her husband *for* her to realize it. She never *knew* it before. But now she knows it, that she never *had* a name, only what was given her by slave traders and slave owners in slavery times. Her real name is *lost* to memory, so she will adopt the name X, because she *has* no name. Because she *wants* no name that is not her own name, her real name!

"Having presented my message I now step aside and turn over this pulpit to Brother Horace Tompkins of the African Baptist Tabernickel who has made such a success of his life that black peoples everywhere are proud of him."

He sat down. The Somerton preacher stood up in his place and began preaching. I nudged the Mayor. He looked at me and shrugged his shoulders. As though to say, "*If that's what they want let them have it.*"

So there it was, the Nation of Islam come to Somerton with the richest woman in town, bar none probably, for its first convert, and another convert on the way. He had announced it right out in the open, too. I thought well, anyhow it beats the In-Double-A-Cee-Pee. At least it's for separation of the races.

STEVE MUNDINE

After all she's been through I can understand it, that she would put away her religion and deny Christianity and embrace this thing, for how could she take it otherwise than that God has forsaken her; how could she console herself otherwise to the murder of this man; for even though she might have been unfaithful to him (but this probably against her will, probably at gunpoint), still she must have loved her husband. Why should she not turn away from this white society and deny the white power structure, yet the pity is that she is driven into the hands of the extremists. Now she's a racist on the other side, but who could really blame her?

NELLA

'Tis pity she's a whore.

MOSBY

He has something right there. He ain't trying to prove nothing, so he must have something. Just because she went for it don't necessarily count it out because he said what he had to say and then he set down. He made sense.

"The Lord giveth and the Lord taketh away," says the Tabernickel preacher, trying to prove something.

"*Amen!*" says everybody but me, clapping and stamping.

"Treat him well, Lord!"

"*Amen!*"

"Show him those streets of gold!"

Streets of shit, that's about what it will be, like everything else they promise one thing and deliver something else. He'll be lucky if it ain't nothing worse than a street full of shit.

Him on the tractor and me running at him carrying the limb. I waved it at him and he stopped like he couldn't hardly believe his own amazement at some nigger, some colored fellow, coming out of the woods at him waving a red oak branch like a flag. Maybe he must have thought I was crazy. I took the gun out of the cigar box and pointed it at him. "Come down," I said.

Him looking at the tree limb and the gun and not knowing which he didn't believe and couldn't understand the most, a big fat black man in overalls, me, or the gun or the limb. It couldn't have made much sense to him, but I let him see me cock the gun, I made sure he saw that. That brought him down, climbing down and me standing back where even if he tried to jump he couldn't jump that far. Anyway, he was too old.

Just a damn dumb old man. I could have broke him in two, not half trying. I could almost let myself feel sorry for him again but I thought about L. B. and that notion was cooled for good. He still thought I was crazy or something, or that it had to be a joke. Probably he expected a bunch of white men to come running out the woods and laugh at him and it would all be some kind of white man joke they had hired a nigger to pull.

"Come and step this way," I told him. He herded on around stepping backwards until he was all the way around back of the baler and it running and going on and chomping so loud I had to yell at him. I said: *"Turn around!"*

He faced it, calm as a cow. I gave him a hard running shove, a hard bump, and he went in and it had him and he blew up like a bum going off, like somebody dropped a bum out of a war plane. He squirted everywhere and it dropped him out and it set there afterwards still chomping and chopping and drippy-jawed. I dropped in the limb and it went through and come out on top of the second bundle of him.

It was all over so fast it was quicker than a man could have thought it would be. I went back around in front of the tractor where I dropped the cigar box. I got the box and put the gun back in it and took off for the woods. I was over the fence before I remembered the gun was still cocked. So I opened the box and uncocked the dog so he wouldn't go off and bite me in the ass like an accident when I wasn't looking for it. Then I got the fishing pole from where I had left it by the holly bush again, and went on back and around the lake going to the car. I was almost nearly to the dam when I saw what I had never noticed, that when he blew up he had soiled and hit me, some of him had, so I had to walk back away to where nobody was watching and take water out of the lake in my hat and wash and rinse off my clothes some. Then when I was washed off I made it to Benny's car and put the box in the back seat and stuck the pole in the window.

He, the man, said: "No luck again?"

"Naw, sir," I said.

"You ain't got enough patience," he said. "You leaving already?"

"Yes, sir," I said.

"Well, it's your money."

"I believe I might try the barrow pits. I saw some peoples fishing there when I come by."

"It's your money," he said.

"Yes, sir." I got in the car and drove on back to town and Jelly ironed and pressed my suit for the funeral.

She said: "You didn't catch no fish?"

Me: "I didn't even get the first bite."

[355]

She: "Well, some peoples just ain't lucky that way."
"It's all different kinds of luck," I told her.

BENNY

Here he comes to the funeral after I *told* him I said Sonny Boy get the *next* train because you can't tell when they might grab you now. I told him you done did what you come for now so catch the next one that rolls. Be on that next one.

He just laughed the kind of laugh that there is nothing funny about it. "It's all different kinds of luck, Benny," he says. "All different kinds."

"Some of it's bad too," I told him, but he wouldn't listen to me. There he sits next to sister and that cop is standing back there by the door. That cop might grab him any minute and when he does that cigar box will open like your eye. Out that dog will come in Sonny Boy's hand and somebody will be bound to get hurt. That's when it's going to hit the fan sure enough. Sonny Boy won't be taken alive.

I said to Lavorn, "Sister you better *put* him on that train."

She said, "Just let me be with him this little bit more and then I'll be willing to give my baby up. Only these few little hours because I might not see him ever again on this side. I might have to wait for him over on that other shore."

"It could be a long wait," I told her.

"I know that too," she said. "Get my gold dress from the funeral home. If it has to be the last time I go anyplace alive I want to look like something decent."

So Jelly got the iron and pressed her hair while I come and got the dress, and nothing could I say to Sonny Boy Mosby changed his mind. There he sets. Wanted for two different murders if anybody knew it. There he sets. By the risk he's taking he ought to be clapping his hands louder than anybody else, but he ain't clapped one clap yet, that I've seen. He ain't hardly what I mean even blinked his eyes.

"Come after one," he told me. "Got two."

LUTHER X, THE NATION OF ISLAM

It wouldn't be no *hard* job if I had to fluff her twice a month. That ain't nothing a man could complain about if he had to drive up once a week to keep her in condition. That's something there that *won't* keep. There can't *be* too much of that to suit me. Something like that could make a man crawl *on* his hands and knees from Memphis, but you don't ever let *her* know it. Play it cool and keep it snappy. Play it non-violent. Keep her happy.

Promise nothing; take everything. Hot damn, look at that. Jesus Christ, just look.

Justice, Freedom, Equality, Islam, and me.

MOSBY

Take the train to Memphis. Walk in the washroom. Pee in the toilet and leave the dog there in his cigar box. Walk out and it's all over. Go home to Kansas and write the policies. Have you a few beers and be easy.

Hello to Isabel Kay Pasco. Hello to my long tall landlady.

Be easy, but how can you ever forget that you stood there like everybody else and you never moved. After you promised him and we all knew that it was.

Benny looking up at me. Benny blowing his nose and reaching for another clean handkerchief. Good-bye to Benny. Good-bye to Lavorn. Hello to Kansas City.

OMAN HEDGEPATH

The March in Review hymn started up front. The whole mob started down the center aisle two abreast, clapping and shuffling, to tell him good-bye. It was just my luck to be watching when Emma bent over the casket and kissed him. I thought I'd have to throw up.

About then the Mayor's elbow nudged into my ribs. "I understand he's got a smile on his face," he says. "You gonna go look?"

"No," I says, "I'll tough it out here. Why don't you and Alf go have a look?"

"Well, pardon me then," says the Mayor, standing up, "me and Alf just will. I got to see this."

"Go ahead," I says. "You can look for me."

He and Alf elbowed their way into the aisle. It took them a good while to get to the casket and almost as long to get back. Finally though they made it and sat back down.

"Well?" I says.

"Smiling just as big as you please," says the Mayor. "You better go look for yourself."

"No thanks," I says. "That's one nigger I've seen just about all I want to see. I've seen enough of him to last me a lifetime and then some."

"I can appreciate that too," says the Mayor. "I'm sure I understand how you feel."

Nella and Steve went down to have a look. Neither one of them so much as glanced in my direction. In two days they had packed and put the house up for sale, so Miss Griggs told me. They were leaving Somerton tomorrow, she said. That's all she knew. Steve hadn't told her where they were going.

"Wherever the Communists have decided to send him," I told her. "That's where."

I didn't see them any more. Steve and Nella must have left after they viewed the body.

MOSBY

When they started to walk and clear out and go for the automobiles to go to the cemetery I hugged and kissed Mama Lavorn good-bye. Benny took her on with him.

It was my chance. I went up to where the big boy was still on the stage and told him I was interested. "I done some pretty hard things though."

"Because of the white man, that made you do whatever it was you did."

"Maybe that's right." He makes sense, I thought.

"I doped and drank and things before I joined the Nation," he says. "What are you doing right now? Maybe we could have a talk."

"Right now I'm catching a train to Memphis."

"Maybe you'd like to ride to Memphis with me," he says. "We could talk on the way down if you would be interested. Do you live in Memphis?"

"Kansas City. Anyway I did live in Kansas City. I was a policy writer."

"There would be work for you in Memphis with the Nation if you decided to stay. Big man like you. I could get you a pad. What's your name?"

"Mosby," I says.

"Mosby X?" He grinned. "Let's cut out of here."

He had his Buick parked behind the building, a black iron top job with air and push-button windows. Getting out of town he doubled way over back of the Crossing. I remarked he wasn't no stranger to Somerton.

"Part of the job. Every place has to be scouted pretty careful ahead of time. You have to pick the right time and the right place. Otherwise you'll blow it, man. You know? Otherwise it's gonna drag on you." He turned down his sunshade once we hit the highway, to get the sun off his face. He slipped on sunglasses. "Otherwise you blow it. You take now once a week or so I'll have to buzz back up here and goose the movement until it really starts rolling. Fluff Emma Jones. She made us a nice opening contribution but she will need to be fluffed. After a while it starts to slide on its own grease, you know?"

He was still making sense. "I got the picture," I says.

"Sure, we can always use a good man with a box like that one. "What size is it?"

"Forty-five," I says.

"That's very good. That's fine."

I tried it out for myself, to hear my own self say it: "Mosby X," I says.

"Right," he says. "Absolutely."

Ahead the road made a long curve and went straight now, straight at the sun so that the way it shined on the road that way, the road looked like pure, solid gold.

2

Oman Hedgepath

Your mind does a double take at the death of an undertaker. Now they leave for the cemetery. Now they put him in the ground twelve feet deep, twice the depth of a normal grave. They lay him to that long sleep.

And I have laid my integrity to rest with him. Time does nothing to bring it back. I dropped it down a well.

In your mind you go back over and over again recounting everything, asking yourself at what point you began the long curve, the sickening slide into error.

The future shapes the past, always. The past is just as you remember it and events will bend memory, will waver it out of shape. Present heat will melt memory a little bit and distort it, as any man who has ever conducted a cross-examination knows.

There was finally, after a long silence, a letter from Steve, mailed from Atlanta but written from the cell of a jail, unspecified, somewhere in South Georgia.

He had marched with a band of blacks and prayed on the courthouse steps with them. Rather than pay his fine he was serving his sentence. Nella, meanwhile, had gone back to San Francisco and given birth to a son.

His letter, in turn, was prompted by another event. He wrote it the day following the Kennedy assassination. He had to tell me again how wrong I was. It was plain that during the intervening months, between the death of Lord Byron Jones and the President's death, Steve had been recounting too.

More than anything else he had wanted to forgive me, but of course he couldn't. When he had been over and over it time and again for my sake and his sake and his mother's sake, he always drew the same conclusion — I killed the undertaker, nobody else.

In a curious way he held me responsible for the President's murder too. The words that stick in my mind are these: "The greatest man of modern times is dead, shot like a hog in the streets of Dallas, Texas. I hope you, I hope Somerton, I hope the South is satisfied. You killed him and don't deny it. You murdered him a thousand times in your hearts."

If he had sent his return address I could have told him Willie Joe Worth was punished anyway, proving the tired maxim that if the law doesn't punish a murderer he will punish himself.

Steve might have gotten a moral out of it, could he have known how Willie Joe would get drunk and try to get somebody, anybody, to hear his confession. It got so white men avoided him. It got so bad that he went stumbling around the Crossing where he'd tell his story to niggers. It go so even the niggers felt sorry for him and would lend him a quarter for a drink of white whiskey. It got so they would walk all the way uptown to Templeton's for him, to buy him a bottle of paregoric so he could keep his whiskey down once he'd swallowed it.

The city hadn't the heart to fire him, yet there wasn't much we could do with him either. He was no good to us. He was no good to himself. He was, finally, as the Mayor said, *weak*. The question Willie Joe Worth asked anybody who would listen to him, the question he asked me over and over again before I finally shamed him and got rid of him for good, was: "Is there any forgiveness? Can anybody ever get that man off my back?"

If he couldn't do it himself, it was strange, I thought, that he would expect that somebody else could do it for him. Least of all me, or the Mayor, or some nigger cafe proprietor.

Another thing Steve might have been interested to know, was how it happened here.

As usual the Mayor got the news first. He phoned me and said somebody had shot the President, out in Dallas; but had failed, that the President wasn't dead.

I ran. I nearly broke my neck running, down through the bank to the sidewalk. The Mayor met me there and we ran together, across Main and down to Johnnie Price Burkhalter's hardware store. Johnnie Price had it on the television.

"God," says the Mayor. "Anybody that would come that close and then botch it. I just don't know. I'll bet twenty-five dollars he don't die!"

"You got a bet," Johnnie Price says. He got the money out of the cash drawer. "Put up or shut up!" The Mayor thumbed the bills out of his wallet. They were ready to hand the money to me to hold when a farmer fetched out five dollars he wanted to bet, so in all it came to thirty dollars the Mayor had to cover. We sat on nail kegs and watched. The store filled up.

There was Alf of course, and then Templeton; Toonker Burkette, the dentist; Chief Fly and a couple of more police, and the usual store clerks — all men.

After the first shock began to wear off I had a moment of tears, afraid he would die and afraid he wouldn't, because no matter how counter your feelings and beliefs run towards those of another man, no matter *how* you hate him, still you don't wish him death. You might want him dead; but you don't wish him death. There's a difference. Those were my feelings, so I got up.

I walked out of the store. I wiped my eyes. The streets were clear and the sidewalks so clean it looked like Sunday. The day felt more like Easter than autumn. The population had vanished indoors to keep watch.

I breathed that November air and lit a cigarette and stood smoking, wanting him out of that office but still not wishing him dead, not this way. I kept thinking that the poor Ku Klux fanatic that did it was probably laboring under the delusion that he had done the South a service. That poor bastard was probably feeling like the greatest hero since Nathan Bedford Forrest, whereas I knew there would be no end to the troops and the punishment they would send on us now. I knew I'd never in my lifetime see an end to the force bills Congress would pass against us.

Templeton walked out where I was standing. Tears were on his face. "Ah," the druggist said. "It's bad."

"Is he still alive?"

"Yes, but it's bad. He's unconscious."

"God help the South," I said.

"God bless the South," said Templeton. "If he dies, if some Southerner has killed him . . ." Templeton started crying. It didn't seem strange, for a grown man to be standing on the sidewalk in front of Price Burkhalter's Hardware Company, weeping like a child.

To let George have his privacy I went back in the store. Somebody had gotten my nail keg. It was too hot indoors. I stood sweating until my feet were numb from standing. Still nobody moved. Nobody spoke.

Then from the television came the announcement, the death sentence, the trump of doom we had been waiting for.

Johnnie Price put out his hand for the money. I had been holding it all that time wadded in my fist like a ball. I opened my hand. It fell to the floor. Johnnie Price scooped it up and unfolded it bill by bill. He paid the farmer his ten and waved the rest of it around. "What did I tell you?" he asked.

I'd had a bellyful. I walked out, past the barber shop, empty except for the shine boy. Nobody had told him yet. I crossed Main Street on the green light. No cars were moving. I walked on down behind the bank and got in my car and sat there a long time without starting the engine.

It came to me that something like the dull pain I felt, the emptiness and sorrow and loss that filled me, that sickened me, must have been much the way Willie Joe Worth felt.

Perhaps a man feels safe in his automobile, I thought. Maybe that's why Willie Joe got the police car that August night and floorboarded it headed south out of town past the Mountains of Gilead. He twitched the wheel and smashed into the bridge. That was his way to get the dead man, the undertaker, off his back.

If Steve had sent a return address I could have written to tell him that Willie Joe's way isn't my way. I could have told him, too, how I miss him, my partner. How for a long time since I watched the postman, hoping for another letter, hoping against hope for a change of heart, or even an apology. Because if you love someone even a curse is welcome. Just so long as it comes from him.

[363]

There ought to be some way to let him know I'm getting old. That like all old people, I dote on the mail.

The months go by. They lengthen into years. The old folks keep hoping, yet the letter never comes. Only in dreams do you find it, open the letter box and see it. You open it and read where Steve says it was all, every bit of it, a mistake. He's back then, bustling and worrying and spinning his wheels in that office you fixed for him, across from yours. Things are like they used to be — until you wake up.

Sometimes I drive down to the Crossing. Ripe black girls walk by with a slow undulant rhythm. Old men watch from the benches, the black and the white and the in-between, watching the sturdy young women; slender shanks and hard breasts and lips that seem to open like the petals of a dark flower. The old men look. A girl is there. They look again. She is gone.

Sometimes a new white Cadillac glides down Fort Hill. Emma X drives it. Beside her in his white car seat sits the infant Victor X, staring at the world from eyes which I am told are hard and calculating, blue eyes that seem already possessed of a secret knowledge of his inheritance.

The wind blows, and it is autumn. The wild grass turns brown. Each tree is like a thorn in the breast of a cold sky. A furze of green appears. It is spring. It rains, and summer is come.

I think of my father.

Thinking of the dead you know how it must be with you. That where your fathers are, there you'll go to join them.

At least I know that when I die I'm going to walk through that gate marked "White Only," be it fire or pearls.